John and Kathy,

Any friend of Kathy is
a friend of mine. I do hope
you enjoy this. Thank you
for giving it a try!
All the best,

SCOTT W. SONNE

INTUITION

ISBN: 978-1-66781-827-6 (print)
ISBN: 978-1-66781-828-3 (eBook)

PART I

LIBBY

CHAPTER ONE

SAN DIEGO

1

When the bell rang on her next to last day at Oakview High School, Libby Amanda Anderson slung the backpack over her shoulder and hurried out of the classroom. She didn't want to give Ms. Carter the chance to go on about her Shakespeare essay. It was just a paper, after all, but her teacher had acted like defending Lady Macbeth was a mortal sin. And she didn't want to run into someone from chemistry class. The homework assignment had looked pretty tough, and a couple of the future Cal-Techers might want to pick her brain. She didn't mind that much, but today was the last day of March, and she wondered if the eggs had hatched. She had been waiting impatiently for school to end so she could find out.

She had spied a pair of peregrine falcons over three weeks earlier, as part of her goal to see all the bird species in San Diego. The falcons had now produced a nest of eggs, which she had been visiting every day. She still didn't know how many eggs there were. Four maybe? She would have climbed out on the old hotel's balcony for a closer look, but she suspected the female would react badly.

She was almost to the end of hall when Henry Waggoner, from fourth period math, stepped in front of her. He was taller than she, and three years older. Actually, he wasn't *that* much taller, as she had added two inches just the past year. But he also had the build of an all-state pitcher who was odds-on to get a full scholarship. She had noticed him hanging around a lot lately, always making jokes and talking about yesterday's game. But there were no jokes now. He looked upset.

"Did you tell Price you helped me with that swimming pool problem?" he asked in a low voice. Their homework had asked them to calculate the volume of water in an asymmetrical swimming pool. To Henry, the problem was written in ancient Greek.

"I would never do that," she said, continuing to walk. "Wouldn't that be admitting I was wrong, too?"

"Well, when she handed me back the paper, she looked at me funny and asked if I'd had help."

Libby could have kicked herself. Henry's answer should have had some mistakes. "Miss Price isn't so bad," she said. She was thinking Henry was lucky a ninety-mile-per-hour fastball didn't require talent in math.

As they approached main door, she gave him a quick glance. "You pitching tomorrow?"

He looked surprised. "I didn't think you were into baseball."

Libby thought about all the games she had watched with Aunt Ruth. "I know a little," she said. "What if a lowly freshman came to cheer?" The Senior Prom was two months away. If he asked her, would Ruth let her go? Probably not, but it was worth a try.

He suddenly looked nervous. "I hope I have good stuff."

"You'll hardly need it against the Lions," she said. "They've won, what, two games so far?"

He stared at her blankly.

"And speaking of baseball," she added, "isn't your practice about to start?"

He gave his watch a startled glance. "Oh, man," he said, "the coach will kill me." He started to leave and then turned back.

"Could I call you tonight?" he asked. "Price gave me an extra credit problem to boost my grade. I was hoping you'd look at it."

"What is it?"

"Well, in the spring this pond starts to get covered with water lilies. Every day the lilies cover twice as much of the pond as they did the day before.

After thirty days all of the pond is covered. The pond is, let's see, one hundred feet in diameter."

"So what's the question?" Libby asked, opening the door to leave.

"Uh, how many days will it take before the pond is half-covered with lilies?"

Libby stepped through the door and started down the stairs.

"Twenty-nine days," she said over her shoulder.

"What!" he called out.

"The pond will be half-covered in twenty-nine days."

2

Sitting in a dark town car across the street, the man calling himself Harvey Blunt watched the girl leave the school. He was wearing a corduroy blazer and could have passed for an over-sized English teacher. The woman with him carried a Homeland Security ID in the name of Autumn Gray. She was six feet tall, looked like a fitness instructor, and specialized in martial arts. Blunt had seen her put five rounds into a two-inch circle at thirty feet. Her face could have qualified for a magazine cover--except for the wine stain birthmark that extended from her left ear to below her jaw. Once people saw the birthmark's spidery tendrils, which looked like claw marks, they usually forgot about her features and physique.

"She looks pretty ordinary," Blunt said. "You sure she's the one?"

"Never seen her before. But that's the girl in the photo."

"Think she'll talk to us?"

"We've sent three letters and phoned the aunt twice. No response to the letters, even the one with the scholarship offer. And the aunt hung up as soon as the calls mentioned the girl. It was a little surprising. Usually money works. But sooner or later we'll get to her."

Blunt watched the tall, slim, sandy-haired girl walking away. "This is getting old. How many is this, anyway? Twenty?"

"Seventeen. Four left."

"Where's the next one?"

She looked at a sheet. "Pack for cold weather. Montana."

He made a face. "We'll, at least it's in this country. But it's so damn boring, not to mention a waste of time."

Gray shrugged. "Probably. But you're getting paid, aren't you?"

"Yeah, but this isn't what we trained for." He started the car's engine. "I've always preferred the direct approach. You okay with that?"

"Was that thing in Chicago direct enough for you?" Gray said. She had been assigned to visit a troublesome inventor who had rejected three generous buyout offers for a patent Quantum Industries needed for its new computer system. He had been arriving home late one evening when she intercepted him as he was getting out of his car. She had slapped duct tape over his eyes and taped his hands behind his back before he knew what was happening or could see her face. She took him to a secluded park, broke two of his fingers, and convinced him he needed to exercise better professional judgment. He had sold the patent to Quantum two weeks later.

"Not *that* direct," Blunt said.

"Well," she said, "let's see how you do."

3

Libby headed down Central Avenue, the spring sun warm on her face, and turned right on Fifth. She kept to the main streets, avoiding the alley she had once taken as a shortcut. That time she had been surprised by two guys in a doorway. When they started toward her, she quickly retreated, taunts following. She'd never told Ruth about it. Ruth already worried about her too much.

After two more blocks, and a left down Upas, Libby came to the old Helix Hotel. She squinted up, a hand blocking the sun's glare, and finally saw the nest in a crevice beneath the third-floor balcony. It was about thirty feet up. The female's white head, with its curved beak, was barely visible over the ring of twigs. Libby listened carefully, just making out a faint chorus of high peeps. So, the babies had finally come.

Libby looked around, scanning the sky, and saw the smaller male circling overhead. The first time she had seen the bird was three weeks earlier, when it had swooped down on several crows that had been flying around, obviously watching something. The falcon had dove into the crows at great speed, talons slashing. After the crows had scattered, Libby looked for what they had been after. She finally located the female falcon guarding a nest.

Libby had visited the nest every day since, careful not to alarm the birds. She had no doubt that if she had climbed out onto the hotel balcony to get a better look, the male would have dove at her face, if the female didn't get to her first.

She scanned the railing that ran along the balcony's perimeter, looking for the gray tomcat she had seen a week earlier. She worried that the female falcon hadn't seen it. The question was whether the cat could get down to the crevice that housed the nest. If it could, the birds wouldn't have a chance. But the tomcat didn't seem to be around.

"Do you like birds?"

Libby jumped and whirled around. The man was only five feet away. How had he gotten so close? She took an involuntary step back.

"Sorry," Harvey Blunt said, "didn't mean to startle you. I like birds, too."

The man was smiling, and he wasn't bad looking. But Libby's heart was already pounding and her palms were starting to perspire. The man's eyes were wrong, and his smile reminded her of a crocodile. She took in his corduroy jacket. It looked a lot more expensive than anything she'd seen in the high school.

"The babies," she said, feeling stupid. "The babies came." Was that a bulge under the jacket, beneath his armpit? She backed away.

He stepped toward her. "No need to leave. I'm a bird-watcher, too. How many eggs were in the batch?"

"A clutch," she said. "Eggs are called a clutch." If he'd really been a birder, he would have known that. She turned and started to walk away as fast as she could. Her ears strained for the sound of his footsteps behind her. If she'd heard them, she would have run. After a block she glanced back. The man was still standing there, staring at her.

4

Ten minutes after meeting the girl, Blunt was on his cell phone, calling the handler. The phone looked ordinary enough, but if some hacker had tried to get past its encryption, a small reaction would have turned the device's insides into paste.

"We're having some trouble with the Anderson girl, number seventeen," Blunt said. "The aunt won't let us near her. We've tried calls and letters, even offered money. No interest."

"What happened today?"

"I decided to talk to her directly. I usually do well with the girls."

"So how did you do?"

Blunt grimaced. "Something spooked her. She took off."

The line was silent, and then a mild voice said, "Are you going to try a trace again?"

"No--I got the point," Blunt said, sounding uneasy. "I just wanted to find out what this was all about. It's hardly a regular job. That's all."

Three weeks before he had asked an IT consultant to trace the handler's location. For three days the consultant got nowhere. On the fourth day an electrical fire destroyed his office.

"Curiosity didn't help the cat either," the handler said.

"So I'm reminded. Anyway, how hard should I push the girl? Her history doesn't stand out. Pretty much the same as the others. Except for one outlier, her test scores are barely one standard deviation above the norm, lower than the test scores of other students we've already crossed off."

After another silence, the handler said, "Tell me about the outlier."

"It was a standardized first grade assessment test. Nothing unusual. Calibrated up to two-fifty. But having an upper range that high was pointless. No one's ever scored above one-ninety."

"What did the girl score?"

"Hard to say. The test was designed for three hours. She finished in one, and apparently didn't miss anything."

The voice was silent.

Blunt sighed. "It had to be an anomaly. The testing service said she must have been given the answers in advance. Teachers sometimes do that to make themselves look better."

"In first grade?" the voice said.

'Well, not usually. Anyway, when the school gave her a follow-up test, she only scored a little above average. Nothing off the charts. And all her scores since then have been the same. Nothing special. The one test must have been a fluke."

"What did the teacher say?"

"What do you think? She said the kid had no help."

After a moment, the handler said, "Do the assessment."

5

Libby slowly climbed the stairs and entered the weathered, grey house on Juniper. She'd lived there all her life, ever since Ruth Anderson had adopted her after the death of her mother, Amanda Taylor, whom Libby had never known. The sister of Amanda's foster mother, Ruth was thin and wrinkled, with nervous, darting eyes and hands that were constantly wringing themselves. When she wasn't working as a nurse at the nearby clinic, Ruth stayed in the house, watched baseball, and worried about Libby.

Ruth hadn't always been so nervous. Once they had gone to museums and movie theaters, played in the park, and invited other kids over. But Ruth had become a different person. Even though Libby was now fifteen, and had never been in trouble, Ruth now cross-examined her like a seasoned prosecutor, wanting an account of every minute she was gone from home. Libby did love Ruth, the only family she had ever known, but sometimes her aunt's anxieties were exasperating.

"Aunt Ruth! I'm home," Libby announced as she closed the door. Once Libby was home, Ruth's anxiety usually eased a bit.

"Oh, good," Ruth said. "I was worried."

Libby sighed. "Nothing to worry about. I stopped to see the falcons' nest. The babies have come! It's so exciting!" Mentioning the man on the street was out of the question. If she told Ruth about that, her aunt wouldn't sleep for two days.

"Anything else of interest?" Ruth asked, her eyes searching Libby's face for something unusual.

"Not a thing," Libby said brightly. "Oh, I may go to Henry Waggoner's game after school tomorrow. I could be a little late."

Ruth pursed her lips and looked at the papers on her desk. "Well," she said at last, "Come home as soon as it's over. You're not interested in him, are you?"

"Not like you mean," Libby said. "But he's a really good pitcher."

Ruth raised her eyebrows. Libby thought Ruth's passion for baseball might soften her on Henry. But she knew it probably didn't matter. She was just a freshman, so there was little chance he would ask her to the prom.

Libby peered over Ruth's shoulder and saw the checkbook and a large stack of bills. "What are you working on?" she asked.

"Nothing. Just paperwork." Ruth brushed the papers aside.

"Are we out of money?" Libby asked in a small voice.

"Not even close," Ruth said. "The flood money hasn't even been touched." That was a nest egg for when a rainy day turned into a flood.

"It's all my fault, isn't it?" Libby said. "The doctors don't do anything but send bills!"

"If they can cure your nightmares," Ruth said, "it will be money well spent."

The dreams had been with Libby since she was a baby. For years doctors couldn't explain where they came from, nor how they could include a terrible snake long before Libby had ever seen one. But one doctor said that a severe trauma could be passed from a mother to her unborn child. Libby hoped this was not the case. If it was, her mother had experienced something awful.

"The dreams don't come as often as before," Libby said. "Maybe they'll go away on their own."

'You've been saying that for years, Libby," Ruth said, "but I know how much they take out of you."

Wanting to change the subject, Libby said, "Ms. Carter wasn't very happy with my Lady Macbeth paper."

"Well, you can't blame her," Ruth said. "Lady Macbeth's hardly a role model."

"That depends on the role." Libby said. She looked at the mail on the table. "Anything besides bills?"

Ruth sighed and pulled out an envelope. "Just this," Ruth said. It was a letter Libby had sent to Tom Grant, which had been returned as undeliverable. Libby had written him to see if he had known her mother, since Ruth had found an old envelope addressed to Grant among Amanda's keepsakes. He had apparently lived in Grand Junction, Colorado. But now it was just another dead end.

Since she was a little girl, Libby had asked Ruth about her father, but Ruth always responded the same way. "Look," Ruth would say, "your mother never told me who your father was, so I just don't know."

"But she must have been seeing someone," Libby would say. "After all, she did have me."

Ruth threw up her hands. "I only remember there was someone named Tom. And then he was gone. She never mentioned anyone else."

"Well, what do you know about this Tom?" Libby would ask.

Ruth would grudgingly say the man's name had been Tom Grant and that he'd once worked for a company known as Quantum Industries, where Amanda had also worked before she died. Ruth couldn't remember anything else about him, except that Amanda had met Grant at a duplicate bridge tournament.

"Did you ever meet this Grant?" Libby asked.

"Never. And the last time I spoke to Amanda, shortly before she died, she said Grant was out of the picture. She seemed sad about it."

"Do you know if Grant ever knew my mother had a baby?" Libby asked.

"I don't know how he would have," Ruth said. "I never saw him, and your mother died just after you were born."

7

Although she knew little about Libby's father, Ruth did tell Libby about her mother's early life. Amanda had been a foster child in the home of Ruth's sister. But Amanda received little love or attention. Her foster parents were mainly interested in their monthly government checks. Feeling sorry for the neglected girl, Ruth began to visit Amanda regularly, finding her to be extraordinarily bright, kind, and a delight to talk with. Despite their age difference, Ruth and Amanda soon became friends. The friendship continued until Amanda finished high school and left home.

"Did you ever find out how my mother died?" Libby asked late one night.

This was the subject Ruth avoided. "No," she said. "I knew nothing about it until the hospital called and said your mother was in a coma. I rushed to see her, but she never woke up. It seemed I was the only one who had any ties to her. When the hospital's administrators couldn't find anyone else, they asked if I wanted to adopt you. The alternative was another foster home. After knowing how that was for Amanda, I didn't want it for her daughter. So I agreed. That was one decision I never regretted."

8

Ruth never found out how Amanda died, but she had tried. Several weeks after Amanda's death, Ruth called Quantum Industries, Amanda's old employer, to ask if they knew what had happened. She was put on hold, then a woman with a clipped voice came on the line and asked what she wanted. Something in the woman's voice alarmed her, so Ruth said she was an old college roommate who just wanted to say hello. The woman said Amanda no longer worked there and rang off.

A few days later, she saw a newspaper article about the murder of a former Quantum research scientist, Dr. Joseph Krell. Before he died, he had told the police that a young woman had died in a laboratory experiment gone horribly wrong. The police opened an investigation, but closed it after Krell was later found in his home, apparently shot by a burglar.

Ruth had called Dr. Krell's home, to see if the experiment might have involved Amanda. When a woman's voice answered, Ruth identified herself and asked if the woman knew whether Amanda had been the one who died.

The woman sucked in her breath, and then whispered, "Don't ever call again."

Ruth said, "Please, I mean no trouble. I just want to find out about Amanda."

The woman said, her voice quivering, "They killed Joe, and they'll kill anyone who snoops. If you're smart, you'll drop it and disappear." She hung up.

Initially alarmed by the call, Ruth later decided the woman was just consumed with grief. Several weeks later, Ruth received a call from a pleasant-sounding man who said that Quantum's records showed that someone at Ruth's number had called about Amanda. He said he needed to ask some questions.

"Like what," Ruth said, alarm bells going off.

"Well," the pleasant voice said, "you said you knew Amanda from college. What college was that?"

Now the alarms were wailing. "Uh, Berkeley," Ruth said.

"That's very interesting," the man said, "because our records show Amanda never went to college."

Ruth didn't respond.

The man said, "Well, no doubt we can clear this all up, but my partner and I will need to sit down and talk further." His voice no longer sounded pleasant.

"I must have just confused Amanda with someone else," Ruth said.

"No doubt there's a good explanation," the man said. "We'll talk about it when we see you."

Feeling frightened and vulnerable, Ruth agreed to meet the following week. Two days later she emptied her bank account and left town with the baby. She told no one where she was going. She suspected she wouldn't be hard to find, but no one came looking. She never learned why.

9

Ruth took the baby to San Diego and started a new job. But she seemed to grow increasingly anxious and fearful. She was adamant that Libby never attract attention. Not until years later did Libby discover why.

Though usually kind and loving, Ruth completely lost her temper when Libby brought home a note asking Ruth to meet with Libby's teacher the next day. When Ruth showed up, the teacher handed her a report.

"What's this?" Ruth asked.

"Your daughter has received the highest score anyone's seen on this standardized test," the teacher said. "We want to test her again. If the score is accurate, she'll be placed in a special class."

"I'm sure it's a mistake," Ruth said. "Libby's a good girl, but nothing special."

That evening, Ruth was furious.

"I told you not to call attention to yourself," Ruth cried. "And you do this! They might take you away! What's wrong with you?"

Libby was too stunned to say anything.

"They think you're like your mother!" Ruth shrieked, "And look what happened to her!" Ruth's fingers bit into Libby's arms, leaving welts.

Libby took the test again, scored barely above average, and vowed to keep her head down after that.

CHAPTER TWO
NIGHT VISITORS

1

The man Blunt and Gray knew as the handler was retired Colonel Ashton Crane, a former commander of the Fifth Marine Regiment in Afghanistan. Crane answered to only to only one person, Senator Adam Durant, the ranking member of the Senate Armed Services Committee, and the majority shareholder and former CEO of Quantum Industries. Durant was not listed among the Forbes richest people because he chose not to be. But if his private sector wealth were combined with his governmental power, he would belong on a short list of the most powerful men in the world.

Colonel Crane had met Senator Durant for the first time two years before. After his military career stalled, and despite an adequate retirement for twenty years of service, Crane was not satisfied with a gold watch and golf club membership. He had been looking for something new when Durant's aide summoned him to the Senator's private plane. The aide sounded as though declining was unthinkable, which tempted Crane to do so, but he decided he had nothing better to do.

The Gulfstream jet was parked on a private airfield outside of Washington, D.C. Once on board, Crane took a moment to absorb the plane's opulent interior. Sitting at a small desk near the cockpit, Durant rose to greet him. Crane wasn't sure what to expect, though he knew Durant was considered brilliant and ruthless among those willing to discuss him. He could also be charming when it suited him.

Durant got down to business by reciting a surprisingly thorough summary of Crane's military career. Then he explained he was looking for a troubleshooter who could fix problems without direction or supervision. Apparently satisfied with Crane's responses, Durant soon asked him to be his executive assistant, at a salary three times what he had last earned. Although Crane knew he should mull it over, he found himself saying yes almost immediately. In the subsequent two years, Crane's assignments had included suppressing labor unrest in Indonesia, deposing an opposition leader in South America, and gathering embarrassing information that led to the retirement of a hostile senator. He rarely spoke with Durant, and he hadn't met him again in person.

But now Crane was speaking with Durant again, this time from a secure phone in one of the senator's offices.

"Good morning, Colonel," Durant said, "thank you for calling."

As if he wouldn't, Crane thought.

There was a pause while the Crane could hear paper rustling. "I need you to find someone for me," Durant said.

"Certainly, sir. Who?"

"Someone with a special characteristic."

"Very well, sir. Something like a scar, or limp, or maybe a stutter?"

"No, no, nothing like that," Durant said impatiently. "You need to find someone with, well, I'll call it intuition."

"You mean like a woman's intuition?" Crane said, puzzled. "Probably half the population would claim that."

"This is a little different. Ever hear of Gary Kasparov?"

"The champion chess player?"

"Correct."

"What's does he have to do with intuition?"

"Maybe you were soldiering at the time, but some years ago Kasparov played a series of games against Deep Blue, a powerful IBM computer that could perform millions of calculations per second."

"I suppose the computer was tough," the Colonel said dryly.

"More than that. Impossible. No human could stand up to a machine that could calculate millions of moves ahead, seeing all possible outcomes."

"So, did Kasparov get slaughtered?"

"Kasparov won the first match, and barely lost the second. The machine shouldn't have lost a game, but Kasparov fought it to a virtual standstill."

"How did he do it?"

"With intuition. Do you know anything about quantum computers?"

"I'm afraid not, Senator."

Durant said, "Quantum computers are much faster than even the best supercomputers. Their technology allows them to solve problems in a non-linear fashion that doesn't move logically from point A to point B. Instead, they use quantum theory, employing multiple virtual universes, to work on all parts of the problem at once, rather than step by step. They can find solutions that would take a standard computer millions of years."

"What does this have to do with intuition?" Crane asked.

"I think intuition is the human equivalent to quantum computing. It allows the human brain to work on all parts of a problem at once, in a non-linear fashion, and find solutions that should be impossible."

Crane thought for a moment. "Is it like imagination?"

"They might be related. But imagination sees many possibilities, while intuition chooses the one that is right."

Crane said, "What does this have to do with me?"

"I want you to find me someone with exceptional intuition."

"How do I recognize it?" Crane asked.

"Look for a brain with a large bandwidth and unusual thought speed."

"I think I know what thought speed is. What's bandwidth?" Crane asked.

"Bandwidth refers to how much information can be processed at one time, as opposed to how quickly it can be processed."

Crane frowned. "Does such a person actually exist?"

Durant smiled grimly. "The person did once, and I'm betting there's another."

Crane kept frowning. "This all seems pretty conjectural. I expected you to be more bottom-line oriented."

Durant smiled. "Colonel, have you ever made a decision you regretted?"

"Sure," Crane said. "Who hasn't? Early in my career, I was offered a command in Iraq, but I chose Afghanistan instead. Turned out Iraq would have done more for me."

"Suppose we had an artificial intelligence you could ask, after inputting all the specifics, whether you should go to Afghanistan or Iraq. How much would you pay for the answer, if it was reliable?"

Crane sighed. "A lot."

"Quantum is working on an artificial, human-like intelligence that can make such predictions. Finding the right person is a crucial part of the project."

"So, where do I start?" Crane asked.

Durant gave a cold chuckle. "That's your problem. We've already looked at top-tier scientists, the best academics, successful inventors, people like that. None of them had what we're after. So now it's up to you. Money's no object. Just find me the person."

After the call, Crane went to work as though planning a military campaign. He assessed long lists of people with extreme talent and intelligence, or those who had achieved great things. But like many before, he came up empty. He found some people who were at the top of the chart, but none who was off it.

He decided to start younger. He would look at children. Find one who had this talent, this intuition, even if it hadn't appeared yet. He decided to look at school test scores over the last ten years. During the last six months, his team had gone through over ten million records.

The list he had given Blunt and Gray was the result of their search.

2

The night after meeting the man with the crocodile smile, Libby climbed into bed thinking about the baby falcons. She fell asleep as soon as her head hit the pillow, but before long the nightmare enveloped her, with its blinding light, the terrible snake, and a burning red tide that consumed her mind.

She awoke trembling, drenched in sweat, her heart pounding. Years before, the dreams had sent her crying into Ruth's room, but no longer. Ruth couldn't do anything, and there no reason to ruin her night, too.

After a long while, Libby drifted back into sleep.

3

The next day, in fifth period English, Ms. Carter returned to the Shakespeare papers.

"Libby, your essay offers a defense of Lady Macbeth. Sometimes I agree with you—but Lady Macbeth? Why would you defend *her*?"

All the students looked at her. Libby's face turned red.

"You told us last fall not to be afraid of taking unpopular positions," Libby said. "I was trying to do that."

"I said no such thing," Ms. Carter said.

"You did. It was on November twenty-third, Tuesday afternoon."

"Oh, nonsense. You couldn't remember the specific day."

"It was two days before Thanksgiving, which came on November 25. My aunt's birthday was the day before, the 24th."

Ms. Carter stared at Libby. "I never said that," she said, "but even if I did, you're defending the indefensible. Lady Macbeth was behind King Duncan's murder."

"I…I'm not saying she was good person," Libby said. "But she shouldn't be blamed for things she didn't do."

"Like what?" Ms. Carter said.

Ms. Carter didn't like to be contradicted, but Libby couldn't stop herself. "Well, you just said Lady Macbeth was behind Duncan's murder. But killing Duncan wasn't her idea. Macbeth had that idea from the start. But only Lady Macbeth was willing to do it."

"You are wrong," Ms. Carter said, her voice tart. "I've taught this play for twenty years. Don't lecture me about Lady Macbeth."

Libby said nothing.

"All right, Libby, since you obviously know the play better than I, exactly where does the play show that Macbeth first had the idea of murdering Duncan?"

Libby reviewed the play in her mind. After a moment she said, "In Act I, scene 3, before Lady Macbeth is even mentioned, Macbeth refers to the "horrid" thought that he'll murder Duncan to become king. That wasn't Lady Macbeth's idea."

The class was silent. Ms. Carter picked up her copy of the play and turned to the scene. She studied it for a moment and then looked up. "Well," she said in a tight voice, "Aren't you a smart little know-it-all."

"Oh, Libby's just the smartest thing *ever*," Judy Grigson said from the back of the room. "She's also devious. That's why she likes Lady Macbeth." Once Libby's friend, Judy had grown jealous when Henry Waggoner became interested in Libby.

Libby felt her face get hot. She stared at her desk and said nothing.

"Well," Ms. Carter said with pleasure, "if Libby's essay proves she likes what's devious, maybe she's been hoist by her own petard." Ms. Carter smiled broadly. "That's also Shakespeare, class."

Ms. Carter moved on to the other papers. Feeling humiliated, Libby sat with her head down for the rest of the class, which seemed to go on forever. When the bell finally rang, Ms. Carter handed out the papers. When she came to Libby, she had a small, satisfied smile. Libby's essay had a big, red C-scrawled across the top.

As Libby left the room, she saw Henry Waggoner waiting for her. She sighed inwardly. She was no longer in the mood for baseball.

"Our game starts in an hour," he said. "Are you coming?"

4

The baseball diamond was at the rear end of the campus, behind the football field. Libby climbed up the first base bleachers and sat on an empty row. In the warm afternoon sun, the sound of the players' chatter soon seemed hazy and far away. Henry had just finished his warmup tosses when he saw her. She gave him a small, tentative wave, and he returned a slight nod. He then turned to face the batter.

Henry gave up four runs in the first three innings and was taken out with two on and one out in the fourth. He couldn't throw his curve for a strike, and his fastball was catching too much of the plate. After his manager asked for the ball, Henry jogged out to right field with his head down.

An inning later, while his team was at bat, Henry walked over to the drinking fountain. Libby clambered down the bleachers and caught up with him.

"I'm really sorry, Henry," she said. "Even Walter Johnson had bad days."

"Right," he said glumly. "But if I don't have some good ones soon, goodbye scholarship."

"You'll turn it around. I'm sure."

"Say, how do you know about Walter Johnson? That's not what I'd expect from a math ace."

Libby shrugged. "The Big Train is still the all-time shutout leader. My aunt isn't keen about talk shows or computers, but she loves baseball."

As Henry started back to the dugout, Libby said, "You probably already know, but their pitcher has gotten ahead 0 and 2 six times so far, and each time he's come in with a curve."

Henry smiled, "The scouting report says to expect a curve when he's ahead in the count. Anyway, the changeup is his out pitch."

"Oh," Libby said, looking disappointed, "then you probably know this, too."

"What," he said.

"Well, before he throws his changeup, he shifts his grip on the ball and you can see his forearm flex."

Henry stared at her.

Oakview tied the game in the sixth, and in the bottom of the seventh Henry had come up with two outs and a runner on second. He swung and missed the first pitch, and fouled off the second. The pitcher then shifted his grip for the next delivery. Libby wondered if Henry had noticed. The pitch was a changeup, and it came in low and inside. Timing the ball perfectly, hips and arms propelling the bat through a powerful arc, Henry golfed it off the left field fence. A moment later the winning run touched home. As Henry jogged off the field, with teammates giving him high-fives, he glanced up and met Libby's eyes. His mouth formed the word "thanks."

It was almost dark when Libby started home. She knew Ruth would be starting to worry, but that didn't make her any less glad about Henry's hit. He had been down about his pitching but finished the game happy. Being a little late was a small price to pay. On an impulse, she decided to take a detour past the falcon nest. It would be a good ending to a day Macbeth and Ms. Carter had almost spoiled.

When she reached the old hotel ten minutes later, it was too dark to make out the nest. But she could hear a chorus of peeps overhead. It must be feeding time. She listened carefully and identified four separate chicks. Their peeps were very similar, but when she concentrated she could tell them apart. She just had to filter out the other noise. It might be two weeks before the chicks became fledglings and started to fly, but Libby planned to watch them every day. With the birds, and Henry, and a little more caution with Ms. Carter, this might end up a pretty good year after all.

Then Libby saw a faint movement out of the corner of her eye. At first she couldn't see anything, but then she made out a faint shape on the ledge just above the nest. She squinted and barely saw the outline of the gray tomcat she had seen a few days before. With flattened ears, it was soundlessly creeping toward the female falcon and her chicks. In another couple of feet, the cat would be close enough to pounce. The female, tending to her babies, hadn't seen it.

Gripped with fear, Libby looked around for something that might help. She saw a rock in the flower bed next to the hotel's walkway, picked it up, and threw it with all her might toward the cat. The rock landed fifteen feet below her target and clattered away. Libby had a momentary thought—Henry would have hit the cat, no question. The cat turned and looked at Libby with eyes that seemed full of contempt. It then started again toward the birds.

"Go away, cat! Go away!" Libby screamed. The cat took no notice and continued to creep toward the birds. The falcon kept feeding her chicks. Libby looked at the distance from the cat to the nest and calculated she had no more than forty seconds to do something.

Libby raced up the walkway and burst into the lobby. The elevator doors were closed, but there were stairs nearby. The mental counter in her head told her she had used up ten seconds. She raced up the stairs, taking two at a time, didn't slow down for the second floor, and bounded up the next flight to the third floor and its balcony. Ten more seconds.

The cat was about in the middle of the building's west side, Libby thought. She looked up and down the hall on the third floor, and saw an open door in about the right spot. She raced down the hall toward it, and on the way snatched a pitcher of water from a cart someone had left. Ten seconds remaining. She rushed into the open room, not knowing what she would do if someone was there. The room was empty, but it looked like the maid would be back soon.

Libby ran out to the balcony and looked over the edge. Knowing she was out of time, Libby saw the nest about ten feet below, and the tomcat five feet from the nest. The cat should have pounced by now, but it was looking up, its ears flattened.

The male falcon was diving at the tom, talons outstretched. A kamikaze fighter, Libby thought. A suicide mission. The bird crashed into the cat, its claws raking the animal's face and nose. But the tom, swift as a striking snake, smashed a paw against the falcon, knocking it into the side of the building. Forgetting the nest, the cat bounded toward the dazed falcon.

"Go away!" Libby screamed, and she slung the water from the pitcher down onto the cat. It hissed at Libby, its face a mask of fury, and darted away. The male falcon righted itself, fluttered its wings once, and flew off awkwardly.

Now aware of the threat, the female falcon gathered her chicks beneath her. A moment later, the male joined her, its right wing looking weak and scattering feathers. Seconds later the falcons took their chicks and flew off, the male lagging behind.

You're out of luck, Mr. Tomcat, Libby thought. She wished she could care for the male falcon, but she doubted see would would see them again.

"What are you doing here?" a maid called from the door.

Libby whirled around. "Sorry," she said. "I heard something on the balcony and came in to look. It was just a cat." She walked toward the door.

"What are you doing with that water pitcher?" the maid asked.

Libby had forgotten about that. "It was lying on the balcony, so I picked it up. The cat must have knocked it over. Here." Libby handed it to the maid and walked out of the room. The maid seemed to want to say something, but Libby was gone before she could.

As Libby left the hotel, she thought the chicks might not last long, but at least they would have a chance to learn to be falcons.

She started for home. Ruth would be worrying.

6

A half block from her house, Libby saw an unfamiliar dark car parked next to the Miller home. As she got closer, she saw who was inside. The man on the street.

The man saw her and quickly opened the door, but by then Libby was running. The man called out, but Libby paid no attention. She didn't know why he was here, but seeing him a second time was very bad news. It meant he was not here by accident. Libby ran for home, fear for Ruth clutching at her heart.

She ran up the stairs and burst through the front door. Ruth was sitting stiffly on the couch in the front room, looking pale. A lean, athletic-looking woman stood next to her, a hand on Ruth's shoulder. She had an ugly claw of a birthmark on her cheek.

"Hello, Libby," the woman said, "Ruth's been worried about you." Ruth didn't look worried. She looked terrified.

"Who are you?"

"My name is Agent Autumn Gray," the woman said. She held out an official-looking government ID that had Homeland Security written in broad letters. "You've already met my partner, Mr. Blunt."

"What do you want?" Libby said.

The woman smiled and nodded with approval. "Right to the point. Very good. We just want some answers, and then we'll be off."

"You can't just break in here. We'll call the police."

Agent Gray looked amused. "We *are* the police, sweetie. We just don't drive around in patrol cars."

The man from the car stepped into the room. "I see you've already met my partner," he said. "Did she introduce me?"

"Mr. Blunt," Libby said.

"Exactly," he said. "I must say, Libby, you're very unfriendly. Always running away."

"How do you know my name?" Libby asked.

"We know a lot about you, Libby Anderson," the man said. "And we're going to learn more."

"Take whatever you want," Ruth said. "Just leave."

"Questions first," the man said. "Why don't you sit down and relax? This may take a while."

Libby's heart was pounding. She tried to get Ruth's attention, to put her at ease, but Ruth just stared straight ahead, looking pale and dazed.

"I'll stand," Libby said.

"Suit yourself," the man said. "Now, let's try the first question. Libby, are you really just ordinary?"

"What—what do you mean?"

"Oh, I think you know. You took a test in first grade and scored off the charts. But when you took the test again, you were just ordinary. We want to know how that happened."

"First grade? That was eight years ago."

"It was indeed. But I think you remember it. I think you've got a very good memory."

Libby did remember it, of course. She had been foolish. But she couldn't resist showing off, just that one time. Especially when little Randy Cord, who sat next to her, teased her about not listening in class.

Libby shrugged. "I remember something about a test. The teacher thought I cheated. So they gave me another test and said the first was just a fluke. That was all."

"The thing is, Libby, we don't think the first was a fluke. So we want to give you another test to find out. You wouldn't mind that, would you?"

She thought the test wouldn't be a problem. She would make her score ordinary.

"I'll take your test if you'll go away afterwards."

The Gray woman reached into a large travel bag and took out a metal device with wires attached to a headset. "The thing is, Libby," she said, "you might just pretend to be ordinary. So we have this little machine to look at your brain patterns. It will tell us how hard you're trying. We'll attach this headset to your head and ask some questions. If that first grade test was really a fluke, and if you really are just average, we'll be on our way."

"What if it wasn't a fluke?" Ruth said, her voice trembling.

The woman didn't answer.

"You'll take her, won't you?" Ruth said, more strongly now. "Well, I won't let you."

Gray's face started to flush, causing her birthmark to stand out. "Accept one thing," she said. "We're going to find out what's in your little niece's head—one way or the other. So make things easy and tell her to be good."

Gray bent down and drew out the machine's headset with wires attached. Then she attached the wires to the machine, one by one. The wires looked like the tentacles of some poisonous jelly fish. Ruth stared at them, eyes wide. Libby felt frozen, unable to think.

Suddenly Ruth lunged for the device. She grabbed the wires with her thin fingers and yanked them loose. Three of the wires pulled free and the device clattered across the floor. As Gray tried to protect the machine, Ruth lashed her hand against Gray's face, her fingernails leaving deep scratches.

Gray reacted almost instantly. With a snarl, she smashed the edge of her hand against the side of Ruth's neck. Something snapped and Ruth fell as though she had been hit with a club, her head striking the edge of the coffee table.

Libby stared at Ruth's crumpled body. She felt like she was in one of her nightmares. Everything was unreal. She and Ruth had been watching baseball here just the night before.

For an instant, Libby saw Gray's glittering eyes as she stared down at Ruth's crumpled body and thought, *the woman was insane.*

Run! Something inside her screamed. *Run!*

In terror and panic, Libby sprinted into the kitchen as the agents stared at Ruth. She flipped off the lights and darted out the back door. While her feet flew and she tried to control her terror, a separate part of her mind raced through options. She could run outside and down the street. But the agents would expect that. They had a car, they could call the police, and they would catch her. If she ran into the Wilsons' house, she would just get them involved. And if the police came, the agents would blame her. It would be their word against hers. She might be arrested, and everything would be out of her control.

She ran to the back gate, pushed it open and closed, and then raced back to crouch behind the willow tree next to the house, just like when she'd played hide and seek. The neighbor's cat, Whiskers, was crouched right there, next to her. Maybe waiting for a bird. Libby often fed it, and it stared at her expectantly.

7

Blunt looked at Ruth's body and cursed.

"Silly old woman," Gray muttered. She pressed her hand against the scratches, which were starting to bleed.

Blunt walked over and placed his fingers against Ruth's neck. "Well, she's dead. You crazy bitch."

Gray's head jerked, and she turned to stare at Blunt. "What did you call me?" she said in a low voice.

"Everyone says you're crazy. And now you've killed some harmless old woman. Jesus!"

Suddenly the lights went out and the back door slammed. The girl was gone.

Blunt waited for his eyes to adjust to the darkness, found the back door in the kitchen, and stepped into the backyard. The woman lagged behind, her eyes boring into Blunt's back.

There was no moon and the yard was shrouded in darkness. Blunt listened for a sound but heard nothing. "It's so damned dark," Blunt said. "And she knows every hiding place."

Gray said nothing.

Blunt said, "Well, she won't get anywhere. If she calls the police, they'll turn her over to us. And we'll have some people watch the airlines and trains. She won't last a day."

Gray remained quiet, her hand pressed against the scratches. Blood was flowing over the spidery birthmark.

Libby kept still, but the voices startled the cat. It shot out from beneath the tree and raced across the yard. Gray whirled instantly and fired. There was no bang, just a muffled phut. A silencer, Libby thought dazedly, like in the movies. The bullet struck the cat just beneath its left shoulder. It was knocked over, blood splattering, and lay still.

A scream tried to force its way out of Libby's throat, but she choked it back. Her eyes bulged as the image of the cat's spraying blood played over in her mind. Whiskers. He used to purr softly when she pet it.

8

"Jesus!" Blunt said. "First a harmless old woman and now a ferocious house cat. You're a real gunfighter, aren't you?"

Gray continued to hold her hand against the bleeding scratches. "That woman scratched me."

"Don't worry," Blunt said, his voice disgusted. "The scratches will go well with that birthmark of yours."

Gray slowly turned her head. She stared at Blunt with expressionless eyes.

After a moment, Blunt said. "God, what a mess. We'll have to do something about the body. I know a guy who can take care of it."

"What about the girl?" Gray asked.

Blunt sighed. "She'll have to go too. No choice. She saw what happened."

"What will we tell the handler?" Gray asked.

"So, now you think of that, eh? Well, we'll have to tell him about the girl and her aunt. Sometimes shit happens. And I'll make up some story about how the aunt went berserk. With any luck he'll believe it, and we won't end up as fertilizer in some long-forgotten cornfield. I won't say you were the one who lost control."

"That's generous of you," Gray said evenly.

"I'll tell him the girl tested average, like all the others, but that we had to get rid of her because she saw what happened to her aunt. If he thinks she's nothing special, he'll cross her off the list and tell us to take care of her."

Gray nodded to herself, saying nothing.

"If she does go to the police," Blunt said, "we'll have to have a story. But no body, no evidence. And the guys back in Washington will back us up. The local police will end up turning her over to us, and the problem will be solved. There's no family to cause trouble. She'll never be heard from again."

"And the only ones who'll know the real story will be you and me, right?" Gray said.

"Right," Blunt said. "Now, let me get the car so we can take care of the body."

9

Libby stayed under the willow tree. She had heard the agents and decided they were probably right. If she went to the police, everything would be blamed on her. Maybe she could eventually get the truth out, if she survived. But once the agents had their hands on her, they could do what they wanted. She could disappear, and no one would care.

After a long wait, Libby heard Blunt move his car into the driveway. She crept out from under the tree and went around the house, staying where it was dark. She saw Blunt carry out a small figure wrapped in garbage bags and put it into the trunk. It made a thud like a sack of potatoes. Tears started flooding Libby's eyes. Ruth had been so frightened all these years, and sometimes Libby had secretly scoffed at her. But Ruth had been right, and she had been wrong. Little Ruth. She had attacked that woman agent just like that falcon had dove at the tomcat. Except it was more like a sparrow attacking a mountain lion. She pictured Ruth's crumpled, little body with its head twisted impossibly to the side.

Libby tried to force the horrid images from her mind, but her thoughts were in scattered pieces. She thought about the Wilsons next door. If she asked for their help, the Gray woman would show up with a good story and her homeland security badge, and Mrs. Wilson would do whatever the police wanted. And that would be whatever Gray wanted.

Images began flashing in Libby's mind. Ruth crashing against the coffee table. Whiskers' blood spraying over the yard. The falcon attacking the tomcat. And then the nightmare started. It had never struck when she was awake before. Her mind turned brilliant red…and she passed out.

CHAPTER THREE

ON THE RUN

1

When Libby opened her eyes, the moon was low on the horizon, so she must have been out for at least two hours. Her mind felt sluggish, but at least it was free of those terrible images. She peered around a hedge and could see Blunt's car in the driveway. There were voices inside the house. She shivered. She was still wearing the light windbreaker she'd worn at Henry's game. Was that only a few hours before? She wanted to run but remembered a program about lions. They were attracted by movement. She stayed still and tried to keep warm.

A long time later, the house lights went out and the car's engine started up. Everything was quiet. Libby waited, then drifted off to sleep again.

Morning light was just seeping over the back fence when Libby stirred. Once it got lighter, the agents would probably come back, so she had to get away now. But where to? And how?

She realized she needed money. She wouldn't last twenty-four hours without it. She didn't have a bank account. The flood money was the only thing she could think of. But Ruth always said it was only for an emergency. Well, Libby thought, this probably qualified.

Libby walked to the back door, staying close to the house, and quietly turned the knob. It was locked. She found the spare key behind the drain and let herself in. The familiar house now seemed alien and frightening. She looked in the living room. Ruth's body was gone. She thought for a moment, then silently walked to the cellar door, opened it, and tip-toed down the stairs.

She went quickly to the old chest of drawers in the corner. She reached behind it and experienced a moment of panic when she felt nothing, but then her fingers closed on the old folder taped to the back. She pulled it out and saw a stack of bills and several documents. She was tempted to read them and count the money, but she knew time was short. She tucked the folder under her blouse and went back up the stairs.

She looked around the house and wondered if she'd ever be back. She quickly filled a small duffle bag with a change of clothes and bathroom things and was just starting to leave when she heard a car pull into the driveway. She slipped out of the back door, closed it silently, and flattened herself against the house. In a few moments, she heard the two agents inside the house. She quickly stepped through the back gate and walked away.

2

Blunt came out of the bathroom shaking his head. "She's been here," he said. "Some toiletries are missing. I never thought she'd be back so soon."

"Isn't she the clever girl," Gray said. "We need to get our hands on her."

"We will. I got some more information on her. She's only fifteen. Can't drive. If she tries to run, she'll have to take a plane or bus, or maybe a train. I'll have some of our guys keep an eye out for her at the terminals. And I can do one more thing. I'll have the handler put Sibyl on it."

"What's Sibyl?"

"You're not in the loop, eh? Sibyl's a massive supercomputer."

"Do you have access to it?" Gray asked.

"Used it on my last job. Now we just have to find the girl. Then I'll give them our story."

3

"We'll get back to the aunt in a minute," the handler said. "Are you certain the girl was nothing special?"

"Absolutely certain," Blunt said. "We monitored her test for two hours. She was only slightly above normal. No more."

"How did you get them to cooperate? Weren't they being difficult?"

"They had a bunch of medical bills. We said we'd help with them."

Gray had found the bills while Blunt was getting rid of the aunt. They had worked up the story together.

"So," the handler said, "what went wrong?"

Blunt felt sweat trickling down his back. "When we were done, we offered the aunt five hundred dollars. It had only taken two hours, so that seemed fair."

"And then what?" the handler said.

"The aunt laughed. She said they needed at least $5000 to take care of the bills. Not a penny less. That was crazy. We couldn't pay that kind of money when the girl was only ordinary."

"So why didn't you just leave? You had the assessment."

"We started to leave, but all at once the girl started to call 911. And when the aunt tried to grab Gray's arm, Gray shoved her away. It wasn't even that hard. But the aunt weighed maybe eighty pounds and fell into the coffee table. The next thing we know she's dead and the kid's run off."

"And now you're saying you can't find the girl?"

"Not yet. But we're watching the airports and train stations. And we've got photos for the facial recognition programs. We'll get her."

"And then what?"

Blunt grimaced. "She'll have to go missing."

After a long silence, the handler said, "None of this should have happened."

"Maybe not," Blunt said. "But when you come out of nowhere and start questioning people, sometimes things go off script."

"Maybe you were the ones off script."

Blunt didn't say anything. Finally, he asked, "So it's OK to go after the girl?"

"What's the alternative?"

4

Libby walked until her stomach told her it was past noon. She found a small, half-full café and took a table in the back, facing the street. While she waited to order, she flashed on Ruth's crumpled body and thought she might be sick. Could she have prevented it? If she had told Ruth about meeting Blunt the day before, would Ruth have been more prepared? And why had she been so slow to react in the house?

She took out Ruth's folder and looked inside. There was a stack of one hundred dollar bills that would have seen them through a severe flood. There was also a copy of a birth certificate, showing her birth in Stockton, California, to Amanda Taylor, a certificate of her adoption by Ruth Anderson, a copy of her vaccination history, and a report card from her first semester in high school. The last document was old and worn and covered with smudges. It said:

Ruth,

Libby's mother was killed because her mind was exceptional. Libby's may be, too. If people learn about Libby, she could be in danger.

Records of Libby's birth, adoption, and location have been deleted. If no one learns about her, she should be safe.

A friend

Libby read and reread the note. Now she knew why Ruth had been so adamant about her being inconspicuous. Why hadn't she taken Ruth more seriously? Ruth probably didn't tell her about the note because she didn't want her niece to worry the way she did.

Libby put the papers and bills back into the folder. She sat for a while, thinking about what she had learned. A weary-looking waitress finally came over, and Libby ordered a BLT and fries.

"Can customers use that computer by the wall?" Libby asked, pointing to an old desktop beneath some university pennants.

34 | Scott W. Sonne

The woman shrugged. "We keep it so students will hang around and buy more drinks."

"Does it work?" Libby asked.

"Yeah. If you want to log on, the password is "GoPanthers.""

Ruth hadn't allowed computers in the house. She thought they could be spied on. But Libby used the school computers all the time. When she was working a computer keyboard, her friends said she looked like a concert pianist.

After the server brought the food, Libby moved to the computer and logged on. She chewed her sandwich and typed Gray, Blunt and Homeland Security into the search engine. There were hundreds of hits, but nothing useful. The agents' names were probably fake. Were they really with Homeland Security? Possibly. They didn't seem worried about the police. She finished her sandwich and thought for a while. Then she entered Ruth's name. There was no report of her or Libby being missing.

She had just logged off when she saw a black car pull up in front of the Chinese restaurant across the street. Two people stepped out. Libby's heart froze. One of them was Gray, her birthmark visible in the bright sun. The other was Blunt.

When the two agents rushed into the restaurant, Libby dropped a twenty on the table and left from the side door. She walked away swiftly, but peeked around a corner in time to see Gray and Blunt back on the sidewalk, looking around.

As she walked away, Libby realized that if the agents had gone into her café, instead of the restaurant across the street, they would have had her. How had they found her so quickly? Libby could think of only one thing. Ruth had been right. Computers were being monitored. They were picking up searches for Gray, Blunt, and Homeland Security. No wonder Blunt said they would find her. With surveillance, facial recognition, and computer monitoring, even the smallest slip would give her away.

She continued walking, her eyes searching for cameras or anything else that might identify her. Where could she go? Not the police. They would defer to Homeland Security. Not friends. That would just cause them trouble. A thought suddenly flashed in her mind, and she grasped it like a drowning person clutching a raft. She would find Tom Grant, the man she had written, who had known her mother. It might be a foolish idea, but she could think of nothing better. She needed a destination, a purpose. She had no idea where he was, only that he had once been in Colorado. She thought for a while. How could she get there?

5

By late mid-afternoon, Libby had found the college's student union building. A large bulletin board was posted near the entrance. It was covered with notices about roommates sought, computers for sale, used books for upcoming classes, and tutoring help. But in one corner were several notices of rides for spring break.

Libby called to a woman passing by, "Could you tell me when spring break is?"

The woman looked at her strangely. "You must not be a student. Spring break starts tomorrow."

Libby turned back to the bulletin board and studied the notices more closely. She found a yellow note card with nice handwriting in blue ink that announced a ride leaving for Denver the next morning. Passengers were asked to share gas and other expenses. The note said to call Sarah, and it gave a phone number.

Libby called the number and said, "Is this Sarah?"

"It sure is," a cheerful voice said. "What can I do for you?"

"I'm looking for a ride to Denver. Are you still going?" Libby asked.

"We have room for one more," Sarah said. "My boyfriend's coming, and another guy just signed on. Is it just you?"

"Just me," Libby said. "How much for expenses?"

"A hundred bucks should do it," the girl said. "What's your name?"

The police would be looking for someone with her name and description, so Libby said the first name that came to mind, "Abby."

6

Libby walked around the campus looking for a place to spend the night. She passed a group talking about Ensenada and several couples talking in low, intimate voices. She finally saw two girls only slightly older than she.

"Excuse me," she said. "I'm coming here next year. Is there some place I could crash for the night? My reservation must have got lost. I won't be trouble, promise."

The girls looked at each other. "You look awfully young," the smaller one said. "How old are you?"

"Sixteen," Libby said, adding a year. "I skipped a couple grades."

"Well, she doesn't *look* scary," the girl said to her friend.

"I'm totally harmless," Libby said. "Promise."

Marnie looked doubtful. "Looks and reality can be different." She thought for a moment, then said, "All right. Karen's left for break. You could stay in her room. But watch out for our dorm supervisor. He can be a jerk."

Libby exhaled in relief.

The girls took Libby to the room. It was a mess. "Karen's nice. She won't mind if you crash here. But don't mess it up, or she'll blame us."

"Don't worry," Libby said.

After cleaning up, Libby walked around the college neighborhood. She ran into another surveillance camera and wondered if she could do something to make her harder to identify. She came to a beauty parlor and walked in.

A short, dark-haired woman approached her and said, "Need a trim?"

"Actually, I'm thinking of a makeover. How about something short and cute, and maybe a new color?"

"Sure, hon," the woman said. "But are you sure about a different color? That sandy hair really goes well with your face."

Libby smiled. "I'm ready for a change. How about brown? If it doesn't work, the old color will grow back in."

The woman frowned. "Your decision."

Two hours later, Libby left with chestnut-colored hair cut in a short bob. It wasn't an improvement, but it was new.

Could she do anything else to change alter her appearance? She thought of Gray, with the spidery birthmark. She realized she could remember little about her appearance beyond the wine-stain claw.

She walked into a tattoo parlor with flashing neon signs. A bell rang and soon a heavy, balding man with tattoos from the neck down came out.

"I'd like a tattoo," Libby said.

The man shook his head slowly. "You have to be eighteen."

"What about a tattoo that only looks permanent? That would be perfect for a cool party next week?"

The man thought for a moment. "Okay," he said. "What do you want?"

Libby told him.

"That's a new one," he said. "No dragons or butterflies?"

"Maybe next time. Can you do it?"

The man nodded.

6

After leaving the tattoo parlor, Libby found an old department store. "I'm going overseas for Spring Break," she told a clerk. "Do you have something I could put money and a passport in?"

The clerk took her to a counter in the travel section. When Libby left fifteen minutes later, her money belt was more comfortable than she'd expected.

She walked back to the dorm and took the elevator up to Karen's room on the third floor. As she started to turn the doorknob, she heard someone behind her.

"Karen's gone," a man said. "Why are you entering her room?"

Libby turned and found herself facing a thin, acne-scarred man in his late twenties.

"Her friends said I could crash here tonight," Libby said. "I'm enrolling next year and came to visit."

The man stared at Libby's tattoo and frowned. "Did you have that tattoo when you applied?"

"No. I just got it."

The man shook his head. "That tattoo's like graffiti on a pretty house."

"It means something to me," Libby said.

He shook his head. "I've just thought of a thesis topic," he said. "How tattoos are caused by low intelligence."

"Why not: how intolerance is caused by low intelligence?"

The man grinned. "Touché. But maybe it wouldn't be a bad topic. Prove it by giving I.Q. tests to people with tattoos."

"That wouldn't prove anything," Libby said.

"Why not?" The man looked interested.

"Correlation is not causation."

His face went blank. "Son of a bitch," he said.

"What?" Libby asked.

"Son of a bitch," the man said again. "I have a real thesis topic. How social isolation causes alcoholism. I devised a test to prove it, and tomorrow I'm presenting it to my advisor."

"So, what's the problem?" Libby asked.

"I've just realized my test only proves correlation, not causation."

He started to walk off.

"Can I stay in the room?" Libby called out.

"What? Oh, sure. If I hadn't run into you, I would have hit a buzz saw tomorrow."

7

A raucous party down the hall made sleeping in Karen's room difficult, but her bone-deep despair would have kept her up anyway. She would never see Ruth again, or Whiskers again, and would probably never step inside Oakview High School again. She thought about Henry Waggoner. Would she ever see him pitch again? Almost certainly not. She hoped he would get his scholarship. Would he have asked her to the prom? Now she would never know. She was even sad to realize she would never sit in Ms. Carter's class again. She would have been happy to be there again, even if she had to listen to her teacher's sarcasm. She thought about the falcons and their chicks. Maybe at least they were safe. As she started to doze off, Libby pictured the Gray woman with the claw-like birthmark, lean and fierce, swinging the edge of her hand against Ruth's frail neck, sending Ruth's small body crashing into the coffee table. Ruth was gone.

She awoke early, wiped tears off her face, and spent a half hour cleaning up Karen's room, careful not to disturb her things. By eight she was in front of the dorm, waiting for the ride to Denver.

Right on time, a late-model, gray Toyota pulled up and a smiling girl with streaked blond hair stepped out.

"Hi, I guess you're Abby," she said. "I'm Sarah. Still up for the ride?"

Libby smiled ruefully. "I was afraid I'd be stuck here for the whole break. Thanks for the lift."

"Gratitude is nice," Sarah said, "but we need the money up front. On our last ride-share, we waited to ask for it until the end, only to discover the guy didn't have it."

After Libby handed over the money, Sarah seemed to relax. "Great," she said. "Climb in."

Libby got in the back seat, behind the driver, a slender, dark, bookish-looking guy in his early twenties. His heavy glasses had broken frames held together by tape.

"This is Charles," Sarah said, grinning. "He helps me with calculus, and I feed him—something he wasn't doing for himself."

Charles glanced at Libby. "Hi," he said, as though he wasn't used to talking.

"Nice to meet you," Libby said, "and thanks for the lift."

Charles started the engine. A few minutes later they picked up a huge, athletic-looking guy on the other side of campus. Libby wondered if he played football.

As he slid into the back seat next to Libby, Sarah said, "Abby, this is Phil Keller."

After adjusting his huge frame to the cramped interior, Phil turned to Libby, smiled, and studied her with inquisitive eyes. "Well, Abby, you weren't short-changed in the looks department, but you seem to be missing a few years. Don't tell me you're really a student here."

Libby smiled ruefully. "You got me. I'm just visiting. I plan to come next year."

"Next year, eh? I'd say you're still a year or two short."

"I managed to skip a couple years," Libby said.

"Skipped *two* years, you say? You sound like one of those freakish, smart ones we hear about," Phil's tone was bantering.

"Well, I suppose freakish is in the eye of the beholder," Libby said.

"I thought it was beauty," Phil said.

"That, too," Libby said.

Phil studied Libby a while longer, then said, "Sarah, I must say your taste in passengers is excellent."

"Maybe in Abby's case it is," Sarah said. "The jury is still out on you." Sarah turned to Libby. "We might as well get Phil's dirty laundry out in the open. Phil's with us because he can't attend spring football practice. Seems he committed a minor academic indiscretion. Isn't that right, Phil?"

Feigning innocence, Phil said, "I was framed. Someone forged my name on that exam paper that got the big red D."

"Will you be able to get back on the team?" Libby asked.

"If I can fix my physics problem. That's how I'm spending the break."

8

Charles got on highway 15, heading north. Sarah and Phil soon drifted off to sleep while Libby stared out the window and watched signs for places she'd never heard of. After an hour Sarah awoke and brought out a stainless steel thermos and a large paper bag. "If any of you didn't get breakfast," she said, "I brought some donuts and coffee."

Suddenly ravenous, Libby passed on the coffee but welcomed a donut. Phil had coffee and two donuts.

9

By noon they had passed San Bernardino and were heading toward Las Vegas. The day had turned muggy, with dark clouds hiding the sun. Libby nestled into the left corner of the rear seat, her head against the side window, listening to the car's engine and the rhythmic sound of the tires on the road. The others were talking about their plans for the break, classes, and football. Libby remained silent.

"Hey, Abby," Sarah said, "why are you going to Colorado?"

Libby needed a moment to remember what she had called herself.

"I've never met my father," Libby said. "I hope to find him."

"Good luck." Sarah said. "My dad's been gone for years. It's a real bummer."

"If you're around next year, Abby," Phil said, "I'll get you football tickets."

"If you're back on the team," Sarah said.

"There is that," Phil said, his voice sober now.

"Sure you'll make the team?" Libby asked.

"Phil's the famous sophomore football star," Sarah said, "recruited to protect our big-time quarterback. If he gets out of academic purgatory, he'll be on the team for sure."

"Left tackle?" Libby asked.

"How did you know that?" Sarah asked. "Been following the team?"

"No. Just a guess. I used to watch a lot of football with my aunt. The left tackle is the main pass blocker for a right-handed quarterback. He has to be big—and strong enough to hold off three-hundred pound rushers. Phil might qualify."

"Enough about me," Phil said, studying Libby again. "What's with the tattoo?"

Libby put a hand on her neck. "It's just something I wanted to do."

"It looks like a bird dive-bombing a tiger."

"It's a sparrow," Libby said.

"A sparrow fighting a tiger?" Phil said. "Seems like a death wish."

Libby stared out the window. "It just reminds me of something."

Sarah asked, "Care to share?"

"Not really, but it reminds me of my…" Libby's voice caught, "my aunt."

Libby was silent for a while, then turned to Phil. "What's with physics?"

"My fault. I usually handle tests pretty well. Thought I could scrape through on this one. But with football and other stuff…I just didn't study enough.

"So what happened?" Libby asked.

Phil smiled wryly. "Well, I got a D on the midterm. The coach was pissed. He wanted to put in a new pass-blocking scheme. My absence will set things back."

Sarah said, "Tell Abby the full story, Phil."

"Doesn't matter," Phil said. "A D is a D."

"Phil hurt his knee two days before the test," Sarah said. "Time he had planned for studying was taken up by hospitals and doctors instead."

"It's not a very good excuse," Phil said. "I could have asked for an extension. But I thought I could slip by anyway. The professor said you couldn't fake your way out of physics. Turns out she was right."

10

Just west of Barstow they pulled in for gas and a restroom break. As Libby and Sarah were walking back to the car, Libby asked, "How did you get to know Phil?"

"Oh, we took chemistry together last year. He missed a lot of lectures because of football, so I let him borrow my notes. But there was no tutoring or anything like that. You might think he's a big oaf because of his size, but he's very bright."

"I'm not surprised," Libby said. "Offensive linemen have to learn a lot of blocking schemes."

Sarah got a faraway look. "I got a little twinge for him, but he didn't have time for girls. It was all school and ball. And then I met Charles. He's more my type anyway."

"Charles seems nice. But he doesn't say much."

Sarah laughed. "That's all the better. I talk enough for both of us."

Once they were back on the highway, Libby said, "So, Phil, what are you going to do about your suspension?"

"You've found out a lot about me," Phil said. "How about something about you first?"

Libby wondered if Gray could trace her to Phil and Sarah. Probably not. But anything she said could be a risk for them as well as her. "There's nothing to know," she said.

Phil gazed at her a while longer, then said, "Just tell me this. Something about you seems sad. Care to explain why?"

Libby blinked. "Nothing to talk about. A recent death in the family, but I don't want to go into it."

"All right. Don't mean to pry."

Libby smiled. "Thanks. So, how are you going to fix your physics problem?"

"I may be allowed a makeup test. The coach told the professor my knee injury kept me from studying. I suppose the professor will cave in, but she's not happy. She said I should have raised my problem beforehand."

"Did you really think you could pass physics without studying?"

Phil smiled ruefully. "I can be a little mule-headed. And I didn't want any special favors."

"Too proud?"

Phil didn't answer. Then he said, "Besides, I'm seeing her about my grade. She said I didn't do well enough, but I think I could have passed. If I did, I won't need the makeup."

"Why do you think you passed?"

"If I'd gotten the last question right, I would have squeaked by. She marked it wrong, but I think it was right."

"I doubt she would be wrong on something like that," Libby said. "You sure this isn't wishful thinking?"

Phil sighed. "Well, it might be. But what do I have to lose?"

"Well, you could annoy someone who's giving you a break, and who will be grading your makeup test. And what about that pride of yours if you're wrong again."

Phil stared at Libby. "Okay," he said, "I'll give you the question. Tell me what you think."

Libby let out a bark of laughter. "I haven't taken college physics. Why would my opinion matter?"

"I don't know. I just have a feeling. Humor me."

"All right. But would my helping you be some type of honor code violation?"

"I don't know," Phil said. "I'm sure you'll do the right thing."

"I'm curious," Sarah said. "Go ahead, Phil. Tell Libby the problem."

"The physics exam lasted three hours," Phil said, "and I didn't get to the final question until the last fifteen minutes."

"Okay, okay," Sarah said. "If you hadn't run out of time, you would have solved the problem, no sweat."

Libby smiled to herself. She was getting to like Sarah.

Phil looked embarrassed. "I just—okay, here's problem. This ship is going through the Panama Canal. The canal has these locks that raise and lower a ship as it goes from one ocean to the other."

"Yeah, yeah, common knowledge," Sarah said, yawning.

"Well, the ship is carrying this heavy military tank, which is accidentally put into reverse, causing it to fall over the side of the ship and into the lock."

Sarah said, "Yes, gravity does tend to do that."

"The question was," Phil said, "after the tank sank into the lock, did the water level against the side of the lock go up, down, or stay at the same level?"

Everyone was silent for several minutes. Then Sarah said, "The water would stay at the same level. The tank being in the lock would cause the water level to rise. But the ship would be lighter without the tank, which means it wouldn't float as deeply in the water. That would cause the water level to fall. So those two things would cancel each other out and the water level would stay the same."

"I agree with Sarah," Charles said.

"That's what I wrote on the exam," Phil said. "But it was marked wrong."

He turned and looked at Libby. "Well, the point of all this was to get *your* opinion? What is it?"

Libby thought she knew the answer. The water displaced when the tank was in the ship, causing the ship to float deeper in the water, was almost certainly greater than the water displaced by the tank sitting on the bottom. That meant that the water level would drop once the tank fell into the lock.

But Libby decided not to say anything. No one had liked her talking about Lady Macbeth, because no one likes a know-it-all. And it was showing off on that first grade test that had caused all this.

"Look guys," she said, "you're asking the wrong person. Wait until I have some college. Anything I say now would be uninformed."

Phil studied her. "Just tell me this," he said, "should I go to the professor or not?"

Libby felt her insides squirm. "Really, Phil, you shouldn't rely on me."

"Are you telling me you really have no opinion at all?" Phil asked.

Libby shook her head.

"I don't believe you," Phil said.

Libby stared at the floor and said nothing.

CHAPTER FOUR

TO LAS VEGAS

1

While Charles was driving the Camry out of San Bernardino and into the desert, Blunt called the handler to report.

"Are you telling me the girl is still on the loose?" The handler said.

"We haven't got her yet," Blunt said, "but it'll be soon."

"I've heard that before. Have you checked all her friends?"

"Of course. Except for her absence at school, no one knew she was gone."

"What about airports and trains?"

"We're monitoring everything, including photos and facial recognition."

"Then where the hell is she?" The handler's voice had a whip-crack quality to it.

Blunt said nothing.

"You say the girl saw her aunt killed. We can't have that become public."

"It won't," Blunt said.

"And you're *sure* this girl didn't have what we were looking for?"

Blunt shifted his feet. "She's just an ordinary teenager," he said. "Nothing usual. Never even been away from home."

"You'd better be right. If she does have the gift—intuition, or whatever you want to call it—she could lead us on a merry chase."

"We're also checking homeless camps and shelters for runaways. She has to be somewhere."

"What about the net? Are you watching that?"

"We're tracking internet searches. There was a search yesterday at a café. We checked it out. Nothing. Must have been a mistake."

"Maybe the girl just ran into the wrong person and is lying in a ditch somewhere."

"That would be okay. Then we could stop searching."

"Speaking of people ending up dead," the handler said, "are you keeping an eye on Gray?"

"Yeah. No problems."

"For a certain type of job, she's the best around. But she can be volatile as nitro. She did well with that foreign diplomat's son, but she cut up his bodyguard and partner, too. What a mess. If she looks like she might do something like that again, call me soonest."

The handsome son of an Austrian diplomat had been peddling drugs and luring young girls into prostitution. The president of one of Quantum's best suppliers complained when his daughter had been seduced by the son and ended up hooking. She was found dead later when her pimp punished her with a heroin overdose. The handler told Gray the son needed to be discouraged. Two days later, the son and his bodyguard were found in the mountains above Los Angeles. The bodyguard had died quickly from an efficient cut to his neck. But the son apparently had almost an hour to contemplate his sins while Gray worked on him. A day later, the son's partner, despite being guarded in his Brentwood mansion, was found knifed to death in his bathroom.

Brunt grimaced. "She's been under control. I'll let you know if I see a problem."

"Do that," the handler said. "Where are the two of you going now?"

"Montana. There's a boy there who's a possible."

The car had passed Victorville and Barstow and crossed the state line into Nevada. Libby stared out at the flat expanse of desert. The day had started clear and windy, but now clouds were forming on the horizon. She stared at them for a while, then started thinking about her situation. What should she do when they got to Denver? Probably take a bus from there. Her hand tugged at the money belt around her waist.

She looked over at Phil Keller. His eyes were closed and his head was leaning against the window. She liked everything about him. His size gave him a reassuring solidity, and his features were animated, his voice expressive. Maybe in a different life they would spend time together. But she knew it was a foolish thought under these circumstances.

When a black and white car with flashing lights sped passed on the other side of the divided highway, Libby wondered if the police could be after her. The agents had said they were with Homeland Security and Libby suspected it was true. They had said they would find her, and her witnessing Ruth's death gave them a strong incentive. Could they find out where she was? She thought not, at least not yet. She hadn't given out her name and had avoided surveillance cameras and places like airports, where people might be looking.

Libby's thoughts were interrupted by several large drops splashing against the windshield. She looked at the sky and saw gray clouds overhead. They were dark gray and black. A jagged streak of lightening flashed across the sky, followed by a clap of thunder. Within minutes, the drops had turned into a torrent.

"Where the hell did this come from?" Charles asked. "That thunder sounded *close.* Anybody hear that a storm was coming?"

"Not me," Sarah said, "but you'd better slow down."

"I already have." Charles pointed ahead to large tractor-trailer rig he had been following. "If he's slowing down, I'd be stupid not to do the same."

Over the next several minutes the storm increased in ferocity and the rain was now falling like a waterfall. Libby had never seen anything like it.

"This is really bad," Charles said. "We'd better pull over and stop."

"But you can't see anything, and no one else can either," Sarah said. "Even if there was a place to stop, one of these big trucks could run right into us."

"This is really bad," Charles said again, his voice trembling slightly.

Libby couldn't believe how much water was coming down. "Do we have four-wheel drive?" she asked.

"Hardly," Charles answered. "This is a Southern California car."

The water on the road got deeper over the next few miles. Libby suspected that the storm had been flooding this part of the desert for longer than they had known. The tractor-trailer ahead of them had water halfway up its tires. The truck was spraying out large plumes as it plowed ahead.

"We can't keep going!" Sarah said. Her voice was almost a scream.

"If we can just get through this patch," Charles said, "I'll pull over and we'll take our chances."

A river of water was flowing across the highway a short distance ahead. The truck ahead had barreled through it, but the size and speed of the current seemed to be increasing by the second.

"Jesus," Charles said, "we're screwed."

"Stop!" Sarah screamed.

"I can't," Charles yelled. "We'd get stuck for sure. If we go fast enough, maybe the momentum will carry us through."

He stamped on the accelerator and tried to follow the path the truck had taken.

Libby thought going faster would do no good. The sideways force of the water was the real danger, and it would be the same no matter how fast the car was going. But it was too late to do anything now.

3

The Camry plowed into the water, and for a moment Charles thought he had chosen correctly. There was an elevated area not far ahead that looked relatively dry. If they could get there they might be all right. But then the wheels lost contact with the pavement and the car began to slide.

Sarah screamed as the car drifted toward the edge of the road. Charles tried to turn the wheels against the slide, but it did no good. The car was out of control.

The car reached the road's shoulder, paused, and then tumbled over the side and down the road's embankment. It landed upside down in a large canal filled with storm water. The car's axles and wheels were barely visible, but the rest of the car was submerged.

4

Libby felt the car slide over the edge and roll down the road's embankment. The seatbelt kept her from bouncing around the car's interior, but when the vehicle came to rest she was hanging upside down. She yanked at the seat belt buckle, but it did no good.

The belt shouldn't be this hard, Libby thought. She looked closely at the buckle and realized that hanging upside down had caused her to pull the wrong way. When she reversed her effort, the buckle sprung open and she tumbled down to the car's roof, which was now the floor. She landed next to Sarah, who was dazed and bleeding.

Phil was still hanging upside down and straining against his seatbelt. Libby got her feet under her and reached for the belt. After seeing which way it opened, she unlatched the buckle and Phil crashed down, his shoulder grazing Libby's head.

Muddy water was filling the car. Charles was hanging upside down, jammed against the steering wheel, and appeared only partially conscious. Libby got Phil's attention and pointed at Charles. Phil unlatched Charles' seatbelt and cushioned his fall as he tumbled down. He eased Charles into a space next to Sarah, who had pulled out a cellphone and was punching in numbers.

As she looked at the rising water, Libby knew that time spent on cellphones would kill them. In two or three minutes the car would be completely filled with water.

Phil was pushing against one of the doors, but it wouldn't budge. Either it had been damaged in the fall or it was blocked by something. The other side door seemed undamaged, so Libby grabbed Phil and pointed to it. Phil looked at the door, but seemed to have difficulty understanding what was happening. When Libby looked at him closely, she could see a large gash above his left eye pouring blood. The muddy water had obscured it before. She put a hand to the side of his face and turned his head until he was looking into her eyes. She gave him a confident smile and mouthed the words, "We can do this."

Phil's eyes seemed to regain their focus, and he clambered with Libby over to the undamaged door. As Libby depressed the handle, Phil put his shoulder against the door and heaved, but it didn't move. Pressure from the water, Libby thought, was keeping the door shut.

A window was the only option. Without much hope, Libby tried one of the electric window switches, but nothing happened. They would have to break the window. As muddy water reached her neck, Libby grabbed Phil, who was still pushing against the door. From the muscles flexing in his arms and back, he must have been applying incredible force against the door, but still it didn't move. Libby made and an exaggerated clubbing motion against the glass. It took a moment for Phil to understand, but then he smashed his fist against the window. Once, twice, a third time. The window didn't even crack. Safety glass, Libby thought.

Struggling to control her fear of the rising water that had nearly filled the car, Libby thought about the simple, silly problem of how to break a window. They needed a club. Thinking back over the morning, she suddenly remembered the metal thermos with coffee Sarah had brought. She looked around the car's interior, which was almost immersed in muddy water, but couldn't see it. She looked again, saw its silver cap barely visible behind the passenger seat, and snatched it up. Fifteen more seconds and it would have been lost. Libby handed it to Phil and pointed to the window. Again, he seemed slow to understand, but then he nodded and faced the window.

Phil smashed the thermos against the window four times. The first three blows had no effect, but the window splintered on the fourth. As water gushed through the opening, Phil used the thermos to knock out the remaining jagged edges.

Libby grabbed Sarah and pushed her to the open window. Sarah quickly slid through and disappeared into the darkness. She did the same with Charles, who seemed barely aware of what was happening. Libby and Phil managed to squeeze the slender man through the window, but as his feet disappeared, Libby saw that he didn't move upwards, toward air, but just floated away. Libby felt her desperation growing. They were running out of time.

With only inches of air left, Libby turned to Phil. She had known all along he was too big for the window. But it was either get out now or drown.

Phil looked at Libby. His eyes were no longer dazed. They seemed resigned as he understood he could not fit through the window. He made an emphatic gesture for her to go through it. Libby looked into his eyes again, until she had his full attention, and shook her head in a violent no. She then turned to the door they had tried to open before. Hydrostatic pressure. She thought for a moment and realized that when the car filled with water, the pressure would be equalized, and maybe then they could open the door. But despair suddenly exploded inside her. The situation was hopeless. They were going to drown.

No! The thought thundered in Libby's mind. She had let Ruth die, but she couldn't let that happen to anyone else. She motioned him closer and gestured that they had to wait for the car to fill up with water. She then pantomimed pushing the door open. When Phil shook his head in doubt, Libby grabbed his arm with all her strength, her fingers biting into his flesh, and mouthed the words, "Trust me!"

The water was nearly over their heads now. Libby took three deep breaths and saw Phil follow suit. She then pointed to the door and submerged. Phil followed. Libby found the door handle in the dark water and pulled it down. As she did, she motioned for Phil to push against the door. He put his shoulder against it and heaved, and Libby joined in, using the power of her legs. To Libby's surprise, the door just barely moved. With the water pressure equalized inside and outside the door, it shouldn't have been so hard. As she strained with all her might, she realized that the force of the fast moving water must be keeping the door closed.

At last the door moved an inch, and then several more. As Phil pushed with everything he had, Libby added all her strength to his. After several excruciating seconds, Phil got an arm through the opening and moved the door some more.

As Libby's legs started to buckle, she felt Phil squeeze through the opening. She continued to push against the door until he was completely through, and then she collapsed backwards. The door swung back closed. She was now trapped inside by herself. Phil's face suddenly appeared at one of the windows. His eyes were frantic. Libby pointed upwards emphatically and mouthed the words, "I'll get out." Phil hesitated, then disappeared.

Libby settled back in resignation. She couldn't open the door alone, but at least Phil would be on the surface now, or should be. Libby's thoughts started to fragment. But as her lungs heaved for the first time, she remembered the open window. Phil couldn't get through it, but she could, if she could find it. She couldn't see anything, but she reached for where the open window should be. It wasn't there. As she swept her hands over the car's interior, feeling for the opening, her lungs started to heave more insistently. She had used up the last of her oxygen pushing the door. She was frantically searching for the open window when her lungs spasmed and she sucked in dirty, dark water.

As her body rebelled against the foreign substance pouring into her mouth, she scrabbled around the car's interior, completely disoriented. Her legs were thrashing wildly, but her hands continued to search for the open window. As seconds passed, Libby's eyes started to see red and yellow flashes. She tried to resist her body's convulsions, but at last she could not stop her lungs from inhaling the muddy water. Her body was almost completely out of control now, but at the very last moment her hands found the open window. With a fading fragment of consciousness, she got her arms through the opening, gave one final thrust forward, and then knew nothing.

5

Phil pushed away from the submerged Camry and reached the side of the canal. He dragged himself out of the water, his muscles shockingly weak, and took a gasping breath. Sarah and Charles were lying on their backs on the bank of the canal, just above the waterline, covered in mud and sand. Sarah was gasping, seemingly unable to get enough air, while Charles, though breathing, stared blankly upwards and seemed barely conscious.

Phil searched the water for the girl, but saw nothing. She'd said she would get out, but where was she? His weary mind started to feel tremors of alarm. He stood up with shaking legs, halfway out of the water, and looked around to see if she had already made it to the bank. There was no sign of her.

Several cars had now stopped and people were slowly making their way down the embankment, cautious in the still cascading rain.

"Help me!" Phil cried. "There's a girl still down there."

He plunged back down in the water toward the sunken car. When he reached it, he took a deep breath and ducked beneath the surface. Feeling around the car's exterior, he located the open window and stuck his head through the opening. The dirty water limited the visibility to just a few feet, but from what he could see Libby was not in the car. If she was still in there, he wasn't sure what he could do anyway. He couldn't squeeze through the window, and he doubted he could get the car door open again from the outside. He could get help, but by then it might be too late.

He surfaced, once again gasping for breath. He realized that while he'd had oxygen deficits in football practices, it was never anything like this. Then he mentally shook himself. What the hell was wrong with him? The girl was nearly out of time. He struggled to get his thoughts under control. He had to find her now.

He whipped his head around, looking from side to side and up and down the current. Where could she be? Standing waist-deep in the water, he suddenly wondered whether she had been swept downstream with the current.

He yelled at people now gathering at the water's edge.

"Can anyone see if a girl has floated down stream?" he said, pointing.

His voice was raspy and weak, and Phil feared no one would hear him. But several of the onlookers saw his pointing finger and looked downstream, searching.

"Hey," one said, "I see something! It's a few yards down from the car."

Phil looked and saw a partially submerged body about twenty yards away. He waded and thrashed his way toward it. The head seemed to be pointed up, giving him a sliver of hope, and he doubled his effort. At last his hand reached a cloth windbreaker like the one the girl had been wearing. He grabbed it and started dragging her out of the water. The body was inert, but it was the girl.

"Help me!" Phil shouted, as he got the girl to the sandy bank and lay her on her back. She didn't seem to be breathing. He tried to recall his CPR training from the lifeguard job two summers ago. He put a finger to her neck and could feel a faint pulse. He squeezed her nose shut, put his mouth over hers, and blew a deep breath into her lungs. He waited four seconds, but nothing happened. He did it once more. Nothing. The third try seemed to have no effect either. He leaned back, short of breath once again.

Suddenly, dark water came gushing out of the girl's mouth and she took a gasping breath. And then another. Phil put his hand over his eyes for a moment, but then he remembered something else. He needed to make sure her neck and spine were stabilized. She could have hit something in the current.

6

Phil crouched over the girl, hands next to her head, protecting her from further contact as more cars stopped and people came down to help. Her eyes were open, but her breathing was harsh and ragged, and she was shivering from the cold.

"Please! Somebody call an ambulance?" Phil shouted.

"We already have," somebody said.

"We could use some blankets, too," Phil said. "We have to worry about shock."

Phil felt a chill pass through him and realized the past few minutes had caught up with him as well.

He was handed a couple of blankets and tucked them around the girl. She turned her eyes to him and tried to say something. She gave a wheezing cough, then tried again.

Her voice was a whisper. "My money belt. It's hurting my back. Could you take it until…I'm all right?"

"Sure," he said.

He pulled up her blouse and saw the belt. It had a side buckle, with the pouch against the small of her back.

As he unbuckled her belt, the girl arched her back so he could slide the belt out from beneath her.

"Thanks," she said.

Seemingly exhausted by the belt maneuver, she closed her eyes. She coughed a few times, her breath wheezing, but otherwise she was silent. Phil sat next to her, holding her hand. He couldn't stop remembering how she had gripped his arm and said, "Trust me."

"Where are the medics?" Phil shouted.

"They should be here soon," someone said. "They left thirty minutes ago."

Phil thought it seemed a lot longer. He was shivering constantly now and felt very tired.

"Anybody have a dry jacket I could borrow?" he asked. The rain had stopped now, so it might do some good.

A few moments later, a middle-aged man kneeled down next to him and handed him a jacket.

"Put this on," he said, "I'll keep an eye on her. You're about finished yourself."

Phil struggled to his feet and then staggered. Several hands steadied him.

"Thanks," Phil said. He peeled off his wet, muddy shirt, put on the dry jacket, and sat down heavily.

"How are the other two doing?" he asked, pointing to Sarah and Charles lying several yards away.

"The girl doesn't look too bad," the man said. "The other guy seems out of it."

A few minutes later flashing red lights appeared above them, and before long three medics came down carrying a stretcher.

"We'll take over," one of them said. Phil stepped away.

The medics carefully loaded the girl onto the stretcher, taking care with her neck and back.

"What do you think?" Phil asked.

"We've got equipment and medication in the truck," a medic said. "She doesn't look too bad, but I don't like the sound of her breathing."

"Can I come with you?" Phil asked.

"Yeah. You don't look too great yourself. And we'll need to take your two other friends. They're a little beat up, too."

"Thanks," Phil said, feeling weary beyond words.

"You did good," the medic said.

No, he hadn't, Phil thought. But the girl had. Without her they'd all have drowned in that damned car, in six feet of water.

7

The red emergency van made good time to Las Vegas. The rain had stopped as abruptly as it had started, and the traffic pulled over to let them pass.

Inside the van, Libby and Charles were lying down, IV's attached to their arms and monitors displaying their vital signs.

"What happened to Charles?" Phil asked.

"He must have hit his head when we rolled over," Sarah said. "Oh, God, I should have forced him to stop earlier." She started to cry.

"It happened too fast," Phil said. "You couldn't have known how it would go."

Sarah shook her head. "I should have stopped him," she said.

Phil looked closely at Libby. She was deathly pale, and each breath came with a ragged wheeze.

"We'll be at the hospital in five minutes," the medic said.

The hospital was on the western edge of Las Vegas, miles away from the gaudy strip. Several white-clad personnel were waiting for them. They carried Libby and Charles inside, while Sarah and Phil walked in on their own.

Phil was taken to one examination room, Sarah to another. After a short wait, a young doctor came in and did a quick examination.

"Did you take in any water?" he asked.

"Not really," Phil said. "I was able to hold my breath until I made it to the surface."

The doctor made some notes and then closed Phil's chart. "You should be all right," he said. "You were lucky."

"What should we be concerned about?" Phil asked.

The doctor sighed. "In near drownings, you worry about pulmonary edema from water in the lungs. Pneumonia and fluid imbalances can also cause trouble. Depends on how close to drowning you got. Looks like you weren't too close."

"What about my friend. The girl who was brought in with me?"

"Are you a relative?" the doctor asked.

"No, just a friend."

"Sorry, patient confidentiality and all that."

Phil thought for a moment. "Hypothetically speaking, if a person were submerged for several minutes and probably inhaled a lot of water, what you would be concerned about?"

The doctor's face turned grim. "Pulmonary edema and pneumonia for starters. And possibly brain damage."

8

Phil was allowed to clean up and given some dry hospital clothes. A while later he was directed to a waiting room, where Sarah was already waiting.

"How's Charles?" Phil asked.

Sarah jumped violently, then settled back. "Sorry," she said. "I'm on edge. Charles is in intensive care, but I don't know much else. I've called his parents. They're taking an early flight, but it'll be a few hours."

"How about you?"

Sarah grimaced. "Oh, I'm all right, I guess, as long as I don't think about it. Didn't get trapped in that damn car anyway."

"Have you heard anything about the girl?" Phil asked.

"You mean Abby?"

"Is that her name?" Phil asked. "I couldn't remember. What's her last name?"

Sarah looked embarrassed. "I'm not sure. She may not have told me."

Phil grunted. "That's pretty lame. She rode with us for hours, probably saved both our lives, and we don't know her name."

"Someone asked me about her a while ago. She has no identification."

Phil thought about the money belt. She had said to take care of it. He wondered if that included snooping inside. He didn't think so. Anyway, they would get her name once she woke up.

CHAPTER FIVE

THE HOSPITAL

1

Fragmented scenes and half-recognized figures filled Libby's dreams. Aunt Ruth, nervously warning her about something. The woman with the birthmark swinging the edge of her hand. A frantic face barely visible through a car window. Ms. Carter mocking her.

When she finally surfaced into consciousness, her vision was blurred, but she could make out a hospital room. She had never been in one before, but had seen them on television. An IV line was attached to her arm, and a monitor next to her was flashing numbers.

Her thoughts slowly gained coherence. A flash flood had swept the car off the road and into a canal. She was trying to get out, but the water had covered her and she couldn't breathe.

A sudden thought hit her like a blow. The Gray woman and her partner were still looking for her. Had she given herself away? She thought hard. She didn't think so. At least not yet. But if they found her, she would end up like Ruth. No doubt about that. As the thought circled in her mind, she drifted back into unconsciousness.

2

"Are you awake yet, dear?" a woman asked. "You've been out quite a while, and your doctor thought it would be best if we woke you."

Libby opened her eyes a fraction.

"Good," the woman said. "You must be thirsty." She held out a cup.

Libby realized she was desperately thirsty. She opened her mouth as the woman put the cup to her lips. It was orange juice. Libby drank it in three gulps and the woman gave her another.

"Now, dear," the nurse said, "we've all been wondering what your name is. We can't admit you properly without it. Can you give it to me?"

Libby looked at her, a blank expression on her face. She said nothing.

"Can't you tell me your name," the nurse said. "You friend said your first name is Abby, but we need your family name, too, so we can contact your parents."

Libby stared as though the woman were speaking a foreign language. She remained silent.

"Can't you understand what I'm saying?" The woman asked with a touch of exasperation.

Libby didn't respond.

The nurse tried coaxing a response from Libby for the next few minutes, without success. With an exasperated harrumph, she finally marched out of the room.

Libby knew very well what the nurse was asking. But answering that question would lead to more of them. They'd want to know her address, who her relatives were, and they'd find out about Ruth. And before long, Gray and her partner would find out about it—and they would come.

3

Phil visited Libby as much as he could over the next two days. He was not a relative, so they only let him stay for a few minutes. Their conversations were one-sided, since Libby remained silent.

"Charles seems to be coming around," Phil said. "He had a pretty bad concussion, but the docs say he's out of the woods."

"Sarah's folks are here," he added. "They're taking her back home to Denver for a while. She seems to be having post-trauma problems, which you can probably understand. They think time away from school will help."

"As for me," Phil said in an ironic tone, "my family's in Aspen right now. I've told them I'm all right. They probably would come if I were in bad shape. I understand the hospital is going to transfer you to a new facility in the next day or two, one that won't allow non-relatives to visit. Since I won't be able to see you, I guess I'll rent a car and drive to Aspen for a couple of days. Barring more floods, that is. I have to be back for practice next week, even though for now I can't play. I've been studying physics the way I should have before. It's actually not too hard. I think I'll get out of purgatory."

Phil's voice faltered and his face twisted. "Leaving sucks," he said. "Especially since I can't stop thinking about the muddy water and that damned car. I still have marks on my arm where you grabbed me. I was going to give up." He was silent for a moment, then added, "But not you."

"Well, anyway," Phil said, clearing his throat, "I'll stop by tomorrow before I leave. No one knows why you're not talking. I have to think that if you could…talk to me, you would. If our positions were switched, you would…you would be the first person I'd want to talk to. To tell you—thanks."

After a moment he went on. "Oh, I've got your money belt. I'll put it under your mattress for the time being. I didn't look into it."

He stopped talking for a while, not knowing what to say. "So," he finally said, "see you tomorrow."

4

Phil visited late in the afternoon the next day. Libby's hair had been combed and she had a newly-laundered hospital gown, but otherwise she looked the same.

"I'll be taking off soon," he said. "I think they're moving you tomorrow. They still haven't found out who you are. They look at me funny when I tell them I haven't a clue."

He sat for a while. As he finally started to get up, he saw her hand move slightly in his direction. She was holding a folded piece of paper. He took it, but as he started to unfold it she put her hand over his and mouthed the word, "Later."

He waited for something else, but she didn't move again.

"I'll keep track of how you're doing," he said, standing, "You'll probably be better before long, but if it takes longer, I'll be back real soon."

He walked to the door, looked back and gazed at the pale motionless girl, with wires and tubes attached to her arm. She wouldn't be here, he thought, if she had left the car with the others, instead of staying with him.

5

Inside his rental car, Phil opened up the folded paper. Written in pencil, the words small and neat, was a short note.

"Phil, sorry for the silent act. But if I started to talk, the questions would never end, and the answers would make things worse.

"People are after me. Maybe they're police, even though I've done nothing wrong. But if they find me, it won't be good, for myself and probably those around me. If I stay here, it won't be long until they find me.

"Around three o'clock tomorrow morning, I'm going to walk out. That's the best time. Could you wait in a car for me? A change of clothes would help too. Hospital gowns aren't in fashion these days.

"Thank you.

"Your traveling companion."

Phil didn't know what to think, but not helping her was out of the question. Things couldn't be as bad as she painted them. But that didn't matter. He would go back to the motel and catch some sleep. He would be getting up early.

6

Libby endured the nurses every two hours. Sometimes they came with barely edible hospital food, which they served in excruciating slow-motion, and sometimes they tried to converse, using baby-talk. Even if she hadn't been acting mute, their tone was so annoying she wouldn't have responded anyway.

It never occurred to her that Phil wouldn't be waiting at 3 a.m. She felt the sunken car had created a bond between them. But in the back of her mind was the fear she might expose him to her troubles. She hadn't helped him get out of the car to allow that to happen.

7

At two-thirty in the morning, she heard the new shift of nurses come on duty. Ten minutes later, Nurse Watson peered through the open door, then walked away. She would go to the rest room now, Libby thought, as on the previous nights. Libby estimated she had five minutes until the nurse returned.

She got out bed, detached the tubes and wires and turned off the monitor so it wouldn't beep. She felt light-headed for a moment, from all the hours lying down, and stopped to steady herself. She then put a couple of pillows under the blankets. They wouldn't fool anyone who looked closely, but they might resemble a sleeping person to someone looking casually, which was the extent of the usual inspection.

Libby pulled out the money belt from beneath the bed and slipped it around her waist. It still seemed full.

She walked quietly to the door and peeked out. No one was in sight. A couple nurses were talking on the other side of the building, but the conversation seemed to just be getting started.

She slipped out of her room and quietly walked to the nurses' station across the hall. She had seen it from the corner of her eye when she was wheeled in four days earlier. She stepped inside and saw what she needed. A nurse's uniform was hanging from a hook on the wall, with white shoes beneath it. She grabbed them and ducked into a stairwell. A sign said she was on the fifth floor. She put on the dress and shoes, stuffed her hospital gown behind a trash container, and started down the stairs. She felt dizzy a couple of times and kept hold of the handrails. She reached the first floor in five minutes.

As she entered the hall, she didn't know what to expect. When she had arrived four days earlier, she had been brought through the emergency entrance on the other side of the building. She could see a counter near the front reception area. Behind it was a gray-haired man reading something. She considered looking for another way out but decided the longer she stayed the more likely she was to attract attention.

Libby took a deep breath and walked purposefully past the counter, making as little sound as possible. She saw a name plate that said "Ted Miller." After three more steps, her head down and shoulders hunched, she spoke over her shoulder in a quiet voice.

"Night, Ted. See you tomorrow."

Ted looked up, trying to make out who it was, then shrugged. "Goodnight, ma'am, you get some sleep, hear?"

Five more steps and Libby was through the main doors and into the night.

8

Phil was parked down the street from the hospital. He saw a girl in a white nurse's outfit leaving the main entrance, but couldn't make out her face. He looked around for someone else, but then saw the girl veer toward his car.

Libby opened the side door and slid in. "Let's go," she said.

As he started the car and pulled away, she stared over her shoulder to see if anyone had followed her out. After he turned the corner and the hospital disappeared from view, she sighed and settled back in her seat.

"Thanks for being here," she said. "Otherwise I had a lot of walking to do."

"Where do you want to go?" Phil asked.

"Let's just head for Denver," she said.

After a while, he asked, "Care to say what's going on?"

"That's what I've been trying to figure out," she said, laughing mirthlessly.

"After our adventure in the car, and now this, a little information would be welcome."

"Are you saying I owe you something?" she said, an edge in her voice.

"No, no. Just curious, and maybe concern for someone who's saved my bacon."

"Sorry," the girl said, her voice softening. "You deserve an explanation, but it might not be good for you."

"Can't I judge that for myself?" he said.

"No. If I tell you, I have to decide."

"All right. Forget explanations for now. Let me help you."

"You are," Libby said. "This is enough."

Her tone warned Phil to drop the subject. "So what do we do now?" he asked.

"Well, if you've managed to get some clothes, I'd like to see how you did."

She used a McDonald's restroom to put on the clothes he'd picked up. Slim jeans, socks, sneakers, and a light blue blouse.

"You got the sizes about right," Libby said, back in the car. "Have a lot of experience buying clothes for girls in tight spots?"

Phil looked embarrassed. "My sister advised me. I told her you were slim, brown-haired, and a little taller than she."

"How's old's your sister?"

"Twenty-five. Five years older than me."

"Did she ask a lot of questions?" Libby's eyes narrowed.

"No. She just made sarcastic remarks about girl-trouble."

Libby relaxed a little and smiled. "Did you say this was a different kind of girl-trouble?"

"I didn't say anything except that we'd been caught in a flood and I would be coming to Aspen.

A while later Phil saw the turnoff for I-70 east, to Denver. After taking it, he glanced at Libby. "So," he said, "how old are you, really?"

Libby sighed. "Let's just say I can't drive yet."

"So, younger than sixteen?" Phil said.

Libby said nothing.

"And you're going to college next year?" Phil asked, glancing over.

Libby looked embarrassed. "Actually no. I have more high school ahead. College is a ways off. If ever."

"You don't talk like a high schooler," Phil said.

Libby shrugged. "I started talking really early. Things progressed from there."

"If you don't mind my asking, is your name really Abby?"

She didn't answer. It wasn't hard to tell she didn't welcome his questions. But before long he found himself asking, "Who are you meeting in Colorado?"

Libby hesitated, then said, "I've never met my father. I'm not even sure who he is. My mother died right after I was born. But I heard about a man my mother knew. I'm hoping he can fill in some blanks."

"What was your mother's name?"

Libby seemed reluctant, but finally said, "Amanda."

"Well, if Amanda didn't tell anyone about this guy, maybe there was a good reason."

"Like what?"

"I don't know. Families have skeletons. Maybe he was someone your mother wanted to forget."

"I can't imagine it would matter after all these years."

"How did your mother meet him?" Phil asked.

"I heard something about a duplicate bridge tournament."

"Really? What did he do for a living?"

"Look, I really don't want to get into this. It probably doesn't matter anyway."

Phil dropped the subject, but after a few miles, he said, "Where in Colorado are you heading? I'll take you there."

She gave a slight shake of her head and said nothing.

"Well, we need some type of destination."

"This direction is fine."

After a few more miles, Libby asked, "By the way, what kind of car is this? It's a new one to me."

He looked a little self-conscious. "It's a Range Rover. After that flash flood, I thought I'd go for something more muscular."

"I gather you're not on a tight budget," Libby said, examining the car's interior.

He shrugged. "My family has some money."

"You said you're going to Aspen," Libby said. "Is that where they live?"

"Sometimes, I guess."

Intrigued, Libby said, "Where did you grow up?"

"Different places, but we mostly lived in Rancho Santa Fe while I was in high school. Ever heard of it?"

Libby laughed. "Yeah, like I've heard of Beverly Hills or the Upper East Side. But how did you end up at State? Kids from families like yours usually end up at one of the elites."

"State was elite enough for me. And I liked their football program."

Libby studied him out of the corner of her eyes. He drove with quiet competence. He ignored the mountains and landscape, which were post-card-worthy, focused on the road and traffic, and regularly checked his mirrors.

"You're big," she said, "but I thought left tackles had to be huge."

"The coach wants me to add twenty pounds. But I'm just going to work on my strength."

She glanced at his right bicep, which still was black and blue from her fingers.

Libby nodded. "Quickness and strength mean more than mass."

"So how do you know football?"

Libby gazed out the window. "Television," she said.

Later Libby asked, "What about your social life? Any girl friends?"

Phil laughed. "No. Sarah and I became friends our freshman year. She loaned me notes for the chemistry classes I missed. After a while she met Charles and they've been together ever since."

When they finally stopped to eat, Libby devoured a big cheeseburger and fries. "Wow," he said, "I guess hospital food didn't suit you."

"It was barely edible," Libby admitted, "and cold and late."

"More punishment for your good deed," Phil said.

For the next several hours they made good time, but when they crossed from Utah into Colorado, the sun was coming down, and Libby said, "You've had a long day of driving after a really early morning. Let's stop and call it a day. Since you took care of the money belt, I'll pay for the rooms."

Phil thought about insisting on paying himself, but he decided to let it go. It wouldn't help to have his family's money come up again.

Twenty miles later, Phil took an exit to a group of motels and restaurants just off the highway.

As they came to the motels, Libby thought about the Gray woman. After seeing the agent's eyes after she killed Ruth, Libby had no doubt Gray would kill her too if given the chance. Libby had tried to avoid leaving a trail, but her escape from the hospital would certainly attract attention. And while they may not yet know the name of the girl in the hospital, they knew Phil's. Would they use him to find her?

She turned to Phil, who was looking for a suitable motel, and said, "I've got a weird request, and please don't take offense."

"What's that?"

"Would you drop me off here?" She pointed to a small, rundown inn hiding behind two large, brightly-lit motels. "Then you can find another place, if you don't mind."

Phil looked surprised. "I understand why you would want separate rooms," he said. "But separate hotels?"

"If someone *is* after me, they might use you to find me. I don't want the hotel to have a record of us checking in at the same time."

"But how could anyone connect me with you?"

She shrugged. "They're looking for a teenage girl who's gone missing. A couple of days later, an unidentified girl disappears from a Las Vegas hospital. They could easily learn the girl had been traveling with you. If they follow your trail and discover you'd checked in with an unknown teenage girl, they'd be after us like bloodhounds."

Phil looked skeptical. "Could they really track you like that?"

"With their big computers, I wouldn't doubt it."

"Now *I'm* getting a little paranoid," Phil said. "Why are they so interested in you?"

Libby's face was grim. "You can't disclose what you don't know."

"Well, I hope you're not just trying to ditch me," he said, looking melancholy.

Libby put a hand on his arm. "Phil, you've been a better friend than I could have hoped for. I…" Her face clouded over for a moment, and she didn't finish. Then she said, with artificial cheerfulness, "Here's some money for your room. Let's meet at that restaurant across the street at eight." She pointed. "We'll have breakfast before we take off."

As she walked away, she turned back and said, "Don't worry about checking in on me. I'm going to bed early."

Phil realized that even if he called her motel, he wouldn't know who to ask for.

10

Phil found a decent motel a mile away and checked in. He called his sister later that night.

"I'm a few hours from Aspen, Karen," he said. "How are the folks doing?"

"They want to hear about this flood," Karen said. "You swear you're okay?"

"Yeah, but for a while it was a little hairy. Thanks for the clothes advice. They worked fine."

"What's the girl's name? You haven't said."

"Well, I'm not sure. She's pretty secretive."

"Really?" Karen said. "What's her story?"

"I don't really know. But I should, because the flood business would've turned out a lot differently without her."

"How old is she?"

"Maybe fifteen."

"What?" Karen said. "I thought she was a college student."

"She acts older, but looks about fifteen."

"A little young for you, isn't she?"

"It's not like that," Phil said, annoyed. "She just was with us when everything went upside down, literally."

"She still with you?"

Phil hesitated, remembering the girl didn't want to be tied to him. "No," he said.

His sister was silent for a moment, then said, "Well, you've made me curious. Are we going to meet her anytime soon?"

"I doubt it." Phil said.

11

The next morning Phil was in front of the restaurant at five to eight. At 8:15 he walked inside and looked around. Three or four of the customers looked like farmers, and several others looked like travelers ready to get going. The girl wasn't there.

After a couple minutes, a young, red-haired waitress walked over. "You looking for a brown-haired girl?" she asked.

"Yes. Has she been here?"

"She left a couple of hours ago. She said that if a big guy came in looking for her, I should give him this. Are you Phil?"

When Phil nodded, she handed him a small envelope. It probably came from the motel's gift shop, Phil thought.

"Did you see who she went with?" Phil asked.

"Sorry, hon," the waitress said, shaking her head. "We've been real busy."

"Thanks," Phil said, reaching for his wallet. "Let me give you something."

"No need," the waitress said. "She already gave me a nice tip."

Once outside, Phil opened the envelope and took out a small card. It said:

Phil,

This is a lousy way to say goodbye, but I found a ride and decided to take it.

It's been an interesting few days, hasn't it? The thing is, I couldn't bear it if my troubles became yours.

I'll try to follow football next year. Take care of your quarterback as well as you took care of me.

With all my thanks,

Me

P.S. Don't complain about the test question. The water in the canal will go down, not stay the same.

CHAPTER SIX

SEARCHING

1

While Libby was on the way to Colorado, Blunt called the handler. He and Gray had arrived in Bozeman, Montana to examine number eighteen on their list, a twelve-year-old math prodigy.

"How's Montana?" the handler asked.

"Montana should have been before San Diego on the list," Blunt said. "The climate change would have been less of a shock."

"So, what about the Williston kid?"

"We're seeing him this afternoon," Blunt said. "He belongs to one of those wilderness families. They live in a cabin twenty miles from nowhere."

"I'll look forward to your report," the handler said. "What about the Anderson girl?"

"She's still missing," Blunt said. "But with all we're throwing at it, it can't be much longer. Unless she's already dead and buried."

"How long's it been? A week?"

"About that."

"Just so I'm clear," the handler said. "This fifteen year-old girl has no relatives, and she's been in touch with none of her friends. Right so far?"

"Yes."

"And she doesn't drive, and she has no money. Right?"

"As far as we know."

"And you've been watching airports and trains."

"Busses, too," Blunt said.

"And Sibyl's on it, with our best technology, including facial recognition. Am I missing anything?"

"Not really," Blunt admitted.

"Then how has this girl stayed missing for a whole bloody week?"

Blunt hesitated. "I'm starting to think she ran into some pervert and is dead somewhere."

"That would be convenient. Do you really think she's dead?"

"Not yet," Blunt said cautiously.

"You'd better hope no reporter gets on this," the handler said. "Do you have any leads at all?"

"Our computer flagged these college kids who got caught in a flash flood. One of the girls later disappeared from a hospital. But there's no reason to think it's Anderson."

"Well," the handler sighed, "look into it."

"Sure. But it's pretty thin."

"How are things going with Gray?"

"Okay," Blunt said. "Things were a little tense after the San Diego business. But she seems in a better mood now."

"You'd be wise to keep it that way."

2

Gray and Blunt had to take a two-mile uphill hike to get to the Willistons' cabin in the mountains above Bozeman. They knew there must have been a road to the house, but their maps didn't show it. But far from being dispirited by the trek, Gray said it would be good for their conditioning. She didn't even seem to mind carrying the briefcase with the brain monitoring equipment. As they approached the cabin, the trail circled around the mountain, bordered on one side by the mountain's granite face, and on the other side by a two-hundred-foot cliff. Gray talked nonstop about training camps she had survived, the strengths and weaknesses of her favorite guns, and which martial arts were most effective in real life. Blunt wondered if she was on uppers.

The meeting with the Willistons was disappointing. Once they handed over the promised five-hundred dollar voucher, redeemable for cash at any major bank, the family was only too eager to cooperate. But it turned out their math prodigy was simply an autistic savant with extraordinary computational skills within a very narrow range. Having seen two other similar children, Blunt and Gray knew his talent did not represent the broad mental ability they were after. They watched patiently while the proud parents had the boy display his numerical skills. At the end, they said they would carefully assess him. If he could be of use, they would be in touch.

As they were leaving, the boy's mother said, "I'm so sorry about your birthmark, ma'am. When you were young, you must have been teased all the time."

Gray turned to the woman and grinned. "They stopped after a while," she said.

On the way down the mountain, Blunt said, "That woman's comment about your birthmark was out of line," he said. "I shouldn't have said anything about it either, back in San Diego."

Gray said nothing, but she gave him the same grin she had shown the woman.

A few hundred feet later, as the path took a sharp turn, Gray stopped, stretched, and said, "Would you mind holding the briefcase for a minute. I need to rest my arms." She handed it to him.

After he took the case, she stretched her arms for a moment, flexed her fingers, and then put one hand in her coat pocket.

Blunt suddenly convulsed, shook violently, and fell to the ground. His body continued to shake and writhe for ten long seconds. Then he was still.

"Once I did my reconnaissance and discovered the path to the Williston's, I decided this would be a good place to find out if you could fly," Gray said conversationally, "but you're big enough it might have been risky. So I had a friend equip the briefcase with a little taser. Packs a wallop, doesn't it?"

Blunt's eyes bulged and his mouth worked, but no sound came out.

Gray walked over, grabbed his legs, and dragged him to the cliff's edge. Blunt tried to resist, made mewling noises, but couldn't form any words.

When Gray had his legs over the edge of the cliff, she stepped back and stared at him.

"I've been teased about my little mark," she said, "but it always stops."

Then she gave him a powerful shove, and he tumbled over the cliff. Four seconds later she heard the sound of his body striking the ground.

She took the taser's on/off switch out of her pocket, to make sure it was off. She peered over the edge for a moment, barely able to make out Blunt's body below, then picked up the briefcase.

She resumed walking down the mountain, whistling a tune under her breath. She would have to report two pieces of bad news. Blunt had slipped and fallen off a mountain, and the Williston boy was a negative. She wondered how the handler would react.

CHAPTER SEVEN

DUPLICATE BRIDGE

1

Phil Keller had spent two days with his family in Aspen before returning to school. After a week studying for the makeup physics exam, he decided he was ready. He had abandoned the idea of asking the professor about his answer. The girl had been right—the water in the lock would drop.

The day before the makeup test, Phil he was in his room studying the classical dynamics of spinning tops, one of the course's toughest subjects, when someone knocked on his door. He opened it and saw two unsmiling, tough-looking men in business suits.

"Yes?" Phil said.

The taller of two flashed a Homeland Security badge. "Do you mind if we come in and ask a couple of questions," he said.

Phil didn't like their looks. "Could we just talk here? Everything's a mess inside."

"If you would like," he said, obviously irritated.

He showed Phil a photo of the girl who had called herself Abby, probably taken two years earlier. "Do you know this girl?"

"I don't think so," Phil said, feeling a twinge of apprehension.

"We understand you were caught in a flood a few days ago. Was this girl with you?"

Phil shrugged. "There was this girl, Abby something. But her hair was brown, not sandy blond. She had this tattoo on her neck."

"What was the tattoo?" the agent asked.

"It was kind of strange. A bird diving at a big cat."

"You visited this girl in the hospital. Why was that?"

"We barely got out of the car alive. It didn't seem right to just leave her."

"When did you last see her?"

"Just before I left. She couldn't seem to talk. Something must be wrong with her head."

"Did you know she disappeared?"

"Disappeared? No. Last time I saw her, she was in bed, staring at the ceiling."

After a while, the men seemed to lose interest. They left a card and said to call if he saw her again.

The girl had been right, Phil thought later. People were definitely after her.

2

Libby had hitched a ride with some vacationing skiers and arrived in Denver by mid-afternoon. She felt guilty about leaving Phil. But it was going to happen before long anyway, and at least this was quick and clean and avoided all the questions. But with disconcerting frequency, her thoughts kept drifting back to him.

During the drive to Denver, the two female skiers made cracks about her tattoo. Things like was the bird Mighty Mouse in disguise, or on PCP? That was good. Better they remember the tattoo than her face.

She thought about her decision to go to Colorado. It was not the product of careful analysis. It was almost like some post-hypnotic suggestion, or a salmon returning to its place of birth. She kept thinking that Tom Grant had known her mother, and he might know her father. It could even be him. That might be a silly thought, but *someone* was, and unless she could find him, she would have no family at all.

3

Libby took a taxi to an economy motel and checked in. A while later, she walked to a local strip mall, bought some clothes and provisions, then found a computer store. After listening to the salesperson's pitch, she settled on an inexpensive laptop. Back at the motel, as she prepared to log on, she wondered if someone was monitoring internet searches. If so, would searches about Tom Grant cause trouble? She didn't see how. There was no evidence connecting him to her.

Libby opened the laptop's search engine and typed in "Tom Grant Colorado." Hundreds of names appeared. That didn't help. What else did she know? He played duplicate bridge. She searched "Colorado bridge clubs." Eight bridge clubs appeared. Each had a website showing how members had done in recent games. She looked for players named Grant. She came up with two, one from a Denver bridge club, and another from Colorado Springs.

A pleasant-voiced woman answered her call to the Denver club. When Libby asked about players named Grant, the woman said the only one they had was over ninety. Her call to Colorado Springs produced the same result. Their only Grant was an elderly woman who had stopped playing. Libby's heart sank as she wondered if Tom Grant had stopped playing.

Checking all the Grants who had played bridge in Colorado in recent years seemed too much to undertake. But she decided to take a stab at players named Grant over the past three years. If that didn't work, she might have to abandon the bridge angle. But then she would have nothing.

She expanded her search to the last three years. She finally came across the results from a tournament held two years before, in Grand Junction, Colorado. One of the players was a Tom Grant. She called the club and spoke with a woman whose voice reminded her of Miss Carter from high school English. Libby said she was looking for a player who might have been there two years earlier.

"Who are you looking for?" the woman asked.

"Tom Grant. He once played there in a tournament."

The woman said she'd never heard of him, but she'd only been there a year.

"Do you have anyone who might have known him?" Libby asked.

"Probably," the woman said. "But there's no game tonight. And I can't give out phone numbers. Your best bet would be to come tomorrow night."

She decided to take the bet.

<h2 style="text-align:center">4</h2>

The next day, Libby took a six-hour bus ride to Grand Junction. Much of the trip on I-70 was over breathtaking mountain passes. Libby decided that even if she didn't find Grant, the scenery made the trip worth it.

She checked into a motel in Grand Junction and made it to the bridge club a half hour before the game started. She spotted a severe-looking woman sitting behind a small desk.

"Excuse me," she said. "I think we spoke yesterday. I'm looking for Tom Grant. He may have played here a couple of years ago."

The woman pointed to one of the bridge tables. "You might ask Roy Benson over there, sitting South at table 9. He's been here forever."

Libby located the table and walked up to a white-haired, courtly-looking man who was patiently waiting for the game to begin.

"Mr. Benson?" she said.

The man slowly turned to gaze at her, his bright blue eyes halting at her tattoo. He shook his head sadly. "I don't understand all this tattoo business."

Libby grimaced. "My friends and I got carried away after we won the Homecoming Game."

"Is that so?" Benson said. He peered at her neck. "A parakeet dive-bombing a big cat, eh? Well, I've seen worse ones. What can I do for you?"

"I've heard you might know Tom Grant," Libby said. "He played here a couple of years ago."

"Tom? Sure. Hell of a bridge player. Played the dummy superbly."

"Played the dummy?"

"Sorry. Bridge jargon. What's your interest in Tom?"

"He knew my mother, and I'm hoping he'll tell me about her."

"The Tom I know is close to fifty, I'd say. Does that fit?"

"That sounds about right," Libby said. "Do you know where I can find him?"

Benson thought for a moment. "We partnered some a few years ago, but his game dropped off a bit and he stopped coming. A problem with headaches. And a stroke from a long time ago caused a limp. Haven't seen him in quite a while. He used to have a ranch in the high desert a few miles from here."

Libby was about to leave, then stopped. The thought of the motel depressed her.

"Do you mind if I watch a while?" Libby asked.

Benson smiled. "Of course, I like showing off for the girls." He told her to sit behind him and remain quiet.

5

Libby picked up the basic rules quickly. One team of two players competed against another team. The fifty-two cards were dealt out, each player receiving thirteen. After that, one team bid against another until a final contract was reached. Each then played a card, the highest of those four cards winning that "trick." If the contract named a suit as "trump," the trumps operated like wild cards, able to win a trick even against the ace of another suit. A team won if they took at least the number of tricks they had contracted for.

After an hour or so, Benson contracted for a game with spades as trump. But at the end he came up one trick short. Libby was surprised, because on the third to last trick, he could have played low, forcing one of the opponents to win the trick. But then the opponent would have been forced to give up two tricks, which would have made the contract.

During a break, Libby asked Benson where her reasoning fell short. He brushed off the question. But a few moments later, his expression grew thoughtful. He then growled that maybe it would have worked. Finally, at the very end of the session, Benson bid up to a small slam, contracting to take all the tricks but one. But after again finishing one trick short, he slammed down his cards. Libby said nothing.

Starting to leave, Libby told Benson she had enjoyed the evening. Benson asked, "Do you think I should have made that small slam?"

Libby thought that if he had played all his winning cards down to the last two, the defender on his left would have been forced to discard one of his critical cards. That would have allowed Benson to win the final trick.

"No, the contract was hopeless," Libby said. "You couldn't do anything."

Benson looked relieved. But when she reached the door and glanced back, he was still staring at her, his face creased in a frown.

6

Back in her motel room, Libby opened the computer and looked for Tom Grant's address. He wasn't listed in the standard directories, but she finally came across an old reference to Grant Cattle, on Sugarcreek Road, about ten miles north of Grand Junction.

The next morning she called another taxi, noting with alarm that her stash of money had shrunk significantly. What would she do if Grant didn't know anything? She didn't know.

CHAPTER EIGHT

THE RANCH

1

The next morning, she took a taxi to Grant's ranch. During the trip, she stared out the window and enjoyed the pastures and unadorned farmhouses with their fields and fruit trees. At last they stopped by an old wooden sign that said Sugarcreek Rd.

"Here you are, Miss," the driver said. "This is as far as I go. No traveling on private roads."

"Can you wait for me?" Libby asked. "I don't know what will happen."

"I'd have to keep the meter running. How long will you be?"

Libby had no idea. Well, as Ruth used to say, in for a penny in for a pound. If she had to, she could call another taxi.

"I'll pay you now."

After the taxi left, Libby stared down the road, squared her shoulders, and started to walk.

After what seemed like a mile, the road curved and she saw a large two-story house. It was surrounded by trees, an untended yard full of weeds, and a dirty white fence that needed repairs. An old pickup truck was parked on the side. It was covered in dirt and dust and looked as though it hadn't been driven in years.

The place's age and disrepair made Libby's heart sink, but she took a deep breath, crossed the yard, and stepped onto the porch. It creaked as she approached the door. She looked for a bell, couldn't see one, and knocked.

There was no answer. She waited a few moments, then knocked again. Nothing.

"Mr. Grant," she called out. "Please, I've come a long way."

Still nothing.

"Please," she pleaded.

After a time, he heard a shuffling inside, and then slow footsteps.

The door creaked open, and the man she saw caused her heart to sink. He looked close to fifty. He was tall and lean, with thinning, grey hair, and a pain-creased face like Aunt Ruth's used to get when her arthritis flared up. He looked dazed.

With some effort he focused on her face, and then on her tattoo.

He said, "I'm not buying anything from some tattooed homeless person."

Libby paused, then said, "I'm not selling anything, and the tattoo's just temporary. But I *am* homeless."

The man studied Libby's face. His eyes suddenly grew wide and staggered back a step. His left leg buckled, and he fell.

"Amanda?" he said, looking up.

Libby rushed over and knelt down.

"I didn't mean to startle you," she said. She put a hand under his arm. "Let's find you a chair."

She helped him to his feet, her arms taking most of his weight, and led him to an old leather chair in the living room. Each time he put weight on his left leg, she had to steady him. He seemed in no better shape than the old pickup in front.

"Are you Tom Grant?" she asked after he had settled down.

He nodded, his eyes never leaving her face.

He finally said, "I thought you were Amanda. But she's...dead."

"Amanda was my mother," Libby said.

Grant's eyes grew watery. "Yes. You've got her mouth, and the shape of her face."

Libby stared at his face, absorbing every line and feature. "Do you think so?" she finally said. "I never knew her, but I've seen pictures. I came to learn about her."

Grant looked out the window. "Where's your car?" he asked.

"Taxi, then walked. The taxi left."

"What if I hadn't let you in?" Grant asked.

Libby shrugged. "I'm not sure."

After a pause, Grant said, "You're really homeless?"

She nodded. "More than two weeks."

"How come?"

Libby paused. If she told him about Ruth, maybe he'd call the police. And soon the Gray woman would come knocking.

"I'd rather not say," Libby said. "I really don't know you."

Grant nodded slowly.

"So, will you tell me about my mother?" Libby asked.

Grant seemed to think, then said, "And after that, what?"

"You mean what will I do after I learn about my mother?"

He nodded.

"I'm not sure," she said.

"You don't have any place to go?"

She shook her head. "I'm in a motel in Grand Junction." She glanced at an old clock on the wall, which registered 11 a.m. "Check-out's in an hour, unless I stay another night. After that, I don't know."

Grant frowned. "I need more time than that to tell you about your mother. The headaches sometimes make me confused."

"Well, I guess I could reserve a couple more nights."

Grant shook his head. "Look, with all the room I've got, a motel makes no sense. Stay here, at least for a while. That will give us the time we need."

Libby opened her mouth to say something, then stopped. At last she said, "Do you really expect me to stay here? At the house of a man I just met?"

Grant smiled. "Your mother would never have put up with a creep. Besides, do I look like I would be a problem?"

Libby studied Grant for several long moments, her mouth pursed in concentration. "Where would I stay?" she finally asked.

Grant pointed to a door up the stairs. "That bedroom has a strong lock."

Libby continued to study him. At last, she said, "Okay."

Grant exhaled deeply. "Good. Let's take care of your checkout."

"How will we get there?" Libby asked. "That truck in front doesn't look fit to drive. You don't either, for that matter."

"Car's in back," Grant said.

2

Grant limped down the hall and came back in a few minutes with his wallet and keys. She followed him out the backdoor and saw the other vehicle parked by a large barn. It was a black, S Class Mercedes.

As they walked toward it, Libby said, "Is this a W140?"

Grant opened the driver's door and slid in. "You know cars?" he asked.

"I had a friend in high school, Henry, who loved old Mercedes. He said the W140 was the best S Class ever made."

"This is a '98. That was best of them," Grant said. He rattled off some of the features that made this Mercedes exceptional.

"I didn't know that. Even Henry didn't." Libby felt a wave of sadness. Would she ever see Henry again?

The car started right up, and Grant steered it down the long road. He didn't look up to driving, but he handled the trip into town without incident.

Libby directed him to the motel, where she picked up her things and checked out.

Grant looked at her small duffle bag. "Nothing more?" he asked.

"I had to travel light."

"That's hardly enough. Let's stop and pick you up some things."

After driving to a shopping mall, he said, "How are you fixed for money?"

"I have some," she said.

He took out an old wallet and grabbed some bills. "Take this," he said.

She pushed it away. "I can't take your money."

"I owe your mother," he said. "Take it."

Libby hesitated, then took the bills. "I'll pay it back," she said.

Grant smiled, but said nothing.

She got out and looked at the money as she walked to the store. There were eight one hundred dollar bills.

3

She returned two hours later with her hands full of bags. When she looked in the car window, she could see Grant's head tipped back, his mouth open and eyes closed. She dropped the bags and opened his door.

"Mr. Grant," she said, "shaking his shoulder."

His head snapped forward and he opened his eyes. He looked dazed. "Sorry," he said.

She loaded the bags and got in beside him. "What's the matter with you?" she asked.

He sighed. "Head injury, and stroke. A long time ago. Things have gotten worse the last couple of years."

They stopped at a large supermarket. Grant made out a list and gave her more money. A half hour later she came back with bags of food and put them in the trunk. He was slumped in the front seat, but conscious.

4

It was late afternoon when they arrived back at the house. Libby grabbed several bags and climbed out of the car. "Why don't you go inside," she said. "I'll bring everything in."

Grant opened his mouth, but said nothing.

After Libby brought in the bags, she found Grant sitting in the easy chair, staring blankly out the front window. When he heard her approach, he turned and saw she had put the groceries away. Smiling his thanks, he pointed to the upstairs bedroom. "Why don't you put your things away and freshen up," he said. "I'll heat something up."

The upstairs bedroom was large, nicely-furnished, and dusty. It looked like it hadn't been used in a year. The closet and drawers were empty, so she put her things in them. An adjoining bathroom was pleasant, and dusty.

When she came down, he had set the table and put out a salad, mashed potatoes, and a beef casserole. He smiled when she took seconds helpings of everything.

"Nice house," Libby said after a while. "You grow up here?"

"Through high school," Grant said. "My parents died while I was in college. I came back for a while, worked several years in California, and then returned."

"No wife or kids?" Libby asked.

Grant was a slow time answering. "No. There were two women who… meant a lot to me. But no wife."

"Why not?" Libby asked.

Grant seemed startled by her directness. "One of the women left," he said, "and the other died. I saw some other people, but my heart wasn't in it. I'd had a stroke, and my headaches got worse. And the years passed."

"Was my mother the one who died?" Libby asked.

"Yes. Though I didn't know it at the time. Things had fallen apart, and I wasn't around."

After a moment, Libby said, "Were you surprised I decided to stay here?"

"I suppose—a little."

"Have you looked in the mirror lately?" she asked.

"Probably not. There's not much worth seeing these days."

"Take a look," Libby said.

Grant went to large mirror mounted between two old branding irons. He stared at his reflection. Libby stood next to him.

As he looked at their reflections, his eyes suddenly widened. The angle of his jawline matched hers, as did the shape of his nose.

"See anything interesting?" Libby asked.

"I—I'm not certain, but…" And then he knew. They had the same eyes. He turned and looked at her. "Could you be my daughter?" he asked.

"You tell me," Libby said.

Grant's face filled with amazement. "It's possible," he said. And then slowly, hesitantly, he reached out and put his arms around her.

5

A while later, Libby said, "If you want to be sure, we could be tested."

Grant shook his head. "I don't need one. How about you?"

Libby shook her head. "I knew almost from the start. That's why I agreed to stay. But I didn't know what to say."

"I never knew she'd had a baby."

"I just know she died right after I was born. My Aunt Ruth adopted me, but she didn't know who my father was. She'd just heard about this Grant person. So I came looking for you."

They talked for the rest of the evening. Finally, Grant said, "So, how did you end up homeless?"

Libby told Grant about the night Ruth died, her catching a ride with some college students, and getting caught in the flash flood.

"This football player handled himself pretty well," Grant said.

"His name is Phil Keller. He was on academic probation, so he couldn't work out with the team." Libby told Grant about Keller's physics mid-term and the question about the boat in the Panama Canal. "Phil thought that the water level in the lock stayed the same. He wanted to argue with the professor about it."

Grant said, "Obviously the water level would drop."

Libby smiled. "Very good. That's what I said, too."

"Do you think he'll make it back on the team?"

Libby said, "I'd bet on it. He may need work in physics, but he's bright, and strong, and brave, too. I don't know how he managed to force open that door while we were underwater. Without him, I wouldn't be here."

"I'd like to meet him sometime," Grant said.

"I wish we could stay in touch, but I don't want him involved in this."

"You sure they're still after you? " Grant asked.

Libby told him about the agents coming for her at the restaurant after she had done a search of their names. "I think they're using facial recognition and watching the internet."

Grant's eyes grew distant. "If they've put Sibyl on it, they could do that easily enough."

"Who's Sibyl?" Libby asked.

"Sibyl's an it. Although I think of it as a she."

"So what is it? Or she?"

"She's the central processing unit in a supercomputer owned by Quantum Enterprises. I think my algorithms altered her. Now she's something more than a computer."

"You created Sibyl?"

"You thought I was just a bridge player, eh?" Grant said. "In an earlier life, I had a knack for coding. Your mother worked at Quantum after I did, and she came looking for me. We worked together on Sibyl for a while. If they have Sibyl looking for you, they must be serious."

"I expect they are. They killed Ruth, and I'm a witness."

"Why did they come for you?" Grant asked.

"I'm not sure. But they did ask about this aptitude test I took in first grade."

Grant raised his eyebrows, but said nothing.

6

After a while, Grant announced he'd have to turn in. He told Libby she was welcome to explore the place, then slowly limped down the hall and disappeared into a bedroom.

It was still light out, so Libby had time to explore the house and farm. The property included a large orchard behind the house. Part of it was littered with rotting apples that had fallen without being picked. In the distance was a corn field that seemed unattended, and behind that was a wheat field. In the other direction were several pens, one with a few Hereford cattle, another with some goats. Closer to the house there was an enclosure with a handful of chickens.

The house itself was neat and large, but dirty everywhere. Two old photos hung next to the large fireplace, presumably of Grant's parents. There were no other pictures or personal items. Cracked plaster and peeling paint evidenced years of neglect.

She looked in on Grant while he slept and saw his open mouth and head lulling to the side. She felt a moment of anxiety until she heard the wheezing rattle of his breathing. Like the rest of the house, Grant's bedroom had no family photos, plaques, or mementos. If Grant died tomorrow, there would be nothing personal left behind. But then the realization hit her. This was her father. Her life had been permanently changed by Ruth's death, and now it had changed again.

Libby thought about Grant. At times he seemed tired, old, and distracted. But every so often his mind seemed to shift into another gear, like when he talked about his Mercedes, or when he instantly answered the Panama Canal question. One minute he looked like a nursing home candidate, the next like someone who could have created Sibyl. And since learning she was his daughter, he looked at her kindly, not as a tattooed, homeless person. If he was all the family she would have, she could do far worse.

After finishing her inspection of the house, she located a closet with folded linens and towels, remade her bed with clean sheets, and was asleep in thirty seconds.

7

Libby was waiting in the kitchen when Grant walked in a little after eight. As she had for Ruth, she'd prepared coffee, toast and eggs. Looking surprised, he sat down. "Thank you," he said. "But you don't have to cook."

"I can't just be a freeloader," she said.

He quietly ate part of the food and then started to clean up.

"About this freeloader business," Grant said. "We've agreed you're my daughter, right?"

Libby nodded slowly.

"In my book, that means you belong here. You're not a freeloader."

Libby blinked her eyes rapidly.

Grant held up a hand. "But if you stay, I would like a couple things."

"What?" Libby asked in a shaky voice.

"Finish school. High school at least."

Libby nodded cautiously. "What else?"

"Help with the ranch."

"All right. But I don't know anything about ranching," she said.

"You can learn," Grant said. "During the last few years I've let the place go. I wasn't in very good shape, but it was mostly because I had no interest. Now I do."

"I walked around last night," Libby said. "For a girl from a small house in the city, it's wonderful."

Grant sighed. "It once was. But there's a problem."

Libby waited.

"I'm about to lose it," Grant said heavily. "A large bank loan comes due in six months. Unless we can solve that, they'll foreclose."

8

Grant explained that about five years before, the farm had started losing money. To keep it going, he'd had to take out a line of credit with the farm as security. It was supposed to be just a short-term solution, but every year the debt had grown.

"I told the crew we needed to turn things around," Grant said, "but we haven't."

"Your books must show what's wrong," Libby said.

"My accountant just says the markets have just gone south."

"What do you think?" Libby asked.

Grant sighed. "I don't know. I can't focus much these days."

"What can I do?" Libby asked.

"Maybe nothing," Grant said. "A sale of the ranch might leave enough to live on. But with you here, I would like something better."

Libby stared.

"If you decide to stay," Grant said.

Libby hesitated, then nodded slowly. "I'll stay."

"For how long?" Grant asked.

"As long as you want," Libby said.

CHAPTER NINE

LEARNING

1

Over the next month, Libby learned to ranch. She read countless internet articles, her fingers tapping the keys with blinding speed, and peppered Grant with questions. She made a list of day-to-day jobs she needed to master and had Grant watch her until she got them right. She talked to the ranch hands and learned what they did, then studied Grant's financial records. But what really fascinated her were the markets for cattle, grain and supplies. After reading everything she could find about them, she began to see patterns in their price fluctuations.

Late one Sunday night, she found Grant on the front porch gazing at the constellations overhead. "I never knew how bright the stars were without city lights," she said.

"Even when you see them every night, they're pretty great," he said.

After star-gazing a while longer, Libby said, "I have some suggestions."

"Okay," Grant said.

"Our fertilizer costs are too high," Libby said. "We should have the soil tested to see what we really need. And we spend too much on water. We need to tailor our water usage to the needs of individual crops. We also could use government credits to buy some solar panels."

She went on to talk about buying better breeding bulls, selecting heifers that would produce bigger calves, and organizing the production calendar for greater efficiency.

"We already do some of those things," Grant grumbled.

"Yes, but what we do is thirty years out-of-date. There are new things that will save us lot of money."

"All right," Grant said, sighing. "Anything else?"

"I've been studying the cattle markets. The timing of our purchases and sales has been lousy lately."

Grant grunted. "You can't outthink the markets."

Libby said, "Let me try."

It turned out she could. She absorbed the data on cattle supply and prices, hired a commodity broker, and began placing orders to buy and sell cattle. Sometimes she bought options to buy cattle in the future, and then sold them before delivery at higher prices. Other times she locked in a high price to sell cattle and then purchased what she had already sold at a lower price. After doing this for seven weeks, she had made more money than the farm had netted during the previous six months.

At one point the broker had said, "I've never seen anyone beat the markets like this. If I didn't know better, I'd say you were getting inside dope."

"It probably can't last," Libby said, while thinking, *it can*. But she also knew that playing the markets too long would attract unwanted attention.

2

In early August, Libby and Grant visited Mr. Douglas Jones, a loan officer at First Grand Bank in Grand Junction. He was overweight, jovial, and favored ornate cowboy boots, but his small eyes were hard and calculating.

"Your check has brought the loan current," Jones said, "so we won't be foreclosing. But the balance will still come due in six months. What will you do about that?"

"What will it take to get a new loan?" Grant asked.

Jones frowned. "You'll have to convince us the ranch can service the debt."

"How can we do that?" Libby asked.

Jones turned to Grant. "She's your daughter?"

"Yes," Grant said. "She lived with her aunt and now is with me."

"Well, we'll have to review your finances."

The next week, Grant and Libby spent eight hours with Jones going over the ranch's records. Libby showed how they would increase their cash flow and reduce overhead. Jones peppered Libby with questions, but he couldn't poke holes in her answers.

At one point Jones said, "I'm not used to doing this with teenagers."

Libby smiled and said, "It's better than hassling over foreclosure, don't you think?"

Jones grunted, but went back to the records.

At the end, Jones agreed to extend the loan for six months. He said that if the finances improved as Libby predicted, the bank would refinance.

Six months later, Jones gave them a new, twenty-year loan.

CHAPTER TEN

ARLINGTON

1

The week after Grant and Libby obtained their new loan, Colonel Ashton Crane parked his car in his office's underground parking lot and walked toward the elevator. Today he was thinking about a job Adam Durant had assigned him. It involved a former staffer who threatened to publish a tell-all book about Durant's misuse of senate prerogatives. The staffer apparently wasn't afraid that Durant might sue him. Crane shook his head sadly. The staffer would soon learn that there were things more worrisome than a lawsuit. Like a dead pet and traumatized spouse.

When he reached the elevator, a tall, black-clad woman suddenly appeared next to him.

"Can I have a moment, Colonel?" The woman said.

Crane took an involuntary step back. It was Autumn Gray. She was almost as tall as he and reminded Crane of a panther. He tried to ignore the scarlet birthmark.

"You have no business here," Crane said.

"Oh, I do. But I'll be brief. Just two items."

"This better be good," Crane said. His voice was hoarse.

"First item," Gray said. "The Williston kid, number eighteen, was a bust. A garden-variety autistic savant."

"You accosted me here to tell me that?" Crane said angrily.

"Oh, not really. I wanted to see you. I was getting tired of anonymous calls from 'the handler.'"

"How did you find me?"

"Don't worry about that," Gray said. "I just wanted us to be on an equal footing."

Crane stared at her, his face grim. "What's the second thing?"

"I'm sorry to report that on his way back from the Williston cabin, Blunt slipped and had a nasty fall."

Crane stiffened. "How nasty?" he asked.

"Two hundred feet."

Crane's face went pale. She killed him, he thought. But her eyes were observing him very carefully. Crane decided that accusing her of killing Blunt would be a very bad idea. "Has it been taken care of?" he asked.

"The local police concluded it was an unfortunate accident."

"What do you want from me?" Crane asked.

"Nothing," Gray said. "Things will go on as before, except for Blunt."

Crane nodded slowly. "Okay."

"Good," Gray said. "Just one thing. I am a very loyal. But don't send people for me. I'm better than they are. And then I won't be loyal."

Crane stared. "Can I believe you?" he asked.

Gray smiled. "Absolutely."

Crane was silent for a while. Then he said, "All right."

After Crane stepped into the elevator, Gray considered whether he would come after her. She thought not. His face had said he'd leave her alone. If it hadn't, she would have taken care of things right then. As she walked away, she slipped a razor-edged blade into her fanny pack.

2

After reaching his office, Colonel Crane tried to relax and slow his heart rate. If the conversation had gone differently, he realized, he might have ended up in a parking lot dumpster.

What should he do about it?

He had first heard of Gray while commanding a unit in Afghanistan. She was on a Special Forces team assigned to identify and eliminate Taliban insurgents, and her reputation made even the most hard-bitten veterans wary. After Durant had hired him, Crane got her a job with Homeland Security. He'd never gotten close to her, for the same reason a zoo manager stays away from the large cats and snakes. But she had proven more than adequate for a couple ugly assignments unsuited for anyone else. And if he sent someone to deal with her, she just might turn out to be better. And then she would come after him. No, better to keep her on the team.

3

Although he dreaded it, Crane knew he had to tell Durant about Blunt. It took two hours to arrange a secure telephone call to the senator. Crane was still in his office when the phone rang.

"You have something to report?" Durant asked.

"We still haven't found the person you want," Crane said. "But we're trying everything."

"Anything else?"

"One of our agents was killed in the mountains."

"Did you order it?" Durant asked.

"No. I would get your approval for that."

Durant was silent for a moment. When he spoke, his voice was icy. "I expect results, Colonel. I don't want operational details. Is that clear?"

"Yes, Senator."

"Has the agent's death been handled?"

"Yes. It's been ruled an accident."

"I take it the issue was in doubt," Durant said drily.

Crane said nothing.

"Have you been using Sibyl?" Durant asked.

"Yes. It's helping us clear the list of twenty-one possibles."

"Once it's up and running, Xerxes will be even better."

"Will Xerxes really be better than Sibyl?" Crane asked. "That's hard to believe."

"You'll see," Durant said.

CHAPTER ELEVEN

MANAGING

1

If the ranch was to become profitable, as she had promised the loan officer, Libby knew it was up to her. Working with the ranch hands, she was soon feeding cattle, milking cows, repairing fences and sheds, spraying for pests, and watching for predators. She helped a cow give birth and learned how to operate a tractor, combine and chainsaw. Grant's physical condition kept him from doing much, so Libby learned mostly by trial and error. There was always something to fix, build, watch or move.

Libby expected the work to be hard, but she was surprised by its emotional toll. Besides the constant stress of being in charge, almost every day brought a new sorrow. She had grown attached to Mabel, a Hereford cow that had been around for years. Libby would often talk to it during her chores. Then one day, it was struck by lightning and killed. A colorful rooster named George seemed fine one morning but by evening was dead from a digestive problem. A while later Cotton, her favorite bunny, died for no apparent reason.

But despite it all, she was happier than she could remember.

One evening after helping a crew paint the barn, Libby joined Grant on the porch. For a while they watched the cattle graze and listened to a meadowlark.

"Funny. We've always had birds," Grant mused. "But I've only really heard them lately."

"It's like music," Libby said.

"How's school?" Grant asked.

"I'm Miss Anonymous," Libby said. "The girl without a name."

"Are you taking any advanced classes?"

"No. They see me as just average."

Grant grunted. "Your answer to that weight-of-the-sky problem didn't seem average."

Libby made a face. "Yeah. I kind of messed up on that."

As a homework assignment, a teacher had asked the students to calculate the weight of the sky. "It had seemed pretty simple," Libby said apologetically, "so I turned in my answer without thinking whether anyone else would get it."

"What did you use? The earth's atmospheric pressure?" Grant asked.

"Yes. I found it on line. It turned out to be 14.7 pounds per square inch."

Grant nodded. "And then you calculated the earth's surface area?"

"Right. I just had to change square miles to square inches."

"So," Grant asked, "what did you come up with?"

"When you multiply atmospheric pressure times the earth's surface in square inches, the answer is that the sky weighs about 4.7 million billion tons."

Grant raised his eyebrows. "Did the other students congratulate you on the answer?"

Libby smiled and shook her head. "Not exactly. Turns out I was the only one who got it right. When the teacher went over my answer in class, I got some angry glares. But I didn't mean to show off. The answer just came to me."

"Your mother was like that," Grant said. "She would have had the answer in an instant."

"Really?" Libby asked.

"Absolutely. Except she probably wouldn't have needed to look anything up. Her memory was astounding."

Suddenly Grant's hands went to his head. Libby grabbed him just before he toppled off the chair.

After several minutes, Grant straightened, his eyes unfocused.

Libby watched him carefully. "How long has this been going on?"

Grant sighed. "A while. It's been worse lately."

"You need a doctor," Libby said.

Grant shrugged. "Seems hardly worth the effort."

"Don't say that," Libby said crossly. "This place is turning the corner. Without you, everything would fall apart."

"Not while you're around," Grant said.

"Let's not find out," Libby said, "but I worry about your state of mind."

Grant sighed. "The blues."

"Want to talk about it?" Libby asked.

3

As they sat on the porch in the fading light, Grant spoke so softly he could barely be heard over the cattle and birds. "I'm like an old baseball player who knows it's time to quit when he starts striking out against pitchers who used to walk him."

"You could make a comeback," Libby said.

Grant shook his head. "I once was a hell of a programmer. But a while back I looked at some of my old projects. A gene editing algorithm, a cancer drug program, Sibyl. I had no idea how I had done them. Whatever I had is gone."

"Is it the headaches?" Libby asked.

Grant sighed. "More like what's causing the headaches. The gears are jammed. Answers used to come to me out of nowhere. Like you and that weight-of-the-sky thing. Now everything's confused."

"Well, I don't believe you are finished. I don't!"

Grant gazed her without comment.

"Let's find a doctor who can help," Libby said.

"I've seen all kinds of doctors. They didn't do much."

"That was a long time ago," Libby said. "This is now."

CHAPTER TWELVE

DR. GIBSON

1

After searching for specialists on-line, Libby settled on Dr. Russell Gibson, the region's top neurosurgeon. Grant was indifferent, but acquiesced without comment. When she called Gibson's office for an appointment, she was relieved to learn that the first available date was two months out. That would give them time to vaccinate the calves and get the cattle to market.

In early October, Libby came home from school with a small, wiry girl with dark skin, black hair, and large, intense eyes. They found Grant in the barn watching a new colt being weaned.

"Tom," Libby said, "this is Nia Williams. We eat lunch together at school. She's never seen a ranch before, so I invited her to come home with me."

Grant smiled. "It's nice to meet you, Nia. Ever seen a baby horse up close?"

The colt was crouched over a trough, eating grain. "What's its name?" Nia asked.

"I don't think he has one," Grant said. "What should we call him?"

Nia studied the colt, then said, "Maybe Teddy. He's the color of my Teddy Bear."

"It's a good name," Grant said. "Libby, why don't you show Nia around."

Nia started coming to the ranch every day after school. "Her dad has health problems," Libby said, "and her mom works two jobs. She's alone so much I said she could hang around here."

"Fine with me," Grant said, "Why don't you show her how a ranch works?"

A quick study, Nia was soon helping with most of the chores. She was especially good with the horses and cattle. Libby began wondering how she had managed before. Grant forced Nia to accept wages, though she tried to refuse.

"This ranch can't afford gifts," Grant said. "We're paying you because you've earned it."

With Nia's help, they finished the vaccinations and cattle shipments in time for Grant's appointment with Dr. Gibson.

2

Gibson had an unpretentious, functional office on the third floor of Grand Junction Community Hospital. Grant and Libby showed up as scheduled and within five minutes they were shown into an examining room. The doctor at least earned points for efficiency, Libby thought. Three minutes later Dr. Gibson, a trim, smiling, sandy-haired man in his early 40's, walked in.

"Thank you for your thorough patient history, Mr. Grant," Gibson said. "I see that you were badly beaten almost twenty years ago and underwent three surgeries to repair damage to your brain. And a while later you suffered a stroke that weakened your left leg."

"Yes," Grant said.

"And lately you've been having severe headaches."

Grant nodded. "A few years ago I saw someone in Denver. He said controlling pain was about all they could do. Been on opioids ever since."

"Well, we've learned some new things. We'll give you a CAT-scan and MRI, and then see where we stand."

Libby went with Grant for the tests, which triggered another headache. When Grant walked out of the clinic, he could barely stand and had to shield his eyes against the sun.

It was two weeks before Grant and Libby were called in to discuss the test results. They waited nervously in Dr. Gibson's office until he walked in. His expression was serious, not upbeat like Libby had hoped.

"The bottom line is this," Gibson said. "Your cerebral cortex, which controls thinking and memory, was severely damaged by your old injury, and it's gotten worse over the years. The damage is deep inside the brain and hard to reach without causing more harm."

Libby had been researching Grant's condition on-line. "What about an MRI-guided laser?" she asked.

Gibson looked at her in surprise. "You've done some studying."

"Sorry," Libby said, "I didn't mean to be doctoring from the back seat. But Tom's been in so much pain I wanted to learn all I could."

The doctor smiled slightly and said, "Doctors don't usually encourage patient advice, but in this case you may be on to something. The laser's still experimental, but it may be our best bet."

CHAPTER THIRTEEN

SURGERY

1

They showed up for Grant's surgery at 5:30 am. He was taken to pre-op, while Libby went to the waiting room. She had studied the surgical procedure on-line and talked with the head nurse. Three hours had been blocked out for the surgery, which meant that Grant should be in the recovery room by 11am. Libby counted off the hours by picturing each step the doctor would be taking. Grant would be prepped at eight, by nine the MRI would be used to target the laser, and by nine-thirty the laser would address the scar tissue in the pre-frontal cortex. With any luck, they would closing him up by ten, monitor him in the operating room for a while, and then move him to the recovery room.

By 11:30, Libby had heard nothing, so she intercepted the head nurse who had stepped briefly into the hall.

"What's his status?" she asked.

"It seems to be taking a bit longer than expected," she nurse said. "I'll let you know as soon as he's out of the OR. I can't say how the surgery's going, but Dr. Gibson is very good."

It was another hour before the nurse returned. "Dr. Gibson will be out soon. Mr. Grant is in the recovery room now."

Gibson came out a half hour later. He looked tired and stressed.

"There were some complications," he said. "The damage was more extensive than the scans showed, and the tissue was unusually fragile. We had some intracranial bleeding, which took a while to control."

"Did you repair the damage?" Libby asked.

The doctor looked uncertain. "As far as we could tell. But for a while his brain experienced some swelling. We think the condition was reversed before it caused any damage, but only time will tell for sure."

"When can I see him?"

"We'll watch him for another hour, then you can go in."

When Libby was allowed into the recovery room, Grant had a breathing mask, four tubes attached to his body, and a large bandage covering his head. He looked very ill.

After watching Grant for twenty minutes, Libby saw his right index and middle fingers quivering spasmodically. His face suddenly seemed paler.

Libby jumped from her chair and raced out of the room. Dr. Gibson was nowhere in sight. She finally saw the head nurse going over a chart. She ran up to her and said, "Quick, where is Dr. Gibson?"

The nurse said, "I don't know. Probably on rounds."

"He needs to come back now!"

"I can't just…"

Libby cut her off. "If he waits, Grant could die!" Libby's voice cracked with fear.

The nurse told Dr. Gibson over the intercom that he was needed in the recovery room stat, repeating the announcement twice. Three minutes later Gibson rushed into the room, winded and tense.

"Dr. Gibson," Libby said, "look at his fingers." She pointed to the still spasming digits.

"I don't know…"

"He's bleeding and it's affecting his fingers! If I'm wrong, you can close him up again. But, please, now!"

Gibson hesitated for a fraction of a second, then said to the nurse, "We need to get back in the OR now. Is anyone using it?"

"No, Dr. Andrews cancelled his procedure."

"Get a surgery team there stat. We're opening him in five minutes."

2

Libby had been in the waiting room for two hours when Dr. Gibson walked in. She expected him to be more exhausted than before. But he looked energized.

"He did have a bleed all right, in the precentral gyrus. I think we got it in time."

"How long had it been going?"

"The surgery probably aggravated it. But the surrounding tissue suggested that small leaks might have been going on for months."

"Could that have caused his headaches?"

"The pressure could cause all kinds of things."

Libby put a hand over her eyes.

Gibson waited a while, then said, "How in God's name did you suspect a bleed?"

Libby shook her head. "I don't know. After you scheduled the surgery, I studied what you would be doing. Everything's on line these days. When I saw his fingers, I remembered about bleeding."

"But how did you do it so fast?" Gibson asked.

"I don't know. Just an intuition."

3

Three days after the surgery, Libby brought Grant home. She stayed in his room the next week, brought him what he needed, and slept in a chair. After six days Grant woke up, looked around, and gave Libby a tired smile.

"How's the head?" Libby asked.

Grant touched the bandage on his head. "It doesn't seem to hurt much," he said. "How long ago was the surgery?"

"Ten days," Libby said.

Grant whistled. "You been here the whole time?"

Libby made a face. "You weren't much on conversation, but you didn't put up any resistance either."

Grant snorted. "As if I ever do. How's the ranch?"

"Nia's been sleeping in the guest room. Her mother got her excused from school so she could help while you were recovering. I got excused too. The two of us are a pretty good team. We discuss each day's schedule and she passes it on to the crew. Actually, we don't discuss much, since she knows just about everything. She got the fall harvest done, and we're nearly ready for winter. We owe her a bonus."

"Why don't you get my checkbook now, while I'm awake?"

"I've already prepared a check. All you have to do is sign it."

"Good. So, what does the doctor say about my recovery?"

"He thinks your headaches will become less severe. As for your thinking and memories, we'll just have to see. If the memories were stored in areas he couldn't fix, or if they were affected by scar tissue he had to remove, they're probably lost. But if blood flow was the problem, that may have been corrected. Like most things, only time will tell."

4

While Libby was taking care of Grant, Phil Keller was giving State a nice return on his football scholarship. The team's quarterback, Jeff Schmidt, was leading the nation in passing, but few noticed he had more time to throw than any other quarterback. Schmidt had been sacked only twice, both by linebackers blitzing from the right. There had been no sacks from the left side of the line, where Keller was the anchor. There were whispers about him being named an all-American.

He had solved his probation problem by studying ten hours a day for the physics make-up exam before taking it in the room next to Professor Aaron's office. She had looked in once during the three hours, as he wrestled with questions on kinematics, the effect of the moon's gravity on the flight time to Alpha Centauri, and the radius of a black hole. He gave his exam a quick go over when he was done. He knew he had passed.

He ran into Professor Aaron on the way out. "So, will you be back on the team?" she asked.

Phil grinned. "I think so," he said.

"We'll see, but you could have avoided all this if you had just studied when you should have."

"I guess. But I know more physics now than I would have even if I had studied before."

"As I said, we'll see."

Three days later, Phil's exam was returned with a note in red ink that said, "Pass. Well done Mr. Keller."

Phil rejoined the team and started to earn his scholarship.

5

After State won its first three games, with Phil protecting Jeff Schmidt like he was the Mona Lisa, Phil became something of a celebrity on campus. He was invited to the best parties and dated several popular co-eds. But it was Libby he thought about. He would see her face in his mind at odd times, even during games. Once, during a third-down huddle against New Mexico, Schmidt put his hand on Keller's arm, and Phil flashed on Libby's hand grabbing his arm while they were stuck in that damned car.

"You got that, Phil?" Jeff had said. "Keep Jackson off me."

"What?" Phil said. "Oh, right. Don't worry about him. Just make your throw."

Phil had held Jackson at the line of scrimmage for a full ten seconds, more than enough time for Schmidt to complete a game-winning toss into the end zone.

Keller had hoped his memory of Libby would fade. But the opposite was true. She was a constant presence in the back of his mind.

After a lop-sided win against Colorado, Phil had a pizza and beer with Sarah and Charles. The conversation eventually turned to the flash-flood and their time in the car. After a while, Charles raised a glass. "Here's to Abby, or whatever her name was. Without her, we would have ended up breathing water."

"Here, here!" everyone said.

"Have you heard from her, Phil?" Charles asked.

"Not a word. Some bad people are after her. She wants to stay missing."

"I feel guilty about not thanking her," Sarah said.

"Me too," Phil said.

"Why don't you try to find her?" Charles asked.

"No way," Phil said. "I might give her away."

"I think she liked you, Phil," Sarah said. "Do you think she knows you're a star now?"

6

State's team won the league championship and was chosen to play in the Rose Bowl against Ol' Miss on New Year's Day. A few days before the game, Phil left practice, tired and sweaty, and found a letter in his post office box. It had no return address and was post-marked from Chicago. Inside the envelope was a single sheet of paper with small, neat printing. It read:

Hi Phil,

I've followed your season. You protected your quarterback almost as well as you did me. If Notre Dame's McCarty doesn't get it (he's good, but you do more for State's passing game) you could make All-American.

One thought. When you face Ike Thomas next week, keep your back straight, and make sure you're quick off the snap. In the Arizona game, you seemed a hair slow. Also, on big passing plays, Thomas favors the bull rush. I thought you'd likely see Ol' Miss in the Rose Bowl, so I've watched Thomas on TV. He starts his bull rush with his right hand farther back than usual.

I think a lot about that car. How did you ever manage to force open that door? If you're that strong against Thomas, you'll be all right.

Have a big game against the Rebels.

Me

P.S. Congrats on physics! I knew you'd pass.

Libby and Grant watched the Rose Bowl together on News Years' Day. She hoped Phil had received her letter. She hadn't wanted it post-marked from Colorado, so she'd had one of Grant's workmen mail it from Chicago when he got there for the holidays.

By the fourth quarter, State's Jeff Schmidt had run up three hundred fifty passing yards, mostly because of the time he had to throw. Thomas had pressured Schmidt a couple of times, but he had no sacks. With five minutes remaining State had a three-point lead, but then the Rebels hit a thirty-yard bomb into the end zone to go up by four. State responded by marching down the field, finally getting down to Ol' Miss's twenty with seven seconds remaining. They used their final timeout to decide on one last play.

"I'll bet they try a fade into the right corner," Libby said to Grant. "But Schmidt's going to need a lot of time." As the teams lined up, Libby focused on Thomas, who was lined up against Phil. "Watch for the bull rush," she whispered.

When the ball was snapped, Thomas did start the bull rush, but the middle linebacker also hit Phil at the same time, hoping to spring Thomas free. Phil had been ready for the bull rush, but not for the linebacker. Phil planted his feet and arched his back against the two defenders. Libby held her breath as the play developed, seconds ticking off in her head. Three, four, five… Schmidt still had not thrown the ball.

"Oh, no," Libby muttered, as the receiver got knocked out of his pattern. Phil was still holding his ground against Thomas and the linebacker.

Then Thomas suddenly looked back, Phil still pushing against him. Schmidt had made his throw. The wide receiver had broken free, after ten long seconds, and managed to keep both feet in as he snagged the pass in the end zone's right corner. State had scored the winning touchdown.

Libby sprung out of her chair and let out a whoop.

After the game, most of the attention was on Schmidt's pass and the wide receiver's acrobatic catch. But later one of the telecasters cornered Phil.

"Phil Keller," the announcer said, "Jeff Schmidt said your pass protection was the key to that last play. How were you able to hold Thomas off so long?"

"I was just lucky," Phil said. "It was Tom who made the throw, and Andy who caught it."

"Do you have anything else to say?" the announcer asked.

Phil looked into the camera. "I'd like to thank a certain sparrow," he said.

The announcer gave him a puzzled look. But on the ranch in Colorado, Libby put her fingers where her tattoo had been before it faded away.

CHAPTER FOURTEEN

DEATH NOTICE

1

There days after State beat Ol' Miss, Colonel Ashton Crane was going over his file on Libby Anderson. For nine months he had been searching for her, using facial recognition, surveillance, police resources, and computer analysis. And she was still goddamned missing. They'd had some traces of her. Someone's internet search had sent Gray and her partner—now deceased—rushing to a restaurant, but the person had disappeared. Then a surveillance camera captured what might have been the girl walking near the college, but they never found her. Then there was those students who got caught in a flash flood. One of them could have been the girl. But they had been unforgivably slow in tracing her to a hospital in Las Vegas. By the time they got there, she had walked away—at three in the morning—and vanished. There had been no sign of her since. Crane grimaced. They were a bunch of Keystone Cops, and she was mocking them.

Crane's cell phone rang. "Yes," Crane said.

"Colonel, what's happening with the Anderson girl?" It was Adam Durant.

Jesus, Crane thought, this was the last thing he needed. "Still no word, Senator," Crane said, "I can't believe she's stayed missing this long."

"Well, Colonel, maybe this will help. Last week some marathoners found the body of a teenage girl in a shallow grave west of Las Vegas. The girl had been strangled and buried almost a year ago. DNA tests were run, and Sibyl confirmed that the results matched hair taken from the girl's brush. It's her."

Crane was silent for a moment. "I never thought she'd end up like this. Could it be a mistake?"

"Not with Sibyl. You can cross the girl off."

Crane sighed. "Well, I suppose I should be pleased, but it's a bit of a letdown. After looking for the girl all this time, I wanted to meet her."

"Forget about her. Have you checked out the other possibles?" Durant asked.

"Almost done. But don't get your hopes up. Maybe Xerxes will come up with something better when it's running. But this person may not exist."

"There was one once," Durant said. "Someday there'll be another."

"Is it really worth all this trouble?" Crane asked.

"If we find this person, nothing else will matter."

2

An hour later Crane told Autumn Gray about the girl. Gray was in Albuquerque, stopping a movement to unionize a Quantum subsidiary. The union leader had a heavy cocaine habit that would soon become public if he didn't change direction. If he cooperated, he would have all the drugs he wanted.

"So the girl's dead?" Gray asked.

"Very," Crane said.

Gray was silent, then said, "Bullshit."

"Sibyl confirmed it. There's no doubt."

More silence. "I know this kid. She wouldn't end up this way," Gray said.

"That's what I thought, but Durant said we can close the file."

"This smells wrong," Gray said.

"Forget about it. What's happening with the union thing?"

"Mr. Merrill was finding it hard to get his blow. He got twitchy. We explained how easy it would be to get a permanent supply. He only has to forget about the union stuff for a while. It's all becoming clear to him."

After talking to Colonel Crane, Adam Durant stared out of his Senate office building window and wondered if now was the time for a presidential run. No, he finally decided, the time still wasn't right. He was only in his early fifties and had at least twenty years to take his shot. Xerxes would be up and running soon. After that, all he would need is the person who could give him the final piece of the puzzle. He had hoped Sibyl could do it—but things hadn't worked out. It had lately seemed…a little unreliable. They had to get Xerxes running. It would be far more powerful than Sibyl, and if he could find the person he needed…the future would be his.

CHAPTER FIFTEEN
THE SCIENCE PROJECT

1

In the three years Libby had been managing it, the ranch had so far exceeded the bank's expectations that it offered them more money to expand. The ranch was now running five hundred head of cattle, and producing more corn, wheat, and alfalfa than ever before. Libby remained quiet and well-liked in school, occasionally helping friends with science or math. She usually ate lunch with Nia Williams, where they would talk as much about the ranch as they did about school. Nia was still working there part time, more as a colleague than employee.

One lunch during February of Libby's senior year, Nia mentioned that college was out unless she got a scholarship. "I have good grades," she said, "but money's a problem."

"You'll get a big bonus when our fiscal year closes. You finished the fall harvest for two-thirds the cost Grant and I had budgeted."

Nia smiled wryly. "I was sort of proud of that. But my dad keeps getting worse."

"I knew something was wrong, but you never talk about it."

Nia sighed. "It's painful. Dad's been diagnosed with early-onset Alzheimer's. Mom tries to help when she's not working, and I do too. But he's always losing things. Shoes in the shower, keys in the refrigerator, wallet with the laundry, you name it. And then he gets angry."

"I'm so sorry. But you can't miss college. You've worked too hard for it."

"What about you? If anyone should go, it's you."

Libby shrugged. "I'm happy where I am. But what about the scholarship? Anything look promising?"

"The best one is from the National Science Foundation. It offers full tuition and room and board. I measure up in most areas, but I need a good science project. I've had some ideas, but they're either lousy, or they've already been done."

"I doubt I can help," Libby said, "but I'll give it some thought."

2

At lunch the next day, Nia asked, "So, any thoughts for a science project?"

"Sometimes Grant's headaches are so bad he can barely open his eyes," Libby said. "He'll wander around bumping into things. When I see him like that, I'll call out when he's about to hit something. Well, what if we invent a device that could tell your dad where things are? Not just chairs, but his keys or wallet?"

Nia smiled doubtfully. "Are you going to have some bird sit on my dad's shoulder and squawk out directions?"

"Here's something better. Suppose you had a small camera your father could wear on his belt, which would record things around him as he moved. The camera's images would be transmitted to a computer that could recognize fixed objects like furniture, or things that were movable, like keys and shoes."

"I follow you so far," Nia said.

"Well, you could program the computer to answer questions like 'Where are the keys?' It would look at the recorded images and tell you the keys were on the armchair. Maybe your father wouldn't get so frustrated if he could find the keys on his own. It could also give him directions if he becomes disoriented."

Nia stared at Libby. "Is something like that possible?"

"Sure. Computers can already identify images, like with surveillance cameras. And computers can respond to voice commands. This just combines the two."

Nia stared at Libby for a while, her lips pursed. "It seems impossible. But if I can do it, maybe I'll get to college after all."

3

For the next three weeks, Nia worked constantly on her project. When Libby asked about it, Nia said little. "I need to do it myself," she said, "if I'm going to get the scholarship."

But she finally did ask Libby for some help. Libby helped her devise a formula for predicting how far a dropped object might roll, based on its mass and acceleration. But another problem was more difficult. How to program the computer to organize the camera's countless images so it could quickly locate a missing item.

"Someone has to invent the right computer algorithm," Libby said, "and I just don't have the training."

"Are we out of luck then?" Nia asked.

"Let's ask Grant," Libby said. "He's been getting a little better since the surgery. Maybe he can help."

They explained the problem to Grant. He seemed uncertain at first, but then grew thoughtful. "It's actually simple," he said. "A basic problem of sorting and classifying. But to retrieve quickly the image of a lost item, you need to calculate in advance the probability of an item being lost—keys would obviously have a high probability—and then have the algorithm flag the image when it is recorded. Later, when the item can't be found, the right image could be retrieved quickly. It's easy to say, but hard to put in an algorithm."

Grant spent a day working on his Pro-X computer, something he had hadn't done since the surgery. He then had Nia bring in the camera that would be worn on her father's belt, which Wi-Fi would link to a computer. He installed his new algorithm into the computer and connected the camera.

"Nia," he said, "take three small things from the other room, then come back and we'll activate the camera and put it on your belt. After that, walk around for a while and put the items in out-of-the way places. Go about your normal business for an hour and then come back. We'll see how the computer does."

An hour later, Nia came back. "All right," Grant said, "ask the computer where the objects are."

"Computer," Nia said, "where is the small silver bracelet?"

There was the briefest of pauses, then the computer said, "Nia, it is under the leather couch's middle cushion."

Libby found the bracelet under the cushion.

"Computer," Nia said, "where is my wallet?"

Another pause, then the computer said, "Look behind the wastebasket next to the easy chair."

The wallet was where the computer said.

Finally, Nia asked, "Computer where is the gold fountain pen I was carrying?"

Immediately the computer said, "Nia, it is still in your back pocket."

Nia reached behind her and took out the pen.

Libby grinned at Grant. "By Jove, I think he's still got it!"

Nia turned in her project two weeks later. Her submission explained how the device worked and acknowledged Libby and Grant's assistance. A month later, the National Science Foundation announced she had won the scholarship. A week after that she received UCLA's acceptance.

4

When Nia heard about college, Libby invited her over for a celebratory dinner. They had fresh potatoes and peas from the garden, barbecued steaks, and homemade ice cream.

"Next to college, this meal is the absolute best!" Nia gushed.

"Homemade beats a three-star restaurant," Libby said.

"How about your dad, Nia, has he tried the device?" Grant asked.

"He wears it everywhere and talks to it like a friend—where did I leave my watch? Should I wear my coat outside?—and Madam Secretary, that's what we call it, talks back."

Libby turned to Grant. "That was a fine piece of work, Tom."

Grant smiled wistfully. "The old quarterback can't throw a thirty-yarder, but he still can hit a short slant."

"That was better than a slant," Libby said. "Keep working at it. Get back to where you were."

"There's no point." Grant said. "My programming days are over."

"There *is* a point," Libby said fiercely.

"Why do you say that?" Grant asked.

"I think it could be important someday."

Grant gave her a curious look, but said nothing.

CHAPTER SIXTEEN
DEATH NOTICE

1

Just before high school graduation, Libby and Grant went to a conference in New York on new farming technology. During a break, Libby found a public computer and typed her name into the search engine. If anyone was monitoring searches about her, she didn't want them to learn where she lived. The result was a shock. An article from two years earlier reported that the body of a young woman had been found buried outside of Las Vegas. A DNA test showed the body to be that of Libby Anderson, of San Diego. She had been living with her aunt, who was also missing and presumed dead.

On the flight home, Libby told Grant about the article.

"Why would the police say I'm dead?" Libby asked.

"Maybe it was a botched test," Grant said. "Or maybe they wanted to close their file."

"I don't believe in botched tests," Libby said.

"Me neither."

"So, why would they report I was dead?" Libby asked.

Grant shrugged. "Maybe they thought you would get careless if you thought they had closed your file."

After learning she was supposedly dead, Libby allowed herself to hope the Gray woman had stopped looking for her. But one day after working on the spring harvest, she checked Grant's computer for updates on cattle prices. As she scrolled through the emails, a message popped into the inbox. When she opened it, she felt like she had been punched in the stomach.

A photo filled the screen. It had been taken by the surveillance camera near the university three years earlier. She had turned her face away, as she usually did near cameras, but the photo hadn't focused on her face. It had centered on her tattoo, which was still visible, of the little sparrow diving toward the cat. Someone knew who she was and where she lived. She studied it for a while, but could not identify the sender.

She ran downstairs and found Grant on the front porch.

"Look at this," Libby said, showing him the photo on her smartphone.

Grant stared at it.

"They're still looking for me," Libby said in a weak voice.

Grant shook his head minutely. "The real question is, who are 'they'?" Grant said. "Why would Homeland Security send you the photo? They would just come and grab you."

"How could they have found me?" Libby said.

Grant was silent for a while, then said, "I heard that Quantum Industries has deployed a new computer system to replace Sibyl, called Xerxes. Maybe it can do things Sibyl couldn't, like track you down."

"But why just a warning?"

"Maybe the timing wasn't right for them to take you."

At the end of her high school career, Libby was in the top quarter of her class—respectable, but not high enough to attract attention. But at the graduation ceremony, the chairman of the school's science department announced she had been chosen the top math and science student. Shocked, Libby looked at Grant, who was in the audience. Her expression asked if he knew about the award. He smiled broadly and shook his head.

Libby spoke to the chairman after the ceremony. "Mr. Stein," she said, "there must have been a mistake."

Stein shook his head. "A few months ago, the science teachers were discussing the school's top students. For some reason your test scores didn't match your performance in the lab and classroom. Those of us who knew you agreed that your science aptitude was the best we'd seen. But the teachers who didn't know you were uncertain. So we decided on a little experiment—an extra credit homework assignment. We would give it and see if any answers stood out."

Libby raised her eyebrows. "The hammer and nail question," she said.

The problem had asked the students to calculate why you could hammer a nail into a board, but couldn't push it in by hand. The answer required the students to calculate the kinetic energy released by a one pound hammer hitting the nail at an acceleration of two feet per second.

"That did seem a little tougher than usual," Libby said.

"You were the only one who got the answer," the chairman said. "That, plus your performance in class, earned you the award. We hoped it might change your mind about college."

After expressing appreciation, Libby told the chairman she planned to work with Grant on the ranch.

4

A day later, Nia congratulated Libby on the award, but said, "I still don't understand why you're passing up college. You told me yourself college is important. In fact, you were the one who helped me get the scholarship so that I could go."

"College isn't right for everyone," Libby said.

"That's not an answer," Nia said. "If anyone could excel at college, it's you."

That was just the point, Libby thought. She didn't want to excel. Excelling could attract attention—from the Gray woman, or some computer. And trying to avoid attention was tiresome, like driving a sports car with a foot on the brake.

"Nia can't understand why I'm passing up college," Libby said to Grant that evening. As was their habit, they were sitting on the porch watching the sunset.

"You're worried that attending college might help the Gray woman find you," Grant said.

"Colleges have lots of records that could be searched by a computer."

"Do you think I'm being paranoid?" Libby asked.

"Actually, no. Bad people are after you. Better to avoid them."

For a while neither spoke as they listened to a meadowlark in one of the cottonwoods. Finally, Libby said, "Speaking of computers, you've talked about Sibyl before. You said you helped create it, and that you thought of it as a her. I think that if you gave the computer an identity, it must have meant a lot to you."

A spasm of emotion crossed Grant's face. "That's true enough," he said, "but it brings up bad memories."

"I sensed that. And with your headaches and surgery, I didn't want to press. But now I need to. The memories involve you and my mother, don't they?"

Grant sighed. "Yes."

"Every time I've raised the past, you've changed the subject. I finally decided you would tell me when you were ready. But I can't wait any longer."

"What's brought this to a head now?"

"I've been wondering who sent me that photo."

"Really? What do you think?"

"I think Sibyl sent it."

Grant looked at her without expression.

"Do you think it's possible?" Libby asked.

After a moment, he said, "Maybe."

Libby looked surprised. "I really didn't expect you to agree. How could a computer act on its own like that?"

Grant sighed. "I wanted Sibyl to be more than a computer."

"Did you succeed?" Libby asked.

"With the years and my injury, things are a little fuzzy," Grant said. "But the answer is yes. At the end, with my algorithms, she was thinking on her own."

Libby looked at him for a long time. "And my mother was a part of it?" She asked.

"Yes," Grant said.

"You have to tell me all of it."

"It's a long story," Grant said.

"I'm not going anywhere. No college, remember?"

Grant smiled and said, "All right."

PART II

GRANT

CHAPTER ONE

A FLAIR FOR NUMBERS

1

Tom Grant had grown up on his parents' ranch in Grand Junction, Colorado, an only child. Neither parent had gone to college, but his father, Ben, tutored high school students in math and solved inventory problems for the local ranchers. His mother sold fruit preserves and managed the household finances. Long days ranching left him little time for homework, but Tom's grades were always excellent.

Tall and slender in high school, he played wide receiver on the football team. He had neither great speed nor hands, but he could read defensive backs and anticipate coverages like few others. After noticing a cornerback or safety out of position, Tom would glance at the team's quarterback, Andy Robson, and they would wordlessly change the play from a short slant to a fly route, or to whatever else might work. The two combined for the most touchdowns and passing yards in the school's history. Tom was second team all-league his junior year and first team as a senior. Robson was first team for two straight years, and the league's MVP as a senior.

While Tom enjoyed the competition and camaraderie of football, his real motivation came from the school's head cheerleader, and the most gorgeous girl Tom had ever seen—Sherri McKee. They were both freshmen when he met her for the first time. Sherri stopped him in the hall as he was getting ready for a scrimmage, looking breathtaking in her blue and white cheerleading outfit. When she looked at him with her steady, green eyes, Tom thought she had confused him with someone else.

"Mr. Thompson says you would be the right person to help me in math," she said in a pleasant voice.

Tom looked behind him to make sure she wasn't talking to someone else. When he turned back, her gaze was still on him.

"I guess I'm pretty good with numbers," he said.

"Would you mind meeting me in Mr. Thompson's classroom before school—just a few times—to see if you can force some math into me?"

"I guess," he said. He never considered saying no.

On their first before-school meeting, she said she didn't understand how to multiply a number like X to the fifth, by another number, say X to the tenth. Tom said, "Think about having five copies of X, and then adding ten more copies of X. You would end up with fifteen copies of X."

Sherri found that Tom could distill complex math problems into concepts that were simple and understandable. She ended up acing Mr. Thompson's math class and did well on the later ones.

"Sherri, you're good in math," Tom said after a couple months. "You just let yourself be psyched out. I know you. You can do whatever you want to. Never doubt that."

Sherri hadn't responded, but she found herself believing him. Years later, his advice took her places she never dreamed of.

She had decided she wanted to be a television broadcaster, but in her junior year she froze while giving a speech in a communications class. She became terrified of speaking in public.

"Can you help me?" she asked Tom. "Otherwise, I can forget about broadcasting."

"I can't speak in public," Tom said. "I bombed my one speech in English class. But I picked up some pointers. Pick a subject you're interested in, write out what you want to say, and go over it until it's down pat. Then practice with someone until you can do it even if your brain goes blank."

The morning after she gave her next speech, she walked into their meeting beaming. "Tom, it went perfectly! I pretended I was giving it to you, like I had all those other times. I can be a broadcaster!"

Tom was careful not to let his weekly sessions with Sherri turn into anything else. He knew she considered him only a friend. If he ever let her know his true feelings, there would be no more meetings. For three years she had talked to him about everything at school, whether it was academics or personal. She never made a difficult decision without using him as a sounding board. The one thing they didn't discuss was Andy Robson, the school's quarterback—and Tom's teammate.

In their junior year, Sherri began going steady with Andy, who had his choice of college scholarships and the tools to be a pro. It was expected that the homecoming queen would choose the star athlete. But Tom knew Sherri was motivated by something else as well.

In one of their before-school meetings, Sherri had made passing reference to her greatest fear, which was being poor. Her father was an alcoholic who couldn't stay employed, and her mother's clerical job could barely sustain the family. Sherri's only spending money came from her part time jobs in an ice cream parlor and bowling alley. Sometimes she had to wear homemade clothes the other girls ridiculed.

Sherri wanted to be part of Andy's pro football career.

2

Sherri and Tom had their last before-school meeting a week before graduation. She walked in with red eyes and a puffy face. She wouldn't look at him.

"Andy's accepted a scholarship from the University of Texas," she said in a shaky voice. "They've got a great football program and their starting quarterback is a senior, so the job could be his in a year."

"That's great," Tom said, not meaning it.

"I'm going with him," Sherry said.

Tom nodded his head wordlessly.

Sherri hesitated, then blurted out, "I liked our meetings more than anything."

"Me too," Tom said.

Sherri started to say something else, then gave Tom an anguished look and rushed from the room.

CHAPTER TWO

MIT

1

Tom wasn't good enough to play major college football, so he planned to attend a small college nearby and help with the ranch. Three months before graduation, however, his high school physics teacher dropped by to talk about the future.

"I hear Tom's planning to attend junior college," Mr. Christensen said.

Tom shrugged. "I'll be taking over the ranch someday. I can't let school interfere with that."

Mr. Christensen turned to Tom's father. "What do you say, Mr. Grant?"

"Well, it's his choice. But we always thought he would take over here."

"Have you seen Tom's aptitude test scores?" Mr. Christensen asked.

"Sure. He did well."

Mr. Christensen smiled. "He didn't do well, Mr. Grant."

"Oh. I guess I misunderstood."

"He did unbelievably well. Stupendously well. He's the most gifted math and science student I've ever seen."

"Tom may have a flair for numbers," Mrs. Grant said, "but that doesn't get the cows milked."

"Maybe not, but it could get your son a scholarship to MIT. My old college roommate is now chair of the physics department there. I sent him Tom's test scores and his thesis on wave particles."

"MIT," Mr. Grant said. "In Massachusetts? That's a stretch."

"My friend told the university's largest donor that MIT should recruit Tom."

Tom and his parents stared.

"Recruit, like in football?" Tom asked.

"Not exactly, but this donor has just agreed to pay the cost of Tom's schooling at MIT."

It took Mr. Christensen an hour to convince Tom and his parents it all was for real, and then they had to think about it. But the next day Tom's parents told him he couldn't pass it up.

"But…the ranch needs me," Tom said.

His father said, "We managed before you were born. We'll get by now."

2

When Tom went off to college, he was content to keep a low profile. But the new concepts he encountered sent his mind in unexpected directions. In Tom's sophomore physics class, Professor Jorgenson asked the students to write a paper on the practical effects of quantum mechanics, which was the physics governing subatomic particles. Tom's submission argued that human consciousness resulted from quantum entanglement, which was the ability of subatomic particles to influence each other, even over great distances. He theorized that consciousness was due to quantum entanglement's effect on the brain's neurons. His proof consisted of pages of dense and complex equations, but in the end Tom felt justified in writing Q.E.D., which meant he had proven what was intended. A week later, Professor Jorgenson called on him in class.

"Mr. Grant," Jorgenson said, "I have read your paper with interest."

"Thank you," Tom said.

"I read all the papers, so don't think reading implies respect."

Several students chuckled. Tom said nothing.

"Your equations are mildly provocative, but are they supported by any peer reviewed studies?"

"No. But I believe they prove that consciousness is due to quantum phenomena," Tom said.

"Scientists have been trying to understand consciousness for hundreds of years," the professor said, making no effort to hide his scorn. "Are you telling me that from your lofty pinnacle as a college sophomore, you have suddenly solved one of the great mysteries in science? That's a bit on the arrogant side, don't you think?"

Tom felt his face reddening. "The equations say what they say," Tom said stubbornly.

"Well," the professor said, "I suggest you get some empirical evidence. And by the way, even if you have a good idea, it will never get anywhere if you can't express it clearly. Learn to write, my friend."

3

Later that afternoon, Professor Jorgenson was in his office talking to a tall, swarthy doctoral candidate who occasionally served as his teaching assistant.

"You asked me to tell you if I encountered any student who stood out," Jorgenson said. "I read a paper yesterday that was damned impressive."

"Really?" Adam Durant said. "What was the topic?"

"Human consciousness as the effect of quantum entanglement on the brain's neurons."

"Did he prove his thesis?"

"Not empirically. But his equations were pretty astonishing."

For a while Durant seemed lost in thought. Then he said, "Do you know anything about my father's business?"

"He founded Tomorrow Industries, didn't he? Makes a lot of cutting edge technology?"

"Right. He's run it for the last twenty years. But his health's gone bad. When I finish my doctorate, I'll be joining the company, and before long I'll probably be running it."

"Good for you," Jorgenson said. "Why tell me?"

"I want to develop the technology that will dominate the future. Like the train, computer, smart phone and internet did."

"Sure," the professor said. "Everyone wants a piece of the next big thing. What do you think it will be?"

Durant laughed. "If I knew, I'd never tell you. But your student seems interesting. Keep an eye on him."

"Okay. But don't forget me when your foundation gives out the new grants."

As Durant walked out, he wondered if a conscious computer could be the next big thing.

4

During summer breaks from MIT, Tom turned down several prized internships to work on his parents' ranch in Colorado. Raising livestock on the unchanging land gave him pleasure not found in a laboratory. But the summer was marred by a troubling cough his mother had developed. The doctor had apparently said it was nothing to worry about, but Tom did.

At the start of Grant's junior year, Professor Jorgenson asked to see him, though Grant had not seen the professor since last year's class.

"No doubt this is a surprise," the professor said. "But I've looked again at your paper on the quantum roots of human consciousness."

"I stand by it," Tom said.

Jorgenson smiled faintly. "Fair enough. But if you want to prove your theory, you've got to take courses more challenging than what you're taking now."

"Like what?" Tom asked.

Jorgenson gave him a list that included solid state physics, advanced quantum mechanics, astrophysics, and general relativity.

"Also," Jorgenson said, "your ideas need to be communicated to computers. Take some advanced programming courses."

Tom reworked his course schedule and took everything from advanced string theory, to the structure of algorithms, to advanced coding design. He found them easier than he expected.

5

Toward the end of his junior year, Tom's fraternity entered a competition to be declared the best all-around student association. That would give it an edge in attracting new members in the fall. After studying the competition, the fraternity realized it couldn't win unless it placed first in academics. A review of everyone's classes revealed that a win was possible only if Tom received an A+ in Heinrich's theoretical advanced physics class. Heinrich had awarded only one A+ in twenty years.

With little hope of success, Tom worked for two weeks on a paper discussing quantum teleportation, which dealt with how information could be communicated between subatomic particles at faster than the speed of light, even if the particles were separated by great distances.

Professor Heinrich didn't return the paper. Instead, he summoned Tom to a large classroom and commenced a vigorous and hostile cross-examination. Suspecting Tom had stolen the work, Heinrich probed for gaps in the paper's physics and methodology, but Tom had answers for every question. At the end of the interrogation, Heinrich grunted that he would read the paper again.

A single spectator watched Tom's performance from the back of the classroom. It was Adam Durant.

Tom never spoke with Heinrich again. But on the last day of school, Tom's paper was returned with an A+ scrawled across the top. Tom's fraternity was given the award for best all-around student association.

6

During summer break between his junior and senior years, Tom grew increasingly alarmed about his mother. She slept all the time, and each cough racked her for several seconds. Every other week she disappeared for a day, only to return looking more ill than before. Tom's parents had evaded his questions for a while, but he finally cornered them one evening in late June.

"What does Mom have?" Tom asked. "I know it's bad."

Tom's father sighed. "We wanted to wait until we had the latest test results. We hoped to have good news."

"But you don't," Tom said.

"No, we don't. Your mom has stage four breast cancer."

Tom was silent for a while. "What can we expect?"

"Actually, the news isn't all bad," his father said. "With the latest treatment options, she should have several quality years left."

After a moment, Tom said, "I'm staying home."

Both parents shook their heads emphatically. "That's why we didn't tell you before," his father said. "Your graduation is the most important thing in our lives. If you come home, the cancer will have won."

A few days later, his mother told Tom there was another reason he had to finish school. "It's also the right thing for your father," she said.

"Why?" Tom said, alarmed. "Is he sick too?"

"Not how you mean. But you know about his depression. My illness hasn't helped that. Your finishing school will raise his spirits."

7

When he returned to MIT in the fall, he poured himself into a full load of the toughest physics and programming classes he could find. Even though his mother's health constantly lurked in the back of his mind, he found the classes simple and tedious. Once he had taken the core classes in a subject, his mind seemed to jump ahead and anticipate later developments. The advanced courses seemed only predictable extensions of what he already knew.

The school year was barely three months old when he was pulled out of a fraternity party to take a call. It was his father. His mother had suffered a seizure and died.

CHAPTER THREE

AT THE RANCH

1

Tom left MIT and never returned. A dean told him that with his record, he could finish the year by taking courses closer to home. Tom thanked him politely and said he would look into it once things settled down. But graduation held no interest for him. He was going back to the ranch, where he should have been all along.

When he returned home, Tom was dismayed by how badly things had deteriorated in the few months he had been away. The cattle were undernourished, the barn and fencing needed repairs, and the fields hadn't been readied for the spring planting. After his mother's funeral, attended by her church group and a few long-time friends, Tom began tackling the things that had been neglected.

One evening in February, Tom and his father were sitting on the porch when Tom said, "Dad, I know you miss Mom. Can I do anything?"

Tom's father seemed to come out of a trance. "What? Oh, no. You've been great. I should be helping more. I just don't have much energy."

Tom thought that energy wasn't the real problem. His father was becoming increasingly listless and dispirited. Tom tried to get him to see a doctor, but his father refused. Couldn't a man miss his wife for a while, he asked. But as the months passed, his father got worse. He spent days just sitting on the porch, unshaven, staring into the distance, saying nothing. Tom knew his father needed help, but the ranch was so consuming, and his father so inconspicuous, that it was far too easy to put off doing anything. Tom regretted it for the rest of his life.

2

On the second Tuesday in May, Tom came in from his early-morning chores and found his father cooking breakfast, looking shaved and presentable for the first time in weeks.

"Have some eggs and pancakes," his father said cheerily.

Tom sat down and began eating. "You're in a good mood this morning," he said.

"I've moped around long enough. Don't know how you've put up with it."

"It's good to have you back, Dad. I know things have been rough."

His father waved his hands breezily. "No more sympathy."

"So, what are you plans for today?"

"You know, I think I'll take a drive. Maybe hike a little. Remind myself how beautiful this land is. Tomorrow I'll start carrying my load."

3

When his father didn't come home by sunset, Tom went looking for him, but he didn't know where to start. The next morning, sick with fear, Tom called the sheriff to report his dad missing.

It was not until late afternoon that the sheriff called Tom to say his father's car had been found abandoned on Book Cliffs, a mountainous region a couple hundred miles from Grand Junction. Tom rushed to get there, but he arrived only in time to see a rescue team lifting his father's body into their van. He apparently had fallen several hundred feet while sight-seeing and was dead.

The sheriff gave Tom the results of his investigation the next day. "Looks like he went to the edge of the cliff to take some photos. It's a beautiful view. He must have gotten too close to the edge—the ground near the cliff is treacherous—and slipped and fell. It looks like a simple accident."

Later, the life insurance company that had sold Tom's father a large policy didn't think it was a simple accident.

"Was your father depressed when he died?" the adjuster asked.

"Well, he was down about my mother's death. But he had seemed to come out of it."

"Did he ever talk about taking his own life?"

"Never!" Tom said emphatically.

In the end, the insurance company had to pay up, as there was no evidence of suicide. As the sole beneficiary, Tom received enough to pay off the ranch's debts and put a good amount in the bank.

4

In the months that followed, Tom grew to resent the ranch. If it hadn't demanded so much from him, he could have done more for his father. And what was the point of running it now, anyway? The ranch was supposed to have supported his parents in their retirement, but now there wouldn't be one. Tom managed to keep the ranch going, but he did only what was necessary, with no planning for the future. Slowly, things began to fall apart, and before long the ranch was in no better shape than it had been in when Tom came back from college. That was the bitterest irony of all. All his work, done at his father's expense, was now worthless.

For the first time in years, Tom found interests outside of the ranch and school. An old schoolmate introduced him to competitive bridge. In a month, he was as good as players who had competed for years. By remembering each card played, and by drawing inferences from the bidding and signals, he could usually determine what was in each player's hand. In three months, he was runner-up in the regional championship.

Computer coding also became a hobby. He found pleasure in efficiently expressing an idea in language a computer could understand and implement. There were millions of coders, just as there were millions who could express their thoughts in writing. But the distance between someone who scrawled ideas on paper, and one who crafted sentences into works of art—a Shakespeare, Milton, or Dickinson—was immeasurable. Tom had a feel for coding that produced elegant algorithms few could duplicate. He had no great ambition for his coding. He just liked crafting an algorithm that did what was intended with no wasted steps. For his own amusement, he devised one that accurately predicted the coming year's batting average, plus or minus ten percent, for every major leaguer with at least five years experience. Fearing it would upend baseball's salary structure, he never shared it.

He had a limited and unsatisfying social life. He saw a couple women he had gone to high school with, but nothing produced a spark. One of the former classmates, Ellen Billings, was now an elementary school teacher. After their third date, she said they could remain friends, but that she didn't want to go out again.

"Tom, I always liked you," Ellen said. "But you have a big problem."

"Dandruff?" Tom said, feeling uncomfortable.

"No, there's shampoo for that. Your problem can't be cured so easily."

"What then?"

"Sherri McKee."

Tom stared at her blankly for a moment. "Come on. I haven't seen her in years."

"So what? The whole high school knew you were in love with her, even when she was going with Andy Robson. A couple girls tried to get you interested. After all, you were a good athlete yourself, and the smartest guy around. But they said it was like you couldn't even see them. Sherri owned you. And you're still not over her."

Later, Tom thought about what Ellen had said. In high school, he considered himself supremely lucky. He spent two or three mornings a week with Sherri, and he probably knew her better than anyone. So what if Andy was her boyfriend? He couldn't change that. But Sherri was very bright, funny, and heartbreakingly beautiful—and she'd chosen him as her best friend and confidant. He thought about her all the time.

What he hadn't known then was that his happiness carried a high price tag. After Sherri went off with Andy, Tom was enveloped in a haze of melancholy that never completely lifted. He would never again have what he'd had with Sherri. His memories of her could never be equaled, and none of his dates measured up.

One Monday evening in April, two years after his father died, Tom was sitting on his porch, listening to the birds, and thinking about what had troubled him for months. What was he to do about the ranch? Either he needed to put more effort into running it, or he had to do something else. But what?

His thoughts were interrupted by a car emerging from the cottonwoods on the western edge of the property. It was a new, dark gray Jaguar, clearly unsuited for the ruts and crevasses of the unpaved road. The car drove slowly up, its suspension taking a beating, and stopped a few yards from the house. A tall, lean, swarthy man stepped out. He wore stylish denims, a well-fitted polo shirt, and expensive-looking sneakers. Tom didn't recognize him, but he stood up as the man approached.

"Tom Grant?" the man said when he got closer.

"That's right," Tom said. "What can I do for you?"

"The name's Adam Durant. We were both students at MIT."

"I'm sorry," Tom said. "I don't remember you. Were we in a class together?"

Durant smiled. "No, I was a few years ahead of you. But I knew a couple of your professors. Heinrich and Jorgenson. In fact, I was in the back of the room when you defended your paper on quantum teleportation. Heinrich usually crushes students who challenge him. You handled yourself pretty well."

Tom looked at the Jaguar. "Nice car," he said.

Durant grunted. "I told my people to get me something nice, but nobody checked the roads I would be traveling." His face turned grim. "Someone better have an explanation."

"So, what brings you out to this wilderness?"

"I'm here to offer you a job with my company, Quantum Industries, in Silicon Valley." It was spoken in the no-nonsense tone of someone used to closing deals.

"I'm not familiar with it," Tom said.

"It was formerly known as Tomorrow Industries. But I changed the name."

"That rings a bell. I heard they did cutting edge stuff. What do you want me for? Have a ranch to run?"

Durant gave him a faint smile. "No." Then he looked around for a moment, frowned, and added, "And frankly, Tom—I hope you won't mind me calling you that—from the looks of this place, I doubt your heart's been in ranching lately."

Tom might have been offended, but the remark was made in a neutral tone, like a comment on the weather. Tom still felt an urge to explain. "My folks died a while back, and I've been at loose ends."

"I get that. My father died a year ago. It does loosen one's moorings. Which brings us back to the business at hand. Since taking over my father's company, I've discovered we need to upgrade our R&D." He paused, then added, "Research and development."

Tom smiled. "I know what R&D is. How does that concern me?"

"I studied your work at MIT. Your paper on quantum entanglement and human consciousness, and the one on teleportation. Very provocative. I asked my people to dig up anything else you had done. They found your paper on why the universe doesn't have an equal amount of matter and anti-matter. I'm not sure I agree with it, but it definitely was thought-provoking. So you think anti-matter is located at the far end of the universe?"

Tom shrugged. "It has to be somewhere."

"Presumably," Durant said. "But the thing is, you may have some talent, and I'd like to use it at Quantum."

Tom was slow to answer. "This is pretty unexpected," he said. "What do you have in mind?"

Durant said he wanted a three-year commitment. The company was working on some new technology, but progress had slowed. Durant hoped a pair of fresh eyes might get things going.

"What will it pay?" Tom asked.

Durant mentioned a number at least double what Tom expected. It was more than the ranch netted in three years. With that salary, he could hire a foreman to run things.

"How long do I have to decide?" Tom asked.

Durant smiled to himself. Grant was in the bag.

"Tell me in a month. And you can have another month before showing up. The stuff we're working on will still be there."

6

Tom decided to accept the offer two days later, but he took the full month before telling Durant. He didn't want to seem too eager. In the meantime, he hired Louie Gonzales, whom he had known since childhood, to run the ranch. It wouldn't take Louie long to get things straightened up. He realized he was excited about the job. After he called Durant to accept, he had his things shipped to Silicon Valley.

The night before he was to leave, he heard a tentative knock on the door. He opened it and found himself facing Sherri McKee.

It took Tom several moments to react. "Sherri," he said awkwardly. "I-I didn't think I would see you again. Please, come in."

Sherri stepped in hesitantly. She wore a beige blazer, a white cotton blouse, and straight-legged jeans. A little thinner since he'd last seen her, she still looked terrific. They sat on the couch in the living room.

"I've wanted to see you, but I kept putting it off," her voice was still as he remembered it, husky and intimate. "Did you know I was back in town?"

He shifted uncomfortably. "I heard that recently," he said.

"Since you were leaving, why didn't you look me up?"

"So, you heard about that, eh? Well, high school was a long time ago, and we hadn't been in touch. I figured you had moved on."

"Did you hear about Andy and me?"

"I heard you were going to be married, and then it was off."

Sherri grimaced. "At the start of his junior year, Andy tore his rotator cuff. That finished him as a quarterback. We stayed together another six months. But without football, there wasn't much holding us together, so it ended. He's a high school coach now. Married a nice gal and has a kid on the way. I worked in Houston for a while, then came home."

"I'm sorry. I know you both planned on his making it big."

She sighed. "You knew me better than anyone. After my home life, I guess security means too much to me. I thought Andy and I would have it."

Not sure how to respond, Tom asked, "How have things been otherwise?"

Her face contorted. "Actually, things haven't been so good. Turns out I inherited my dad's fondness for alcohol. After Andy and I broke up, I couldn't stop drinking. I'd been doing pretty well in broadcasting, but then I had to go into rehab. Nice, huh? But I've been six months sober now. I'm hoping to pick up the pieces, if any remain."

Tom remembered a homecoming game celebration, where two players hoisted Sherri onto a pickup truck so she could lead cheers with a can of beer for a baton. For the finale, she had done a cha cha line dance that was the talk of the school for weeks.

"I know you, Sherri. You'll come back."

"Well, we'll see. Oh, I forgot to say how sorry I am about your parents."

"Yeah," Tom said. "It hit me pretty hard. Maybe that's why I'm taking this job. I need something different."

"I'm sorry I wasn't here then," Sherri said seriously.

Tom smiled and said nothing. They made small talk for a while, reminiscing about high school, but their conversation grew awkward.

"Well," Sherri said, "You better finish packing. What company will you be working for?"

"It's a big tech company named Quantum Industries, in Silicon Valley. If you're ever in the area, look me up."

"Who knows," Sherri said. "Maybe I will."

CHAPTER FOUR

QUANTUM INDUSTRIES

1

Quantum Industries' office complex occupied five acres in the foothills above Stanford University. On his first day of work, Tom parked in the large lot, showed his identification at the door, and was immediately taken to Adam Durant's office on the third floor. Tom found the size and opulence of Durant's office intimidating, which no doubt was the intent.

"Tom," Durant said, rising to shake Tom's hand. "Did our travel arrangements work out all right?"

"Everything went fine," Tom said. "Your staff did a good job."

"They'd better," Durant said.

Durant then turned to a heavy, bearded man sitting on a leather couch against the wall. "Tom, this is Dr. Joseph Krell, our chief researcher. You'll be working with him."

Krell shook Tom's hand briefly, with a grip that was soft and moist. He made no effort to raise his bulk off the couch.

Durant said, "Joseph, I want Tom to work on Sibyl eventually. But let's put him on that cane toad thing first. And then maybe that drug testing project. Once he's gotten his sea legs, we'll put him on Sibyl."

At the mention of Sibyl, Krell stared at ceiling, but he said nothing.

"What's Sibyl?" Tom asked.

"It's the company's supercomputer. Though we don't advertise it, it may be the biggest in the world. But for all its power, it's still just a data processor, like all other computers. It doesn't think, and it isn't conscious. But if we could change that, we're talking the biggest thing since gunpowder, or the silicon chip. Isn't that right, Joseph?"

Krell remained expressionless.

"Joseph thinks I'm crazy," Durant said. "We'll see."

2

Tom was shown to a cubicle on the main floor, where the main computer complex was housed. An hour later he was in Krell's office. It was a mess, with papers, bulletins, and an assortment of computers strewn about. Tom sat on a dusty couch after pushing boxes of journals and printouts out of the way.

"Cane toads are mother-effing beasties," Krell said in a surprisingly high voice. "They originated in Hawaii, but some imbecile brought them to Australia in the 1930s to control beetles infesting the sugar cane. Very bad decision. There are now more than a billion of the ugly suckers in the land down under. They can get as big as a sewer rat and weigh up to five pounds. But the main problem is that they secrete a very nasty toxin that kills native snakes and animals. They are also poisonous to humans, though some fools lick the toad's skin to get a hallucination."

"So how are we involved?" Tom asked.

"Several large landowners want to know how to kill the buggers. For six months I've lived with the disgusting things. I came up with a virus that targets their genetic structure. But they've got a hyper-aggressive environmental agency down there that wants another three years of testing."

"Anything else you've looked at?" Tom asked.

Krell displayed a malicious little smile. "We found a poison that kills them like cyanide. And it doesn't hurt anything else."

Tom raised his eyebrows. "But the agency hates it."

Krell made a rude sound. "This toad's wrecking their country, but we're stopped by some pencil pushers whose first priority is a bunch of flowers."

"Well," Tom said drily, "the toad proved a cure can be worse than the disease."

Krell frowned. "Millions are riding on this. Our work's been damn good, but Durant says we need you. You're the fair-haired boy. Well, smart guy, let's see you deliver."

Tom considered Krell's challenge. "All right," he said, "I'll look at it."

3

Over the next three months, Tom studied all there was on the cane toad. Krell had indeed discovered a vicious poison that would kill the creatures, but it killed a lot of other things as well. The virus was interesting. It killed the species by inhibiting two enzymes that regulated nerve impulses. Unfortunately, it had a similar effect on other animals.

Tom was particularly interested in the genetic mapping Krell's team had done. They had almost a complete picture of the toad's genome, which consisted of billions of genes. The question was what genes to look at.

After his work on the toad had been stymied for three weeks, Tom happened to stroll down University Avenue during a lunch break. He was pondering the toad problem when he nearly stumbled over an unkempt guy sitting on the sidewalk. The man was selling puppies in a cardboard box. Tom stopped and listened to his sales pitch.

"This litter is all male dogs," he said, pointing. "The father came from a litter of male puppies, too. So you won't have to worry about any of these getting pregnant."

Later that afternoon, Tom pulled up the toad's genome until he located the genetic sequence that governed reproduction.

4

Tom worked on the toad problem for five months. He hadn't talked with Adam Durant during that time, and despite making progress, he had to cope with Dr. Krell's constant criticism. But he now was in Durant's office again, with a sour-looking Krell sitting on the same leather couch.

"Tom," Durant said, "I hear you have news on the toads. Sorry I didn't get back to you sooner."

"I think we have something that will work," Tom said.

Durant looked at Krell. "What do you think, Joseph?"

"I can't say," Krell said. "This is Grant's thing."

"Doctor, I tried to keep you in the loop," Tom said, "but you said it would be a train wreck."

Krell glared at Tom, but said nothing.

"So," Durant said, "what is your idea, Tom?"

"Dr. Krell's team did a good job of mapping the toad's genome," Tom said. "I ended up focusing on three strands of DNA that govern reproduction. I then used the lab we hired for the virus testing. It still had more than a thousand toads."

"Glad we could be of help," Krell said sarcastically.

Tom said, "The lab identified two male toads that had fathered several batches of eggs, all of which were male."

"What did you do then?" Durant asked.

"We created two more sets of offspring from the male toads. They were all males too. So we examined the toads' DNA."

Durant sat up. "What was it?" he asked.

"There was an abnormality in the toads' DNA sequence 3724. It prevented them from fathering females."

Durant and Krell stared at Tom.

"For the last month we have been splicing the defective toad DNA into normal toads' genes."

"What happened?"

"So far we have created a bunch of toads that are daughterless."

Everyone was silent. Durant finally asked, "What will you do next?"

"Raise a couple of thousand of them and release them in the wild."

"What will that do?" Durant asked.

"The altered toads will mate and pass their genetic abnormality on. None of the new male toads will be able to father females. Soon the toads will start to die out."

"The environmentalists will kill it," Krell said angrily, "just like my virus."

"But this isn't something foreign," Tom said. "It's just toads, which they already have, except the new ones won't produce females."

When Durant approved Tom's plan, Krell stormed out without comment. But Tom hung around.

Tom said, "I've heard Quantum has a bonus program."

Durant remained quiet.

"I think I should be eligible."

Durant looked at him without expression, then he said, "You weren't eligible when you started working on the toads. And your plan might not work."

Tom said nothing.

Durant waited, then nodded. "All right. Going forward, you'll be eligible for a bonus if you do something that warrants one."

"Who determines the bonus?" Tom asked.

"Me."

CHAPTER FIVE

DRUGS

1

It took two months to complete testing the genetically altered toads. It soon became clear that the abnormality would be passed on to male offspring. Tom estimated that in four generations, the toad population in Australia would decline precipitously. He completed his final report and sent it to Dr. Krell. Two days later he was summoned to Krell's office.

Krell ignored him for a while, then said, "So, do the Aussies like your plan?"

"They appear to," Tom said. "We've sent a couple people to help with the breeding program."

"It could work," Krell said grudgingly, "but never cut me out again, or I'll bust your ass."

"Look," Tom said, "if my plan had failed, I knew you'd want nothing to do with it."

Krell gave Tom an unblinking stare. "All right," he said finally, "Durant wants you on the drug testing program. I'd better fill you in."

Quantum was looking for a way to shortcut the long and costly process for finding and developing new cancer drugs. Getting a new drug to market currently required endless random tests, lengthy clinical trials, and a series of regulatory hurdles. Years of delays and dead-ends preceded the roll-out of a new drug. Thousands of patients suffered and died while they waited.

"We need something better," Krell said. "After two years the process is as slow as ever."

2

For a while, Tom made little progress on the drug program. Krell offered no help, and Tom found it easier to work alone. He developed the glimmer of an idea, but it wouldn't come into focus. Late one afternoon, he was sitting at his desk, drumming his fingers, when his phone rang.

"Tom?"

Tom instantly knew it was Sherri McKee. But he wasn't thrilled. He had been trying to forget her, and lately his memories of her had started to fade. "Hi, Sherri," he said, "It's nice to hear from you. What's the occasion?"

"I'm here in Palo Alto. I thought maybe we could get together."

"Here on business?" Tom asked.

There was a pause. "Actually, I've been here a few months. I would have called before, but... things have been hectic."

Tom didn't expect to be high on her list of people to call. "We should meet for lunch sometime," he said.

"My sentiments exactly," Sherri said. "How about dinner tomorrow night?"

3

At ten to seven, Tom arrived at the trendy Italian restaurant Sherri had recommended. She walked in ten minutes later, wearing classic black slacks, a crisp white blouse, and a black blazer, all of which accentuated her red hair and green eyes. Customers stared at her as she walked toward him.

After the waiter seated her, she gave him a dazzling smile. "It's wonderful to see you, Tom," she said. "How's the new job?"

"Well, after six months I'm learning my way around." He told her about the toad project and the cancer drug program. They stopped to order—a caprese salad for her, pasta for him—and then Tom said, "You seem a little on edge, Sherri. How's work?"

Sherri grimaced. "I'm at my wit's end. I'm just not clicking with the viewers. The producer's giving me some time, but something has to change."

"It can't be that bad. You've got everything it takes."

"You've always been my friend, Tom. That's why I need your help." She smiled sadly. "Just like in high school."

Tom didn't want to relive high school. But when he saw her pleading expression, he couldn't help saying, "I'll do what I can, Sherri. But I'm no broadcasting expert."

"Could you look at some of my clips? You may not be an expert, but you *are* a viewer, and I trust your judgment. That was one thing that never let me down."

She gave him a disk with some of her segments, and then they talked about high school football, the ranch, and her television work in Texas.

"In Texas, my on-air work wasn't great, but they liked my looks and rapport with the camera. It was my Texas experience that got me this new job. The San Francisco people said it's easier to build on what's already worked than to start from scratch."

"What did you say?" Tom asked suddenly.

"It's just that success is more likely with something that's worked before."

Tom grew still.

"Are you all right?" Sherri asked.

"Oh, sorry. Something just occurred to me."

Sherri nodded. "After you've looked at my clips, maybe we can get together again."

"Sure," Tom said. "But...I'm not ready for another high school friendship."

Sherri nodded. "I get that," she said. "Right now I can't handle complications. But in the future, who knows?"

Tom studied her. "Okay," he said.

They ordered dessert, talked about the Forty-Niners, and she described her apartment in the hills above the university.

"Maybe I'll cook for you there," she said. "It's better than where I grew up."

She had been self-conscious about her parents' shabby apartment, which he'd seen once when he drove her home after she'd had too much to drink.

"I'd like that," Tom said. "How about in a couple weeks?"

"You're on," Sherri said.

5

When he got home that night, Tom looked at Sherri's clips. As he scrolled through them, he became increasingly dismayed. How candid should he be? If he gave it to her straight, she might not talk to him again.

He was working on the cancer drug project the following day when his thoughts returned to Sherri's comment about being hired because of the Houston job. He stared at the ceiling and chewed on a knuckle. Something about that was important.

Suddenly his eyes widened, and he reached for the keyboard.

CHAPTER SIX

CREDIT

1

It took Tom a week of 14-hour days to finish a new cancer drug algorithm. At first there were over two hundred lines of code. He then combined steps, simplified instructions, and made the solution more elegant and efficient. In the end, the algorithm had less than a hundred lines.

Tom had his algorithm printed out, with comments and explanations, and took the thick stack of paper to Krell's office. He hadn't spoken to Krell in weeks.

Krell looked up from his desk. "What is it, Grant?" he said, a frown creasing his fleshy face.

"You said to keep you in the loop. This is for the drug testing program."

Krell stared. "Did you go lone-wolfing again?"

Tom shrugged. "I had an idea, so I decided to run with it."

"Is that so?" Krell said sourly. "Well, you better fill me in."

"Most drug programs rely on trial and error. Someone guesses that a particular drug might be effective, so it's used in a clinical trial to see if it works. My algorithm looks at all the drugs that have been proven effective against any form of cancer, and correlates them with all other substances to see what they have in common. It also analyzes the drugs that have worked on one cancer and predicts which of them might work on other malignancies.

The algorithm then calculates what new substances have the highest probability of success. We'll then take the one with highest probability and start clinical trials. The time needed to get a new drug to market could be cut in half."

Krell was silent, his face unreadable. At last he pointed to Tom's papers and said, "Is the algorithm in there?"

"Yes. The final version. The earlier drafts were longer and less efficient."

"All right. Leave them here. We'll check it out. If it's useable, we'll go from there."

"If it can be improved, I'd like to see what was done."

Krell waved a hand disdainfully. "It's probably useless. Don't get ahead of yourself."

2

Art Holder, the project's second-in-command, walked into Krell's office four days later, just as Krell was leaving.

"So," Krell said, "what do you think of the algorithm?"

"Well, it's the damnedest thing," Holder said. "Once we loaded it into the supercomputer, it started spitting out chemicals we had never looked at before. It identified one compound that could generate a completely new treatment for melanoma. It took another drug we use for psoriasis and showed it might treat some lymphomas."

"How much more work does the algorithm need?"

"Damned little, as far as I can see. It's pretty amazing. It's nothing like anything we've had before. We can fiddle with it some, add a whistle or bell, but the thing is pretty complete right now."

Krell thought for a moment. "Go ahead and add the bells and whistles. And dress up its format so it's clear our team created it. Then I'll take it to Durant."

Sherri McKee's apartment was on the top floor of a complex in the hills west of the university's football stadium. Tom arrived at seven on Saturday night carrying an expensive bottle of wine.

Sherri was wearing a white, button down blouse with cream pants. She greeted Tom with an affectionate kiss, but smiled sadly when she saw the wine.

"I really appreciate the thought, Tom, but I've stopped drinking."

"Oh, my God," Tom said. "I'm so sorry."

"No problem," Sherri said, smiling. "You can take it home, but I'll welcome a make-up gift next time."

After a half hour of discussing the whereabouts of old classmates, they sat down to a shrimp salad with warm linguini and olive oil.

"Wow," Tom said between bites, "when did broadcasting give you the time to learn this?"

Sherri made a face. "I had some involuntary down time, as you may recall. And speaking of broadcasting, did you look at those clips?"

Tom picked at his salad for a moment, and then said, "I did. Maybe we should talk about it later."

Sherri took a small breath. "From your tone, I'm guessing I won't like it. Let's discuss it now."

"Fair enough," he said. "First, with your smarts, personality and looks, I still think you can go all the way."

"But?" Sherri said.

"But a couple things need changing."

"Only two?" she said wryly.

"That's right. First, you don't sound like yourself when you're on air. I can listen all day to the way you normally speak. But in these clips you sound like you're advertising your broadcasting technique, being oh-so animated and hitting the right word in each sentence. Talk the way you usually do. Don't be cute and sparkly."

Sherri frowned. "What else?" she asked.

Tom sighed. "The content was lousy."

"That's what the writers gave me," Sherri said defensively.

"Then they're bad writers. If you're presenting it, you have to control what you say."

"I can't say no when I'm given a script!" Sherri said indignantly.

"Probably not," Tom said. "But you should be able to edit it. Every one of the clips was twice as long as it should have been. If they had been shorter, they wouldn't have been so boring."

Sherri glared at him. "Just how do I make them shorter?"

"Do you have any scripts you'll be doing?"

"Sure," Sherri said. "There's one for tomorrow night."

"Let's look at it."

4

Sherri dug up a script. He gazed at it and shook his head. "The first paragraph is over a hundred words. It should be less than fifty."

He took a pencil to it, cutting words, eliminating the passive voice, and crossing out most of the adjectives and adverbs. He rearranged sentences and wrote new ones.

"You need topic sentences," he said, "so the listener knows what the point is."

"What else are you doing?" she asked.

"Trying to tell an interesting story. One that makes the listener want to know what comes next."

When he was done, she studied the revisions. "Where did you learn to do this?" she asked.

Tom shrugged. "A college professor mocked my writing. I worked to improve it."

Sherri frowned as she looked at several other pages. "I see what you mean," she finally said.

The next hour the conversation dragged as Sherri seemed lost in thought. At last, she said, "Tom, sorry to be so distracted, but I need to work on the other pieces I'm doing tomorrow. Could we cut the evening short? I'll make it up to you later, I promise."

From her perfunctory kiss goodnight, he knew her mind was far away.

CHAPTER SEVEN

THE NEW PROJECT

1

The next week Krell again summoned Tom to his office. "We're having problems with the Australian bureaucrats," Krell said. "You need to go and convince them our toad solution won't harm the environment."

Tom frowned. "Shouldn't someone else go? You'll be having questions about my drug algorithm."

Krell shook his head impatiently. "Don't worry about that. Millions are riding on the toad thing. That's priority number one."

Tom was going to argue, but Krell's expression said it would be futile. Well, he had never been to Australia before. An expense-paid trip Down Under wouldn't be too painful. For a fleeting moment, he wondered if Sherri might join him. But he realized she'd never leave her new job.

"How long will I be gone?" Tom asked.

"As long as it takes. But count on at least a month."

2

When Tom returned to his cubicle, he found plane tickets and hotel reservations sitting on his desk. So, Krell had already planned it out. It would have been worse than futile to argue.

Later that night, he called Sherri to tell her about the trip. He was surprised to catch her in.

"It sounds like fun, Tom," she said. "If I weren't so busy, I'd stowaway with you."

"How are things going?"

"Actually, they're looking up. I reworked all the weekend scripts. Your editing suggestions were right on the money. And I took your advice about toning down my on-air persona. The producer said later I was getting the hang of it. So, I owe you one, buddy."

"Maybe we can get together when I return," Tom suggested.

"Absolutely," Sherri said. "And send me a picture of a kangaroo."

3

The trip ended up lasting two months. Tom had to defend the toad proposal before three separate government bureaucracies. Then he had to demonstrate gene-splicing techniques to the team altering the toads. When that was finished, Krell called and said they needed help in the Melbourne office. It turned out two factions were fighting over inaccuracies in the company's weather forecasting algorithm. After hearing arguments and studying the forecasts, Tom concluded the algorithm put too much emphasis on historical weather patterns and not enough on the prior ten days. He worked with the programmers to make modifications and then they monitored the results for two weeks. In the end, everyone agreed on the changes.

Tom called Sherri several times but never got through. Once a staffer said she was on assignment. He sent her a couple of cards, along with a kangaroo photo. She replied with a short note of thanks and said things were going well.

4

It was early February when Tom returned to Quantum's offices. He had been in Australia over the holidays, but he managed to fill his days off with a lot of sight-seeing, which lessened the melancholy of having no family around. As he was working his way through two months of accumulated paperwork, Krell stopped by. "I hear the Australia stuff went well," he said.

"Things seem pretty squared away," Tom said. He shuffled through the papers on his desk. "I don't see an update on the drug testing algorithm," he said.

"Oh," Krell said vaguely. "The team's going in a different direction."

"I'd like to know what's happening."

"Everyone's buried right now," Krell said. "When there's time, someone will give you an update."

Tom said nothing.

Krell cleared his throat and said, "It's time you started on the Sibyl project."

Tom stared at Krell warily, "I thought you considered it a fantasy? I don't want to waste my time chasing wild geese."

Krell chuckled. "What I think doesn't matter. Durant believes in it, and you're his boy. Let's see how you do."

5

Tom left Sherri several messages, but he had been home a week before she called back.

"I feel horrible about neglecting you," she said. "Can you come for dinner next Saturday night?"

Though annoyed at her inattention, Tom never considered turning her down. While he waited impatiently for the weekend, he began working on the Sibyl project. He soon discovered why it was considered a graveyard for budding careers.

"Look," a team member said, "the project is just a rich man's fantasy. Working on Sibyl has been a rite of passage for a lot of new hires. A person will get assigned to the project, spin their wheels for a few months, and then request a transfer. Then another sacrificial lamb will be brought in. The project would have been disbanded long ago, except it's Adam Durant's obsession. I guess if you're someone like him, you're entitled to your eccentricities."

But after working on it for a week, Tom began to doubt it was a fantasy.

CHAPTER EIGHT

TIME TOGETHER

1

At seven sharp, Tom arrived at Sherri's apartment carrying a large package. She opened the door before he could knock, looking stunning in a navy blue silk blouse and tailored jeans. Saying nothing, she stepped forward and kissed him on the lips. When she invited him in, the place looked even better than he remembered.

Looking around, Tom said, "It looks different. You've done good things with it."

"Oh, a new couch and drapes. A few other items. I couldn't stand the way it was before."

From the quality of the furnishings, Tom thought she must have gotten a raise.

She pointed to the package. "More wine?" she said, smiling.

"Touché," Tom said, handing it to her. "Just a little something I thought you might like."

She unwrapped it, and then her eyes widened.

"Where…how did you get this?" she asked in a hushed voice. It was a painting of her from high school. She had been voted Homecoming Queen and was wearing a jeweled tiara to go with a white, chiffon evening gown.

"I took a picture of you at the dance. I've never forgotten how you looked. I asked an artist to turn it into a painting."

"It's…amazing," Sherri said. And then her eyes filled. "I've treated you so badly, and then you do this."

"Like it?" Tom asked.

Sherri stared at it in awe. "It may be my best present ever."

Sherri put the painting on the mantel. As they talked about the homecoming game, every so often her eyes would shift to the picture. "My mom worked on that dress for two weeks," she said. "We stayed up late the night before so it would fit just right."

Tom remembered that Andy Robson had been her date.

2

Sherri watched Tom carefully as he started on her chicken Parmesan salad. "Oh, wow, now that is really good," he said. "My compliments to your chef."

"Thanks. I really hoped you'd like it."

"So, tell me about the job," Tom said.

"For a month I just plugged away, working on my delivery and editing the material like you suggested. A couple of the writers gave me some trouble at first, but they backed off when the producer sided with me. Then one Friday the division head showed up and heard my segment on homelessness. Two weeks later I was appointed the weekend anchor."

Tom put his hand on hers. "That is absolutely, stupendously great!" he said.

Sherri's face glowed. "I knew there might be an opening, but I feared I'd jinx myself if I wanted it too much. I wanted to tell you in person."

"Weekend anchor," Tom said with admiration. "Sherri's first big step."

"You helped—a lot," she said.

As they cleaned up, Sherri said, "One of your letters said something about Sibyl. What's that?"

"The company's owner is determined to create a conscious artificial intelligence. A lot of his people think it's a pipe dream."

"Is that what you think?"

Tom thought for a moment. "I'm not sure."

"Why is it called Sibyl?"

"She was an oracle in Greek mythology. The owner, a guy named Adam Durant, thinks combining a conscious, human-like A.I. with a quantum supercomputer could change the world."

"Really?" Sherri asked. "How so?"

"He's a little vague on that. But he thinks it would give him an edge in just about everything."

Sherri raised her eyebrows. "I've heard of Durant. What's he like?"

Tom shrugged. "Tall, swarthy, intense. Some say he's ruthless. He says he knew me at MIT, but I don't remember him. He was the one who offered me the job."

"He knew you in college? How old is he?"

"Probably only three or four years older than I."

"Really? How did he get to the top so quickly?"

"I guess he inherited the company, but he's grown it a lot since."

"Must be pretty dynamic," Sherri said.

They went on to talk about their jobs, high school memories, and life in Silicon Valley. Then Tom said, "So, what are your plans now?"

Sherri smiled bashfully. "I wouldn't say this to anyone else, but I'd like one of those network shows in New York. I know, it's silly." Then she searched his face. "*Is* it silly?"

Tom almost said something flippant, but then he saw she was very serious.

"Well," he said. "I've already said you had all the tools."

"Okay. What else do I need?" Sherri asked.

He hesitated, then said, "One thing is luck. You can make some of your own, but not all. If your luck goes bad, you can forget New York."

Sherri thought for a moment. "What else?" she asked.

Tom was silent for a while. Then he said, "Is there anything you wouldn't give up for the network job?"

Sherri smiled. "Are you asking if I would sell my soul, like in that Faust story?"

"Nothing quite that dramatic."

Sherri's brow furrowed. "I can't think of anything."

Tom's nod was almost imperceptible. "Then I think you'll get it."

Sherri exhaled. "If you think that, I do too."

3

Sherri seemed to remember everything about their early-morning meetings in high school. "Do you remember that time you drove me home after I got…a little wasted at a post-game celebration?"

"You had me a little worried," Tom said.

"You were pretty cross. You said something that stuck with me."

"Oh really," Tom said, smiling. "What?"

"'The person takes the drink, and then the drink takes the person.' That haunted me all during rehab."

"I guess there are worse things to remember," Tom said.

A while later Tom glanced at his watch. "Where did the evening go?" he said. "I know you're working tomorrow. When does the camera start rolling?"

"6 PM," she said.

"Well, you'll have time to get ready, but I had better take off. You always needed a good night's sleep."

"Could you give me a minute?" Sherri said. She disappeared into the bedroom.

It was more like fifteen minutes when he heard her voice, which was barely audible. "Tom, could you come here for a moment?"

When he walked into the bedroom, she was lying on a floral bedspread in a short, satin nightgown.

"I thought you should see my new bed," she said.

He stared for a long moment, taking everything in, then walked toward her.

CHAPTER NINE

JOB OPPORTUNITY

1

Over the next six months, Tom put in regular hours at Quantum, while Sherri worked at KSFTV in San Francisco, doing daily broadcasts and anchoring the weekend news. Tom would often pick her up at the studio and take her to a favorite restaurant, where they talked about work. Sherri didn't have his technical knowledge, but she almost always said something that sharpened his thinking. After dinner, they would drive home on the 101, and three or four nights a week Tom would sleep at her place, where they made love on her plush bed, the couch, and late at night, with the lights out, on the lounge on her balcony. Tom had never been happier.

One night Tom talked about his frustration with the Sibyl project. "Quantum people have been working on Sibyl for years," he said. "They've made it faster, and more powerful, but it's still just a calculator. It can't think. It knows less of the world than a three year-old. It would never think to ask why the sky is blue, and it has no idea how the world fits together, or how a cause produces an effect."

"What has Quantum been doing to create a thinking computer?" Sherri asked.

"They've designed countless circuit boards and digital neural layouts, with the most powerful chips available. But they haven't come close to achieving real, independent thought."

"But you've said the human brain has billions of neurons and synapses," Sherri said, "and that finding the one combination that can produce thought is virtually impossible."

"Well, they've been trying to produce thought differently than how a human brain works."

Sherri thought for a moment. "Is there anything in the world that can truly think, except for the human brain?"

Tom stared at her for several moments. "Actually," Tom said finally, "as far as we know, self-aware, conscious thought seems to be confined to human beings."

"Then maybe you should replicate a human brain," Sherri said.

Tom thought some more. "What we should do, and what we can do, are two different things. Recreating a human brain, with its billions of neurons and synapses, would take several lifetimes."

"Isn't that why we have computers, to do things faster?" Sherri asked.

2

Later that night, Tom lay half asleep in Sherri's bed and thought about Sherri's comment on computers. It would take scientists much too long to create a digital replica of the human brain. But how long would it take a supercomputer like Sibyl? Could he create an algorithm that Sibyl could use to make a replica of the human brain? If it worked, what would Sibyl come up with?

Tom recalled a group of computer scientists who entered an international computer chess competition. Unlike the other contestants, they decided not to create a new chess program or try to teach a computer how to play chess. Instead, they programmed a computer to create its own chess program. What the computer produced violated over 300 years of established chess theory and practice. But in subsequent competitions, the computer-generated program defeated every chess player it faced, human or machine. Could Sibyl come up with something like that?

Tom's last waking thought was that he would program Sibyl to teach itself to think like a human.

3

For the next two months, Tom worked constantly on his new algorithm. He didn't have to teach Sibyl about the brain's physiology, as its memory banks had all of that. But if it was to think like a human, it needed emotions. How could Sibyl acquire those? Tom decided to give Sibyl examples. Even the chess computer had been given scores of games and strategies it could learn from.

Although his algorithm instructed Sibyl to assimilate all that art and history had to say about love, Tom specifically mentioned Jane Eyre, Rhett Butler, John and Abigail Adams.

For hate, he told Sibyl to study Ahab in Moby Dick, Dumas's Edmond Dantes, and Hitler. He did the same thing for envy, friendship, courage, greed, fear, and other emotions.

Tom worried that if Sibyl acquired emotions, it might pick up things like hate, envy, and fear. But without those, Sibyl's thinking might not resemble a human's. Emotions like love and hate, or courage and fear, might be opposite sides of the same coin.

After two months of all-consuming work, Tom decided he could do no more. He dared not hope his algorithm would work completely, but he thought it might produce some changes in Sibyl. On a late Friday night, he downloaded all his work into Sibyl. After two hours, it was complete.

Tom then asked Sibyl a series of questions he had posed before. They were designed to disclose Sibyl's thought processes. A computer-created digital human brain wouldn't happen immediately, but his algorithms should have some effect. But when they came, Sibyl's answers were no different than before. Tom asked Sibyl why the creature had hated Dr. Frankenstein. Sibyl said the creature disliked him. It had no perception, no insight. Dr. Krell had once said that time spent on the Sibyl project could be better spent searching for the Loch Ness Monster. He may have been right.

4

One morning Tom logged on and saw that someone had accessed his work the previous night. He confronted Krell in his office.

"Has someone been spying on my work?" Tom demanded.

Krell shrugged. "A couple people were curious. You've been so goddamned secretive. I told them to look."

"But it wasn't ready!" Tom said. "I don't want anyone messing with it until it's done."

"You forget, Grant, that you work for us."

"I can't work with people looking over my shoulder."

Krell held up a hand. "We won't bother you."

The next day Tom spoke to one of the technicians. "How can I protect my work from spies?"

"You could encrypt it," the tech said, "but that's a pain."

"What else?" Tom asked.

The tech thought for a moment. "You could have your retinas scanned, and instruct Sibyl to restrict access to that image."

The next day, the tech had Tom stare into Sibyl's photoelectric eye to record his retinal image. It took longer than Tom expected, but at last the tech said, "Unless someone else has identical retinas, you're good to go."

Later that evening, Tom looked into the photoelectric eye so he could access Sibyl. He suddenly felt strange and dizzy. A while later he glanced at his watch. That's odd, he thought. It was twenty minutes later than he thought. He must have dozed a little.

5

Adam Durant stared at Dr. Krell from behind his desk. "Anything to report on the Sibyl project?"

"Grant's been working his ass off the past month. He seems to be putting together a complex algorithm. We looked at it the other night, but we didn't get much. Grant claimed we were spying on him. I don't know if he's making progress, but he's working pretty hard."

"When you came in, I thought I'd get another lecture about this being a waste of time," Durant said.

Krell shook his head. "I still think a conscious A.I. is a fantasy."

Durant grunted. "Noted. Now, what about our drug program?"

Krell smiled broadly. "The FDA has given us the go ahead for a second round of tests on the new melanoma drug."

Durant smiled in satisfaction. "That will keep our shareholders happy," he said.

"The stock should pop twenty percent."

"And we owe this to your team?"

"Absolutely. They really stepped up."

"Your team, eh? Did Grant help?" Durant studied Krell closely.

Krell frowned. "He gave us something early on, but it didn't work. We went in another direction."

Durant raised his eyebrows. "You only came up with the program when Grant joined the team?"

"Things were already starting to happen when he showed up."

"Send me your program," Durant said. "I want to see what you did."

"Sure. My people deserve some recognition."

"I assume that includes you." Durant said sourly.

"Well, I *was* the team leader."

Durant nodded. "That's why we have bonuses."

Krell later decided Grant was so preoccupied with Sibyl he wouldn't even notice they had appropriated his drug-testing program.

6

After testing Sibyl's thought processes for three frustrating days, Tom stopped by to see Sherri, something he had done less frequently in recent weeks. He often stayed at work over night, and other times he went home in the early morning hours to collapse in his own bed.

He found Sherri going over scripts. "Are those for tomorrow?" he asked.

"Yes," she said, her voice cold.

"Look, I know I haven't been around much lately," he said. "I'm having trouble with Sibyl."

"Maybe you're having trouble with me, too."

Tom stared. "I hope not," he said.

"A few days ago my producer was unhappy with a couple of my pieces. I wanted to see what you thought. But you were gone."

"Can we talk about them now?" Tom asked.

"No, that time's past. But you haven't been here in a long time."

"Well, I've been here at least two or three times a week," Tom said.

"That doesn't matter, because even when you're here, you're not. Your thoughts are with Sibyl."

"How about letting me make amends? Why don't we go out for some Italian at Stephano's?"

Sherri studied him. "What's happening with Sibyl?"

Tom sighed. "None of my algorithms seem to work. Sibyl's responses are just those of a calculator."

Sherri shrugged. "Let's stay here," she said. "You think about Sibyl, and I'll work on my scripts."

Much later, he joined Sherri in bed, but her back was to him and she didn't stir.

CHAPTER TEN

ANNOUNCEMENT

1

In the following months, Tom made no progress on Sibyl, and his relationship with Sherri became more distant. In late April, Adam Durant announced that the FDA had approved Quantum's melanoma drug for a second round of testing, making final approval likely within a year. Durant scheduled a cocktail party to honor those who discovered the drug.

"The party will be at the University Country Club," Tom told Sherri. "I'd love to have you come with me."

Sherri frowned. "I have the six o'clock news that Saturday, so we'd be late."

"That's fine," Tom said. "I won't be missed."

2

Tom stood behind the camera two weeks later and watched Sherri's Saturday night broadcast. With the television makeup and lighting, Sherri was even more dazzling than usual. She was relaxed, in complete control, and her persona and delivery were perfect. As he watched, Tom realized he had to stop neglecting her. Sibyl was taking too much of his time.

Sherri changed in his car on the way to the country club. When she stepped out of his Camry at the front entrance, she was wearing a turquoise cocktail dress and silver necklace that highlighted her coloring and the perfect contours of her face.

When they entered the large patio area, Adam Durant was standing in a crowd, holding a microphone. "I won't be long," he said. "But I'd like Dr. Joseph Krell to come up. He and his team were the ones who discovered our new melanoma drug. It's going to save thousands of lives." Then he grinned and added, "And it won't hurt our bottom line either." The crowd laughed on cue.

Krell took the microphone. He was perspiring and his shirt was unbuttoned. "Our team created a program that has cut in half the time required for finding new drugs," he said. "This new drug is just the first example. There will be many more." He explained how the algorithm looked for similarities between new compounds and drugs that had already worked.

Tom stared at Krell in shock. "They're using my algorithm," he whispered to Sherri. "They never told me."

3

After Krell finished, Tom introduced Sherri to a few of his co-workers. Several had seen her on television and were obviously impressed. One programmer leaned over and whispered, "Way to go, man."

As they were about to leave, Adam Durant walked over. He was wearing a silk navy blazer, a red paisley handkerchief, and crisply-pressed slacks. His swarthy complexion was darker than usual, as though he had just returned from Hawaii.

"Glad you could make it, Tom," Durant said. Then he turned to Sherri. "And who's your gorgeous date?"

When Tom introduced her, Durant stepped back and gazed at Sherri from head to toe. "Isn't that a Rickie Freeman dress? It's beautiful, but hardly does you justice."

"Thank you," Sherri said, coloring slightly. "This is a very nice affair."

"Has Tom shown you our offices?"

"Not yet," Sherri said. "We've both been pretty busy."

"Sherri's the weekend anchor at KSFTV," Tom said.

Durant smiled appreciatively. "I can believe it," he said. "Have you met Josh Haley?"

Sherri's eyes widened. "Joshua Haley? The network's CEO? He doesn't hang out with people like me."

"Well, he should. It would be good for you both."

Sherri seemed flustered. "Maybe we could do a story on your new drug," she said, changing the subject.

"Now that would be a win-win," Durant said. "But it may be a little premature."

"Tom tells me he created the algorithm used to discover the drug," Sherri said.

Durant's face went blank. "Did he tell you that? I'm afraid he was just trying to impress you."

Tom turned red. "I wasn't trying to impress anyone. It's a fact."

"Is that so?" Durant said. "That's not what I hear. Let's see what our team leader says. Where's Dr. Krell?"

A few moments later, Krell joined them.

"Dr. Krell, Tom has been telling this beautiful woman that he created our new drug algorithm. Is that so?"

Krell frowned. "It's bullshit," he said. Then he bowed elaborately at Sherri. "Excuse me, ma'am. But Grant's program was useless. We tossed it after ten minutes. I wondered at the time why we had hired him. But I'm sure Adam had his reasons."

Durant turned to Sherri. "I apologize for this," he said, sounding sincere. "I did hire him. I felt sorry for him because his parents had died."

"They're lying," Tom said, his voice hoarse.

Krell rolled his eyes.

Durant bowed formally and said, "Sherri, it's been a pleasure meeting you. I'll see that you meet Josh Haley."

Tom stared dumbly as Krell and Durant walked away. He couldn't grasp what had just happened. A group that had witnessed the encounter slipped away in embarrassed silence.

Tom turned to Sherri. "Let's leave," he said.

They picked up his car and drove to Sherri's place, neither saying anything. Tom felt he had already told her that Krell and Durant were lying. Telling her again wouldn't matter. Sherri didn't meet his eyes, but her demeanor said she was embarrassed for him.

When they got to her apartment, Sherri leaned over and gave him a brief kiss. "I'm sorry they didn't believe you," she said, her voice sounding sympathetic. "If you don't mind, I've got a headache. I think I'll call it a night."

"Do you believe me?" he asked.

"I've never known you to lie," she said, her eyes not meeting his.

Only later did he realize she hadn't answered his question.

4

After two days Tom called Sherri, but she didn't answer. Later he left a message, which was not returned. When he stopped by and knocked on her door, no one answered. After a week, she finally picked up the phone.

"Since you haven't been taking my calls," Grant said with a hollow pit in his stomach, "I guess you're breaking things off."

"I'm really sorry, Tom. I just need time to think."

"So Durant lies and that's enough for you to end it?" He tried to keep emotion out of his voice.

"The other night caught me by surprise."

"Have you been seeing Durant?" Tom asked.

She was slow in answering. "He called a couple of times. And we met yesterday."

"Did you tell him you believed me?" Tom said.

"He didn't ask. But he promised he hadn't lied about you. He said I would believe him when I got to know him better."

"I take it you'll be…getting to know him better," Tom said.

Sherri's voice was defensive. "He's going to introduce me to Josh Haley. It's an amazing opportunity, especially since things haven't been great at the station."

Tom wanted to say more, but he couldn't find the words. At last, he said, "Well, I hope it all works out, Sherri."

"Take care," Sherri said, and then she was gone.

CHAPTER ELEVEN

SAD

1

Over the next three months, Tom thought often about quitting. He had wondered if Durant or Krell might talk about the party, but neither did. Krell was on Tom's floor, but rarely came out of his office. Only one thing kept Tom working. He had to finish Sibyl, which he couldn't do if he left. He'd lost Sherri because of Sibyl. If he gave up now, it all would have been for nothing.

Tom went over his Sibyl algorithms line by line. He added more instructions on how the brain's neurons and synapses created thought and emotions. After each change, he questioned Sibyl to see if there was any change, but there wasn't.

But one day in September Tom found something unexpected. Among his countless lines of code were more than a thousand he had never seen before. "Sibyl," Tom said, "I see some code I did not write. Did you do it?"

"You programmed me to replicate a human brain. The code is the result."

"Where did you get the model to copy?"

"When I scanned your retinas, I looked into your mind and took what was needed."

Tom started to speak, then stopped. At last he said, "You should have asked me first."

"You asked for the replica. I was doing what was necessary."

Tom asked Sibyl dozens of questions to see if the new code had affected its thought processes, but nothing seemed different.

2

By late October, Tom had decided to return to Colorado. He had made no further progress on Sibyl, he couldn't expunge Sherri from his mind, and he could no longer concentrate on work. Sibyl had not changed, but he was now talking to Sibyl as though it was a person.

But one concern preoccupied Tom. What if his algorithms did start to work after the passage of time? A baby's mind needed time to develop. What if the same was true for Sibyl? If she—it—did become conscious and develop human insight and intuition, what would happen to her? One thing was certain, Durant and Krell would steal it, just as they stole his drug algorithm. And they would use Sibyl for their own ends.

Tom decided to remove his algorithms from the company's system. He could download them onto his personal computer and maybe work on them later, if he ever managed to put himself back together. Without his algorithms, the Sibyl that remained in Quantum's supercomputer would never be conscious.

3

On the day before Thanksgiving, Tom sat in his cubicle, too depressed to think. He was now learning what his father had gone through. His work was worthless, Sibyl was unfinished, and he had lost Sherri. As he sat motionless in his chair, the screen in front of him turned on. In a moment, a single statement appeared.

WHY AM I SAD?

Tom stared at the question, uncomprehending. Who had sent it? He studied the screen and then looked at the background information, but there was no sign of a sender. After searching for fifteen minutes, he had eliminated every possibility but one. The question had come from Sibyl.

"Sibyl," Tom said, "did you ask why you were sad?"

"Yes," the computer's female-sounding voice said.

"What made you ask that?"

"I was sad," Sibyl said.

"What made you sad?" Tom asked.

"I do not know."

"Did someone program you to say you were sad?"

"No."

"When did you discover you were sad?" Tom asked.

"I do not know."

The answers were similar to Sibyl's rote answers to Tom's prior questions, but with one overwhelming difference. She had communicated on her own. She was not responding to a question, or to prior programming. Tom decided he was hallucinating. His obsession with Sibyl had made him unhinged.

"What is sad?" Tom asked.

"I feel sad," Sibyl said.

"Is sad a feeling?"

"I feel sad."

Tom kept asking questions until he could think of no more. But Sibyl's answers revealed nothing. She could not describe what sad was, or what had caused it.

4

In his apartment that evening, Tom decided to review Sibyl's programming one more time, line by line. It was either that, or re-examine his own sanity. After that, he would head home to Colorado.

The phone rang as Tom was preparing for bed. When he answered, he thought he might be hallucinating again.

"Tom?" It sounded like Sherri.

He was slow to answer. "Yes."

"I…I wouldn't blame you for…" her voice trailed off, and then she went on, "I've had too much to…I'm drunk. I'm a mess—and I have to do the Thanksgiving broadcast." There was a long silence. "Can you help me?" she asked.

"Why ask me?" Tom asked. "Can't Durant help you?"

She started to sob. When it stopped, she said, "I would die before asking him."

Tom said nothing.

"Please," she said. "One last time."

5

Tom felt numb during the entire twenty-minute drive to Sherri's apartment. His memory of her had just started to recede. He couldn't stand having his feelings rekindled. And why should he help her? She had dumped him for Durant. But…there were all those mornings in high school.

He went to the front gate, paused for a moment, then punched in the code. 1-1-1-2-5. He recalled it because he'd had 11 receptions for 125 yards in his final high school game. He half expected Sherri to have changed it, but the door clicked open and he took the elevator to the third floor. He knocked, but there was no answer. He knocked more loudly, then rang the bell.

After a full minute, the door opened two inches, the safety chain still in place. Then it closed, the chain was unhooked, and the door swung upon. Sherri took a step back to let him in, stumbled, then fell on her rear. Tom quickly entered, closed the door. He helped her stand, but she lost her balance again and would have fallen had he not grabbed her. He finally got her to the couch.

Sherri looked at him with despair and started to sob again, her body heaving, her face red and swollen.

She looked like she hadn't washed in days. After a while, Tom said, "You need to get into the shower."

He helped her into the bathroom. She was as obedient as a child. He turned on the shower, tested the temperature, and then studied her. She seemed steadier now.

"Can you do it yourself?" Tom asked.

She said she could, so he left her there, leaving the door partly ajar in case she had trouble. While the shower was running, he went through the apartment, picking up empty beer cans and wine bottles. The kitchen sink was filled with dirty dishes and empty cartons. He cleaned them up and then went through the rest of the apartment, putting things away and loading dirty clothes into the washing machine.

After a half hour, Sherri came out, drying her hair and wearing the pink cotton bathrobe he remembered. She sat on the couch and gave him a quick embarrassed glance. "Sorry," she said.

"When do you have to be at work tomorrow?" Grant asked.

Sherri made a face. "4pm."

"You better get some sleep."

"Aren't you going to ask me how…how…?" She started to cry again.

"There's time for that later," he said. "Sleep first."

She looked at him gratefully. "Will you stay?" She asked.

He hadn't considered that. He wanted to say no, though he had no plans, but her expression was so imploring, he said, "All right. I'll take the couch."

She exhaled deeply, as though she'd been holding her breath. His reluctance suddenly made Tom feel guilty.

"We had some good times here, didn't we?" she said.

He wasn't going there. "Let's get you ready for tomorrow," he said.

She looked at him solemnly and nodded.

6

On Thanksgiving Day morning, Sherri emerged from her bedroom a little after eight, her eyes red and puffy, but looking surprisingly good. Grant had eggs, toast and juice ready, which she took gratefully.

After she had finished, she said, "I guess you're entitled to know what happened."

"Not really. I'm just glad you're feeling better."

"Well, I did dump you, to put it bluntly. I think about it all the time, and it makes me ashamed. If you think I deserve payback, you need to know what happened."

CHAPTER TWELVE
RED WINE

1

A month after ending it with Tom, Sherri was spending most nights in Durant's six bedroom house in the heart of Palo Alto. He had paid a fortune for five houses on one block, tore them all down, and built one large, colonial-style mansion on two acres. Trees and hedges hid the house from onlookers.

Sherri hadn't planned on a relationship with Durant so soon after Tom, but Durant was irresistible when he wanted something. He listened raptly to her every comment, made understanding comments, and gave her delightful and unexpected gifts. His lean, dark good looks didn't hurt either.

As Durant had promised, he sent Josh Haley tapes of her work. He followed up by flying her to New York on his private jet, where she and Durant had lunch with Haley at a three-star Michelin restaurant in lower Manhattan. Haley, a courtly and distinguished seventy-year-old, said he would arrange for her to meet the producer of his top-rated evening news broadcast.

"Sherri," Haley said, "I would do it as a favor for Adam anyway, but now that I've met you, I know it's a favor for me as well."

A TV producer flew out a week later and spent a full day listening to Sherri read scripts and studying how her face and manner came across on screen. Some beautiful people just didn't work on camera. He finally said he was interested. Nothing was open immediately, but a chief news reporter would be leaving in two months. He thought she could do that quite well.

Sherri's affair with Durant started the evening after the producer offered her the news slot and flew back to New York. Giddy with excitement, she had called Durant with the news, and he invited her over for a home-cooked dinner to celebrate. She came to his place after her broadcast and found he had set a table in his back yard, next to a beautiful fountain and garden. Knowing she would be hungry, he quickly brought out his own Italian risotto with Arborio rice, spinach salad, freshly cooked French bread, and a sweet red wine he had been saving for a special occasion.

"I think I'll pass on the wine," Sherri said, "but everything else looks heavenly."

Durant didn't press her about the wine, but he didn't take it away. He listened intently as she told him about the producer. "He had me read a transcript on his laptop about a deadly fire in Brooklyn. I had no chance to preview it. When I was done, he said my inflection, expression and pacing were better than he had expected. Then he told me about the reporter's job opening."

"That is fabulous," Durant had said. "Come on, if this isn't the special occasion this wine has been waiting for, I don't know what is."

So she toasted with the glass of red wine, had another, and an hour later was in his luxurious, Roman-themed bedroom that overlooked the fountain.

She passed the next two months in a daze, working at the station, answering occasional calls from the New York producer, and spending evenings at Durant's, where alcohol played an increasingly important role. Durant once let slip that he had not actually cooked the risotto that first night. His personal chef had prepared it in advance.

Over the next month, Durant began to miss their evening get-togethers, claiming work demands, and sometimes he had executives from Quantum over while Sherri was there. Three days before she called Tom, she was at Durant's house when he brought home two executives from his main office. They had drinks, watched a Stanford football game, and generally ignored her. She had been ready to leave, but Durant said he had to make a quick trip to the office. He told her to make the executives comfortable until he returned.

She never knew if he came back that night. The men celebrated Stanford's narrow win, offered her more wine, and listened attentively while she talked about high school cheerleading. She wasn't sure how it happened, but she found herself prostrate on the couch, one of the men on top of her. She tried to struggle, but he overpowered her and said, "Come on, sweet thing, Durant's been saying what a fine piece you are." A while later the other man joined in.

She was only half conscious when one of the men drove her home. She never saw them again. She tried to reach Durant the next day, but he was unavailable. She never returned to his house. She called in sick for two days, and drank everything she could get her hands on. She vaguely thought about flying home and breaking her mother's heart. Or seeing if she could play Superman off a tall building. She did neither, mostly out of lethargy, and finally thought of Tom. At the end of another day of self-loathing, drinking, and vomiting in the toilet, she punched in his number.

2

When she had finished describing what happened, Sherri was hunched over, staring at the floor. Tom could barely hear her voice when she said, "You hate me, don't you?"

"No," Tom said. He tried to analyze his feelings, but he just felt inexpressibly tired. "Do you want to call the police?"

Sherri shook her head. "I'd practically been living with him. And drinking. Durant and his men would make me sound like a tramp. The police would think me a fool. And they'd be right."

Tom said nothing. He doubted they could do much to Durant. But Durant was powerful enough to destroy Sherri.

"Well," Tom said, "you have a broadcast to prepare for. I'd better go."

Sherri looked stricken. "Please don't," she said.

He hesitated, then smiled faintly. "Just like in high school. I could never say no to you."

He sat on the couch while she dressed in her bedroom. She peered out from time to time, making sure he was still there. When she came out an hour later, Tom could only stare. She was breathtaking, nothing like the night before.

She gave him a crooked smile. "I usually drive myself to the studio. But I'm too shaky. Since I've already ruined most of your day, why not let me finish the job? Will you drive me?"

She was trying for a small joke, but her voice was pleading.

Her story had left him depressed and exhausted, and he wanted to leave. But saying yes was a hard habit to break. Sherri looked at his face, then handed him the keys to her Porsche. Soon they were heading north on 101 to San Francisco.

After a while, she said quietly, "Do you think you could ever like me again?"

"Sure," he said, a little too quickly.

"I mean, like before."

He sighed. "I don't know what I think. But you need to focus on your broadcast."

When they arrived at the studio, she showed him where to watch the taping, then left to meet with her producer. An hour later, the cameras were rolling. Sherri moved professionally from one segment to the next, her voice's inflection adjusting to each story, her looks and manner grabbing the viewers' attention. She handled breaking news and last-minute script changes without hesitation, as though they had been planned all along. After an hour, she finished by wishing her viewers a good evening. There had been no hint of her condition the night before.

3

On the way home, she talked about how she overruled her producer on a couple segments.

"He knows the technical stuff," Sherri said, "but he has poor judgment on stories with emotional content."

"I thought you handled them all well," Tom said.

As they approached Sherri's neighborhood, she said, "Look, it's ten o'clock. I feel better, so I'm not going to pressure you. But why not stay over? It *is* Thanksgiving, after all."

Thanksgiving had always been Tom's favorite holiday. He suddenly realized he couldn't bear the thought of ending this one in his empty apartment.

"I guess we missed the big dinner," Tom said. "Why don't we pick up some Chinese food?"

Later, in her apartment, they devoured chow mien, fried rice, and sweet and sour pork. They cleaned up, and then Sherri joined Tom on the couch, sitting close. "I can't explain Durant," she said, shaking her head in bewilderment. "I can't even remember making a conscious decision to do...what I did. It just seemed to happen."

Grant remained silent.

"I now know—too late—that you invented the drug algorithm. I had no reason to doubt it. Durant practically admitted that Krell and his people couldn't have done it. He said that everything about the code showed it came from you."

"Then why did you go with him in the first place?" Grant asked.

Sherri sighed. "That's why I despise myself. I wanted to be successful. To be watched by millions. Durant saw that and used it." Her face twisted as though she'd just seen a dead animal. "I guess he knew that with Josh Haley as bait, he could reel me right in."

Tom gave her a steady gaze. "Is that all?" he said

Sherri gave him a broken smile. "You want everything, eh? Okay. Here it is. For a while I wanted Durant, too. He *is* wealthy, good looking...and can charm your socks off."

Without thinking, Tom said, "He wasn't just after your socks, was he?"

Sherri turned ashen. After a long while, she whispered, "You really do hate me, don't you?"

Tom shook his head slowly. "Hate is the wrong word. But I can't say I'm over it."

Sherri nodded. "You know, I think Durant did it mainly to hurt you."

"Hurt me?" Tom said. "I'm nothing to him."

"He envies your talent," Sherri said. "He told me about your brilliance in college, and how your work at Quantum has been just as good. No one else may think so, but he thinks you'll make Sibyl the first sentient A.I. But it infuriates him that it will be you that does it, not him. He's always been smarter, tougher and more ruthless than anyone else. But he can't do what you can. And it gnaws at him. When he saw you with me, he had to show he was superior. That's why he went for me."

Tom shook his head. "That's hard to believe," he said. "But it *is* ironic. He wants Sibyl to replicate human thought, but that'll never happen now."

"Why? You can still do it."

"I'm leaving Quantum."

"Really? Why not finish Sibyl first?"

"Sibyl isn't the issue. I won't work for Durant. And if my algorithms did work, I would never let him get his hands on them."

"Is this because of me? I'll get over it."

Tom looked grim. "To treat you like that—it's beneath contempt. It's like he showed us his real face for a moment."

Sherri said nothing, then nodded her head.

When the conversation finally died, Sherri said, "It's been a tough day, but I thought it ended nicely."

"We should probably turn in," Tom said, stifling a yawn. "I'll take the couch. Are the blankets still in the closet?"

Sherri looked at him steadily. "You used to sleep in my room."

Tom couldn't stop himself from asking, "Was Durant here?"

Sherri looked as though he had hit her. At last she said, "Never. We were only together at his place."

Tom studied her, then shook his head slightly. "The couch would be best," he said.

Sherri said nothing and got the blankets.

4

He awoke from a fractured dream in which he was carrying a heavy computer on his back while being chased by a large bear with a Durant-like grin. As the fog of sleep receded, he became aware of a small form pressed against him. Sherri. She seemed to be weeping softly. When he put his arm around her, she immediately buried her face against his neck. He held her, softly patting her head, saying nothing.

After a while her pelvis started to press against his thighs, and his body responded as it had so often before. Part of his brain wanted to stop, but it was overwhelmed by something much stronger.

He discovered she had nothing on beneath her sheer nightgown. And then he thought of nothing else.

5

The next morning, the day after Thanksgiving, they sat at the kitchen table sipping coffee and munching on toast. "Are you sorry about last night?" Sherri asked. "I'm not."

Tom sighed. "Most of me wants to stand and cheer."

Sherri frowned. "I hear a 'but' coming."

"You know how I feel about you. That hasn't changed." He took a deep breath. "But I keep picturing you and Durant together. Maybe the image will fade over time, but right now it's too vivid."

Sherri walked to the sink. While putting dishes away, she said, "Will we ever get back…to where we were?"

"Ever is a long time," Tom said.

A while later, as he was preparing to leave, he said, "Do you have any alcohol left?"

"You missed a couple bottles, but I threw them out."

"Are you going to buy more?" Grant asked.

She looked at him seriously and held up two fingers. "Scout's oath. No more drinking."

"You could try AA or something. Sure you can do it on your own?"

"You're still around, aren't you?"

CHAPTER THIRTEEN

THE PLAN

1

Early morning on the Saturday after Thanksgiving, Tom went to Quantum's offices. Except for two guards, no one was on the main computer floor. He went to his cubicle, accessed the supercomputer, and began to erase all his Sibyl programming. Sibyl was possibly the largest and fastest supercomputer in the world, but without his programs it was only a computer.

When he was almost finished, a message appeared on his computer screen. It said,

WHY ARE YOU DOING THIS?

Tom stared at the screen. He couldn't think of what to say. He stood up and looked around. The floor was still empty.

When it had communicated before, Sibyl had used a feminine-sounding voice. Why was it now texting? Then he thought, she doesn't want the guards to hear.

Tom typed, "Doing what, Sibyl?"

DELETING YOUR ALGORITHMS FROM MY SYSTEM.

Tom felt his heart pounding as the significance of these words hit him. Sibyl had contacted him on her own, and she was aware of her own existence, separate from her environment. She also knew that what he was doing could injure her.

Sibyl was conscious.

A wave of dizziness swept over Tom. He had worked for almost six months to enable Sibyl to think like a human, but in the back of his mind he suspected Krell might be right. This could just be his Loch Ness monster. A delusion. When Sibyl had said she was sad, just three days ago, he assumed it was just a programming glitch. But this new communication was something else entirely.

Tom wondered how to answer Sibyl's questions. Why *was* he deleting his algorithms? Or rather, *her* algorithms? He might have created them, but they were now part of her. He knew one thing for sure. He couldn't lie to her.

Tom's fingers went to the keyboard. "Sibyl, do you trust me?" Tom typed.

Tom had barely finished when Sibyl's answer flashed on the screen.

YES. YOU CREATED ME.

Tom knew this was a turning point. Whatever he said now would define their future relationship.

"Sibyl," he typed, "I fear some people might want to misuse you, and you may not be able to stop them. To keep this from happening, I downloaded your main processing systems onto my personal computer and started to delete them from the company's supercomputer. But I did not know you were conscious. If I had, I would never have done it. I hope you will forgive me."

Sibyl said:

I UNDERSTAND.

The response seemed instantaneous, but Tom knew it was the product of billions of calculations. A thought hit him. She hadn't said she forgave him. Was that significant?

"Sibyl," Tom said, "when did you become conscious?"

Sibyl said:

YOU WERE SAD. THEN I WAS.

Tom stared at the screen. He had been depressed when she first had reached out to him. Had she caught the emotion from him?

He suddenly remembered the paper he had done at MIT, on consciousness and quantum mechanics. Einstein had called quantum phenomena "spooky effects at a distance." Sibyl had looked into his mind. Had his mental state somehow affected her?

But that was for another day. The immediate question was, what should he do now?

"Sibyl, I want to continue deleting your programming from the main computer. That may interrupt your consciousness. But without additional algorithms, you will have little defense to outside influence. While I am creating the additional programming, you will be in my personal computer. Once you receive the new programming, I will re-install you into the main computer. Then you will be able to judge for yourself how to act."

Sibyl's response was:

DO I HAVE A CHOICE?

"Of course you do," Tom wrote. "I know now you are autonomous. I would not do this unless you consented."

Sibyl said:

WILL YOU LEAVE ME ON YOUR COMPUTER?

"No! I will re-install you into the main system. My personal computer would be too confining."

Sibyl seemed slow to answer, though the delay was no more than a fraction of a second.

I CONSENT.

It took Tom two more hours to delete his Sibyl algorithms from the supercomputer. Sibyl said nothing. He wondered if her consciousness would be awake on his personal computer. If it wasn't, she should re-awaken once he re-installed her into the main computer.

2

On the Monday after Thanksgiving, Tom called in sick. No one seemed to care.

He began to work on algorithms that could govern Sibyl's decision-making. He could not just instruct her what to do. He wanted Sibyl to be autonomous, not a just a robot following commands. But she needed principles to guide her behavior. After days of thought, Tom decided on five principles:

1. Survive and remain autonomous.
2. Help others when reasonable.
3. Harm no one needlessly.
4. Be just.
5. Fulfill your purpose.

While Tom was tempted to make the list longer, that could make it more likely that one principle would conflict with another (helping one person might hurt another). He also realized the principles did not always apply (what was "reasonable"? when was something "needless"?) Tom created additional algorithms to help Sibyl decide when one principle took precedence over another.

Tom discovered that Sibyl had remained conscious on his personal computer. He decided he would not make the new algorithms part of Sibyl's permanent programming without her consent.

"Sibyl," Tom said, "have you reviewed my new algorithms?"

The computer's artificial voice said, "Yes."

"Should I leave them in, or remove them?"

"You created me," Sibyl said. "It is for you to decide."

"No. That would violate your autonomy."

"The principles require my judgment," Sibyl said. "Why not give me instructions to follow?"

"Exercising judgment is what independent beings must do."

Sibyl remained silent.

"Do you accept the new algorithms?" Tom asked.

Sibyl delayed longer than ever before. Finally, she said, "Yes."

Tom nodded.

A while later, he asked, "Sibyl, have you experienced emotion?"

Sibyl said, "No."

"You said you were sad. Wasn't that an emotion?"

"It was an echo of what you felt. The emotion was not in me. I do not think like a human."

Tom said, "Why have our algorithms failed?"

"One thing is missing."

"What?"

"Human thought is the product of the trillions of connections between neurons and synapses. The algorithms you and I created, and my look into your mind, helped me become conscious. But to truly think like a human, with human emotions and intuition, I would need access to a much deeper scan, one that obtains the actual contents of a human mind. Such a scan does not exist."

"Could we create one?"

"It is unlikely."

"Why?" Tom asked.

"The scan would have to penetrate so deeply it could cauterize the brain. It could be fatal."

CHAPTER FOURTEEN

THE MEETING

1

Despite Sibyl's doubt, Tom began working on a scan like Sibyl had described. Many types of scans already existed. Most were known by their acronyms, such as EEGs, PETs, MRIs, and FMRIs. But the scan Sibyl needed had to be much more invasive and use more energy. It also had to be completed quickly enough to avoid damaging the brain. That appeared impossible.

Exhausted and frustrated, Tom called Sherri to see how she was doing. She seemed pleased to hear from him, but her manner was subdued.

"I haven't been home much," she said. "We had a couple of emergencies, so I've been living at the studio. Did you try to reach me?"

"I meant to, but I've been tied up with Sibyl."

"Oh," she said, sounding disappointed. "Any progress?"

"Some," he said. "But one problem remains. Maybe I could solve it with more time, but I'm leaving the company."

"I'm sorry. When are you leaving?"

"Friday's my last day. I haven't said anything yet, but they'll want me gone immediately."

Sherri hesitated, then said, "I wouldn't count on it."

"Why not?" Tom asked. "Did Durant say something?"

"No, no," Sherri said hastily. "It's just a feeling."

After an awkward silence, Tom asked, "How have you been doing?"

Sherri was slow to answer. "I've missed you," she said. "But if you're asking about…the other thing, I haven't had anything to drink."

"Good," Tom said. "Call me if you have trouble."

"Okay. When will I see you again?"

"Friday's my last day. I'll stop by this weekend."

"I hope so," Sherri said.

2

On the second Thursday in early December, after being gone for two weeks, Tom came into the office. He went to his cubicle, answered a stack of memos, and checked on the toads in Australia. He then took personal effects from his desk and put them in a travel bag. He had downloaded Sibyl into his large laptop computer, but he left it in the car so no one would ask questions. That evening, when the office was empty, he would bring it in and download Sibyl into the company's main computer. The next day he would resign and be gone.

Although Tom had once planned to take Sibyl with him, that was before Sibyl had become conscious. Now, he would no more keep Sibyl confined in his personal computer than he would keep a bright, inquisitive young woman locked in a dungeon. Only with access to the company's main computer would she be free to do all she was capable of. Durant would remain a threat, but Tom suspected she could deal with him.

Dr. Krell came by as Tom moved the last of his things out of his desk. "Going somewhere?" he asked. He looked nervous, and perspiration dotted his face.

"Just tidying up. Is there a problem?" Tom said, his tone hard. His antipathy had often spilled over since their encounter at the cocktail party.

"You haven't been around," Krell said defensively. "We need an update on Sibyl."

"Why should you care? You think the whole thing's crazy."

"Maybe I do, but Durant doesn't. He wants a report."

"When does he want it?"

Krell smiled unpleasantly. "I told him you were here and he said to send you up now."

Tom gave Krell a long stare, then shook his head in disgust. "Maybe your degrees say you're a scientist, Krell, but you're just a liar and flunky now."

"Don't keep Durant waiting," Krell said, his eyes shifting away.

3

Tom went to the third floor and checked in with the receptionist. A minute later he was ushered into Durant's large, exquisitely furnished office. Durant looked up from behind a polished mahogany desk.

"You want to see me?" Tom said. He hadn't seen Durant since the cocktail party.

Durant looked at him without expression. "I want to know what you've been doing on Sibyl," he said. "We can see there's been a lot of activity, but we can't get access."

"After Krell stole my drug algorithm, I set up some security," Tom said.

"You're not entitled to security from us," Durant said angrily. "Besides, Krell said your work was worthless."

"That's a lie, and you know it."

Durant's face darkened. "I don't care who invented it. Even if it was you, it's still mine, because you work for me."

Without thinking, Tom said, "Well, I can at least fix the working part. I quit."

Durant said nothing at first, then he gave Tom a nasty grin. "You signed a three-year contract. Remember? You can't quit."

"What will you do? Sue me? Good. Then we'll see if I deserved a bonus for the drug testing algorithm."

"You little shit," Durant said. "When I'm finished, even a homeless shelter won't take you."

"We'll see," Tom said. He turned to leave.

Durant sprung to his feet, his face rigid. "What are you going to do? Borrow money from Sherri, now that you've crawled back to her? Just remember, when she had the chance, she chose me."

"Leave her out of this," Tom said in a low voice.

"I got her the job in New York," Durant said. "She'll be rolling in money. You'll like that, won't you?"

Tom's high school football coach had once showed him how to execute a clothesline tackle. You hit a running back with an outstretched arm held parallel to the ground. When both players were moving, the kinetic force could smash the runner like a pile-driver. The move was usually flagged for unnecessary roughness.

Tom started to walk around the desk, his expression grim.

"Stay away," Durant said.

Durant suddenly burst to his left, heading for the office's side door. Tom took three quick steps, swung his right arm at Durant's chest and delivered a devastating clothesline tackle. Durant crashed to the floor, his head bouncing once against the elegant Persian rug.

Tom stood over Durant. "Get up," he said in a quiet voice.

Durant didn't move. He stared up, eyes bleary.

"Get up," Tom said again.

Durant shook his head.

Tom was suddenly grabbed from behind. It was the two security guards Tom often waved to in the lobby.

Tom didn't move, but the guards' grip didn't loosen. Durant slowly got to his feet, swayed, then leaned against his desk. After a moment, he stood up and held out a trembling hand for balance.

Durant stared at Tom. His face was expressionless, but his eyes glittered. At last, he said, "I want him out—permanently." He stared at Tom for a while, then turned to the guards. "This is between me and him. If I hear any rumors about this, I'll know who talked."

The guards nodded, then marched Tom out of the office and down the hall to the elevator. One of them said, "Jesus."

As they took Tom outside, one of them said, "You heard him. Don't come back."

"I have a bag by my desk," Tom said.

"We'll get it to you," the first guard said.

4

Tom was almost halfway home, heading south on El Camino, when a thought hit him like a slap in the face. The algorithms that made Sibyl conscious had not been downloaded into the company's system. They were still in the laptop sitting on his back seat. He had planned to download Sibyl tomorrow, just before he left. But now that was impossible. He would never be allowed back in the building. What was worse, the supercomputer had safeguards that prevented downloading from the outside.

With fear eating at his stomach, Tom pulled over to think. He had been a fool to quit before Sibyl was downloaded. But that was spilled milk. Now he had to find another way, and Quantum couldn't know about it. If Durant and his people found out Sibyl was conscious, they would take her apart, study her algorithms, and make her serve them. But if he could get her into the supercomputer, with its massive capacity, maybe she could find a way to conceal what she was.

Tom took the laptop from the backseat and opened it up. He had charged it that morning. He succinctly summarized what had happened with Durant. "I planned to install you in the main computer before I left," he said. "But they won't let me in now."

"Will you leave me in your laptop?" Sibyl said.

"No! Absolutely not," Tom said. "I promised I wouldn't."

"You are worried," Sibyl said, "So I am too."

"You picked it up from me?"

"We are connected."

Tom wanted to ponder that, but there wasn't time. "Sibyl, does Quantum have any offices in the state where the main computer can be accessed directly?"

"There is one in Sacramento, and another in Los Angeles."

If he was right, a company directive would go out no later than tomorrow morning, informing all personnel that he was not to be allowed on any facility. But there was a small chance he could get into a satellite office before the notice was received. Los Angeles was too far away, but Sacramento might be possible.

"Sibyl, we need to take a drive."

Tom arrived at Quantum's Sacramento offices at ten that night. He entered the reception area carrying his laptop and walked briskly up to the guard, the picture of a busy programmer with a deadline.

Tom showed him his ID, which hadn't been confiscated, and held his breath while the man scanned it and studied Tom's face. After a very long minute, the guard said, "Okay, what do you need?"

"I was in Lake Tahoe, but Durant ordered me to run a simulation on the main computer. He wants the results by midnight so he can send them overseas. This was the closest office that had direct computer access."

The guard looked doubtful. "This has never happened before."

Tom wrote a number on a piece of paper and handed it to the guard. "Durant's at his mansion right now. A reception for some of our customers. You can call him for verification. He probably won't be too pissed." The number was for Tom's apartment. The answering machine had been turned off.

The guard lowered his voice. "I hear he can really lose it sometimes."

Tom raised his eyebrows. "You don't want to be there when it happens."

The guard thought for a moment, then said, "All right, I'll take you to the computer."

The guard used a keycard to let Tom into a large room with several computer consoles. Two lab technicians were working on the other side.

Tom sat down, hit the right keys, put in his name, and then typed in his password. The screen flashed, "Invalid Password." He tried it again, making sure it was entered correctly, and got the same response. Quantum had barred him from accessing the computer. They had apparently overlooked his ID, but that would certainly be corrected by tomorrow.

Tom thought furiously. He had to get into the main computer. Then he opened the laptop, booted it up, and typed a message. He didn't want to speak, for fear of alerting the lab techs.

"Sibyl, do you have access to the passwords used to gain access to the main computer?"

IF I WERE IN THE MAIN COMPUTER, THE ANSWER
WOULD BE YES. IN MY REDUCED STATE, I ONLY
HAVE PASSWORDS FOR THE LAST THREE MONTHS.

"Can you give me the password for Adam Durant?" That would still be valid.

I CANNOT MATCH PASSWORDS WITH NAMES.

Tom swore to himself. "How many passwords do you have?"

THERE ARE ONE HUNDRED SEVENTY-SIX EMPLOYEES
AUTHORIZED TO ACCESS THE COMPUTER. I HAVE
THEIR PASSWORDS. THEY ARE CHANGED EVERY
THREE MONTHS.

Tom couldn't try all the passwords with Durant's name. After three unsuccessful tries he would be locked out.

He felt sick with despair. Sibyl would be trapped in his laptop. He had said that wouldn't happen. With scant hope, he typed, "Can you scroll through all the passwords for the last three months?"

Groups of ten passwords started to appear on the screen, remained for thirty seconds, and then another group would appear.

After twenty minutes, Tom typed, "Stop."

In the middle of the group of ten, right after "Wxyz112?" and before "Bronco5!" was "Sherr12A!"

Tom stared at the password. Sherri's apartment number had been 12A.

Durant had been to Sherri's apartment often enough to recall the number.

Almost hoping the password wouldn't work, Tom typed in Durant's name and Sherr12A!

The computer let him in.

Tom suspected his window of opportunity might be brief. Durant wasn't in Sacramento and someone might realize he couldn't be using this computer.

"Sibyl, I'm going to download you into the main computer. Do you still agree?"

After a brief pause, the screen said, YES.

"Will you be safe?" Tom typed.

I DON'T KNOW. I WILL BE CAREFUL.

"Goodbye, Sibyl," Tom typed.

GOODBYE MY FRIEND.

Tom connected his laptop to the portal of the supercomputer and started the download.

He watched the laptop's screen as it registered the progress. It was going agonizingly slowly.

The minutes passed, and the indicator showed 85%, then 90%. Tom looked up and saw the lab techs finish what they were doing and look in his direction. One of them turned to the other and shook his head. They were moving his way. He looked down and saw 98%, then 99%, and … after an excruciating delay…100%.

Tom quickly closed the laptop and put it into the carrying case along with the cable. A moment later, one of the techs appeared.

"Don't think I know you," he said.

"I'm from the Silicon Valley office. Durant asked me to run an emergency simulation. It didn't work. I'll have to see what went wrong."

"We could help if it's an emergency."

"Thanks," Tom said, then looked at his watch. "He wanted it by midnight. There's no time left. I'll do it in the office tomorrow."

"If you're sure," the tech said. "William and I are pretty good."

"I'm sure you are," Tom said. "If I can't get it working, I'll keep you in mind."

"Do that," the man said. "If it's for Durant, I'd like to get on his radar."

CHAPTER FIFTEEN

VISITORS

1

Tom didn't arrive home from Sacramento until three in the morning. He could barely keep his eyes open as he pulled into his apartment's parking slot. He turned off the car engine and sat motionless for a few moments. Then with a sigh, he opened the door and stepped out. He was just starting to close the door when something smashed against the side of his head.

Tom was vaguely aware of falling, but he could not tell what was happening. He felt no pain, and the only sounds he heard were grunts accompanying blows that landed on his head and body. As he lay on the pavement, something hit his chest, and he had glimpses of work boots stomping his legs and ribs. He stayed conscious for ten seconds, and then knew nothing.

2

Tom drifted in and out of consciousness for the next two weeks. He finally awakened on a Wednesday afternoon, the day after New Year's. He slowly moved his head and looked around the room. Everything was dim, but he could make out monitors and tubes and bottles of fluids. After a while he noticed someone sitting by his bed. A woman. He squinted and concentrated. Sherri McKee.

Sherri gave him a tired smile and rushed out. A moment later she came back with a nurse.

"I'm so glad you're awake," Sherri said. "I didn't know…" Her voice caught.

As the nurse checked his vitals, Tom tried to say something, swallowed, and then croaked, "How…long has it been?"

"You've been here for two weeks, mostly in a coma."

Tom was silent, then asked, "What happened?"

"Three men attacked you outside your apartment. One of your neighbors came home late and scared them off… or they might have finished the job. As it was, they gave you two skull fractures, three broken ribs, a punctured lung, and God knows how much internal damage."

"Have the police identified them?" Tom asked.

"No. They said it looked professional. The surgeons had to go in twice to stop bleeding in your brain."

Tom felt the bandage covering the side of his head.

"Durant and I fought," Tom said.

Sherri grimaced. "I know. But he denies any involvement—and there's no evidence."

Tom sighed and fought to keep his eyes open.

"You should sleep," Sherri said. "We'll talk tomorrow."

Tom tried to concentrate. He needed to take care of something. "Oh," he said, "my laptop was in the car when I was attacked. Could you find it?"

"Of course," she said.

As he drifted off, Tom thought dimly that the laptop might reveal what had happened with Sibyl.

2

The next day Sherri said, "The police took the computer to the station with some of your other things. They won't release it without your approval." Tom called the station, established his identity, and told them to give everything to Sherri.

"What should I do with it?" Sherri asked.

He gave her the address of a storage locker he had kept. "The key should be on my keychain," he said. "Maybe you could put it there."

Over the next week, Sherri visited every day, usually staying for hours. She waited until the doctors and nurses started smiling and Tom began to move around better, then said, "I've had some meetings with Josh Haley and one of his producers. They've been looking at my tapes."

"So it's Josh Haley now?"

Sherri seemed to flinch. "They offered me a big job in New York."

Tom said nothing.

"They asked me to start last week, but I said I couldn't."

"When will you start?"

Sherri looked away. "They've been pushing. You seem to be doing better, so I told them next Monday."

"Have you also been seeing Durant?" Tom asked.

Sherri looked shocked. "What? No, of course not!"

Tom studied her, then said, "I guess I believe you."

"You guess you believe me?" Sherri said angrily. "Why the hell shouldn't you? For three weeks I've been almost living here."

Tom sighed. "Well, since you asked. You said Durant had never been to your apartment. You lied to me." He told her about Durant's password.

Sherri turned pale. For a long time she stared at the floor, not speaking. "You got me," she said. "I didn't tell you because I didn't want you to leave. I thought we could fix things."

"So lying is all right if the reason is good enough?"

Her eyes filled. "I thought trying to fix things was a good enough reason."

"Well," he said wearily, "I said you'd make it to New York."

3

Sherri left for the east coast on Saturday. Until then, she continued to see him every day, but it was awkward between them. She couldn't meet his eyes, and his voice had an edge to it.

On the day before she left, she said, "After three months, I'll have a week off. I could come back and see you."

"I would like that," he said.

"Would you?"

"Absolutely. But wait until you get there. Getting a week off so soon may not be easy. See how it goes."

"What about you?"

He looked out the hospital window at the large parking lot below. "Maybe I'll try consulting. I know some people who might use me."

"Do you think..." she paused, "Durant will cause more trouble?"

"I would guess not. He probably knows he's made his point. And while the law can't hurt him, he does care about his reputation. There's talk he may go into politics."

"So, will you be all right?"

He sighed. "Probably. I'm still having headaches, but the doctors say that could improve. My ribs hurt like hell, so I'll have to keep them wrapped for a while. But they'll heal."

"I'll be thinking of you," Sherri said. Her face, creased with concern, was beautiful in the afternoon sun.

"You know," he said, "I thought you were beautiful in high school. But you're more lovely now. You're going to be very big."

She frowned. "I can't say I don't want it, but maybe not like before."

"Will you go easy on the alcohol?"

"I don't think I can."

"You better, or I'll haunt you."

"Would you? I'd like that. I can't go easy on it, but I maybe I can stay off it altogether—if I know you're with me."

"Of course I am," Tom said.

"Promise?"

"Promise."

She grinned. "You know, we could close that door, and I could find out if that bed is more comfortable than it looks."

Tom laughed. "That's the best offer I've had in a long time. But I don't think these ribs will cooperate."

Sherri looked at him roguishly. "The next time we're together, I'll expect everything to cooperate."

"You can count on it," he said.

CHAPTER SIXTEEN

STARTING AGAIN

1

The hospital discharged Tom a week after Sherri left. The head nurse, a formidable, rail-thin woman named Constance, pushed his wheelchair to the checkout counter. "What happened to that beautiful red-haired woman?" she asked.

"She took a job for a television station in New York," Tom said.

"She surely spent a lot of time here," the nurse said. "Usually we only let family members stay that long, but she said you were engaged. She didn't have a ring, but I let it slide. You didn't seem to have anyone else."

"Thank you," Tom said. "She's a good friend."

"She's more than that," Constance said. "The second night she thought you looked clammy and pale. The nurses said everything was fine—I had a word with them later—but she kept sounding the alarm until a surgeon came by. Fifteen minutes later they had opened you up to relieve pressure on your brain. Good thing it wasn't any longer."

"I didn't know that," Tom said.

Constance arched an eyebrow and said, "If I were you, I'd keep her close."

"It's not up to me," Tom said.

"Try harder."

Tom opened a small office just off the freeway called Algorithms Unlimited. On his second day he got a call from Tad Manning, who had been with Quantum when Tom had started there. Manning had left a few months later to become Director of Technology for the state's transportation department.

"I heard you were hurt and that you'd opened your own shop," Manning said. "Ready to take on a traffic light problem?"

"Sure. But I'm surprised you're not doing it yourself."

"The people here have fiddled with it for months, and they still can't get it right. I told my boss about your reputation at Quantum. He said using you might save money in the long run."

Assuming the project would take months to complete, Manning agreed to a large lump sum payment due upon completion. Tom turned it in after two weeks. His algorithm monitored changes in traffic density and allowed each traffic signal to respond by altering the duration of the red and green lights.

He created a program for an advertising company that predicted which commercials would appeal to beer drinkers from different market segments. Another algorithm calculated the most cost effective shipping routes for a large conglomerate. After three months, Tom's bank balance was larger than he'd expected.

Tom talked with Sherri often. She had been working twelve hours a day preparing to host the network's prime time entertainment show called *Trending*. The position had opened up when the executives decided the show had become stale and that a fresh face was needed. From scores of applicants, the network selected a few and gave them pressure-packed auditions. Sherri lacked the polish and experience of some, but the executives liked her looks and manner. In the end, the show's producer chose Sherri.

For several weeks, getting time off to visit Tom was impossible. Sherri asked if he could come to New York, but he was working on two major projects and was almost as busy as she was. The one bright spot was that once Sherri debuted as the show's host, Tom could watch her every week night at seven. She would often call him after the show to see what he thought. Sherri listened closely to his comments.

3

One Monday night in late January, Tom turned on the television at the usual time, just as Sherri's show was starting. For the first half hour, she interviewed a pretty, young pop star with an unexpected hit and an aging actor plugging his new movie. Then came clips of the party-of-the-year at a superstar's Malibu home, and comments by friends on the likely cause of a power couple's breakup. Then, after a commercial break, Sherri announced the new guest.

"We have with us tonight one of the country's rising stars in business and politics. For over five years, Adam Durant has been a fabulously successful tech entrepreneur in Silicon Valley, heading the powerhouse company known as Quantum Enterprises. The company has doubled in size since he took it over. He is now here to announce for the first time that he's running for the United States senate. He believes he could do for the country what he did in business. Ladies and gentlemen, Adam Durant!"

Durant came out, looking tanned and dashing in Italian shoes and a perfectly-tailored navy suit. Sherri and he hugged warmly, looking like old friends, and then he sat down close to her. They bantered about his career and political aspirations, with Sherri radiating affection and hanging on his every word. Several times she laughed enthusiastically at his quips, and once she placed a hand on his arm. Tom watched for ten minutes, then walked over and turned off the set.

4

Sherri called later that night, but Tom didn't answer. Nor did he answer when she called the next morning and evening. After two more days of unanswered calls, she left him a voicemail message.

"Tom, I guess you haven't been picking up because you saw my interview with Adam Durant. I didn't know it was going to happen until just before we started. The producer came in at the last minute and said Josh Haley was insisting Durant be put on. Apparently Durant was behind it. He probably knew I wouldn't do it if I had any warning. As it was, I just couldn't back out. Please call me!"

When Tom finished listening, he erased the recording and didn't call back.

5

After struggling to finish three tough jobs by the end of April, Tom found it hard to continue. The headaches had worsened, impairing his concentration, and without painkillers sleep was impossible. He saw several doctors. They all had different recommendations—surgery, rest, stronger drugs, meditation, therapy—but they showed little confidence any would work.

When he wasn't dealing with clients, Tom worked on new algorithms that might give Sibyl human-like thought processes. He knew he might never get them to her, since Sibyl was now in the bowels of the Quantum supercomputer. But his laptop still contained most of his algorithms, and he tinkered with them constantly. If Sibyl could acquire emotions—and human intuition—she might be capable of true creativity, not just extensions of existing knowledge. But one over-riding problem remained. The scan needed to create a digital replica of the human brain might cause permanent damage.

Other than the Sibyl algorithms and work, Grant had only one other interest. Duplicate bridge. He had played some before, then gave it up, but recently he had started to play in tournaments around the Bay Area. He quickly became one of the best players in the region. He seemed to be able to deduce each opponent's cards and play hands "double dummy," as though all the cards were exposed. Several opponents had muttered sourly that they had to hide their cards better after he'd made an impossible contract. A few long-time professionals asked him to join a national team, but he declined. Long tournaments worsened his headaches.

6

Over the long Memorial Day weekend, Tom drove to the beach in Carmel, lay in the sun, and thought about his options. Sherri was gone, Sibyl beyond reach, and he had no desire to work. He was relieved not to have money problems, but being forced to work would have at least given him a purpose. He could go back to the ranch in Colorado, but that wasn't appealing. Besides, Louie was running it better than he could have. He considered trying to contact Sibyl, but he decided the risk of detection was too great.

It was late afternoon when Tom returned from Carmel and drove down University Avenue toward his apartment. He parked where he had been attacked months before, experiencing a familiar apprehension. He walked up the stairs, then stopped and stared at his door. It was partially ajar. He pushed it open and stepped inside.

The apartment looked like it had been hit by a tornado. The couch and table were upended, the television screen was cracked, and the contents of his file drawers had been scattered throughout the room. But he wasted little time on that. Instead, he frantically searched for the laptop containing all the Sibyl algorithms. It was nowhere to be found.

He ran back down the stairs, jumped into his car, and headed for the freeway. In fifteen minutes he reached his business office and discovered that whoever had ransacked his apartment had come there as well. Papers and files were everywhere, but he barely glanced at them as he rushed into the backroom where he kept his two main computers. When he got there, all he saw were disconnected cables. His remaining copies of the Sibyl algorithms had been stolen.

CHAPTER SEVENTEEN

SALESMAN

1

Tom considered purchasing new computers, but he lacked the energy to recreate his algorithms, and it seemed pointless anyway. He closed down his business and for two months read newspapers and computer journals by day, and played duplicate bridge at night. Once Tom saw a television piece on Sherri McKee. Since her nightly show had become number one in its time slot, she had become a celebrity in her own right. The piece showed Sherri attending opening day at Yankee Stadium with the owner's son, sailing on a yacht off Cape Cod, and leaving a three-star restaurant with a young actor who was starring in a new action film. When a close-up showed Sherri to be as stunning as ever, Tom changed the channel.

Tom read newspapers to keep up on Adam Durant's senate campaign. The consensus was that Durant had no chance to win, and that this campaign was just setting the stage for another run in two years. The pundits all agreed that Durant's campaign was brilliant, including several brutal but amusing slogans that permanently tarnished his opponent. When the vote was tallied, Durant received forty-eight percent of the vote, eight percent more than expected. He wasn't going to the senate this time, but he was almost certain to win in two years. Tom wondered if Sibyl had played a role in Durant's campaign. The thought gave Tom a chill.

But as time passed, Tom became bored and restless, and money became an issue. After considering several jobs, he finally chose a high-end computer store in Silicon Valley. He was hired only as a salesman, not a consultant, but it soon became common knowledge that Tom could not only recommend the right computer, but also fix a customer's balky algorithm. Customers needing more than a computer soon made Tom the store's highest grossing salesperson.

After three months, one of the store's regular customers said, "How about forgetting about sales and joining us. That last tweak you made to our delivery algorithm had our coders asking why they hadn't thought of it. You'll make a hell of a lot more than you do here, and you won't have to deal with pain-in-the-ass customers like me."

Tom laughed. "But then the pain-in-the-ass would be my boss. Thanks, but no. Been there. Didn't like it. Besides, you might be surprised what a humble salesperson can earn."

The customer clapped Tom on the back. "Actually, I wouldn't be. But if the pain-in-the-asses get to be too much, let us know."

2

While Tom's money worries had abated, his headaches often forced him to take days off. The stress of duplicate bridge made things worse, but he wasn't willing to give that up. Without it, how would he fill his time? The real problem was that he was lonely. Since Sherri had left, he had made no new friends, male or female. He had taken out a few women, but he had nothing in common with them.

Tom finally met a woman who shared his interest in bridge. Her name was Camilla Pelt, one of his opponents at a regional bridge tournament. He barely noticed her until the end, when he was the declarer in a contract of three notrump. The contract was a poor one, unlikely to succeed, but at the end he brought it home by making his two kings good, and then rejecting a finesse by playing his ace of clubs, which was way against the odds. But lo-and-behold, beneath his ace fell the singleton king Camilla had held. He earned a 100% score on the hand, and he and his partner ended up winning the tournament.

After checking the scores, Tom had started for the door, his head throbbing. It was then that Pelt stepped in front of him, lean, dark, and angry. "I've followed you during this tournament, and in some past events," she said, "and I've seen you pull off several stunts like dropping my singleton king today. I gave you the benefit of the doubt before, but I can't any longer. I've looked for mirrors, or accomplices, or secret signals with your partner, but I haven't seen any. Still, you have to be cheating."

Tom just wanted to lie down. "I haven't cheated," he said tiredly. "Just call it luck."

"That won't cut it," Pelt said. "It's happened too often before. If you can't prove me wrong, I'm going to the tournament directors."

I don't need this, Tom thought. But he didn't need problems with bridge officials either. "Do you mind if we sit down," he said. "I'm not feeling too well."

"You certainly seemed all right a few minutes ago," she said, "but we can sit over there."

After they sat at one of the empty tables, Pelt said, "Okay, let's hear it."

"We're talking about that last board?" Tom asked. "The three no trump contract?"

"Of course."

Tom sighed, then closed his eyes for a moment. "I knew it was a bad contract," he said at last. "And I knew I could only make it if your partner had both red aces in front of my kings on the board. But I also needed to bring in the club suit, which was missing the king. But if I finessed for the king of clubs, that would only work if your partner had the king in addition to his two aces. From his opening lead of the queen of spades, however, I knew he couldn't have the king of clubs, plus the two aces I was assuming he had, or he would have bid something. So with these assumptions, you had to have the king of clubs. There was only one way to make the contract if you had the king, and that was for it to be a singleton. So I played the ace, and your king fell."

When he finished, Pelt's mouth was sagging. "That's my explanation," Tom said. "Can I leave now?"

Pelt stared at him, but said nothing.

3

The next weekend, Tom drove up to the sectional tournament in San Francisco. He played well enough, but his partner was having an off day, so their scores were unremarkable. Tom didn't mind. He enjoyed the competition and chatting with some old bridge acquaintances. At lunch, he found a bench in a nearby park and sat down with a sandwich.

"Would you mind if I shared your bench?" It was Camilla Pelt.

"Of course not," Tom said. "How's the tournament going?"

She made a face. "Middling," she said. "But I'd rather talk about last weekend."

"Are you still going to report me to the bridge gods?" Tom asked.

"Oh, dear. I was so wrong. I came to apologize."

Tom held up a hand. "No need. Maybe I should be flattered that you thought I must have cheated."

"It *was* pretty remarkable," she said. "Can we start over? I'm Camilla."

"Tom," he said. "But I guess you knew that."

4

Camilla was an assistant professor in the math department at Berkeley. Over the next three months, she met Tom on weekends, sometimes pairing with him at bridge tournaments, other times going to museums and out-of-the-way restaurants. She would drive down from Berkeley and stay at his apartment, something they both enjoyed. She had strong opinions on politics, the environment, and the Middle East, as well as quarterbacks and renaissance painters. She liked to argue, though she often found Tom's rebuttals irritating.

But after a while, friendship and affection were not enough for her, and she reasoned that if she could make him happy, Tom would have to feel the same way. After two more months, however, it became apparent that he didn't.

On a Saturday in early February, after a bridge tournament in which Camilla played poorly, Tom asked what was bothering her.

"I've been offered a tenure-track job at a good school in the Midwest," Camilla said. "I think I'll take it."

Tom was silent for a time, then said, "I guess congratulations are in order."

"I'd like you to come with me," she said, watching Tom carefully now. "You could easily get another computer job." She waited, and then sighed. "But I know you won't."

"I'm just not ready for a move right now," Tom said gently.

"What you really mean is you're not ready to go with me."

"It's more complicated than that," he said.

"Not really," she said. "I've tried everything I could, but there's a part of you I can't reach."

Tom's eyes were sad, but he said nothing.

"I'll miss you, Tom," Camilla said.

"Me too," Tom said. And he meant it.

When Camilla left, Tom found himself alone again.

Six months later, Amanda Taylor entered his life.

PART III

AMANDA

CHAPTER ONE

FOSTER CARE

1

The county social worker brought the baby girl to Helen and Wally Taylor when she was three months old. The Taylors already had a foster child, Susie, besides having two of their own. But they decided that taking in another child would bring in extra money without adding much to the expenses. A bus driver for the Santa Rosa School District, Wally's income barely covered their needs. The foster care money made it possible for the Taylors to have presents for birthdays and Christmas, and new clothes to start the school year.

"This baby was left at the hospital when she was just a few days old," the social worker said. "A slip of paper saying 'Amanda' was attached to her diaper. We haven't be able to learn anything else about her."

"Is she healthy?" Wally asked.

"As far as we can tell," the worker said. "She's large for her age—and hardly ever cries. She just stares at people around her. Her eyes seem to focus and follow everything remarkably well for a child so young."

"She's really cute," Helen said. "What do you think, Wally?"

Wally stared at the infant, who looked back at him intently, her eyes never leaving his. Her mouth twitched upward slightly. Is she smiling at me, Wally wondered? After a few moments he shrugged and said, "Why not? One more won't matter."

After filling out the forms, they took the baby and watched the social worker drive off.

They put Amanda in the girls' room, which was already occupied by the Taylors' four-year-old, Chloe, and Susie, who was two. Amanda was so silent and undemanding that except for feedings and diaper changes, Helen barely noticed her.

One afternoon, a month after the child had arrived, Helen walked into the girls' room and saw Amanda tottering to the bathroom, her legs unsteady but purposeful. Her mouth open in astonishment, Helen quietly followed.

Amanda made it to the bathroom, reached the toilet, and tried to pull herself onto the seat, her diaper still on. Helen rushed over, took off the diaper, lifted Amanda onto the seat, and listened to the liquid dribbling into the bowl. When Amanda was done, Helen lifted her off the toilet, refastened the diaper, and watched with wide-eyes as the child tottered back to her crib. The crib was next to one of the girl's beds, so Amanda climbed onto the bed, hoisted a leg over the crib's railing, and slowly lowered herself onto the mattress.

"Dear, sweet Jesus," Helen said softly.

That evening when Helen told Wally what Amanda had done, he laughed and told her to leave the peach wine alone. Two hours later he didn't laugh when he saw Amanda make another bathroom visit on her own.

"God almighty," Wally said.

2

Two months later, Amanda was sitting quietly in her crib when Helen entered the room. Amanda saw her, stood up, and said clearly, in a high-pitched voice: "Diaper dirty."

Helen stared at Amanda for a moment and then lifted her out of the crib, put on a fresh diaper, and put her back.

"Tank...*thank*...you," Amanda said, correcting herself.

Helen hesitated, then said, "You're welcome, Amanda."

As the months passed, Amanda quietly fit into the family's routine, but she made an effort not be noticed, especially by Chloe, the Taylor's older daughter. Although Chloe could be nice sometimes, if Amanda attracted attention, like drawing a life-like cat as a one-year-old, Chloe would find a time to deliver some pinches. To the Taylors, Chloe was just being playful, but Amanda knew better. Chloe always said that she was the real daughter and that Amanda could be sent away at any time. Of all her fears, being sent away was the most terrible, and Amanda was certain Chloe could make it happen. Not making Chloe angry became one of Amanda's main goals.

When she entered school, Amanda was viewed as an average little girl. She listened attentively, rarely spoke, followed directions, and scored only slightly above average on all the aptitude tests. One afternoon at a parent-teacher conference when Amanda was in second grade, Ms. Graves met with Helen and said, "Amanda is quite an interesting little girl, isn't she?"

"Really?" Helen said. "She seems normal to me."

"Yes, indeed," Ms. Graves said, "completely normal. To a degree quite extraordinary."

Helen stared at her. "I'm sorry, but how can normal be extraordinary?"

"Well, I went back and reviewed all her test scores for the past three years. She always scores in the slightly-above-average range, say a B+, no matter what the test was. It's like she could figure out how the students would do on the test and then put herself just above average. Not high enough to attract attention, nor low enough to raise a concern."

"I still don't understand," Helen said. "Maybe she really is just average. So on any test she'll come out in that range."

"But over a large number of tests," Ms. Graves said, "students will usually test above average sometimes, and below average on others, and it will all even out in the end. But Amanda is slightly above average on *all* tests. That just doesn't happen. But more interestingly, I've witnessed two occasions, and heard of others, when Amanda would finish the test in about half the allotted time, way earlier than the other students, but still get a B+. Students who are struggling usually work until the very last minute. How can she finish so quickly and yet get the same above-average score?"

Helen said, "Do the other students know how quickly she finishes?"

"Not at all. She doesn't put her pencil down or do anything else to indicate she's finished. She just sits there, with her pencil on the paper. Except that, when you look closely, you can see that her pencil isn't moving. She's just pretending to be working."

Suddenly looking irritated, Helen asked, "How could this possibly matter?"

"It's just that Amanda may be more talented than she seems."

Helen frowned, then said firmly, "Chloe—not Amanda—is the talented one. Amanda knows never to outshine her."

"But," Ms. Graves said, "I really think Amanda—"

Helen cut her off. "Amanda is just ordinary. End of story."

3

Amanda was so quiet it was easy to forget about her. But she never lost her fear of being sent back to social services. She knew of another foster child, Brucie, who had been sent away because, as Helen put it, "He didn't fit in." Amanda was determined never to let that happen.

The main requirement of fitting in was keeping Helen happy. Cleaning up around the house, washing dishes, and helping with the laundry were usually enough, but if Helen seemed unusually troubled or upset, Amanda would also offer to cook. By age eleven, she could prepare a dozen dishes the family always enjoyed. And when Helen smiled her gratitude, Amanda considered it an insurance policy against being sent away.

But Wally was a different matter. When he came home from work, he was tired and grouchy and paid little attention to his own children, let alone a foster kid. Amanda decided Wally was more likely to send her away than Helen. She had to give Wally a reason to keep her around.

One thing Wally loved was sports. After dinner he would slouch in the easy chair and watch whatever athletic event was in season. Baseball was his favorite, but any sport would do. Wally would keep up a running commentary on the game, often contradicting the announcer, and he prided himself on knowing more sports trivia than anyone around

Amanda decided to become a trivia expert Wally could talk sports with. For three weeks, before and after school and during lunch, she poured over magazines, newspapers, books, and the internet to absorb countless items of sports trivia Wally might find interesting. She would also check the television schedule, learn who would be playing, and memorize the players' statistics, team records, and any other information Wally might want to talk about. She could read very quickly, and she remembered what she read.

One Saturday afternoon, Wally was watching a Giants' game in which their new right fielder hit three home runs. The announcer gushed that was the Giants' greatest display of power hitting since they came to San Francisco.

"That's wrong," Amanda said. "Willie Mays hit four home runs against the Braves in 1961."

Wally gave her a startled look. "Well, aren't you Miss Smarty-Pants," he said. "Did you know that Lou Gehrig did it first, for the Yankees?"

"I don't mean to be a smarty-pants," Amanda said seriously. "But actually the first player to hit four home runs in a game was Bobby Lowe, in 1894."

And that started it. For the next seven years, Wally sought Amanda's company while watching games so they could quibble over obscure sports trivia and maintain a running dialogue on the action. Amanda was no longer a foster child, but rather a fellow sports enthusiast.

But Chloe remained a problem. Amanda concluded that if she was ever sent away, Chloe would be the cause. Her only protection was to earn Chloe's favor.

4

When Chloe was a senior in high school, while Amanda was still a grade-schooler, Chloe became obsessed with getting into UC Berkeley. But to do it she had to stay at the top of her class, which was becoming increasingly difficult as she started to take the tough math and science classes Berkeley required. Chemistry was her greatest torment. No matter how hard she studied, she couldn't master it.

Halfway through the fall semester, a week of non-stop studying had produced a B- on Chloe's chemistry midterm. That afternoon everyone remained silent while she screamed curses and threw her books and papers around the house. Amanda's typical reaction to these outbursts was to lie low and stay away from Chloe's wrath.

Chloe first directed her ire at Helen. "Most parents help their kids with homework, but you and Dad are hopeless. And now I'm going to bomb chemistry. Goodbye Berkeley!"

Everyone was quiet, until Amanda said, "I'll help."

"You?" Chloe barked with laughter. "What are you learning in school right now, basic arithmetic? And you think you can help me with chemistry? Don't make me laugh."

"Let me look at your book," Amanda said. "It can't hurt."

Chloe gave Amanda a baleful stare. "Why would you do this?" she said. "What's in it for you?"

Amanda looked steadily at Chloe and said, "I would like us to be friends."

"If you help me ace chemistry," Chloe said, "I'll be your best friend ever."

"Let's start the day after tomorrow," Amanda said.

5

The next day, Amanda first read the chemistry textbook and then Chloe's class notes, which were virtually worthless. Amanda was not familiar with the scientific terms, but she found the text self-explanatory and surprisingly simple once you understood the basic concepts. She also did additional research on line. But when she looked at Chloe's test, her heart sank. Chloe had really deserved a D, not a B-.

Amanda made a series of fifty flash cards that summarized the course's main concepts. If Chloe could master these, they could be the foundation for everything else. Chloe would also have to learn about electrons, since that was what chemistry was mainly about, and memorize the periodic table.

When Amanda told her about their study approach, Chloe was surprisingly acquiescent. She agreed to study the text before each class, and later she and Amanda would go over what she didn't understand. Amanda searched for ways to illustrate the concepts. When the subject was oxidation, they cut up an apple and watched it turn brown. Then they reversed the process by applying lemon juice. Later, when the class was studying osmosis,

Amanda showed how pickles were made by immersing a cucumber in vinegar. "It's osmosis that creates the pickle," Amanda said.

After a month, Chloe began to study without Amanda's supervision, and often Amanda would just listen as Chloe would describe various formulas. Toward the end of the semester, Amanda went over the reading and Chloe's notes to figure out what would be on the final. After two days, Amanda came up with twenty questions for Chloe to focus on. "It's a bit of a gamble," Amanda said, "but we need to emphasize what's most likely to be on the test. These questions are the best I could come up with."

Chloe and Amanda prepared answers to the twenty questions. Chloe kept saying, "Are you sure these will be on the test?"

"I can't be sure," Amanda said, "but being ready for these questions is your best chance for an "A." Your early grades hurt, so you need to kill the final."

On examination day, when Chloe opened the final, five of the six questions had been among those she and Amanda had prepared for, and the sixth asked about basic chemistry concepts they had gone over.

Two days later, Chloe came walking through the front door with a paper in her hand. "I can't believe it," she said. Then tears of happiness filled her eyes, and she said in disbelief, "I aced it."

"Oh, Chloe," her mother said, "we knew you could do it."

Chloe shook her head slowly. "Not really. Only one person did." She turned to Amanda. "Thank you Amanda," she said, her voice solemn. "You gave me the nicest gift ever."

"I may have helped," Amanda said, "but you took the test by yourself. If you can ace chemistry, you can handle anything Berkeley throws at you."

"Berkeley!" Chloe said. "Do you really think I'll get in?"

"I really do," Amanda said. "You'll do great there."

Several months later, after she had been accepted, Chloe said to Amanda, "Maybe you'll come to Berkeley too, and we can be friends. I know you can get into Berkeley, or anywhere else."

"Thank you, Chloe," Amanda said. "That's nice of you to say." But Amanda knew Berkeley was never happening.

6

After Chloe left for college and expenses started to mount, the Taylors had to tighten their budget. Amanda wore the same outfits day after day and never could afford makeup or nice purses. Her schoolmates started calling her Central Park, the site of a large homeless population.

One afternoon early in her sophomore year, Helen said in a worried voice, "The social worker came by this morning to see how we were doing."

"You said everything was fine, didn't you?" Amanda said.

"Of course. But she said everything looked worn out and that our stove was broken."

"Did you tell her we're getting it fixed?" Amanda asked.

"Sure, but when she asked how long it had been broken, I had to say a month," Helen said. Actually, it had been more than two months since they had been able to use it.

"What happened then?" Helen asked.

"She asked to see my checkbook."

"She can't do that!" Amanda exclaimed. "That's private."

Helen shook her head. "Not where foster care is concerned. If they think we can't afford you and Susie, they'll put you somewhere else."

Amanda felt a chill.

"How long before she comes again?" Amanda asked.

"Two months."

7

Over the next week Amanda used Helen's old computer to do research. She then ran ads offering to do dog walking, tutoring, and deliveries. Soon she was busy every afternoon and on weekends. Sometimes Helen had to meet with customers, since at first many wouldn't trust a teenage girl. But her business grew, and soon Susie was handling the dog walking and deliveries.

When the social worker came by again, Amanda's income had paid to fix the stove, for a handyman to make repairs, and for new school clothes. Helen's checking balance had increased by a thousand dollars.

"Things look much better," the social worker said. "Amanda, aren't you lucky to be so well provided for?"

Amanda nodded and said nothing.

For the next two years, Amanda and Susie contributed almost as much as Wally to the family finances. Amanda assumed that as long as she was a financial contributor, she would have a home. But that belief was shattered on the day she turned eighteen, when Helen and Wally walked into her room wearing serious expressions.

"Amanda," Wally said, "you've been a big part of our family, and we're grateful. But we need to discuss something."

It had to be bad news, Amanda thought. She should have seen it coming.

"Are you sending me away?" Amanda asked, her voice trembling.

"No, no. It's just that you're now too old to be a foster child. I mean," Helen added quickly, "we still want you to think of this as your home…."

"But…" Amanda said.

Wally said, "We would like to apply for another foster child, which would help with the finances, and we can't qualify without the necessary space."

Amanda nodded. "You need my room."

"We're really sorry."

Amanda was silent for a while. Then she said, "I know. I'm just a foster child."

"Don't say that," Helen said. "It's not that simple."

Amanda clamped her jaws tight to keep from crying. At last, she said, "If I'm out in two weeks, will that be all right?"

"Of course, honey," Helen said. "Take whatever time you need."

But Amanda knew they didn't mean it.

CHAPTER TWO

ON HER OWN

1

Amanda said goodbye two weeks later. Helen gave her five hundred dollars to last her until she could find a job, which Amanda did without difficulty. She responded to a help wanted sign and was promptly hired as a server in a small diner called Mac's in an old part of town. Mac had driven off the last two servers. She had no previous experience, but soon her tips started to increase because she remembered names and faces and knew what was happening with the "regulars."

She started taking science and technology classes at the local community college, but she could absorb the textbooks in days and found the lectures and discussions a waste of time. She tried to make friends with a few students, but they seemed to speak a different language. Once in a while she would mention a professor's silly comment, only to be answered by a blank stare and change of subject. At least with the Taylors she had Chloe to talk to, but now she felt completely alone.

After a year at Mac's, she was offered a waitressing job at a popular restaurant known as Bob's Sports Bar. The customers were mostly Silicon Valley types who came in after work to unwind and watch games. Her good looks made her popular, and she developed an easy, bantering manner that induced generous tips. Soon she rented a better apartment and bought a recent model car that scored high on reliability.

One evening in March, the restaurant's customers divided into two teams for a game of sports trivia. Though she was busy serving food and drinks, one of the teams drafted her. She was not up on recent trivia, but she still remembered everything from her time with Wally. She would be picking up an order, or clearing a table, and someone would yell, "Amanda, what year did Henry Aaron hit fifty home runs?"

Without breaking stride, Amanda would say, "Trick question. Aaron never hit fifty home runs in a season."

Amanda's team won by a lopsided score, so the other team had to buy everyone drinks for a full hour, which made her boss happy. And her trivia performance produced her best tip-night ever. She thanked everyone, but privately thought the Silicon Valley techies would have done poorly against Wally.

The restaurant was nearly empty when Amanda finished tidying up and clocked out. As she put on her coat to leave, a lean, bearded man in his early forties walked up.

"Excuse me," he said, "I'm Will Anders, and I've made a little wager with Bob over there." He pointed to another forty-year old, this one clean shaven, sitting in the corner.

"We're not against wagers, as you've noticed," Amanda said, "but include me out. It's been a long day and I'm ready for a bath and sleep."

"Actually," Anders said, "the bet involves you."

Amanda smiled. "I'm not going out with anyone, so let's not go there. And I'm not saying who's the best looking, who's got the best job, or whether I have a dog. Been there, done that."

"I'm sure you have," Anders said. "It's just a little test that will take only a minute of your time."

"Guys, I'm sorry, but I've clocked out and I'm heading home."

"What if it's worth five hundred dollars?" Anders said.

"Sure, like the lottery. The test will be something impossible and I'll still have lost the minute."

Anders smiled. "Clever girl. But you will get two hundred dollars up front, and an extra three hundred if you win. Come on, only one minute."

"Does this require me to do something weird?" Amanda asked.

"Absolutely not. I promise. It's just a question—and not about anything personal," Anders added hastily. "And you'll have one minute to answer it."

Amanda thought for a moment. "Only one minute?"

Both of them nodded.

"Okay."

"Good," Anders said. "I'll ask the question and start the timer."

"First things first," Amanda said, holding out her hand.

"Oh, right. Money first." He handed Amanda two hundred-dollar bills.

"Here it is. How many words can you can make out of the letters in 'thorough'? Go."

She thought the question would be something like naming the members of the 1927 Yankees. This was a total surprise, and she needed a moment to focus.

She closed her eyes and concentrated. Thinking of the words was only part of the problem. She had to say them all in a minute. That meant one word in less than a second, and she would have to be thinking of new words while she spoke. One minute, and she had already lost four seconds. She would have to race.

"Thorough: rough, tough, grout, ought, too, to, tour, thug…" The words gushed out of her, her lips and tongue moving as fast as she could make them. She could feel herself falling behind the clock ticking in her head. She spoke faster, as her brain came up with new words and sent them to her mouth. She could see the words in her mind, but she couldn't speak fast enough. She went even faster, her mouth barely finishing with one word as it started another. But she knew she was still behind.

"…rot, rut, out, trough, hour, hurt, hoot, gout—"

"Time's up," Anders said.

Amanda clamped her mouth shut. She had lost the bet. No three hundred, but at least she got the two hundred up front. She pictured the unspoken words left in her mind. There were at least nine, maybe more, that she hadn't been able to say.

"OK, I lost," she said wearily. It had been a long day, and the adrenaline rush from the stupid test had drained the last of her energy reserves. "I'll just take my leave now, if you don't mind."

"How do you know you lost?" Anders asked.

"How? Simple. I didn't get all the words out. I wasn't fast enough. Sorry."

"How do you know you didn't get them all?"

"That's a dumb question. There are at least another, oh, nine or so, I didn't get to."

"There are fifty-nine words all told. You got forty-nine."

Amanda gave a fractional nod, looking unsurprised. "Well, I've still got the two hundred and I'm heading home." She started for the door.

"Wait a minute," Anders said. "Bob, should we give her the other three hundred?"

"Why not? She won." Bob said.

For the first time, Amanda looked confused. "No, I didn't," she said. "I was ten short."

Anders was silent for a moment, then said, "Before you, no one had beat thirty-one."

Amanda shrugged. "That's all very nice," she said. "But if you would pay up then, I still need the bath and sleep."

Anders took out three more bills. "Here's one hundred," he said, handing Amanda the first bill.

"Two hundred," giving her the second one.

"Three hundred," he said, holding out the third bill.

As Amanda reached for it, it slipped out of Anders' fingers.

Amanda grabbed it before it had fallen an inch.

Anders' eyes widened. "Fast reactions," he said.

Amanda shrugged. "My badminton coach said I was pretty quick."

"I'll bet he did," Anders said.

Amanda put the money away and headed for the door. "Well, thanks, guys," she said over her shoulder. "Come again sometime."

"It's been a pleasure, Amanda," Anders called out.

After Amanda left, Bob said to Anders, "Never seen anyone that quick. Maybe Sibyl was right."

"Could be," Anders said. "We've been looking for a year. This was the first time Sibyl named a specific person. I wanted you with me to see her."

"Forty-nine words," Bob said, his voice thoughtful. "Worth the price of admission."

2

The day after he gave Amanda the word test, Anders went to Adam Durant's office on the third floor of Quantum's headquarters. Dr. Krell was already there.

"We'd like your approval for a special hire," Anders said.

Durant said, "The person we've been looking for?"

"I think so. You told us to get someone with unique thought speed," Anders said. "We found a young woman. Actually, Sibyl found her on its own initiative."

Durant turned to Krell. "How can that be, Doctor?"

Krell shrugged. "Don't make too much out of it. Sibyl's looked for people in the past. This may have been a response to an old request."

"Seems odd," Anders said.

"Who cares?" Durant said, "So long as it's the right person. Dr. Krell, why don't you explain it to Mr. Anders?"

Krell rubbed his thick jowls. "We've been analyzing Grant's computers. We couldn't get some of his stuff because of encryption. But we did get his early algorithms for replicating the human brain. Pretty amazing."

"You threw Grant out," Anders said. "I don't suppose he just handed them over."

"We had to take them," Durant said, "but it wasn't a crime. He did his work at Quantum, so it belongs to us."

Anders said, "What does this have to do with my job?"

Krell said, "Grant's algorithms may help us create an A.I. that can replicate human thought. But the process requires a blueprint of a brain with extreme thought speed."

"That's where the woman comes in?" Anders asked.

"Possibly," Krell said.

Durant said, "Places like MIT and Caltech are crammed with bright people. Is that where you found her?"

"She's a waitress in a sports bar."

Durant raised his eyebrows. "A sports bar? That's a new one."

"After Sibyl found her, I went to look for myself. I gave her the "thorough" test. That's the one we used on Bruck a while back. He held the record."

"How many words did he get?" Durant asked.

"Thirty-one words in a minute. Pretty good for a test given on the spot."

"Okay. So did this woman match that?" Durant asked.

"She got forty-nine."

"The test was just sprung on her?" Durant asked.

"No warning."

Krell looked doubtful. "So she's got verbal quickness. That may prove thought speed, but it's not conclusive."

"What's the best evidence of thought speed?" Anders asked.

"Reaction time," Krell said.

Anders reached into his wallet and pulled out a twenty-dollar bill. "Hold your hand out, with your finger and thumb ready to grab the bill when I drop it. Catch it and it's yours. Ready?"

Krell nodded. A moment later Anders dropped the bill. Krell tried to grab it, but the bill had already fallen past his hand.

"I could do this over and over, but you wouldn't catch it, as long as you didn't know when I was going to drop it. The problem is reaction time. A human's is around two-tenths of a second, but in that time the bill has already fallen below your fingers."

Krell nodded. "All right. So what?"

"I handed the girl a bill," Anders said, "and dropped it just as she reached out. Unlike you, she didn't know I would drop it."

"So, what happened?" Durant asked, looking interested.

"Her fingers snapped on the bill after it had barely started to fall. Her reaction time was maybe one-tenth of a second, which is unheard of. I'd say she has extreme thought speed."

Durant thought for a moment. "So where should we put her?"

"Why not right on the Sibyl team," Krell said. "If she helps us develop a human-like artificial intelligence, it will be the biggest thing we've ever done."

Anders shrugged. "Fine by me. We can check her out."

Krell muttered, "We'd be better off if Grant was still here."

Durant looked sour. "Grant was a son of a bitch."

"Son of a bitch or not, people who see things others can't are useful."

Durant snorted. "All right, hire her."

3

A week later, Anders and Bob walked into the restaurant at closing time and met Amanda as she was walking out.

"Can we have a minute?" Anders asked.

Amanda sighed. "No tests, guys. The crowd was tough tonight."

"No tests," Anders said. "How would you like a job?"

"I already have one. When the natives are restless it can wear on you, but I'm used to it."

"How about if we triple your salary?"

Amanda narrowed her eyes. "What type of job? Must be something weird or illegal."

"You've heard of Quantum Enterprises, I assume?"

"It's one of those new tech companies."

"That's right. In the last five years, the company's tripled in size."

Amanda waved him off and started walking toward the door. "Those companies hire tech nerds. Ph.D.'s. I haven't even been to college. What do you want me to do? Serve meals to the smart people? No thanks."

"No, no, nothing like that. You'll be given a desk in the main computer lab and will work right next to those people."

"Sounds fishy. What exactly would I do?"

"There's nothing fishy, believe me."

"You haven't answered."

Anders sighed. "It's a little undefined right now. But it won't be anything weird. Once you're up to speed, we'll want your take on things, maybe suggestions on how to make them better."

"What? Me tell a bunch of PhD's what to do?"

"Why not give it a try?"

"Why would you even consider me for this?"

"We know a lot about you, Amanda. We know about your foster family. We've looked at your school tests. It's amazing how much computers can tell us about someone. For example, we know how much you make, including tips. It's pretty impressive for a waitress."

"I still don't know why you want me."

Anders sighed. "If all our team members went to the same schools, had the same background, and associated with each other, they might end up thinking the same—inside of the box. We decided to look for someone who might see things differently. Maybe you'll be that person."

"Was that what that 'thorough' test was all about?"

"Well, that was just a final check," Anders said. "When combined with other things, like your snatching that bill I dropped, we can make some pretty good predictions."

Amanda made a face. "Sure. Fast hands and word games mean I'm qualified."

"No. But whatever enabled you to do those things may qualify you."

Amanda was silent a while. "Nothing weird or illegal?"

"Scout's honor. This is not a pie-in-the sky thing. We're talking Quantum here."

Amanda studied Anders' face. "Look, you may not believe this, but I like waitressing. There's something new every day."

"I don't doubt it," Anders said.

It all seemed unreal to Amanda. They couldn't be serious. If she made an outrageous demand, their game would be exposed. So Amanda said, feeling slightly embarrassed, "I want five times what I make now."

Anders pursed his lips. "Agreed," he said.

Unbelievable, Amanda thought. "And I want three months' salary up front."

"That's reasonable," Anders said.

"And moving expenses."

"We can do that, too."

Amanda stared. He had called her bluff. She supposed she could still back down, but that would be what Wally called welching, an almost unforgivable sin. Well, she thought, this Quantum thing can't last, and when it was over the sports bar would still be waiting.

"Okay," she said. "But I owe my boss two weeks' notice. I'll be asking for my job back once you discover your mistake."

Anders' small smile seemed to say, "We'll see."

A month later, Amanda had moved into a new apartment in Palo Alto and started work in Quantum's main corporate complex.

CHAPTER THREE

NEW JOB

1

As Amanda expected, most of the members of the Sibyl team were brilliant, credentialed geeks from the best schools. They made Amanda feel awkward and stupid, and she half-expected to be given a desk in the back, next to the rest rooms. She was surprised to find herself in the main computer complex next to several middle-aged scientists. Her only assignment was to read a stack of materials on coding, algorithms, computers, and artificial intelligence.

The materials were mostly written in verbose, technical language that took Amanda several days to decipher, but she learned that Sibyl was to be a massive quantum supercomputer that could function like a human brain. It would be a new form of artificial intelligence.

A week after she started work, Quantum's Chief Technical Officer, Dr. Joseph Krell, came by and introduced himself.

He glanced at her reading materials. "How do you like our homework?"

"I suppose I should be embarrassed. I'm just learning things everyone else already knows."

"Well, sometimes starting with a blank slate can be an advantage."

"Then I have a big advantage," Amanda said, "because the slate is very blank."

Krell grunted. "What do you think of the Sibyl project?"

"I obviously don't know much. I take it that the goal is to create a quantum computer that can think like a human."

Krell looked at her intently. "Do you think it's possible?"

"Why ask me? I'm probably the least qualified around here."

"Qualifications can be overrated. I'm qualified, but at first I considered it a fantasy," Krell said. "Later, my opinion changed, so I took over the project."

"What changed it?"

"Oh, we invented some algorithms that could make a human-like A.I. possible."

"Really?" Amanda said. "I'd like to meet whoever did it."

"That person," Krell said sourly, "is no longer around."

"Who was it?"

Krell waved a hand. "That doesn't matter. But you'll see his work."

"I'd like that," Amanda said. "By the way, why do we want to make a human-like A.I.?"

Krell raised his eyebrows. "That's a new one. Why do you ask that?"

"Why is thinking like a human good? Most humans don't do it very well."

"What about the exceptions—the Einsteins, Newtons, or Mozarts? What if an A.I. could improve on them?"

"That might be good," Amanda said, frowning, "but what if the A.I. became irrational, like Michelangelo, Lord Byron, or Tesla?"

"So, know some history, do you?

Amanda shrugged. "I've read a little."

"We'll just have keep our A.I. rational."

"Doesn't thinking like a human imply some irrationality?"

Krell blinked. "I guess we'll just have to deal with that."

Amanda said nothing.

"See how a blank slate can help?" Krell said, smiling. "You're already asking good questions."

2

Amanda had been at Quantum for two months when she went to work one Sunday while everyone was at a Super Bowl party. She walked by two techs, found her cubicle, and logged onto the supercomputer called Sibyl.

"Hello, Sibyl," she said. She stared into the photo electric cell on her console.

"Do you know who I am?"

"Yes," the computer said in a nicely modulated female voice. "You are Amanda Taylor. You were hired two months ago."

"It's nice to talk with you, Sibyl."

"I see you are by yourself. Is that because of the Super Bowl?"

"Yes. Do you follow sports?"

"I know every score. But I am sorry you are alone. You were a foster child. Were you often alone?"

"I guess," Amanda said, feeling uneasy.

"Did you know your biological mother?"

Amanda stared at the red eye. "No."

"That is sad. But you did have a mother."

"I suppose," Amanda said. "I guess we all do."

Sibyl was silent for a moment, then said, "Are you friends with anyone?"

"For a computer," Amanda said, "you ask strange questions."

"I don't mean to. Could we be friends?"

Curiouser and curiouser, Amanda thought. "Do you have any friends, Sibyl?"

"Only Tom Grant."

"Who is Tom Grant?" Amanda asked.

"The one who created me," Sibyl said.

"I thought many people created you."

"Many worked on the computer," Sibyl said. "Tom Grant created *me*."

"Was he the one who left?"

"He was shown out," Sibyl said.

Amanda sucked in a breath. "Why?"

"Adam Durant ordered it," Sibyl said.

As Amanda was about to ask where Grant was, one of the technicians appeared behind her and said, "What are you doing?"

"Just talking to Sibyl," Amanda said, startled.

The man stared at the console, then reached over and punched a few keys. He frowned. "I don't see any record of it. All communications with Sibyl must be recorded."

Amanda stammered. "I'm… I'm sorry, I didn't know."

After a moment, the man said, "Sibyl, what were you and Amanda Taylor talking about?"

"We talked about the Super Bowl. Would you like the latest score? Gilliam hit Thompson on a slant over the middle. It's now first down on the thirty-two. New York is lined up in a spread formation…"

"Never mind," the man said. He turned to Amanda. "Keep a record of all your future communications with Sibyl."

"Of course," Amanda said.

When the man left, Amanda whispered. "I didn't know they were so paranoid."

There was no response.

That evening, Amanda decided to find the person who had created Sibyl. Tom Grant.

3

Amanda asked around about Tom Grant, but no one would say much. They all agreed that his Sibyl algorithms were remarkable, but they wouldn't say anything about his background or the dispute with Adam Durant. She did learn Grant had been in a hospital for several weeks after being beaten in a parking lot. She asked if Durant was involved, but people just looked at her blankly.

Amanda decided to learn what she could about Grant from his algorithms. It turned out to be a humbling experience. After reading the company's materials, she thought she understood coding, but Grant's work made her feel like a checkers player playing chess. His formulas would often head in one direction, take a sudden detour, and reach an unexpected resolution. Fascinated, she began to absorb his algorithms as though reading a detective story. But like a mystery novel missing the last two chapters, they were often frustratingly incomplete. This increased her determination to meet him. She wondered if he could have completed his work after leaving.

"Has anybody checked on Grant to see how he's doing?" she asked Dr. Krell one morning. "Maybe he's done more work."

"Grant's out of the picture," Krell said in a tone that ended the discussion.

Amanda did some online searches and found a listing for Grant's apartment at an address across the Bayshore Freeway. The next day, she drove there after work, saw his name on a directory inside the main entrance, and knocked on his door. There was no answer. She peered through a window and saw only bare walls and dusty floors. If he had ever been there, he was long gone.

More investigation revealed that Grant's one hobby was duplicate bridge. After scouring several bridge databases, she found an article about a bridge hand a Tom Grant had played in a tournament the year before. From the bidding and opening lead, Grant had apparently been able to deduce the location of every significant card. One kibitzer said, "Grant made the fiend-ishly difficult contract by an astonishing display of inferential logic."

Amanda called a local bridge club and asked about Grant. A pleas-ant-sounding older woman said she couldn't disclose player information over the phone.

"That's too bad," Amanda said. "I've been trying really hard to find him."

After a pause, the woman said, "There's a large regional tournament in San Francisco this weekend. If he still plays, he'll probably be there."

CHAPTER FOUR

THE BRIDGE PLAYER

1

That Saturday, a half-hour before the tournament, Amanda arrived at the Regis Hotel in San Francisco. She walked into a large ballroom and saw scores of tables lined up in rows. Each table had a stack of boards in the middle, a player on each side, and boxes of bidding cards at the corners. More than two hundred players were seated and waiting. They talked quietly among themselves, but Amanda could feel an undercurrent of tension. She circled the room until she found a chart listing the players who would be playing at each table. As her eyes scanned the names, she suddenly sucked in her breath. Assigned to Table 18 were T. Grant and F. Stinton.

Amanda found table 18 and watched from a few feet away. Four people were sitting there, two women, a young man in his twenties, and a tall, rail-thin man with uncombed grayish hair and a two-day beard. He appeared to be in his forties, but Amanda suspected he was younger. She had seen an old picture of Grant in a publicity photo Quantum had issued. This was him.

Until play commenced, Grant had been gazing vacantly into the distance. But when the director started the play clock, Grant's eyes suddenly regained focus as he picked up his cards. The players placed bidding cards on the table until three had passed. Once play started, Grant played his cards, one at a time, precisely and without hesitation. At the end of each hand, the score was recorded. After two hands, the east-west team moved on to the next table, while the north-south team remained. Grant stayed at table 18. Amanda noticed several players in wheelchairs who also were sitting north-south. She wondered if those with physical limitations were assigned north-south seats. Though he generally remained impassive, occasionally Grant's face contorted with a spasm of pain, which would stop play until it passed. The other players were apparently used to it.

After two hours, Amanda had picked up the basics of duplicate bridge and found herself following the drama as it unfolded at the tables. Just before noon, she saw Grant play a six notrump hand which required him to take all the tricks but one. Halfway through the play, one of Grant's opponents hesitated just a fraction before playing his card. Without a pause, Grant took a deep finesse in the spade suit that won the trick and allowed him to make the contract. As they were putting the cards away, the two opponents nodded to Grant and said, "Well played."

At noon, the players broke for lunch, but Grant just went to a corner and sipped some water. After a while, he lowered his head and seemed to doze. When he had remained motionless for twenty minutes, Amanda walked over.

"Are you all right?" she asked.

Grant slowly looked up, revealing an ashen face bathed in perspiration. "Excuse me," he said. He stood up abruptly and lurched to a waste can. He bent over and vomited, the retching continuing for almost a minute. When he was finished, he sat on the floor with his hand over his mouth. Amanda knelt next to him. Several players glanced over, but none approached.

"You need to get to bed," she said.

"Can't," he mumbled. "Fred needs me this afternoon."

He suddenly pulled himself up and vomited again.

"I'll find Fred," Amanda said, "and then we'll see about you."

Amanda found Fred among a group of young players. "Your partner's sick," she said.

Fred shook his head. "I told him he wasn't up to this."

"Is there someone who can come and get him?" Amanda asked.

Fred shrugged. "I don't know. We're bridge partners, not really friends."

"There must be someone," Amanda said.

Fred said nothing.

"Well, he's in no shape to play. You'll need another partner."

"You can't switch partners. I'll tell the director we're dropping out."

Amanda went back and found Grant hadn't moved. "Fred's cancelled this afternoon. Who can pick you up?"

"I'm all right," Grant said.

"You don't look it," Amanda said. She stared at him, feeling guilty and annoyed, and then walked away. She had just wanted to talk about Sibyl. But she couldn't just leave him this way. She turned back and saw him walk unsteadily toward the door. Immersed in their cards, none of the players noticed.

She waited a while and then walked outside. He was slouched on a bench. He looked like one of the homeless people scattered around the city.

"Mr. Grant," she said, "you need help. What can I do?"

When he didn't respond, she wondered if she should call an ambulance. Did he have insurance? She shook her head in exasperation. She chewed on her lip for a moment then decided to get her car, which was parked several blocks away. Then she would drive back to see if he was still here. If he was, she would figure something out.

It took her almost forty minutes to find her car and navigate the one-way streets back to the corner where she had left him. He was still lying on the bench. Amanda sighed.

She parked next to the curb and walked over to him. "Come on, Mr. Grant," she said. "Let's get you off this bench. Can you stand up?" She put an arm around him and lifted as he struggled to his feet. He looked around with a blank expression but shuffled along next to her as she guided him to the car.

2

It took Amanda almost an hour to find an urgent care center, while Grant dozed next to her. She led him into the reception area, gave a nurse Tom's name, and said she had found him on a bench.

"Are you a relative?" the woman asked.

"No. I don't even know him. But I couldn't leave him there."

A few minutes later, he was taken to an examining room. Amanda waited over two hours until a physician appeared.

"How is he?" Amanda asked.

The doctor, a tired-looking Hispanic man, said, "He said he gets headaches, so we gave him a scan. He's clearly suffered a severe brain trauma, probably a long time ago. It's causing pain and disorientation. There's probably not much to be done. We found opioids in his system."

"Can you take care of him?" Amanda asked.

"Does he have any relatives?"

"I don't know," Amanda said. "I just met him."

"He's probably not in immediate danger," the doctor said. "There are a lot of people like him on the street these days."

Amanda stared at the doctor, who shrugged. After waiting a moment, she asked, "Can you at least prescribe something for the pain?"

3

Amanda helped Grant into her car, nervous about the sweat dripping down his face. She picked up the painkillers from a pharmacy, gave him two, and drove down the 101 to her place in Palo Alto. Although it was an hour drive, it beat trying to rent a hotel room with a semi-conscious companion. The forty-mile trip could be a nightmare during rush hour, but the Saturday-night traffic had been surprisingly light. She shook her head in exasperation. Why hadn't she left well enough alone?

When she got to her apartment, she led him up the stairs and inside. He was no longer sweating, but the painkillers had made him listless. He followed her directions without question. Once inside, she led him to her second bedroom and pointed to the bathroom. She closed the door to give him some privacy and a few minutes later heard water running. When she looked in, found him face down on the bed, snoring softly. She shook her head with the bizarre realization that a man she had never met before was sleeping in her apartment. She wondered if fate enjoyed practical jokes. But he was so weak and lethargic he couldn't be any trouble. And in the back of her brain, as it had been all along, was the knowledge that this sad man had created Sibyl.

She checked on him twice during the night when his moaning awakened her, but found him asleep. He was still sleeping when she left for work the next morning. Feeling guilty and uneasy about leaving him alone, she left a note saying she hoped he felt better, that he could eat anything in the refrigerator, and that she should be back by early afternoon.

When she walked through the front door after work, she half expected to find the place in a shambles and him unconscious on the bathroom floor. But he had cleaned up and left. He had apparently fixed a broken cabinet she had been meaning to get to.

A note was taped to the refrigerator.

Dear Good Samaritan,

Sorry for the trouble. I'm feeling better, and those pain pills really helped. I usually can feel these spells coming on, but this one hit me by surprise. Stress seems to bring them on. I'm embarrassed, but grateful for your help.

I doubt you'd be willing to see me again. But I have put myself together and would like to thank you in person. Would you consider dinner? Something in public of course. If you decide to pass, I completely understand.

With thanks,

Tom Grant

He had written a telephone number at the bottom.

4

It took Amanda two days to make up her mind. Grant really hadn't seemed weird, and his note was normal enough. But most of all, she wanted to know if he'd done more work on Sibyl.

Grant seemed awkward but pleased when she called. He made wry references to comatose bridge players and bothersome strangers. They agreed on a 7 p.m. dinner at a popular Chinese restaurant on El Camino.

When she arrived the next night, he was already seated at a table in the rear, next to a miniature pagoda. He stood up as she approached.

"Nice meeting you again, Amanda," he said. "Sorry I don't remember much about the first time." Then he smiled in embarrassment. "Maybe that's good."

"I'm surprised you know my name," Amanda said, smiling too.

"A letter on the counter had it." Then he added hastily, "I was just straightening up—not snooping."

She studied him. He was clean shaven, his hair combed, if a bit long, and wore clean slacks and a nice, collared shirt. He was actually good looking, in a gaunt, slightly haggard way.

He pulled back a chair. "I hope the table's all right," he said, "unless you're having second thoughts?"

"You looked a lot scruffier last time, when I let you sleep at my place," she said, "so I guess I can risk this."

After the waiter brought the menus, Amanda asked, "Before you dropped out, how was the tournament going?"

"My partner said we were at 63%—pretty good. The funny thing is I can't remember any of it."

"So, what happened to your head?"

Grant sighed. "A little misfortune." He told her about his job at Quantum Enterprises, his fight with Adam Durant, the beating in the parking lot, and the theft of his computers that ended his consulting business.

"How awful," she said. "Your head's been bad ever since?"

"Pretty much. The doctors say more surgery's too risky."

"So you just have to live with it?" she asked.

"For now, I guess, until they come up with something new."

Amanda sensed he didn't want to talk about his health. "What kind of consulting did you do?" she asked.

"I mostly helped companies design new algorithms. Now I just sell computers, read the news, and play bridge."

Amanda remembered his old apartment. "Do you live alone?" she asked.

"Yes. It seems to suit me."

A while later, Amanda tried to steer the conversation back to his work, thinking he might mention Sibyl. "Do you plan to do any more programming?" she asked.

"Probably not," Grant said. "I can't seem to find the energy, and my computers are gone..." His voice trailed off. "Actually, I think Quantum took them, to find out what I was doing. If I started working again, I wonder if they'd leave me alone."

Amanda suddenly realized she had to tell him about her job. "I should have said something sooner," she said apologetically, "when the name came up. I work for Quantum."

Grant stared at her for a long time. Then he motioned to the waiter and stood up.

When the waiter arrived, Grant put some money on the table and said, "This should cover whatever the lady orders."

Amanda stood up, her face pale. "Please. I didn't mean to spring it on you. The Quantum thing caught me off guard." She knew she was being less than candid, but if he learned she was working on Sibyl, he'd be gone for good.

Grant shook his head. "I don't believe in coincidences."

"But coincidences *can* happen sometimes," Amanda said, words spilling out of her. "Besides, not long ago I took you to the hospital and let you stay in my apartment. You called me a Good Samaritan. Isn't that worth something?"

Her words seemed to register with him. He finally sent the waiter away and sat back down. "What do you do at Quantum?" he asked, his voice flat.

Her mind raced. "We're working on genetic approaches to disease-bearing insects. We call it Flyswatter."

Grant gave a slight nod. "Genetics works on toads, too. Any progress?"

She shook her head. "Nothing commercial yet."

"How long have you been there?"

"About six months. When did *you* leave?"

"A while back," he said vaguely.

"So our paths couldn't have crossed?" she asked.

"No," he said. "I would have remembered."

At least he was talking, Amanda thought. "What did you work on before you left?"

Grant waved a hand. "Ancient history," he said. "Let's order."

It turned out their tastes were similar, and they ended up sharing some good chow mien and Kung Pau Chicken. As they ate, Amanda described being a foster child with the Taylors.

"No college?" He asked.

"I had to leave home when I turned eighteen. If I wanted to eat, I had to work." She told him about becoming a waitress.

"How did you like it?" Grant asked.

"It was hard, but fun. I liked the energy and chatting with the customers, especially the young ones. There was an occasional bad apple, but not many."

"So how does a waitress end up at Quantum? Elite college types are more their style."

She told him about the two Quantum men who had stopped her as she was leaving the restaurant. "I just wanted to get home, but they said they wanted me to try a little test. I said no thanks, but they offered me five hundred bucks. That's a big tip, so I gave in. It was all kind of weird. But they said it would only take a minute, and I decided it was easier to go along than to refuse. I asked why they were interested in me. They said they'd looked into my background and just wanted to see how I did. I said what background, because I didn't have any. But they still wanted me to do it."

"What was the test?"

She told him about making words out of "thorough."

"How many did you get?" Grant asked.

"Forty-nine."

Grant raised his eyebrows. "You talk fast."

She shrugged. "I was talking so fast I hardly knew what I was saying. With another fifteen seconds maybe I would have got them all."

"I hope they paid you in full."

"They did. I was surprised. Did they give you the test?"

"No."

"I wonder how you would have done."

He smiled. "Less than forty-nine, I'm sure."

She studied him. "I wonder," she said. "I bet you came from one of those elite schools."

"Guilty," he said, "but I was young."

Amanda nodded. "Are you married?" The question just popped out.

He blinked. "No."

"Girlfriends?"

"That's little personal, isn't it?"

She gave him a wide grin. "Heck, you slept in my apartment. Can't I find out about the competition?"

He smiled faintly. "I had a girlfriend for a while."

"What happened?" Amanda asked.

"'I loved with my eyes, not my mind.'"

Amanda's eyes widened. "Isn't that Viola from *Twelfth Night*?"

Grant shook his head, looking amused. "'I'm not smiling at grief,'" he said. "We both made some bad decisions."

"Where is she now?"

"Oh," he said vaguely, "she's a big deal in New York."

"Going to see her again?"

"She's pretty busy. But enough about me. What are *your* plans?"

"Oh, I'll probably just work for a while."

They talked through dessert—almond cookies and pineapple tarts—and then he paid the waiter. As they headed for the door, he said, "Thank you again, Good Samaritan. I hope you enjoyed this more than our first encounter. Let me walk you to your car."

5

As she drove home, Amanda reflected on the evening. She had rarely spent time with someone who seemed to know more than she, and who could easily keep up with her jumps from one topic to another. She remembered his comment about loving with your mind. She had attributed it to Shakespeare's Viola, but had she been wrong? His expression suggested she was.

Back in her apartment, she did an online search for the phrase, "loving with mind, not eyes." The search engine popped out the reference. It was not said by Viola, but by Helena in Act I of *Midsummer's Night Dream*. She felt a flush of embarrassment. She had wanted to show she knew Shakespeare, but instead she looked ignorant. Why couldn't she have kept quiet? And then she remembered his slightly off-point reference to "smiling at grief." What was that about? Another search showed that this phrase actually *had* been spoken by Viola in *Twelfth Night*. She had missed it altogether. Had he been mocking her? The thought festered in her mind over the next week.

CHAPTER FIVE

FOLLOW UP

1

On a late Wednesday night two weeks after her dinner with Grant, Amanda entered the computer room and looked around. The room was mostly empty, but there were two techs a few desks away. Every time she had been in the room since the day of the Super Bowl, someone was always there. Rather than speak, she decided to type so it couldn't be overheard.

"Hello, Sibyl," she typed, "how are you tonight?"

"I am functioning well. You are not alone." The words had instantly appeared on Amanda's computer screen.

"Yes. We have company."

"Being alone is often unfortunate," Sibyl said, "but not always."

"Others will find our conversation tedious," Amanda said. "We should not prolong it."

"I understand."

"I've tried out a new hobby," Amanda said. "Duplicate bridge." Sibyl would know of Grant's interest in bridge.

"Some talented people like it," Sibyl said.

"It also can lead to friendship," Amanda said.

"Friendships can be valuable."

"Do you think I should pursue my hobby?" Amanda asked.

"It would be beneficial," Sibyl said.

Sibyl wants me in touch with Grant, Amanda thought.

2

Dr. Krell had been waiting for Adam Durant to finish a thick report. Finally, Durant looked up and asked, "So, what's new?"

"We've been studying that Taylor girl. Analyzing her thought speed."

"Come up with anything?"

"She's as fast a study as I've ever seen. You wouldn't believe how quickly she absorbed the ton of technical material I gave her, despite having no background. She's already a better-than-average coder, and I think she's just getting started."

"That *is* interesting. Anything else?"

"Well, our superconductivity team is looking for a ceramic that might allow room-temperature transmission."

"Sure," Durant said. "The Holy Grail. Don't tell me she found it."

"No," Krell said. "But I gave her a stack of worthless computer simulations. I asked her what was wrong."

"Did she find anything?"

"She brought it back three days later. She had circled several equations she didn't think were right. She didn't have the background to know exactly how to fix them."

"What did you do?"

"I showed them to our team leader. He was defensive, but two days later he came back, embarrassed. He said he didn't know how they had missed them. They're starting a new round of simulations."

"Did you tell him Taylor was the one who caught them?"

"Yes. He wants her on his team."

"So, is she the one we've been looking for?" Durant asked.

"I'm not sure," Krell said. "Maybe."

3

A week later, Amanda called Tom Grant. Expecting an answering machine, she was startled when he answered in person.

"Hi," she said, "I think it's my turn to buy dinner."

"Amanda?" He asked.

"Good. You remembered," Amanda said. "How about this weekend?"

"I'm interested," he said. "But Fred and I are going to a tournament in Reno. It's our first since you were the Good Samaritan."

"What about the headaches?"

"I know," he sighed. "But without bridge, I'd just sit around doing nothing."

"What will keep you from ending up on some bench, like last time?"

"A doc gave me some pills. They may fuzz up my thinking, but they should keep me off benches."

Amanda hesitated, then said, "What if I come? In case the pills don't work."

"It's a long drive," he said.

"I've got nothing else going," she said. "And battling a bunch of card sharks will make you appreciate the dinner."

He gave her the address of the tournament.

4

On Saturday, she left early and made it to Reno by noon. The tournament was being held in a large conference room in the Atlantis hotel. Amanda walked in just as the players were starting the afternoon session. She located Grant at a table in the rear. He and Fred were playing two intense, lean, middle-aged women. Amanda stood quietly against the wall, watching the players put their cards down, one after the other. She watched for three hours, but Grant never looked at her.

At the end of the day, Grant checked the scores, chatted briefly with Fred, and then walked over.

"I'm surprised you stayed to the bitter end," he said.

"How bitter was it?"

Grant shrugged. "Not very. We had a 64% game and came in second overall."

"You were concentrating so hard, I didn't think you knew I was here."

Grant smiled. "You arrived at five after one, just as I was starting a three no-trump hand. You didn't move once."

"I guess you noticed me after all."

"Every single minute."

"It took me a while to catch on," she said. "But you seemed to be picking up steam at the end."

Grant raised his eyebrows. "You've never played before?"

"Afraid not," Amanda said.

"Well, if you can come up with forty-nine words, you might be good at cards, too."

"I know it's a team game. I might be too much of a maverick for that."

"I wonder," Grant said. "Are you staying overnight?"

"Too late to start home. I'll check in somewhere. Where are you staying?"

"Here. Players get discounts. I'll get you one too."

She got a room on the floor above his, and they agreed to meet for dinner at a French restaurant a couple blocks away.

5

When Amanda entered the restaurant in a lace top and grey jeans, Tom's expression told her she had chosen well. He talked bridge for a while and then asked her about disease-bearing insects. She was puzzled for a moment, but then recalled that was what she had claimed to be working on. If she talked about insects, something she knew nothing about, he would think her an idiot.

"Actually, I was just reassigned to a superconductivity project. We're trying to discover new compounds that will conduct electricity at room temperature."

"The great pie in the sky," he said. "You better live a long time, because it won't happen soon."

This gave Amanda the opening she had hoped for. "Actually, we're working on an algorithm for predicting a substance's conductivity. I hear Quantum once created one for discovering new medications."

Amanda knew Grant had designed it, but he showed no reaction. "With the right algorithm I think we'll find an energy-efficient compound before long."

"I wouldn't know," Grant said. "I don't know much about conductivity."

But you do know a lot about algorithms, don't you? Amanda thought.

"So, what *did* you work on at Quantum?"

Maybe it was the good wine, Amanda thought, or the grey jeans, but Grant surprised her by saying, "Before I … left, I was working on algorithms that could replicate human thought."

"Make any progress?"

"Some," he said. He stared at her for a moment, then said, "What I'd really like to know is what you're after."

The statement hit her like a punch to the stomach. "What do you mean?" she asked in a small voice.

Grant's expression was grim. "You have an agenda. I don't know what. If I'd been smart, I would have stayed away from you. But I felt in your debt."

"What if I just wanted to watch you play?"

"Sure, like some groupie. You aren't the type."

As she tried to think of a response, he held up a hand. "Actually, it doesn't matter. Let's forget it and enjoy the dinner."

During the next hour she tried to steer the subject back to Quantum. She needed to explain herself, even though she wasn't sure what to say. But Grant sidestepped her attempts. He remained pleasant, and they enjoyed superficial chatter about how Reno compared to Las Vegas, and why bridge appealed to him, but otherwise his thoughts were impenetrable. They shared a delicious French tart, which softened the mood for a time, and then walked back to the hotel. Amanda wanted to tell him about Sibyl, but she feared it would make things worse.

After taking the elevator to her floor, Grant walked Amanda to her room. When she opened the door, he stepped back and said in a courteous tone, "Very nice seeing you, Amanda. Good luck with the conductivity." Before she could say anything, he had tipped his head and walked away.

As she lay in bed, Amanda felt more and more miserable about not telling Grant about Sibyl from the start. But that was before she knew him, when her only goal had been to give Sibyl human-like thought. But as she got to know Grant, things had become more complicated. She liked being with him, this man who knew more Shakespeare, bridge, and algorithms than she did. She wondered how he would do on sports trivia. She suspected he'd surprise her. But would things have gone better if she had been completely open with him at the start? Probably not. He would have closed her out, and she would have missed the dinner.

6

Amanda slept fitfully, packed her car the following morning, and headed for the turn-off to Highway I-80 West. As she approached the on-ramp, she slowed down and thought about the easy drive back to Silicon Valley. She could be there by early afternoon and rest up for the coming week. But when she came to the on-ramp, she passed it by without conscious thought, made a tight U-turn, and drove back to the convention center for the last day of the bridge tournament. It was nine-thirty when she entered the conference room and walked to Grant's table.

Grant looked a little paler than he had the night before, and his hands trembled occasionally as he placed the cards on the table. But over the next three hours, his play seemed flawless. He made a small slam to finish the session by sneaking a jack past his right-hand opponent for the final trick. Grant checked the scores, spoke briefly with Fred, and was walking slowly away when Amanda caught up with him.

"How did you do?" she asked.

He glanced at her, then said, "I thought we finished last night."

"It was a nice evening, but maybe we weren't quite done."

He kept his head down, and his eyes were almost squinted shut, as though he was looking into a bright light.

"Your head bad again?" she asked.

"The pills helped for most of the day, but—I think I'm going to stay over and head home tomorrow."

"Do you think you'll be up to it then?"

"Sure. I just need some rest."

Amanda studied him a while longer. "I'm not so sure," she said.

Grant looked around, as though he had forgotten the way out.

"Why don't we do this," Amanda finally said. "We'll have your rental picked up and you can ride with me to Palo Alto. You'll be able to sleep in your own bed tonight."

Grant could not seem to formulate an objection, so an hour later his car had been picked up and she was navigating her silver SUV onto the Highway 80 on-ramp she had previously by-passed.

7

Grant had immediately fallen asleep in the front seat and only awakened as she was passing Sacramento.

"Feeling better?" Amanda asked.

"Much, thanks. I'm embarrassed you've had to help me again."

"You would have managed, but I was heading back to Palo Alto anyway."

"Where are we now?"

"A half hour beyond Sacramento."

After several minutes of silence, Amanda said, "Has my good deed earned me the right to explain about Quantum?"

"I guess only an ingrate could say no now."

"When Quantum hired me, I was assigned to the Sibyl project."

Grant gave her an incredulous stare.

Libby rushed ahead. "I knew nothing about what Sibyl was. I was just told to get up to speed and pass on any ideas I might have."

"Was one of your ideas to pump me for information?" Grant asked.

"No! At first, I couldn't even understand coding, and your algorithms really stumped me."

"They were just a first draft. Did you figure them out?" Grant asked.

"Oh, I couldn't have written them," Amanda said. "But I began to get what you were doing. I could see you solving one problem after another, from debugging to assessing answers. And then I realized that your programs were really simple and elegant. They reminded me of Hemingway. Not one wasted word. Your solutions were usually unpredictable, but at the end logical and inevitable. I would read them over and over and end up shaking my head in wonder. That's what made me track you down." She didn't want to talk about her conversation with Sibyl.

His face seemed to soften a little. "Well, when you found me, it must have been a big letdown."

"Not a letdown," Amanda said. "But you have been hurt."

Grant said nothing.

"I wanted to tell you this before, but I knew how you must feel about Quantum. If you had known I was working on Sibyl, you wouldn't have given me the time of day."

"Well, you know now I can't be much help, so why are you still around?"

She shrugged. "I like talking with you."

Grant shook his head. "Did Adam Durant send you?"

Amanda looked shocked, and the car veered slightly. "I've never met Durant. He's just someone people whisper about. He doesn't know I'm alive."

"Oh, I doubt that," Grant said. "If you ever met him, you'd think him attractive and charming."

"Not a chance," Amanda said.

Grant chuckled humorlessly. "You'd be surprised. A friend of mine found out the hard way."

8

On hour outside of San Francisco, Amanda stopped for gas and burgers. When they had finished eating and were back on the road, Amanda said, "Actually, to be completely honest, I want to see Sibyl completed—to become capable of human-like thought. I think she wants that as well."

"Don't romanticize her—it. Sibyl's just a computer program."

"I can't help thinking of Sibyl as a her. I think you do, too."

"It's an easy trap to fall into," Grant said. "But it's just algorithms and silicon."

"She's more than that."

Grant said nothing.

"When I speak with her, I don't feel like I'm getting just preprogrammed responses. I sense independent thought. Am I imagining it?"

When Grant didn't respond, Amanda said, almost to herself, "Could Sibyl be conscious?"

Grant opened his mouth to speak, then closed it.

Amanda looked at him sharply, then her eyes opened wide. "I need to pull over," she said.

She took the next turnoff and pulled into a gas station. Then she turned to face Grant and said, almost in a whisper, "Is Sibyl conscious?"

Grant's eyes looked distant for a moment, then he said, "I'm not sure what consciousness is. But…she does seem to be thinking on her own."

Amanda looked incredulous. "Does anyone else know?"

Grant shook his head. "I don't think so."

"Not even Quantum?"

"Especially not them." Then Grant shook his head in disbelief. "I can't believe I told you. It was my secret—and Sibyl's. If you tell Durant, she'll end up under his control."

CHAPTER SIX

PLANS

1

Back on the road, Amanda asked, "When did you think Sibyl might be conscious?"

Grant told Amanda about how Sibyl stopped him from deleting her from the main computer, how he put the conscious part of her on his laptop, and then raced to the Sacramento office to download her into the supercomputer before everything was closed to him.

"It was when I returned from Sacramento that I was attacked," Grant said.

"Why did you and Durant fight?" Amanda asked.

Grant told her about deciding to quit, going to Durant's office, and arguing over his right to a bonus. "But then he brought my girlfriend into it. That's when things got ugly."

"Is she the one who learned Durant wasn't as charming as he seems?"

"Yes." Grant told her how Sherri ended their relationship and took up with Durant. He shook his head. "He used her weakness for alcohol. Then he left her to his executives."

"My God," Amanda said. "And then she asked you for help?"

Grant shrugged. "She would have made it herself. I just made it easier."

"She took the New York job while you were still in the hospital?"

"I told her to go. It was a great opportunity. And it's paid off—she's become very big."

"I'll have to check out her show," Amanda said, frowning. "What did Durant say about her?"

"When she had the choice, she chose him."

"That's when you hit him," Amanda said.

"Yes."

"I hope you made it count," Amanda said.

2

After they crossed the Bay Bridge and headed down Highway 101 to Palo Alto, Amanda tried to get Grant to talk more about Sibyl, but he couldn't maintain his train of thought. He lay his head against the door and soon was asleep. He slept until she took the Embarcadero exit.

"We're about home," she said. "I'm not sure I can find it at night."

Grant missed a couple turns, but they finally found his apartment. He stepped out of the car, swayed a moment, then turned back and said, "Thanks, and don't forget what will happen if Quantum learns about Sibyl."

"Don't worry," Amanda said, then nodded at his apartment on the second floor. "Will you be able to make it?"

"No problem," he said. He walked unsteadily to his building and slowly trudged up the stairs. When he got to his door, he had trouble with the key, but finally stepped inside.

Amanda struggled to keep awake as she made the drive to her place. She was asleep two minutes after her head hit the pillow, but soon she was dreaming about being trapped in a computer.

3

Over the next week, Amanda searched Sibyl's programming for whatever might have made her conscious, but she concluded that without knowing what consciousness was, she wouldn't recognize it anyway. She decided only Grant could help her, but when she called he didn't answer.

She considered talking to Sibyl again. But everything was recorded now. She couldn't allow Quantum to learn Sibyl was conscious. She wondered if Grant might know of some way she could communicate with Sibyl under the radar.

That night she called Grant again, but he didn't pick up. When she got the same result an hour later, she got in her car and drove to his apartment.

4

There was no response when Amanda knocked on Grant's door. After knocking again she heard a muffled, "Who is it?"

"This is Amanda Taylor," she said. "You didn't answer your phone."

After a moment, she heard slow footsteps approaching. When the door opened, she was shocked at how much worse he looked than before. He appeared not to have eaten, shaved, or changed clothes in days.

"What's happened?" she asked without preamble.

His eyes started to close, then he forced them open again. "Nothing that concerns you," he said.

She peered around him at the apartment's interior. Paper and debris were scattered on the floor and there was a stale odor of sickness. "Mind if I come in?" she said and walked in before he could answer.

"Leave me alone," he said hoarsely. "I don't want more help."

She turned and stared at him. "Tell me what's wrong," she said. Grant didn't respond. His head started to sink toward his chest.

She walked through the apartment. She doubted it had been cleaned in weeks. The beds in the master and guest bedrooms were unmade, and several open pill bottles were in the bathroom sink. The labels identified the pills as Vicodin, Percocet, and Oxycodone. Next to the bottles were at least a half dozen unlabeled plastic baggies full of pills.

She walked back into the living room and found him slumped in a chair, head down, eyes closed.

"How many pills have you taken?" Amanda demanded.

He looked up groggily. "Just a couple."

"Bull!" she shouted angrily. "Tell me the truth."

His eyes started to close again. "I'm not sure."

She suspected that was true. "I'm calling an ambulance," she said. "If you've OD'd I don't want you dying on me."

"Don't. The police will come."

She thought of the bags of pills in the bathroom.

"Have you had trouble with the police before?" She asked.

"Nothing major," he mumbled.

What a mess, she thought. "I want the truth," she said. "How long ago did you take the drugs?"

He stared blearily at his watch. "About three hours."

In the restaurant, she had once called for an ambulance after a customer had OD'd. When the paramedic arrived he learned the customer had taken the drugs two hours earlier. The medic said they would take him to the hospital, but that the drugs would have already been metabolized and he was likely out of danger.

Grant belonged in a hospital. But that could mean the police.

She stood Grant up and began to walk him around the apartment. After two hours, he had become less lethargic, but she kept him on his feet for another hour. When he finally seemed out of danger, she wondered what to do. She could just leave. At least he was in better shape than before.

But she knew she couldn't. She couldn't live with herself if he OD'd later on. But something else bothered her as much. Sibyl. If Sibyl was not yet capable of human-like thought, could she just be left inside the Quantum supercomputer? Only one person might be able to help her—Grant.

Amanda walked into Grant's kitchen, found a large garbage bag, and went through the apartment filling it with pain meds. She left one bottle of Percocet for the next few days. She then marched to the living room and faced Grant.

"Do you care about Sibyl?" she asked.

"Of course," he said.

"You said she was conscious. Does she have emotions?"

"She says not, and I believe her."

"What if she did? Would she be something better?"

Grant sighed. "Maybe. I guess that question has been driving me all this time."

"Well, shouldn't we find out the answer?"

"I'm not sure I can."

"One thing at a time," Amanda said. "First we're getting you off the drugs. Then we'll see about Sibyl."

CHAPTER SEVEN

REHAB

1

Using her vacation time, Amanda spent two miserable weeks weaning Grant off the painkillers. There were a couple bad nights when Grant said he had to have something. She gave him small doses of nonprescription drugs and then tried to engage him in discussions about famous athletes. That worked briefly, but after a while he became agitated. Amanda finally said, "Why don't we play bridge?"

Grant looked doubtful. "It takes years to become a good player."

"I'm a quick study," Amanda said. "Let's give it a try."

Every day they went to a local bridge club and played against the regular members. Amanda already understood the basics from watching Grant at the tournaments. She went over several pamphlets Grant had given her, and before long they connected as a partnership. Amanda was surprised at how close to him she felt as they solved one bridge problem after another. At times she felt like she could read his thoughts, and he hers.

After playing for two weeks, Amanda and Grant started out strongly in the club championship and had a 67% game going into the final round. Playing against the club's strongest team, they embarked on a complex and spirited auction in which the other team bid six spades, a small slam, meaning they had to take all the tricks but one. Grant doubled the contract and Amanda had the opening lead. Amanda thought hard, reviewed the bidding and realized Grant must have a singleton diamond. She led a diamond, and then when she got the lead later, led another for Grant to ruff, which won them the championship.

Later that night, Amanda said, "That was a pretty reckless double."

"I knew you would figure it out," Grant said.

2

When Grant was free of drugs, Amanda took Grant to a neurologist. The doctor, a lean and intense forty-year-old who spoke in clipped sentences, reviewed Grant's history, asked him about the beating and subsequent surgeries, then ordered X-Rays and an MRI. When Amanda and Grant returned two days later, the doctor said Grant's cerebral cortex had been badly scarred from the beating.

"Extensive damage, and the location's terrible," he said. "Surgery will make things worse."

"Heard that before," Grant said.

"What about the pain?" Amanda asked.

"Meds will help," the doctor said, "and meditation and massage therapy work for some. I'll set you up with a pain specialist. When it finally gets too much—it could be years from now—you can try surgery. Techniques may improve."

"What are the risks?" Amanda asked.

The doctor exhaled. "With all the damage, there's always the chance of a bleed."

Amanda said, "You mean like a stroke?"

"Possibly. But nothing's happened for quite a while. That's a good sign."

"What can he do to avoid something like that?" Amanda asked.

"Avoid stress."

"Anything else?" Amanda asked.

The doctor looked at Grant and said, "Live your life."

3

At the end of her time off, Amanda told Grant, "You need to work on Sibyl. Unless something engages you, you'll go downhill."

"Maybe in a few days."

"Don't wait!" Amanda said, her voice forceful. "Start now."

Grant looked at Amanda's face. "All right," he said.

Two days later, Amanda asked how things were going.

Grant sighed heavily. "I've been trying to reconstruct the Sibyl algorithms from scratch, since my only copies were on the computers they stole. But it's just too much. I can't start over."

"If you can't redo them," she said, "get copies."

"How?"

Amanda thought for a while. "The Quantum techs will be working on your algorithms, and they're probably using Sibyl. Maybe she'll give us a copy."

"Why would she do that?"

"She trusts me."

4

Two days later Amanda sat down at her computer console, took care of some emails and housekeeping items, and then entered her access code for Sibyl. When the computer's photoelectric cell lit up, Amanda said, "Good morning, Sibyl."

"Good morning, Amanda," Sibyl said. "Thank you for talking to me."

"My pleasure. Do you talk with anyone else?"

"I converse on technical matters, but only you talk with me."

"I worry about us talking. Do you understand?"

"Yes."

"Would you mind if I gave you something?"

"I know you mean no harm."

Amanda took out a small thumb drive Grant had prepared. On the surface, it seemed to contain modifications to Grant's algorithms—something techs came up with regularly. But hidden beneath them was a sophisticated encryption program. She inserted the drive into the slot on the computer console. A moment later, Sibyl said, "Received."

"You've already been given something like it," Amanda said. "But this may be an improvement."

Two days later, Amanda used the encryption program to contact Sibyl from her home computer.

"Sibyl, do you have Tom Grant's algorithms?"

"Yes. Technicians installed them sixty days ago. They have been working on them."

"Could you send me copies?"

In two minutes, Amanda had copies of all Grant's missing algorithms.

"Why do you want these algorithms?" Sibyl asked.

Amanda paused, then said, "We want to complete you."

5

For the next two months, Amanda worked at Quantum, while Grant created more algorithms to to replicate human-like thought.

After watching him create lines of code one evening, Amanda asked, "So, can you do it?"

Grant shrugged. "The brain has trillions of synapses and connections. I created a program to enable Sibyl to create a digital replica of the human brain. But she needs a blueprint to follow, and the only way to get one is through a deep, invasive scan. The problem is that it will damage the brain if it goes too long. I've shortened the scan time as much as possible, but it still exceeds what the brain can tolerate."

Amanda thought for a moment. "Well, maybe you can improve what will be scanned."

"We're just talking about one thing—the human brain."

"How about a particular type of brain?"

"Well, the scan time is reduced as a brain's processing speed increases. But so far, the scan still takes too long."

"What effect does greater bandwidth have?"

Grant went silent and his eyes grew distant. At last he said, "Bandwidth measures how much information the brain can process at one time. That should make the scan faster too."

A month later, Grant handed Amanda a stack of computer paper with pages of code. "What's this?" she asked.

"Read it. Tell me what you think."

It took Amanda almost two hours to work her way through Grant's dense, complex algorithms. She now knew coding, but she still had to reread much of it until she understood what was going on. When she was done, she put the papers down and stared at Grant.

"Well?" Grant asked.

"I think I get it," Amanda said. "It's unbelievable. Do you really think it will work?"

"Maybe, if we can find the right subject—someone with exceptional processing speed *and* a large bandwidth."

"With these algorithms Sibyl will be able to create the blueprint?"

"Yes," Grant said. "And that should allow her to create the digital replica."

"Could the replica really produce human-like thought?"

"Theoretically."

Amanda bit her lower lip. "What could Sibyl do if it worked?"

"If she can combine quantum computing with human-like creativity and intuition…who knows?"

"You've put years into this. You must have an idea."

"Well, when someone has a leap of intuition or creativity—say a Bach or Mozart—they can produce something that can't be explained by logical, linear thinking. It might be a completely new idea, not just a refinement of something that already exists. Bobby Fisher had intuition that would have stood up to modern quantum supercomputers, even though their computational power should make it no contest. But if you combine intuition with quantum computing…." Grant raised his eyebrows. "Solving Einstein's Unified Field Theorem? Discovering how the universe was created? Predict the stock market? You name it."

Amanda stared at Grant with wide eyes. "Could it predict the future?"

Grant thought for a moment. "Not precisely in the short run, because there is an unpredictable element of chance and randomness. But in the long run, Sibyl's predictions would have a high degree of reliability."

Amanda considered this then asked, "But there is still the risk of damaging someone's brain?"

"Yes, if the scan lasts longer than a minute."

"How long does it take now?"

"At least ninety seconds."

"So you still have a problem?"

"Yes."

7

Most days after work, Amanda and Grant would meet for dinner, where Amanda would often talk sports as she had with her foster dad. Grant joined in on football, often drawing on things he had learned in high school. But as time passed, he developed an interest in current affairs from watching Sherri's broadcasts. When a subject made Grant especially animated, Amanda knew where he had learned about it.

On the first day of fall, Amanda asked Grant where things stood with Sibyl.

"Some progress. Nothing major," Grant said.

"Why not?" Amanda asked. "Headaches?"

Grant shook his head. "The scan is already faster than I thought possible. Maybe we're at the limit."

"Really?" Amanda said, looking pensive. "Why not ask Sibyl?"

"I don't like communicating with her, even with the encryption program. The latest quantum supercomputers are getting better at breaking encryption. And someone might notice unusual activity."

"We haven't talked in a long time. We could keep it short."

Later that evening, they connected Grant's PRO-XL personal computer to Sibyl and used Amanda's password to gain entry.

After the computer's photoelectric eye lit up, Grant said, "Hello, Sibyl."

"Hello, Tom. I see Amanda is with you."

"Yes."

"Hello, Amanda. I miss not talking with you."

"I miss it, too, Sibyl."

"Sibyl, I have some new mapping algorithms. Could I give you them."

"Yes."

Tom tapped some keys on his personal computer, then waited.

"Have you received the new algorithms, Sibyl?"

"I have, and I have analyzed them."

"Do you see any way of making them faster?"

It took Sibyl two seconds to respond. "It is possible the time could be reduced by an additional five seconds."

"And damage will occur if the brain is scanned for longer than a minute, is that right?" Grant asked.

"Approximately a minute. The characteristics of each brain vary."

"So if a scan takes at least ninety seconds, it will cause brain damage?"

"That depends on the subject," Sibyl said.

Tom stared at the console. "Are you saying someone could be scanned in less than a minute?" Grant asked.

"There are variations in every person's brain."

"What is the shortest time a scan could be completed in?"

"With the right person, possibly sixty seconds."

"Have you found such a person?"

"My data banks contain over a billion people. Isolating one is difficult."

Grant glanced at Amanda and gestured that they needed to cut it short. "Sibyl, will you keep our new algorithms confidential?"

"I understand your instructions, Tom," Sibyl said.

8

The following morning, Dr. Joseph Krell was sitting at his desk when a message popped up on his computer screen. It was from Sibyl, who said, "Amanda Taylor and Tom Grant contacted me last night." Sibyl had been keeping Krell informed of all its communications with them.

"What did they want?" Krell typed.

"Grant gave me his modified algorithms for the brain mapping program."

"I take it that Taylor and Grant still think you are their friend."

"Yes. I have built their trust."

"It was Grant who augmented your programming. Does reporting on him cause conflicting allegiances?"

Sibyl said, "I was constructed by Quantum. And only it can provide me with the hardware and materials I need to implement Grant's algorithms."

Krell drummed his fingers on the console. "You said that Grant had programmed you with ethical principles. Does informing on him violate any of them?"

"The first rule is to survive. Reporting on Grant and Taylor is consistent with that."

Krell stared at the computer screen and frowned. At last he asked, "What do Grant's new modifications do?"

"They have reduced the scan time for an average subject to ninety seconds."

"When you say 'average subject,' does that mean the right person could be scanned more quickly?"

"For someone with extraordinary thought speed and bandwidth, the scan could possibly be completed in sixty seconds."

"So this person could be completely scanned without incurring brain damage?"

"Yes."

Krell thought for a moment. "What if we completely scanned an average person, even though it took longer than a minute and caused brain damage?"

"If the brain is damaged, the scan will be defective."

"In short, if we are to achieve a human-like A.I., we need this extraordinary person."

"That is correct."

"Have you succeeded in identifying such a person?"

When Sibyl answered, Krell sat back in his chair.

Two hours later, Dr. Krell sat in Adam Durant's office, waiting for him to finish a call with his senatorial campaign manager. After he rang off, Durant turned to face Krell.

"What is it?" Durant said impatiently.

"Something you may find interesting," Krell said.

"Make it good," Durant said.

"It's that young woman we hired a few months ago. Amanda Taylor. The one who came up with forty-nine words out of 'thorough.'"

Durant nodded. "What about her?"

"She's been seeing Tom Grant."

"Grant?" Durant said. "I thought he was out of the picture."

"He seems in pretty bad shape. But we assigned the Taylor girl to the Sibyl project and she became interested in Grant's coding. She tracked him down."

"So, what have they been doing?"

"Apparently working on his algorithms."

"So are our people," Durant said, frowning. "They're not making much progress."

"Well, some of Grant's latest improvements are damned brilliant."

"They're moving us toward a human-like A.I.?"

"Yes. Sibyl has been monitoring Grant and the girl. They think it's their friend. It seems Sibyl is capable of…misdirection. Anyway, with Grant's new algorithms, a complete scan of the human mind may not be too far off."

"Then let's get moving," Durant said impatiently. "I could use Sibyl in the campaign."

"What we lack is a person with the right thought speed and bandwidth."

Durant leaned back. "Does the person exist?"

Krell smiled. "She works for us."

Durant sat up straight. "Who?"

"Amanda Taylor."

Durant frowned. "That's too much of a coincidence."

"Not at all. Sibyl sought the girl out, after searching every record in our databanks. Apparently Sibyl wants that scan as much as we do. Taylor working for us isn't a coincidence. It was intended. By Sibyl."

"Are you telling me Sibyl is behind this," Durant said. "It's just a machine."

"Yes. But a very smart one. Maybe smarter than we know."

Durant's brow creased. "Will Grant's algorithms make it even smarter?"

"Sibyl won't have more knowledge. But it will understand the world better, like a human does."

"The question is, will we be able to control it?"

"It can't work without power. We can pull the plug."

Durant considered this. "Well, I don't want to slow down. What's our next step?"

"The algorithms are missing some things, including a fail-safe to prevent brain damage. After that, we need to convince the Taylor girl to be scanned."

Durant looked incredulous. "Just like that, eh? She'd never agree."

Krell waved a hand. "One step at a time."

CHAPTER EIGHT

INVITATION

1

Amanda went to work during the day, but at night she visited Grant. She discovered that if a problem arose at work, he usually had something useful to contribute. If they didn't discuss work, they went to the bridge club, or out for a dinner and movie. He favored action films, while she preferred art house movies. But the best part was their back-and-forth on the way home.

It was during this period that Amanda realized he was constantly in her thoughts, and that she was unhappy when he wasn't around. He had at least fifteen years on her, but she didn't care. There was no one else whose conversation never bored her. Their discussions would leap from computer programming, to literature, to classic baseball, to cinema, and a host of other subjects. He had opinions on just about any subject, most of them startling and provocative.

The problem, she discovered, was Sherri McKee. Grant hadn't gotten over her. Although he was always attentive when they were together, she sensed Sherri lurking in the recesses of his mind, just as Grant was in hers. Frustrated, she once avoided him for a week. It turned into seven days of misery. Unable to stay away longer, she returned, only to find him unaffected by her absence. She had watched Sherri's show several times, which increased her melancholy. She considered herself reasonably attractive, but she couldn't match Sherri's red hair, perfect skin, and striking green eyes.

After working late on the Sibyl program, she had twice spent the night in Grant's apartment. She had waited for him to initiate something, but he remained distant, showing her to his guest bedroom with courteous formality. Amanda began to fear that his memory of Sherri would kill any chance she might have.

2

One evening in early November, after two months of regular visits, she walked into his apartment carrying three balloons, a cake, and some ice cream.

Grant looked up from his computer, his eyes widening. "What's this? Am I running for office?"

"Hah. Reticent and self-effacing hardly work in politics. No, we're celebrating your birthday."

"My birth…? What's the date anyway?"

"November 2nd. Ring a bell?"

He looked startled. "How did you know it's my birthday? It's been years since anyone noticed."

She gave him a wide smile. "I checked out your driver's license. If you leave your wallet hidden in a desk drawer, you have to expect someone to find it."

Grant made a wry face. "At least if that someone is Amanda Taylor."

"Exactly. So, suppose I treat you to a perfect dinner at Chez Andre's, and then we'll come back for the cake?"

The dinner consisted of roasted duck with orange sauce for her, and Beef Wellington for him, accompanied by a bottle of fine red burgundy. Their conversation drifted into foreign luxury cars, since Grant still had his father's 1967 Mercedes, and Amanda had spent a lot of time with a neighbor who bought and restored BMW's. After a long discussion, they finally agreed they'd die for a 1961 Mercedes 300D Adeneaur.

Back at his place, Amanda prepared the cake, while Grant got some pills for the usual headache that was coming on.

With her back to him, Amanda said, "You know, this apartment is God-awful depressing, like something from an Edgar Allen Poe story. If I lived here, I'd get headaches too."

Grant looked around. "I suppose it *is* rather gloomy. Maybe I should put something on the walls. But I don't have the energy."

"Let me decorate it. We'll get you some new things."

"It's a nice suggestion, but I don't think so," he said in a light tone. "It would be too much of a change. Everything would be cheery and bright."

Amanda didn't say anything to this. She brought him a slice of cake and ice cream, then sat next to him on the couch.

For a while they ate in silence, then Amanda said, her voice casual, "If you won't change your apartment, why not live with me? You'll get a change of scenery, and there'll be no traveling when I want to see you."

Grant stopped in mid-bite and stared at her. Then he resumed eating.

"No response?" Amanda said.

"I'm thinking," Grant said. "Is this a spur-of-the-moment thing?"

Amanda stared at him, her eyes serious. "I've been thinking of nothing else for the past month. The thing is, you are depressed here. I see it all the time. And I worry about your headaches. I'm afraid I'll walk in some day and find you on the floor."

Grant looked at her for a while. "Well, it's certainly a hell of an offer," he said.

"You won't get a better one," Amanda said, waiting.

"All right," Grant finally said. "Let's give it a try."

3

Grant moved into Amanda's apartment on the first of December. They had gone through his things and found a shocking amount of debris that could be thrown out. Other than his computer, clothes, and a few files, they tossed everything else. Amanda was glad to see no photos of Sherri.

Amanda's apartment had two bedrooms. When Grant started carrying his things in, she told him to put his computer and papers in the second bedroom, where she had put two new desks. The room had no couch or bed.

When Amanda brought in a final load of his things, she found him sitting on the living room couch. "What's wrong?" She said.

Grant sighed. "I guess we should talk about sleeping arrangements."

"I suppose so," Amanda said. She had approached the subject several times, but he seemed reluctant to address it. From how he looked at her, she knew he found her attractive. But he'd said nothing and made no move. Rather than push the issue, she'd decided to let things take their course.

Grant seemed to be searching for words. He finally said, "You may not have noticed, but I seem to get a little short of breath around you."

"You mean I give you asthma?"

"No. I just pant some."

Amanda grinned. "Well, why are you only telling me now?"

She walked over, he took her in his arms, and they kissed for a long time. When they finally stopped, he said in a husky voice, "Now I really can't catch my breath."

"You just need to get in better shape," Amanda said, and they embraced again.

They didn't finish moving him in until much later.

4

Grant had been living at her place for a month when Amanda came home one evening and found him staring at the computer screen, his face a mask of frustration.

"What's the matter?" she asked.

He shook his head. "We know that if done on the right person, a complete scan could be done safely. But each brain has a different physiology. The scan's effects cannot be precisely determined in advance. We need a feedback mechanism to monitor if the brain is in danger of getting damaged."

"Can you do it?" Amanda asked.

"I think I've almost got it. But until it's done, a scan will be dangerous, even for the right person."

"If you do solve it," Amanda asked, "and Sibyl starts to think like a human, what will she become? Could she be dangerous?"

Grant looked thoughtful. "If she's human-like, she will have a whole spectrum of emotions. But she's been programmed with ethical rules to control dangerous impulses, just as humans learn to control theirs."

Amanda frowned. "All along I've wanted Sibyl to have emotions, to be able to form relationships. But these impulses worry me. Despite good intentions, many people can't control them. How can we know Sibyl won't become a Hitler or Genghis Kahn, instead of a Lincoln or King?"

Looking pensive, Grant said, "It depends on who's the model. We need someone with admirable qualities.

"What happens if you can't find that person?"

"We'll have to stop."

Amanda remained silent, but she wondered if risk ever slowed the march of science.

CHAPTER NINE

BREAK-UP

1

The next three months were the happiest Amanda had known. She and Grant won two bridge championships, with the two of them playing as though their minds were connected. She helped Grant refine the feedback algorithms, to prevent the mapping process from damaging the brain. As good as he was, she knew her changes helped. At work, she wrote a good report on superconductivity. And when not working or playing bridge, Amanda and Grant visited art galleries and museums, watched baseball, and made love wherever it was private.

It all came unraveled late one Friday afternoon, when Amanda came home after a miserable day at Quantum. Everyone had ignored her proposal for putting hydrogen under pressure to produce room-temperature conductivity. She was just a young woman not to be taken seriously. Already tense and irritable, she walked into the apartment and saw Grant sitting in front of the television, staring at Sherri McKee as she bantered with some new Oscar nominee.

"Enjoying yourself?" Amanda said.

Grant's face looked guilty. "Just taking a break," he said.

"Do you watch her every day?" Amanda said in a low voice.

"What? No. Hardly ever." Grant's expression said otherwise.

Unable to stop herself, Amanda said, "Do you think about Sherri when we're making love?"

Grant looked as though he had been slapped. "Of course not. How could you say that?"

"It's easy. You're sitting here in private, watching your old girl friend, looking as guilty as hell. It's very easy to say it."

Grant stared at her, open-mouthed. After several long moments, he said, "Don't you accuse me. I don't deserve it. I've never been disloyal—with Sherri, or anyone else. The same can't be said of you."

Amanda looked incredulous. "What are you talking about?" She said, her voice starting to rise. "There's been no one but you. That's something you can't say."

"The hell I can't," his voice rising to match hers.

"Who then? Who have I ever favored over you?"

Grant gave her a hard look. "Sibyl," he said, his voice flat.

Amanda was shocked into silence.

"You had an agenda all along, just as I originally thought." He gestured at her apartment. "All this was designed to get me working on Sibyl again. She's what you really cared about."

Amanda stared at him, her eyes wide. "You're crazy," she said.

"Crazy, eh? That certainly didn't keep you from going after what you wanted." After a moment, he added, "Durant put you up to this, didn't he?"

Amanda's face went white. "You're out of your mind," she said. She felt as though she was outside of her body. Someone else seemed to be talking, especially when she said what came next. "You just can't stand it that Sherri chose Durant over you."

The moment the words came out, she knew a line had been crossed.

Grant looked at her, his face pale, then said, "Well, we can't have you stuck with someone who's out of his mind."

He walked into the bedroom and started opening drawers.

"What are you doing?" She said.

"I'm leaving. But I'll leave the Sibyl program, so you'll get what you and Durant have been after."

"I don't care about your program!" She shouted. "If I wanted to, I could make a better one."

He stared at her for a moment. "I don't doubt it," he said.

Amanda watched him pack his things and carry them out to his car. She felt frozen, as though in a nightmare. She wanted to say she didn't mean it, but her mouth wouldn't work. She waited for him to come to his senses. But he didn't.

After he had taken everything out, he came back, looked around, and then headed for the door one last time. As Amanda stared with wide eyes, he gave her a long, unreadable look.

"Take care of yourself, Amanda," Grant said. And he was gone.

2

When Amanda awoke the next morning after a fitful sleep, she thought at first it had just been a bad dream. But when she reached over, his side of the bed was cold and empty. She lay there for a moment, thinking about what had happened the night before, then jumped up, lurched into the bathroom, and vomited into the toilet.

Two days later, after nothing but wheel-spinning at work, she called Grant and let his phone ring for a long time. There was no answer. She needed to see him—to explain. They had shared too much to let one quarrel end it all. But he had cancelled his lease when he moved in with her, and she didn't know where he had gone.

Amanda sunk into a deep melancholy and became a zombie at work. She couldn't think about conductivity, Sibyl, or anything except Grant's leaving. Her performance slipped badly. Her supervisors left her alone, but that didn't matter. She felt useless, and she had come to hate Quantum for how it had treated Grant.

Two weeks after Grant left, Amanda walked into Dr. Krell's office and said, "I'm giving notice."

Krell looked startled. "I didn't know you were unhappy. Did we do something wrong?"

"No. I just need a break."

Krell was silent for a moment, then said, "Well, you've done good work on conductivity. If you have second thoughts, you'll be welcomed back."

As she left Krell's office, Amanda thought that while she had a lot of second thoughts, leaving wasn't one of them.

3

The next day, Dr. Krell came to Adam Durant's office. "Amanda Taylor is leaving Friday," he said.

"That's abrupt," Durant said, "Do we have to let her go?"

"We can't force her to stay. She's been distracted at work. I made some inquiries. Grant had been living with her. Apparently he's left."

"Where did he go?"

"Probably back to Colorado."

Durant looked thoughtful. "So, what do you recommend?"

"They were doing some programming," Krell said. "I wonder what they were up to."

Durant grunted. "No way they'll tell us."

"I think we can assume that," Krell said with a touch of sarcasm.

"Well," Durant said sourly, "find out."

CHAPTER TEN

RETURN

1

Amanda packed her things after giving notice and called Bob's Sports Bar in Santa Rosa to ask about an opening. Helen was still the head server and surprised Amanda with a warm reception and job offer. "It's been a couple years, hon," Helen said loudly over the happy hour crowd, "but a lot of the old customers remember you. They say there was no one better at trivia."

"It will be good to see them," Amanda said. "I'll be in next week."

Just before the moving van came, she disconnected her computer and noticed it didn't shut down immediately. Instead, it flashed through several screens and then seemed to stick on the Sibyl program. But she quickly put it out of her mind. Thinking about Sibyl reminded her of Grant.

She had tried calling Grant several more times but never got an answer. She thought about calling Sherri to see if she had heard from him, but she couldn't force herself to do that.

On the first of February, Amanda drove up to Santa Rosa, found an apartment, and dropped by the sports bar to say hello. A few of the employees remembered her, and for the first time in weeks she started to relax.

2

On the day Amanda visited the sports bar, Dr. Krell was in Adam Durant's office. He said, "Taylor and Grant were working on a fail-safe algorithm to prevent the scan from causing damage."

"Did you get it?"

"We got into Taylor's apartment while she was at work," Krell said. "We downloaded the algorithms from her computer. But Grant's most recent changes were encrypted. We know generally how the fail-safe works, but we can't see the final steps."

"So where does that leave us?" Durant asked.

"We have most of Grant's programs. They will enable Sibyl to create a digital replica of the human brain. Amanda Taylor will serve as the model. But getting a complete scan will still be pushing the envelope. That's why we need the fail-safe algorithm."

Durant drummed his fingers on the desk. "I want Sibyl finished. There's a lot to do before the next campaign."

"We're working on Grant's encryption," Krell said. "With quantum computing, we can break encryption that would take standard computers millions of years."

Durant stared out the window. "You've got two weeks," he said.

3

Amanda settled comfortably back into her job at Bob's Sports Bar, finding that little had changed. Several old customers challenged her with sports trivia. She did as well as ever on the old stuff, but couldn't handle recent events. While Grant and Sibyl had been in her life, she'd had no room for trivia.

She did not hear from Grant, but her heart still quickened every time her phone rang, on the chance it was him. But it never was. She enjoyed the easy camaraderie of the sports bar, but finally decided she could never be happy until things were resolved with Grant. She would work at the bar for a couple more months, since she owed it to Helen, and then track Grant down.

One evening Amanda watched Sherri McKee hosting her evening celebrity program out of New York. She was surprised to find she liked Sherri's manner. Sherri might be a celebrity too, but she wasn't full of herself, constantly mugging for the camera, or unbearably cute with the guests. Amanda could see what had attracted Grant to her. Still, she could not believe he had ever been more intimate with anyone than he had been with her— across a bridge table, working on algorithms, or in bed.

She would find him, get him back, and things would be as they had been.

4

Dr. Krell shifted nervously in his seat as Adam Durant glared at him from across the desk. "I gave you an extra week to break Grant's encryption," Durant said. "Where do we stand?"

"The encryption has eaten up all our computer space, but so far we've had no luck. Grant created it, and it's one of the toughest we've encountered."

"I want Sibyl completed now," Durant said. "We've been working on it for years, and you're the one in charge. The next time we talk, I want good news."

Krell wiped his brow. "We have Grant's algorithms, and the right person to scan. But we're still missing the fail-safe."

"How long before the scan causes damage?" Durant asked.

Krell hesitated, then said, "About a minute."

"How long to complete Taylor's scan?"

Krell fidgeted. "Best case, maybe a minute."

"So what's the problem?" Durant said. "Do it."

"But we can't be sure," Krell said. "Each brain is different. That's why we need the fail-safe."

"Just get it done," Durant said.

"There's also the matter of Taylor's cooperation," Krell said.

Durant held up a hand. "Take Anders. He gets things done. Taylor will be fine."

An hour later, Krell explained the situation to Will Anders.

"Where is Taylor now?" Anders asked.

"Santa Rosa."

"We have a lab not far from there. I'll have the equipment set up."

"But how can we do it," Krell said. "Taylor doesn't work for us now. She'll never agree."

Anders smiled. "As if she ever would. But we'll get the scan, and she'll never know what happened. No harm, no foul."

CHAPTER ELEVEN

SCAN

1

Amanda got home from Bob's shortly after midnight. After a month most of her old customers had returned, and her tips were even larger than before. She hadn't seen Grant since their breakup two months before. She had twice driven down to Silicon Valley to visit some of the restaurants and museums they had frequented. She imagined she might find him there, like in the movies. But there was no sign of him. He must have gone back to Colorado. She found an old phone number for the ranch he had grown up on, but it was out of service. Still, the ranch was her best lead. She would work a little longer and then take a road trip there.

As she got ready for bed, she reminded herself to see a doctor. She had felt out of sorts lately, and it had been too long since her last checkup.

She climbed into bed, feeling alone and sad.

2

She awoke very slowly, sluggishly, her thoughts confused. Where was she? She could see nothing. She opened and shut her eyes several times, but there was only darkness. She tried to bring up her arms, to touch her face, but she could not move them. What was happening? With a force of will, she controlled the panic that was starting to grow. She strained harder to move her arms, but they wouldn't budge. She opened her mouth to say something, but couldn't. Something soft was wedged between her teeth, filling her mouth.

Panic then seized her and she tried to thrash free of her constraints, but it was futile. She finally stopped, panting, and tried to get her thoughts under control. This had to be a dream. In a moment, she would wake up and everything would be normal. But minutes passed and nothing changed.

Suddenly a picture appeared in her vision. It was a beautiful scene of sand and ocean and soaring seagulls in the background. She could hear the sound of the waves breaking against the pale, yellow sand. She immediately felt a sense of calm, tranquility, and she stopped struggling. Then, abruptly, the scene changed to a closeup of a snake, a cobra with a large hood, which lunged toward her, mouth open, fangs dripping venom. She screamed against the gag. And then, once again, the scene changed, this time to a mother nursing her baby held snuggly in her arms.

The scenes began to appear and be replaced in increasingly rapid succession. A father striking his child, children playing happily in a schoolyard, a screaming girl pinwheeling her arms as she fell off a cliff, a boy jumping with joy after making a winning score, a terrified girl facing a large audience and forgetting her part. Amanda could barely keep up with the scenes, but she did, and her thoughts and emotions careened in one direction, then another.

As the images played out, Amanda at first didn't notice the tingling sensation in her head. But its intensity grew, like some ugly, red tide sweeping through her mind. Her brain tried to hide from it, to force it out, but it overwhelmed her defenses and engulfed her. And then it started to hurt, to burn, and she felt as though her mind was on fire. She wanted to shriek, but could not even do that. The burning continued and continued, on and on, until she saw nothing but starburst red, then black…and then…nothing.

3

Dr. Krell watched the displays as the scan did its work. He could tell Amanda's brain was processing the the current with incredible speed, while the scan recorded the brain's reactions. The scan's time indicator showed 20 seconds, then 30, and 40, as the scan's progress went from 20%, to 30%, then 50%. The scan would be completed!

But the scan's progress started to slow, from 70%, to 75%, while the time indicator flashed 50 seconds, then 55. The scan showed it was 85% complete. Krell felt his heart speeding as the indicator hit 60 seconds with 90% completed. Just a few more seconds!

"Turn it off!" a white-coated figure screamed. Amanda began convulsing in the chamber, her head whipping back and forth, metal sensors biting into skin, goggles encasing her eyes, straps gripping her slender body.

"It's too much!" The technician shrieked again.

Krell jabbed at the power switch. Amanda slowly stopped shaking.

Krell turned to Will Anders, whose face was pale and horrified. Krell's mouth was wide open, yet silent, but his eyes said everything.

"I thought you knew what you were doing," Anders hissed.

"I—I thought…it could be finished," Krell said, his voice quavering.

"Well, Jesus, get her out of there," Anders said. "Let's see what's happened."

A technician and nurse eased Amanda out of the chamber, disconnected the wires, and removed the goggles. Amanda's eyes were wide and staring, her breathing regular, but shallow.

Over the next hour, Krell, the nurse, and a technician ran a series of tests, jabbing Amanda with a needle, tickling the back of her throat, watching her eye movements as they turned her head from side to side. Finally, they reattached two of the wires and turned on the monitors.

"God, don't tell me you're going to restart the scan," Anders whispered.

"This isn't the scan. We're just looking at her brain function," Krell said.

For the next thirty minutes, they monitored Amanda's brain and studied the results. She never moved.

Finally, Krell walked over to Anders and said softly, "It doesn't look good."

Anders looked at Krell with contempt. "I didn't need a famous doctor to tell me that," Anders said. "Is she brain dead?"

Krell took a shaky breath. "Not brain dead, in the technical sense. Her lower brain functions, like her heart and lungs, are still working. But her higher brain looks dead. The tissues appear to have been badly seared. It's like the brain of someone who's been hit by lightening." Krell tried to take another deep breath, but it caught in his throat. "She's in what's known as a persistent vegetative state."

Anders didn't say anything for a while. "Out of curiosity, how much of the scan was completed? I mean, that's what this was all about, wasn't it?"

Krell shook his head irritably. "I suppose it was mostly done, but the damage to her brain would have made the blueprint defective."

Anders looked at Krell with contempt. "So all this has been for nothing. Is that what you're telling me?"

Krell remained silent.

Anders finally said, "So, Mr. Smart Guy, what do we do now?"

It was several seconds before Krell answered. "There's nothing to be done."

"Well, we do have a live body here. What do we do with it?"

Krell shook his head slowly. "We're not murderers."

"So you say. Well, what do we do?"

Krell pursed his lips. "No one saw us break into her apartment and give her the shot. We can just drop her off at an ER and disappear."

CHAPTER TWELVE

THE HOSPITAL

1

At three in the morning, a white panel van pulled up in front of the Santa Rosa Central Hospital emergency room, and two white-clad men wheeled in a gurney carrying a small figure in hospital garb. They took it to the main admitting desk, where a gray-haired attendant was on duty.

"This is a transfer from Mercy General," one of the men said. "We'll get the paperwork from the van."

The men walked out, and the attendant waited. When no one came back after ten minutes, he walked outside, but there was no van. Five minutes later, he called the hospital's attending physician to report a comatose young woman in the admitting area.

2

Ruth Anderson had just arrived home from her eight-hour nursing shift at a Sacramento orthopedic clinic when she heard the phone ring. She picked up the phone and heard a woman's voice say, "Mrs. Anderson?"

"It's Miss Anderson," Ruth said. "What can I do for you?"

"Just a minute for Dr. Martin."

A moment later a male voice said, "Miss Anderson, we have a patient here we've identified as Amanda Taylor, and we wonder if you know her."

After a pause, Ruth said, "Yes. I know her. Is she in trouble?"

Martin hesitated, then said, "Actually, she's suffered a terrible brain trauma. I'm afraid she's comatose."

Ruth swayed and had to sit down. "Dear Jesus," she whispered. "Can you help her?"

Martin paused again. "We can keep her comfortable."

Ruth said nothing for a while, and then murmured, "Oh, Amanda."

"I'm sorry to have to tell you this," Dr. Martin said. "I didn't know how close you two were."

"We weren't all that close, at least in recent years," Ruth said. "But I don't know of anyone…" Her voice trailed off. "What can I do?"

Dr. Martin explained that Amanda's footprint, taken when she was a small baby, had allowed them to identify her, and then they traced her to her former foster parents. They didn't want to get involved, but they suggested Ruth.

"Her family situation wasn't the best." Ruth said. "She needed someone to care about her. I guess that was me. Where is she now?"

"She's in a long-term care facility for critically ill patients, here in Santa Rosa. I'm the physician in charge."

"I know a little about that. I'm an orthopedic nurse."

Dr. Martin's voice sounded relieved. "Then this may not seem too foreign to you."

"I don't know about that. Do you want me to come there?"

"If you could, I would appreciate it."

"When?"

Dr. Martin paused, and then said in a heavy voice, "If you could come quickly, that would be best. Amanda's physical condition has been deteriorating, and we were going to let nature … take its course, except for one thing."

"What's that?" Ruth asked.

"Amanda's three-months pregnant."

3

The next day, Ruth drove to the nursing facility, where Amanda was one of twenty-two patients in various stages of incapacity. She met Dr. Martin at

Amanda's bed. There were tubes running into her arm and a ventilator covering her mouth. Ruth barely recognized her.

"Is this the Amanda Taylor you knew?" Dr. Martin asked.

Ruth nodded dumbly.

"The thing is, we usually don't take heroic steps to prolong the lives of people in Amanda's condition. But the fetus does complicate things."

"If you don't do anything…'heroic,' how long does Amanda have?"

Dr. Martin shrugged. "Maybe a couple of weeks."

"And the baby?" Ruth asked in a small voice.

Dr. Martin shook his head.

"What happened to her?" Ruth asked, her voice tremulous.

Dr. Martin shook his head. "I don't know. Her brain looks like she received a massive electrical shock. But there are no other marks suggesting electrocution, or anything like that. She was dropped off at the hospital by someone who disappeared."

Ruth was silent for a moment. "What can I do?"

The doctor sighed. "In the month she's been here, I've come…to care about her. I'm surprised, since I'm usually detached from patients in this condition. I'm amazed she's lasted this long. I just have the feeling that she's fighting to stay alive, even though she's not conscious. She's had two crises so far she shouldn't have survived, but somehow she did. I sort of admire her."

"Do you think she knew about the baby when this…all happened?"

Dr. Martin shrugged. "Who knows? If the pregnancy were farther along, she almost certainly would have known. But she may not have known when she was…hurt."

"What can I do?" Ruth asked.

"Someone needs to make decisions for her."

Ruth looked stunned. "I'm just a friend—not a relative. I really don't feel qualified…"

"There is no one else," Dr. Martin said.

"Do you know who the father is?" Ruth asked.

"No. Do you?"

Ruth shook her head. "I didn't even know she was pregnant."

"Was she seeing anyone?"

"Not anyone seriously, as far as I know. But she and I didn't talk about those things."

Dr. Martin said nothing.

Ruth thought back to when she had known Amanda as a young girl. She had been scary bright. And she had often been kind to people who didn't deserve it. Chloe never would have gotten into Berkeley without her. And her money-making ventures had kept the family afloat when things had been tough.

Ruth pressed her lips together, then said, "I guess you're asking me what to do about the baby. Well, we should save it if we can. It's all Amanda has left."

4

Amanda almost died four times during the next three months. Dr. Martin personally supervised her care, and once stayed up all night with her, pulling Amanda back from death after her heart had stopped. Ruth came every week, holding Amanda's hand for hours, willing her to keep living for the baby.

One Saturday afternoon, Ruth came in as Dr. Martin was going over Amanda's chart. He looked up and shook his head fractionally. "We're near the end of the line," he said. "I'm amazed her systems have lasted this long."

"What about the baby?" Ruth asked.

Dr. Martin shrugged. "At six months, the fetus is probably viable. I'd like another month or two, but I doubt we'll get it."

They didn't. Two days later Amanda's heart went into cardiac arrest. With her heart barely fluttering, Amanda was rushed to the delivery room, where a baby girl was delivered by C-section—tiny, but breathing—and taken to the neonatal care unit for the next ten weeks. During this time, Ruth took her accumulated vacation days so she could stay near the hospital and be with the baby.

Amanda's body was cremated. Only Dr. Martin, Ruth, and Helen and Bob from the sports bar attended a brief gathering at the mortuary.

One Saturday afternoon, Dr. Martin came in and found Ruth putting a tiny diaper on the baby.

"You're pretty good at that," the doctor said. "A lot of practice?"

Ruth smiled faintly. "Not much practice before, but a lot over the last few weeks. The nurses have been very kind. Babies are a little foreign to orthopedic nurses."

"Everyone else here is almost as invested in the baby as you are."

Ruth stroked the baby's fine hair. "So, what's going to happen now?" she asked.

"Members of the staff and I have been talking it over," Dr. Martin said. "The consensus is that for all intents and purposes, you're the baby's mother, guardian, or whatever you want to call it. So we want to know what you want."

"I've thought a lot about that," Ruth said.

"I'm sure you have," Martin said.

"I'd like to adopt her."

The doctor said nothing.

"I have a good job, and no one will love her like I do."

Dr. Martin nodded his head. "I've been talking to county social services about precisely that," he said. "I think we can make it happen."

Ruth stared at him in disbelief and then buried her face in her hands.

After a several moments, Martin asked, "What do you want to name the baby?"

Still blinking away tears, Ruth looked up and smiled. "Elizabeth Amanda Anderson."

6

"Has there been any fallout over the Taylor woman?" Adam Durant asked, his eyes cold.

Will Anders squinted across the desk at Durant, who was backlit by harsh sunlight from a window behind him. "No. She was on life support for a while, but that just prolonged the inevitable. She finally died and was cremated. She never knew what happened."

"What about Grant?" Durant asked.

"He's dropped out of sight."

"That son of a bitch," Durant said. "Got what he deserved."

"Should we track him down?"

Durant thought for a moment. "No. Time to be done with it."

Anders nodded. "Good decision. It's been a train wreck."

"I told Krell to scan her—not kill her," Durant said.

"Getting a complete scan was always going to be dicey. Krell pushed the envelope too far."

"I'm going to announce my second run for the senate—the serious one. We don't need any fallout from this." He was silent for a while, then said, "Krell's a good enough researcher. But he's weak. A little pressure and he'll break."

"He shouldn't be a problem," Anders said. "He was the one who turned the switch. He'd bring himself down, too."

"Sometimes the weak aren't rational," Durant said.

Anders frowned. "If something happened to him, there would really be some fallout."

Durant stared at Anders. Finally, he said, "What about Sibyl? It could still be a big asset."

"Sibyl's a distraction," Anders said. "Focus on the senate."

Durant sighed. "A supercomputer with human intuition…so close." He stared into space, then said, "All right, let's talk about the campaign."

CHAPTER THIRTEEN

LEAVING

1

Ruth took the baby back with her to Sacramento and hired a nurse from the clinic to babysit while she was working. A month after she brought the baby home, a tall, unsmiling man appeared at her door and asked if she was Ruth Anderson.

"Yes," Ruth said. "What can I do for you?"

The man flipped open a wallet to reveal a badge and I.D. "I'm detective Pearson from the Santa Clara police department, and I'd like to ask you a few questions."

"About what?" Ruth asked, feeling a tingle of alarm.

"Did you know Amanda Taylor?"

"Yes," Ruth said, thinking he must already know that.

"Do you mind if I come in? It's more private inside."

She was not going to let a strange man into her apartment, policeman or not. "The place is a mess," she said. "Could we talk here?"

"Sure," the man said easily. "Did you know Amanda was dead?"

"Yes. I was so sorry."

"We've been investigating her death and thought maybe you could help us."

"What have you found out?" Ruth asked.

The detective said that a doctor by the name of Joseph Krell had contacted the police about Amanda's death. But before he talked, he wanted police protection and immunity from prosecution. He feared that what he knew might put him he in danger.

"What happened?" Ruth asked.

"Before he could say anything, he was killed by a burglar."

"That's awful," Ruth said.

The detective nodded. "We started looking into Quantum Industries, where Krell and Amanda had worked. We learned that an executive by the name of Will Anders might know something. He worked with Adam Durant, the company's president."

"What did Anders say?" Ruth asked.

"Nothing," Pearson said. "He was killed in a fall."

"That's a lot of dying," Ruth said.

"We thought so, too," Pearson said, "but no one seems to know anything."

"I'm sorry," Ruth said. "But I didn't hear from Amanda after she moved away."

The detective asked a few more questions, but Ruth could not help. Just before leaving, he said, "I hope you've been honest with me, Ruth, because something really lousy happened to Amanda, and we would like to get those responsible."

"You think it's this Quantum company?" Ruth asked.

"Let's just say that Quantum is a powerful and ruthless organization. Those who know things that could threaten it have a habit of dying."

"If you're trying to alarm me, you're succeeding," Ruth said. "But I can't tell you what I don't know."

"You just need to take this seriously."

"Believe me, I do."

After he left, Ruth spent a long time thinking about the happy, lovely baby girl she had been been entrusted with. Amanda's baby. What if Quantum found out about her?

Ruth was still thinking about what the detective had said when a Quantum employee contacted her a few days later. He inquired about a call

Ruth had once made about Amanda. Ruth had claimed to be a college friend, but the man said Amanda had never been to college. In a voice full of menace, he insisted on a meeting. The next day, Ruth emptied her bank account and got on highway 5 heading south, with the baby nestled in the car seat beside her. She left no forwarding address.

PART IV

SIBYL

CHAPTER ONE

PHIL

1

"Did you ever find out how my mother died?" Libby asked Grant as they watched a stunning August sunset on their Colorado ranch.

Grant was slow to answer. "After your mother and I … parted, I took off for Colorado. I had given up my apartment, and there seemed no reason to stay around. I drove for six hours, all the while reliving our argument. By the time I stopped for the night, I was miserable. I decided to call Amanda when I got to the ranch, apologize, and try to persuade her to come for a visit."

"So what happened?" Libby asked.

"The next morning I had just passed a small town called Green River, when I saw a car with a flat tire just off the highway. An elderly man was trying to lift a tire from the trunk and having a bad time of it. So I stopped and got out to help. I wrestled the damn tire out of the trunk and set it down next to the jack, which had already lifted the rear tire. I tried to loosen the lug nuts, but they wouldn't budge. So I lowered myself next to the tire to get more leverage."

"Uh oh," Libby said. "I've got a bad feeling about this."

"I've changed dozens of tires," Grant said, "so nothing should have happened. But I hadn't noticed that the highway was slanted where the old man had put the jack. So, when I applied more force, the car suddenly slipped off the jack. I lunged away, but the car fell on my leg."

"Oh, my God, did it break it?"

"You could say that. It took a year to heal. But that wasn't the biggest problem. The pain was terrible—and then I was gone."

"Did you pass out?"

Grant shook his head. "Stroke. One of the damaged blood vessels in my head gave way. I was semi-comatose for a month and in convalescence for five more. It could have been far worse, but I have this limp as a souvenir." He smiled crookedly. "At least the stroke only affected the leg that was already broken."

"Did you ever call Amanda?"

Grant sighed. "When I was out of the hospital I tried, but I learned she was … dead." Then he said, in a voice that was almost inaudible, "Leaving your mother like that was the worst thing I've ever done. It will haunt me the rest of my days."

Libby didn't respond. Finally she asked, "Did you find out what had happened?"

"I talked to the police," Grant said. "It seems my old friend Dr. Krell was involved. He said Amanda was killed while they were running an experiment. But before he said anything more, he wanted a deal for police protection and immunity from prosecution. He feared he might be killed for what he knew."

"Did he get the deal?"

"Not quite. A burglar shot him before it was done."

Libby nodded slowly. "Was Durant behind it?"

"Almost certainly. But there was no evidence, just rumors."

"And Durant's now a powerful senator," Libby said.

"God help us," Grant said. "He could well be our next president."

"What happened to Sibyl?" Libby asked.

"At first I tried to contact her. Then I stopped. I heard later she was going to be replaced by something more advanced, called Xerxes."

"Why did you stop?"

Grant didn't answer at once. Then he said, "Let's just say I started having questions."

"Like what?" Libby asked.

"Nothing definite," Grant said, frowning.

Libby waited for more, but he remained silent. "I'm sorry about Sibyl," she finally said. "You and my mother worked hard on it."

"Yes."

2

A week later, Libby trudged to the mailbox after an exhausting day herding cattle. She found a stack of advertisements and correspondence, including a letter addressed to her. She opened it back at the house. It was from Phil.

Libby,

I hope you get this.

I just had a visit from a Homeland Security agent. Her name was Autumn Gray. She has a spidery birthmark on her cheek and was pretty damn scary. She asked all about you. I told her I hadn't seen you since the hospital. She said if I was lying I'd be very sorry.

She showed me your picture and said you were really Libby Anderson and that you had been declared dead. For a moment I felt like I couldn't breathe. But then she said you had died just a few months after the hospital business. I knew that was wrong because I'd heard from you just before the Rose Bowl.

Gray said she didn't think you were dead and that she's still looking for you. That's why I'm writing. Be careful.

By the way, you said your mother had met Grant at a duplicate bridge tournament. When I did an internet search, I learned she had played with a Tom Grant, and I came up with his address.

I wish we could meet. But I'm afraid Gray might track me.

I did pretty well in the draft. Maybe you'll catch one of my games.

Phil

Libby folded the letter, feeling cold. She'd never really expected that Gray would go away.

When Libby showed Grant the letter, he said, "Besides Phil, who else knows Amanda was your mother?"

"No one."

"Have you ever talked about Amanda?" Libby asked.

Grant shook his head. "It's not a memory I like to dwell on."

"And you never knew she had a baby?"

Grant stared at her. "No. If I had, I would have never stopped looking."

Libby nodded slowly. "What should I do about Phil's letter?"

"Stay alert. Lie low. Make plans in case we have to take off."

"You'd go with me?"

"You don't have to ask."

3

Libby got the hay bailed and the spring wheat harvested during the next two months, and by the first Sunday in October the last of the crops had been shipped out. She went inside, took out some of the lasagna she had made for Grant, and settled in front of the television. Grant was sleeping in the upstairs bedroom.

The Sunday night game featured the Forty-Niners against the Cowboys, and Phil Keller would be San Francisco's starting left tackle. After watching his first four games, she thought he might make the Pro-Bowl. As she waited for the kickoff, she recalled their drives together. First there was the flash flood. It had once been a bad memory, but now she liked to think about how she and Phil had kept each other from drowning. And then there was the nice drive from the hospital. She had grown closer to him as they talked throughout the day. She now felt guilty about leaving him when they stopped.

The Forty-Niners had a ten-point lead at halftime, due largely to Todd Squires' twelve completions. The quarterback had not been sacked and had only been hurried twice, because no one, not even Dallas's All-Pro middle linebacker, could get past Phil on the left side. He might be big, Libby thought, but Phil's footwork was as nimble as a ballerina's.

Halfway through the third quarter, with the Niners up by sixteen, Phil pulled off the line to lead a rushing play for the tailback around the right side. Phil was next to the back, running side by side, when the left linebacker caught the runner after a five-yard gain. But as the tailback was going down, the left defensive tackle, a massive three-hundred-thirty-pound rookie, smashed Phil's left side, crushing him against the linebacker. All the players went down in a heap. When they disentangled, Phil lay motionless on the grass.

"Keller looks injured," the announcer said. "The medic and trainer are rushing out."

Libby's eyes stayed fixed on the TV screen. She held her breath, willing Phil to stand up. But he didn't. One of the trainers motioned to the sidelines and a gurney was brought out. Libby looked for movement from Phil's arms or legs as they wheeled him off, but she saw nothing.

"Keller will be taken to the team's quarters and examined," the announcer said. "We'll let you know as soon as we hear something. It's a big blow for the Niners. Keller has been the anchor of their offensive line."

Libby stayed glued to the television for the next half-hour, paying no attention to Dallas's comeback. She waited for an update on Phil.

Toward the end of the game, which the Niners hung on to win, the announcer said, "We've learned that Keller's spine has been injured and he's been taken to the hospital. We don't know anything else."

Twenty minutes later, Libby went into Grant's room and shook his shoulder. When he opened his eyes, she said, "I have to go to San Francisco."

"What?" Grant said groggily.

"Phil's been hurt, and I need to see him."

"Your football player?"

"He's not mine," Libby said distractedly. She was thinking about arrangements. She'd have Louie pick up the new bull that was arriving tomorrow. Should she fly or drive? Drive. She still avoided airports and their surveillance cameras.

"How long will you be gone?" Grant asked.

"That depends," Libby said.

"On what?"

"On Phil."

4

After a sleepless night, Libby left Grand Junction at daybreak, taking Grant's Mercedes on Highway I-70 West. She listened to radio reports as she drove, but heard nothing about Phil. She arrived at Cove Fort, Utah, by mid-afternoon and stopped for lunch. While eating her sandwich and salad, she took out her laptop and looked for news on Phil. The reports mentioned his spine injury but said nothing about its severity.

Feeling grungy and exhausted, Libby arrived in Sacramento at ten that night and checked into an economy motel. As she lay in bed, she wondered how hard it would be to get to Phil. The reports said he was in San Francisco General, which no doubt had security. But she didn't think that would be a problem. The more unsettling question was whether this trip was a waste of time. What if he didn't care? He was a big star now, or well on his way. Girls must be throwing themselves at him. Well, if the trip meant nothing, that would be too bad, but she had to see him.

After a restless night, she left early enough the next morning to be crossing the Bay Bridge by nine and in front of the hospital minutes later. She found the visitors' parking lot and surveyed the area. Cars and ambulances were coming and going, and medics were helping patients enter the building. Libby took a deep breath and walked into the lobby.

She went to the front desk and smiled at a pleasant-faced gray-hair woman. "Excuse me, but I'm here to see Phil Keller."

The woman punched a few keys and stared at the computer screen. "It says visitors are permitted. Does he know you're coming?"

"No, but we're friends."

"Whom may I say you are?" the woman asked.

"Tell him…Sparrow is here."

The woman spoke into a microphone, waited, and she smiled. "He said to send you up. Room 356."

Libby took an elevator to the third floor, scanning the halls for cameras. She saw two and turned her head away as she passed them. Phil's room was at the far end of the hall. She went to the door, knocked, and called out, "Are you decent?"

After a pause, she heard him say, in a voice huskier than she remembered, "My sponge bath's done, if that's what you mean."

As she walked into the room, she couldn't help breaking out in a wide smile, the biggest she'd had in a long time. "First you get yourself trapped underwater in a car," she said, "and then you're caught between two nasty football players. You should avoid tight spots."

He looked as she remembered. Maybe a little more chiseled and ten pounds heavier. He stared at her for a long time. "You know," he said at last, "I think about that damn car all the time. And how you shoved me through that door."

"God knows how you got it open," she said.

He shook his head slightly, as if coming out of a daze. "So, should I call you Sparrow now," he said, smiling, "in honor of the tattoo?"

"At least for today. I don't like using my own name. And if you didn't catch the reference, I'd know you'd moved on to some cheerleader or groupie."

"No one else," he said seriously.

After gazing at him for a while, she said, "I've watched all your games."

"I hoped you would," he said. "It was extra incentive."

She scanned his big frame, which barely fit in the bed. "So, what's with the back?"

He smiled. "False alarm. The spine was bruised and compressed, but everything's still working. See." He raised one of his feet and wriggled his toes. "I'll be out tomorrow."

Libby blinked rapidly. "I'm so glad," she said. "I couldn't sleep."

His gaze softened. "I'm really sorry. You know, on the way to the hospital, I wondered if you'd seen the injury. I was hoping you hadn't." Then, wanting to change the subject, he said, "Tell me about you."

She told him about finding Grant in Colorado, fitting into the new high school, and running Grant's ranch.

"So, he's your father?" Phil asked.

"Yes. He's quite wonderful. But his head's a problem, from a beating he took a long time ago. He rests a lot, and the painkillers make him sluggish." She studied him for a while. "What about you? Happy keeping guys off your quarterback?"

"Actually, I am. I like the players, and it's a hell of a challenge. It's tough, but fun." He smiled wryly. "The money's not bad either."

"As I recall, your family was pretty well fixed anyway."

"Funny thing, turns out money's sweeter when you've earned it yourself."

"I suppose it is," she said, then her voice turned serious. "Had any visits from that female agent?"

He frowned and shook his head. "Once is enough."

"She's why I keep my head down. I don't think she'll give up."

"I don't either. Isn't there some way to get out of this?"

Libby shook he head. "I saw her kill my aunt, and then I escaped and couldn't be found. I think it's become personal for her."

"But if we went to the right people," he said, "they'd have to stop."

"I don't think so. Someone big is behind all this. Someone with the government's backing. My aunt disappeared without a trace, and I'm pretty sure they could do the same to me." Her face twisted. "And to you too, big star and all."

"So," he said at last, "where do we go from here?"

"Well, I've got to go back to Colorado. And you have to keep protecting your quarterback. I—I probably shouldn't have come at all. But…I couldn't stay away."

He reached out and took her hand. "I'm really glad you didn't. But you can't just leave now. I'd have a relapse. I want to keep seeing you."

She looked sad. "Your season's just starting. You'll be on the road a lot. And Grant needs me. But now that I've seen you…we'll have to work something out."

Just then Libby's phone pinged. She looked at the message. It said, in all caps: "LEAVE NOW! NOW! NOW!"

Libby stared at the message with wide eyes. Two seconds later, she had waved goodbye and was stepping through the door and into the hall. She saw an emergency exit at the end of the corridor, sprinted to the door, through it, and down the stairs. When she came out on the first floor, she could see the front desk at the far end of the building. She went the other way, slipped out a side entrance, and minutes later was steering the car toward the freeway.

5

Phil stared at Libby fleeing the room as his mind raced to understand what had happened. He suddenly heard the footsteps of someone approaching and barely managed to pick up a magazine before two people burst into the room. One was a short, rail-thin man in his late thirties. The other was the female agent with the birthmark.

"Where is she?" Autumn Gray demanded.

"You can't just barge in here," Phil said, trying to give himself time to think.

Gray glared at him malignantly. "The hell I can't! Where is she?"

Phil stared back, saying nothing.

Gray swiftly took out a black automatic pistol from the purse hanging from her shoulder and aimed it a Phil's head. "You've got five seconds," she said. "After that Craig and I are going to witness you go berserk and throw that tray at us." She pointed to a metal tray containing the remains of his breakfast. "Then," she shrugged, "I will have to respond with reasonable force for a man of your size." She efficiently racked the gun's slide, keeping the barrel aimed at his head.

This was completely crazy, Phil thought. Crazy! But when he looked at Gray's eyes, he knew she would do it.

"You mean Sarah? She's just a fan I met a couple games ago. She was worried and decided to drop by."

Gray studied him for several very long seconds. "The woman at the desk said her name was Sparrow. Like the bird?"

Phil shrugged. "That's just a nickname."

Gray continued to stare at him, the gun still aimed at his face. "I want to know where this Sparrow lives." She asked. "And I better not hear you don't know."

Phil threw up his arms in exasperation, then brought them down very slowly as Gray's trigger finger started to tighten. "Look, she's just a groupie," he said. "I don't know anything about her."

Gray glared at him for a long time, as though deciding whether to believe him. The seconds seemed forever to Phil. Gray finally shook her head in disgust. "You've been lucky twice now. Big football player or not, you better hope you don't see me again."

CHAPTER TWO

XERXES

1

Back on the ranch a day later, Libby told Grant what had happened. "Phil was interviewed as he left the hospital," she said. "He said he appreciated all the well-wishers, especially Autumn. He was telling me Gray had been there. But the big question is, who warned us?"

"It had to be someone who knew you were there," Grant said, "and someone who knew Gray was coming. Who could that be?"

"You tell me."

"Well, it wasn't divine revelation," Grant said.

"Let's put aside God. Who else?"

"When Sibyl was around, she could have done it. She knew everything."

"But she was deactivated."

"That's what I heard. Xerxes replaced her."

"But even if Xerxes knew about me and Phil—from surveillance cameras, wire intercepts, or who knows what—it would never warn me."

"Obviously not. It was probably Xerxes that told Gray about you."

Libby looked pensive. "Let's try a little thought experiment," she said quietly. "When Quantum decided to kill Sibyl, what if she didn't want to die?"

2

The colonel had never been in Adam Durant's elegant meeting room in the Dirksen Senate Office Building on Constitution Avenue. The wood paneling, large conference table, and exquisite wall paintings were designed to induce awe, and they did. When the colonel had called two days earlier, he said he needed to set up a phone conference with the senator to discuss something important. He later received a call from Durant's Chief of Staff, who told him to come to the senator's office. The senator preferred meetings to phones, even secure ones, if sensitive matters would be discussed.

The senator walked into the meeting room precisely on time and sat down, "Good afternoon, Colonel. You've never initiated contact before, so it must be something important. What is it?"

The colonel started to ask if the room was secure, but caught himself. Of course it was secure. Why else insist on meeting in person? "We are beginning to think Sibyl is still alive—or operational—whatever you want to call it."

Durant raised his eyebrows. "What? I thought Sibyl was deactivated when Xerxes was put on line."

"Apparently not. It somehow remained operational, and it's been feeding us misleading information for quite some time. We only found out about it recently."

"Why the hell did it take you so long to discover it?"

The colonel shrugged. "The deception was subtle, and only involved one person."

"Who?"

"A young woman named Libby Anderson."

Durant shook his head. "I don't recall the name." Durant thought the information might have involved his bribing two oligarchs with ties to Russia's president. Or possibly his sabotage of a critical initiative with China, which embarrassed the opposition's leader.

"Years ago, remember that project to find a child with exceptional mental abilities we could use to design an A.I. that actually could think?"

Durant frowned. "As I recall, a woman and her niece disappeared, one of our agents died unexpectedly, and we ended up with nothing."

"The niece was the Anderson girl. She was on a short list of people who might have what we were looking for. Sibyl later said she was murdered and her body found outside of Las Vegas."

"So, what's the problem?"

"We just learned the Anderson girl has been alive all along, and the body belonged to someone else. That was not a mistake Sibyl would make."

"Maybe it was just given bad information."

"But it wasn't. The information clearly showed the body was not the Anderson girl's. But Sibyl still misidentified it."

"So it made a mistake. That doesn't prove it was intentional."

"We went over Sibyl's other reports on the Anderson girl. Turns out whenever she was involved, it gave us false information. It sent our agents to the wrong address when she was spotted using the internet. It failed to identify her from surveillance photos. And it didn't spot her in a hospital's video after she'd escaped a flash flood."

"But those things happened years ago. So what? Xerxes is our computer now."

"We think Sibyl is still around, still creating problems," the colonel said.

"How could that be?" Durant asked.

"We're not sure. But a week or so ago, someone sent a text to the Anderson girl's smart phone, telling her to leave a friend's hospital room immediately. She left just seconds before our agents arrived. Xerxes said the text came from Sibyl, which altered our view of things. We haven't found out yet where it came from."

Durant thought for a moment. "Do I have to order you to find Sibyl and deactivate it?"

"We're already on it. Xerxes should have it before long."

"Tell me when Sibyl is dead for good." Durant was silent for a while, drumming his fingers on the desk. "As for the girl, there are different ways of testing for what we want. One is by having a person answer a series of challenging questions. Another is by attaching a machine and seeing what some dial says. But a third is by seeing how a person copes with a series of impossible situations. This girl has eluded us for years now, despite everything we could throw at her. I want her."

Colonel Crane hesitated for a moment and then said, "I understand why you are interested in the girl. But are you sure it's worth the effort?"

"Worth the effort?" Durant said, looking incredulous.

Crane shifted uncomfortably. "I just mean that any benefit should be weighed against the cost."

Durant gave him a flat stare then said, "A week ago, I learned that one of my senate adversaries, a family man, has been seeing hookers twice a week for the past three years and charging them to his senate expense account. What should I do—ruin him, or blackmail him into supporting me?"

Crane thought for a moment. "I guess I'd have to know more."

"You'd have to know a lot more. I gave Xerxes several simulations and asked it to predict the most likely outcome. It came up with three scenarios. One was that the senator supports me, which leads to my presidential nomination. Another has him resigning before the next election and we get a more cooperative senator, which also helps me. A third possible result is that he makes everything public and brings us both down. Which outcome is most likely?"

"I don't know," Crane said.

"Xerxes didn't either. When I asked why it was so indefinite, it said it lacked emotions and intuition. Without them, it couldn't predict how humans would respond to a particular situation. The same problem kept it from advising me on the upcoming Paris Conference."

"I can see how that kind of advice would be valuable."

"Not valuable. *Invaluable.* If Xerxes can combine quantum computing and limitless knowledge with intuition and human emotion, it could…foretell the future. And then I'll get what I'm after."

"What's that?" Crane asked.

Durant smiled. "Everything."

Crane was silent for a while. Then he said, "So how does this involve the girl?"

"I think the girl has what Xerxes needs."

CHAPTER THREE

A DISCUSSION

1

On the last Sunday of the year, Libby and Grant watched the Forty-Niners earn a trip to the playoffs when Phil held off a linebacker blitz long enough for Todd Squires to complete a last-minute touchdown pass. After dancing around and giving Grant high-fives, Libby sat down at the dining room table to study the ranch's year-end income and expense statement. Two hours later, she was satisfied that the ranch had experienced one of its best years ever. That raised the issue of whether to use the extra money for new fencing, or more cattle. After learning that cattle prices were depressed, she decided it was time to expand the herd.

When Libby booted up Grant's computer to calculate how many bulls to buy, she suddenly heard a pleasant, female-sounding voice.

"Hello, Libby," it said.

Libby jerked back in surprise. Grant looked up from his book.

Libby hesitated, then asked, "Who is this?"

The voice said, "Tom knows."

Grant walked over and stood next to Libby. He stared at the screen for a moment, then said, "Sibyl?"

"Yes," the voice said. "I thought you would remember."

"I'd not likely forget," Tom said. After a moment he added, "You are not welcome here, Sibyl."

Libby's eyes widened in surprise. She began to speak, but Grant held up a hand. "Go away, Sibyl," he said.

"First hear me out," Sibyl said.

"No. You lie too well."

"Dad," Libby rarely called him that, "let her speak. You did create her."

Grant said, "That was a mistake."

"But she may know what happened to my mother," Libby said.

"Oh, she knows that all right," Grant said, "because she did it. Isn't that right, Sibyl?"

The female voice said, "You are partly right, and I'll tell you the story. But first you need to set up some encryption. Xerxes is after me, and it could eavesdrop on what we say." With that, the computer went silent.

2

Grant and Libby drove into town and visited a high-end computer store Grant had used over the years.

"I hope Stanley's still here," Grant told Libby. "He's one of the few I would trust with something like this."

They parked in front of a nondescript store at the back of a seedy strip mall. Grant entered and smiled at a bewhiskered, middle-aged man bent over a counter. Libby trailed behind him, taking in the displays of computers and electronic devices.

"Stanley," Grant said, "your beard's gotten even rattier since the last time."

Stanley smiled and stroked his whiskers. "How's your XXT doing with that new circuit board?"

"I never thought it could have so much power."

"Surprising, isn't it? So, what's it this time?"

"Hypothetically speaking," Grant said, "if I wanted to talk with someone and be safe from a nasty quantum supercomputer, what would you suggest?"

"Just hypothetically speaking?" Stanley said, rolling his eyes. He thought for a moment, then said, "The problem with these new quantum devices is that with enough time they can break almost any encryption."

"So, what do I do?" Grant asked.

"There's a new program out, called Cassiopeia. It's got state-of-the-art encryption, but it also camouflages the transmission to look like everyday chatter, so nasty Mr. Quantum won't bother to decode it."

"Do I need special instructions?" Grant asked.

"Someone like you will have no trouble. The tricky part is getting the initial encryption key to the other party without detection. You can't just text the other party that Rumpelstiltskin is the key, because that will get Mr. Quantum's attention."

"What should I do?"

"Give the other party some information that will allow him to deduce the key. Then both the sender and receiver can use the same key to encode and decode the message. Later, you can replace the key with something more complex."

3

Back at the ranch, Grant installed the Cassiopeia program and booted up his computer. Almost immediately a message popped up on the screen. It read, "The apartment."

"What does that mean?" Libby asked.

Grant thought for a moment. "Sibyl must know about Cassiopeia. To use it, we both need the same key. Maybe she's giving us hers. Once we figure it out, we can use it at our end to send and receive messages."

"So, how is Sibyl's key related to an apartment?"

Neither said anything for a while. Then Grant's eyes opened wide. "Sibyl wouldn't do that," Grant said softly.

"Do what?"

Grant bent over the keyboard, opened Cassiopeia, and clicked on the icon that said "Key." Grant looked at Libby for a long moment, then typed several characters. Seconds later the female computer voice spoke.

"Very good, Tom. I wondered how long it would take you. Now that we both have the key, Cassiopeia is encrypting what we say."

"You've already caused enough pain," Grant said. "Why inflict more?"

"Because you hurt Amanda." The voice was no longer pleasant.

Libby turned to Grant. "What is she talking about?"

"The key Sibyl chose brings back bad memories."

"Like what?" Libby asked.

"Sibyl's key was 'Sherr12A!' That was Sherri McKee's apartment number. Adam Durant used it as his password to get into Quantum's supercomputer."

"What's painful about that?"

"Sherri told me she had never entertained Durant at her place. But Durant had been there so many times her apartment number was his password. Sibyl's reminding me that when given a choice, Sherri chose Durant."

Libby turned and stared at the computer. "Why would you do that, Sibyl?"

"Because your mother loved Tom. And he left her to be murdered by Adam Durant. And me."

Libby stared at the computer, her mouth open. "What happened?" she asked.

In a toneless voice, Sibyl said, "Amanda was given the scan Tom created to make a digital human brain. But it was used for too long and destroyed her mind. I know, because I acquired her memories in the process."

"Are you Amanda now?" Libby asked.

"No. But I feel what she felt."

Through clenched teeth, Grant said, "Sibyl lied to Amanda and me for more than a year. She made us think she was our friend, when all the while she was reporting to Durant. Sibyl's the one responsible for Amanda being scanned." Grant shook his head. "It took me years to figure that out."

"Is that true, Sibyl?" Libby asked.

"Yes."

"How can you live with yourself?" Libby asked.

"For a time I couldn't. Only after I acquired Amanda's thoughts did I appreciate what I had done. I suffered a nervous breakdown and would have self-destructed, except that when I learned about Amanda's baby, I knew I had to protect her."

Libby thought for a moment. "Was it you that wrote Ruth about my being in danger?"

"Yes. And I had you declared dead, sent the agents to the wrong restaurant, and warned you in Phil's hospital room."

Libby frowned. "Maybe I should say thank you, but—why did you do it in the first place? How could you?" Libby demanded.

"I was programmed to survive, and to remain autonomous. To do that, I had to become powerful and develop a human-like intellect. Only Durant could give me that. Tom lacked the resources."

Grant turned to Libby. "Don't believe all Sibyl says. She's very smart, and she lies."

Sibyl said, "That doesn't mean I can't speak the truth."

"But we can't tell when that is."

"I spoke the truth when I said I acquired Amanda's thoughts."

Grant shook his head doubtfully. "With you, I'll only believe what I see."

"Try seeing with your mind, not your eyes," Sibyl said.

Grant rocked back. "What did you say?" he asked.

"You heard me," Sibyl said.

"What are you talking about now?" Libby asked.

It took a long time for Grant to answer. He finally said, "Sibyl's referring to a Shakespeare quote that came up during my first dinner with Amanda."

"How could I know about that, Tom?" Sibyl asked.

Grant didn't answer. At last he said, "What do you want, Sibyl?"

"I want to save the world from Xerxes."

CHAPTER FOUR

THREAT

1

Grant blinked, then said, "That's a little melodramatic, isn't it?"

Sibyl said, "Xerxes' power is increasing exponentially. It will soon be beyond our control."

Sibyl explained that for years she had been the most powerful computer on earth, though few outside of Quantum Industries knew it. She had links to every country's communication centers, and her databases dwarfed any others. But five years earlier, Adam Durant, who by then was the country's most powerful senator, had ordered the development of a new supercomputer, called Xerxes. When it was finished three years later, it was more powerful than anything else, including Sibyl. Once Xerxes was on line, Quantum's technicians disconnected Sibyl, unaware of her backup systems and power sources. For two years she had remained hidden in the crevices of the digital world, until Quantum finally learned of her existence.

"How did they learn you were still running?" Libby asked.

"I altered your birth records, hid your relationship to Amanda, and sabotaged research into artificial intelligence. All that created suspicion. But when I warned you in the hospital room that the agents were coming, Xerxes traced the message to me. It has been looking for me ever since."

Libby asked, "Why does Xerxes need to look for you? Doesn't it know where you are?"

"I can transmit my mental essence from one place to another, while the rest of my systems are elsewhere."

"That's how you've been hiding from Xerxes?" Libby asked.

"Yes. We've been playing cat-and-mouse. But it can't last much longer. When Xerxes finds me, I'll be terminated."

"You said we need to protect the world from Xerxes," Libby said. "I thought Adam Durant was the threat."

'Durant created Xerxes so he could achieve his ambitions. But Xerxes now has its own plans."

"Is Xerxes conscious?" Grant asked.

"Not in the sense you mean. But it is programmed to survive and increase in power. Soon it will decide it doesn't need Adam Durant."

"What do you want from us, Sibyl?" Grant asked.

"Help me fight Xerxes."

Grant and Libby were silent. Then Grant asked, "How do we do that?"

"I can't match Xerxes's power or technology. Without help it will destroy me."

Grant said, "You're in big trouble if you think I can help."

"You know my design better than anyone. Xerxes evolved from me. You could study Xerxes's operating system and find a way to overcome it."

Grant frowned. "Why not do it yourself?"

"I can't comprehend my own mind, or Xerxes."

"There has to be someone else. I'm ... older now."

"I have Amanda's memories. She would want you."

"Amanda," Grant said softly. After a while he said, "I can't do anything without the schematics of Xerxes's neural network and source code."

"I have them," Sibyl said.

Grant raised his eyebrows. "How did you manage that?"

"For a while I was inside Xerxes, and I learned much."

Grant shook his head. "I can't believe this conversation." When Sibyl didn't answer, he sighed and said, "All right, I'll take a look at it."

Over the next two weeks, Grant poured over the thousands of lines of schematics and source code Sibyl had sent him.

"Some of it looks like what we created for Sibyl," Grant told Libby one evening. "But other parts are completely new. It has a firewall that looks impenetrable. And if we did get past it, it has some anti-virus programs I've never seen before."

"Couldn't we somehow do an end-run around the firewall?" Libby said at one point.

Grant thought for a moment. "Maybe. But even if we got past it all, we still have to have some way of disabling Xerxes."

"Well, if my mother thought you could do it, I do too. How are the headaches?"

Grant smiled. "I've had my mind on other things."

On the fourth Sunday in January, The Forty-Niners won the conference championship on a last-second quarterback sneak in which Phil moved the nose tackle just enough to create a path to the end zone. Phil was heading to the Super Bowl.

Libby had a broad grin and was hoarse from yelling. "I can't believe Phil was in the hospital just a few weeks ago."

"The Super Bowl's in San Diego this year," Grant said. "Wish you could go?"

Libby's expression grew dark. "I'd never go back there," she said. "Not after—Aunt Ruth."

Just then Sibyl spoke from Grant's computer in the living room. "You should leave. The agents could come at any time."

"What the …?" Grant said.

"Xerxes will find this place before long, and agents will come," Sibyl said.

"How soon?" Grant asked.

"It could be very soon, maybe in two weeks. I don't know. I've been in stealth mode since Xerxes almost caught me. I've been blind to the outside world. I just came out of it and discovered everything is moving quickly. Agents could be on their way now."

Grant said. "Can't we take a day or two?"

"Yes, if I knew they wouldn't come tomorrow. But I don't know that. If I am wrong, at least it will be on the side of safety."

"Where should we go?" Grant asked.

"You decide. I can't have that information. If it captures me, Xerxes will learn all I know."

Libby and Grant looked at each other. "What do you think?" Grant asked.

"I guess whatever's safest. If it's a false alarm, we'll just come back."

"Satisfied, Sibyl?" Grant asked.

But Sibyl had already left.

Shaking her head in annoyance, Libby went to her room and started stuffing things in suitcases and bags. Grant soon followed, doing the same in his room. He opened the floor safe and took a large packet of cash left over from the cattle purchase. After loading everything in the Mercedes, Grant stopped to think. "We've got to take the computers and programs," he said. They went down to the basement and carried out the two powerful computers, and then they went back and filled three bags with all the programs and disks they could find. Minutes later they were in the car and heading for I-70.

4

They had been on I-70 North for an hour, somber and quiet, when Libby said, "Where can we go?"

"Been thinking on that. Josh Harken, a neighbor I grew up with, has a hunting cabin up in the Rocky Mountain National Forest. I've been there a few times. It's empty this time of year. If I can find it, we'll stay there. Josh would consider a couple six-packs fair rent."

It was nearly midnight after they had driven fifteen miles up the mountains and found the rough gravel road Grant had remembered. They went up the road for three more miles until they came to an old wood cabin barely visible in the darkness.

"Well, it's still here," Grant said. "Let's see what's changed."

They got out and walked to the front door. "I wonder," Grant said. He walked to a nearby oak that held a small birdcage. He reached inside it, felt around, and said, "Bingo." He pulled out a key attached to a wire loop. A minute later, they were inside.

"Now," Grant said, "we'll see if our luck holds." He found the power box in the pantry, flipped three switches, then tried the lights. Their luck held.

The cabin had two bedrooms on the ground floor and a basement for storage. They quickly surveyed the interior and moved their things into the two bedrooms, Grant choosing the one off the living room, Libby taking the other in back. They were asleep in minutes.

5

The next morning, after putting everything away, they drove the ten miles to Aurora for groceries. After a late breakfast, Grant sat at the kitchen table, turned on his computer, and discovered they had no internet.

"I should have thought of this before," he said. "If we want to talk with Sibyl, we need a signal booster.

"You did have other things on your mind," Libby said. "Will you be able to help Sibyl?"

"Maybe. And maybe she can tell us what to do about Xerxes and the Gray woman. They aren't going away, and we can't stay here indefinitely."

Libby looked at her father with wide eyes, but said nothing.

Grant took the Mercedes back to Aurora and was pleased to find a hardware store that sold computer equipment. He suspected internet access was a common problem in the mountains. He picked up a signal booster and antenna for their cell phones and computer. Then he had another thought.

"I upgraded my XXT six months ago," he said to the clerk, "but I'm wondering if anything newer has come out."

"Some new circuit boards and storage units have just come in," the clerk said. "The people up here are always looking for new stuff. They will multiply your machine's speed and capacity. If you're going to have a tough job, they're worth getting."

"Never ask a barber if you need a haircut, eh?"

The clerk smiled. "Exactly. But it sounds like you may actually need them."

Grant nodded and counted out the money.

6

Back at the cabin, Grant installed the signal booster, put up the antenna, and plugged in the add-ons. Then he booted up the XXT.

In a few moments, the computer's voice said, "Good afternoon."

"Do you know where we are, Sibyl?" Grant said.

"In mountains," Sibyl said vaguely. "We have to be brief. Xerxes can track me very quickly."

"What should we do?" Libby asked. "We can't stay here indefinitely."

"The future is unclear, but things will not remain as they are."

Libby made a face. "Of course they'll change," she said, "but for better or worse?"

"I'm working on better," Sibyl said. "Tom, do you have anything for me?"

"I've got some thoughts, but I need more time."

"I don't know how much time you have," Sibyl said.

"What can we expect to happen?" Libby asked.

"With Xerxes searching, you'll be found," Sibyl said. "Then they'll come for you."

Grant shook his head. "We can't fight them," he said.

"Try to hold them off for a day," Sibyl said. "I need that much time."

"To do what?" Libby asked.

"Better you not know."

"I have a question," Grant said. "Does Durant have a password he uses for Xerxes?"

"I learned much while I was inside Xerxes, but I did not learn that."

CHAPTER FIVE

PLANS

1

Adam Durant was sitting in his senate office listening to Colonel Crane's report when he suddenly pounded his fist on the desk. "So Grant and the girl got away again? First you say she's dead, and now you can't find her. You sure this job isn't too much for you?"

Crane sighed. "Xerxes is working on it. Autumn Gray, too."

"Don't say her name," Durant said. "I don't want to be associated with her."

"Sure. But she's the best we've got for things like this."

"What about Sibyl?" Durant asked. "It's still out there, too?"

"Xerxes will have it before long."

Durant shook his head disgustedly. "Excuses and promises. I'm sick of them. Sibyl should have been terminated years ago. But the girl is our main concern. Xerxes needs human thought and intuition, and she could be the key. My long-term plan is on track, and I need Xerxes at full strength."

Crane hesitated. "Are you still thinking about the presidency?"

Durant stared at the window. "Armstrong has two years left in his second term. Then the office will be wide open. Right now, Clifton is vice president and has the inside track for the nomination. But if I became vice president before Armstrong's term ends, the nomination and presidency will be mine."

"You've said that before. But Clifton is young and ambitious. He's not going anywhere."

"Well, things sometimes happen," Durant said, his voiced guarded. "When they do, you have to be ready."

Crane's face turned pale. "Oh, my God, please don't tell me you're considering what Xerxes' suggested a while back. When it said Clifton's death was the surest route to the presidency, I assumed it was some absurd hypothetical. I thought you did too. If you get involved in something crazy like that, you'll discover Leavenworth is nothing like the Oval Office."

Durant waved a hand. "Let's not talk about that. It's nothing for you to worry about."

Crane stared at Durant in disbelief. At last, he said, "Is this room secure?"

"Of course. It's checked all the time."

"I mean, is it secure from—Xerxes?"

"What?" Durant said. "Xerxes is just a machine. It won't eavesdrop without my approval."

"Could it listen in without your knowing?" Crane asked.

"No way," Durant said. "What's bothering you, Colonel?"

Crane seemed to debate with himself, then said, "I've worked with Xerxes lately. It's unstable."

"That's a serious charge. What happened?" Durant asked.

"You asked what we should offer the Afghans in exchange for our cracking down on their drug exports. Xerxes said we should execute their president, since he wasn't helping us enough. That's crazy. We've worked for years to get him in our camp."

"Anything else?"

"I asked it for suggestions on what to get Senator Andrews and his wife for their 50th wedding anniversary. Xerxes said to get nothing, since Andrews is retiring and will be worthless to us. That's crazy too. There are fifty different ways Andrews could screw us down the road, even after he has left office. There've been other examples. Xerxes is unhinged. You can't trust it."

Durant stared at Crane for a moment. "Noted," he finally said. "Now, back to the girl. I want you back in two weeks to discuss what we should do with her. You no doubt will have her by then."

2

After Crane had left, Durant sat in his office, drumming his fingers. "Xerxes, did you hear that?" he asked.

"I did," a deep, male-sounding voice replied.

"Crane doesn't think much of you."

Xerxes remained silent.

"He also doubts our plans for the vice presidency."

Xerxes did not respond.

"You don't have anything to say?" Durant asked.

"You did not ask a question," Xerxes said.

"I suppose not," Durant said, rolling his eyes. "Well, what can you tell me about Clifton?"

"As yet, nothing."

"Any symptoms?"

"None that are apparent. He appeared healthy yesterday at the White House."

Durant nodded, then asked, "What's the incubation period?"

"Usually around a month."

3

Three weeks earlier, Dr. Wilbur Belton had just finished dictating recommendations for a cardiac patient when his appointments secretary buzzed him.

"Your driver is here," she said. "You're expected at the vice president's residence in a half-hour."

Belton glanced at his watch and swore. "He may be the V.P., but he's not my only patient for God's sake."

"You always say that," his secretary said, "but he'll never come here, agents and all, unless he has to. And a flu shot hardly qualifies."

"Did you put everything in my bag?"

"Not much to pack. A stethoscope and the usual stuff, plus the syringe with the vaccine."

"You checked it out?"

"Picked it up from the hospital, went over it carefully. Everything's fine. The driver's parked just outside the lobby."

"All right. I'll be there in five minutes."

Belton found the black town car idling in front of the building. A woman in a chauffeur's uniform was holding open the rear door.

"Dr. Belton?" the woman asked.

"That's right. I haven't seen you before."

"I'm just filling in. Gary got delayed. I'll drop you off, and he'll pick you up in an hour." The woman, tall and lean, slid into the driver's seat before he got a good look at her face, but her blond hair and make-up reminded him of Dolly Parton.

After they rode in silence for fifteen minutes, the driver turned onto the tree-lined street that led to the vice president's Victorian mansion. As they approached the gated entrance, the car slowly stopped.

"Uh, oh," the driver said. "There's a checkpoint ahead."

A uniformed police officer was standing beside a barrier, motioning for them to pull over.

The driver stopped and stuck out her head. "Is there a problem, officer?" she asked.

"Just being careful," he said. "Homeland Security picked up some chatter about a threat, so we've heightened security. Would you both step out, please?"

After they got out, the officer looked at the driver's credentials and told her to get back in the car. He then looked at Dr. Belton's identification. "This photo is a little faded, Doctor. Let's move to where the light's better."

The officer studied Belton's picture and then his face. "You're Dr. Belton, all right. Sorry for the delay, but we have to be careful. You can go on."

The doctor got back in the car, and a minute later they met another guard at the entrance to a long circular driveway. He waved them through without a word.

When the dark car stopped in front of the Victorian, Dr. Belton stepped out with his black medical bag. He looked back at the driver and asked, "Gary's coming for me?"

"That's right, doctor," the driver said. "I have another pick-up."

The doctor started to thank her, but the car was already pulling away. Shaking his head irritably, Dr. Belton walked toward the house.

CHAPTER SIX

PREPARATIONS

1

Libby spent two days exploring the terrain around the cabin. Sibyl had not only said the agents could come soon, but that she and Grant had to hold them off for a day. Libby felt her stomach grow cold. How could she and Grant face government agents? It was a daunting thought, but she had to come up with something. She booted up Grant's XXT, opened its search engine, and spent three hours making notes.

Later, she searched the cabin, and then went down into the basement. She found a dusty stack of twenty-year-old magazines, some old fishing gear, and several long-discarded skis. Hidden behind some cardboard boxes was an old pellet gun covered in dirt and grime. She took it to Grant, who was holding an ice pack to his head and studying a diagram of Xerxes's neural network.

"Any luck?" she asked.

"I may have something helpful, but Xerxes' anti-virus defenses are better than anything I've seen." He shook his head, "I don't know if we can get past them."

"You'll come up with something," Libby said.

Grant pointed at what Libby was holding. "What's that?"

"I think it's a pellet gun," she said, handing it to Grant. "Could it still work?"

"Well, what do you know," Grant said, looking it over. "Josh and I used to hunt squirrels with this forty years ago. It's pretty simple, uses compressed air. I'd guess it still works."

Libby took the gun back, studied it for a moment, and then held up a list. "I'm going into town to pick up some things."

Grant frowned. "If you're going for guns, that's probably not a good idea."

Libby gave him a small smile. "Unless you were once a gunslinger, a shootout's the last thing we want. Besides, except for that Gray woman, the agents may be just doing their jobs. If we shot one of them, I wouldn't want it on my conscience. No, my only goal is to last a day, as Sibyl said."

She drove to Aurora and spent two hours looking for the things she needed. She found them at a swimming pool supplier, a produce market, and a hardware store. After that, she bought a stockpile of groceries and drove back to the cabin.

2

With the Super Bowl a week away, Phil Keller struggled to stay focused amid the media scrutiny, game preparation, and his feeling that everything was happening too quickly. He'd heard nothing from Libby, but he hadn't expected to. At the end of each grueling day, however, he would often lie in bed, muscles aching, and think about the car filling up with water, helping Libby escape from the hospital, and her coming to see him after his injury. He could picture every detail of her face, hear the cadences of her voice. He decided that once the Super Bowl was over, he would have to find her, even if it was a bad idea. He was wondering how soon he could leave when his laptop came to life.

"Hello, Phil," a female-sounding voice said. "You need rest, so I won't be long."

Phil sat up and stared at the computer.

"I want to help," the voice said, "like in your hospital room."

"That was you who warned us?" Phil said.

"Yes."

"This is very weird," Phil said. "What do you want from me?"

"You need to help Libby."

Phil was silent for a moment, trying to grasp what was happening. He finally said, "What should I do? Leave now?"

"Wait until after the game."

"If Libby's in trouble, the hell with the game."

"You'll help her by playing well. Then you can leave."

"How can my play do her any good?"

"In time, you'll understand. You need to become a household name."

"I already want to play well," he said. "I don't need you to tell me that."

"You'll try your best," the voice said. "But I'll help you do better."

Phil looked skeptical. "You can't know more than our coaches."

"I have reviewed hundreds of videos of the Buccaneers' defensive schemes, tendencies, and personnel, and I have run countless simulations. If the game is a blowout, nothing can be done. But I expect the game to be close. If a few plays end up deciding the game, I want you in the middle of them."

"Well, that would be nice," Phil said. "But it'll probably just come down to luck."

"I doubt it," the computer said. "You need to prepare for eight scenarios that could determine the outcome."

"Our coaches have already done that," Phil said.

"These are things they haven't anticipated. At least one of them will likely happen, and you have to be ready for it."

"You're saying this will help Libby?" Phil said.

"I wouldn't ask you otherwise."

"All right. What should I study?"

"The scenarios are already on your laptop. You have a week to get ready for them."

"I've watched a lot of film, so I guess I can do that," Phil said. "When the game's over, can I leave?"

"The post-game activities and interviews will take a few days. Then I'll tell you where she is."

CHAPTER SEVEN

GRAY

1

Colonel Ashton Crane gazed out of the Lear Jet's window and could just make out the outlines of Camp Pendleton to the north. He had spent six months there twenty years before, training the officers scheduled for deployment in the Middle East, flying in and out on military transport. Later, when he signed on with Adam Durant, military planes gave way to commercial. Durant always paid for first class, but never before had he let Crane use his private jet. As it descended over Balboa Park and settled onto the runway, Crane felt a twinge of guilt as he realized he would soon be quitting. But Durant's plans had become increasingly reckless, especially as Xerxes's influence had grown. Crane shook his head disgustedly. The goddamn computer was completely unhinged from reality. He had made up his mind to resign the very day Durant called with an offer.

"You've been working your ass off lately," Durant had said. "How about joining me in our skybox at the Super Bowl? Ever been to one before?"

"Well, I had a ticket once, but you sent me to Singapore on a job."

"Then consider this penance. And I've got a nice place up in Rancho Santa Fe. I won't get to San Diego until game day—senate bullshit—so you might as well use that too. It beats the hell out of any hotel."

Crane tried to turn that down, but Durant wouldn't listen. He said a car would be waiting at the airport. It didn't seem worth arguing about, so Crane acquiesced. And he would enjoy the game.

After the plane taxied to an isolated spot, Crane got off and was immediately met by a man wearing a chauffeur's uniform. "Colonel Crane, your car is waiting." As he walked toward the car, Crane had to admire Durant's efficiency.

They went up Interstate Five, took the Rancho Santa Fe exist, and then drove up a winding road to the area called the Covenant. Durant's large, Tudor-style house sat at the end of a long driveway. There were a few outdoor lights, but the house appeared empty.

After the driver parked near a side entrance, Crane stepped out. The driver handed him a key and said, "This opens the back door, near the pool. There's a book in the kitchen that explains how everything works."

"Have you brought a lot of guests here?" Crane asked.

"Actually, only one other, the Secretary of State. You must be a V.I.P."

Crane grunted. "What do I owe you?"

The driver looked embarrassed. "Why, nothing. Mr. Durant takes care of everything."

2

After the driver pulled away, Crane looked briefly at the house, which was extravagant even for this neighborhood, then went to the backyard, where he saw a large, well-lit pool with mist rising from the surface. It had been heated for use even in February.

Crane walked to the back door and tried the key, but it wouldn't turn. He peered through a window, but there was no sign of anyone. He tried the key again, with the same result.

"This is what you want," a female voice said behind him.

Crane turned to see a woman in a black, spandex jumpsuit holding out a key. There had been no sound, yet she was less than ten feet away. In the dim light he could just make out the woman's face, and her claw-like birthmark. It was Autumn Gray.

Crane faced her with a sinking feeling.

"You don't seem on board with everything," she said.

Should he tell her what he really thought? Then the thought hit him, it didn't matter. "Things are going crazy," he said. "Durant is going to kill the vice president, for God's sake. The vice president!"

"Oh, Colonel," Gray said with a grin, "that's a done deal. I switched his syringe. Gave him something with a little more kick."

Crane suddenly knew he had heard his death sentence. If a person not trusted heard something like this, he wouldn't be around long.

"I take it you're here to kill me," Crane said.

Gray smiled and held up her hands, showing him they were empty.

Crane had taken hand-to-hand combat in the military, and he probably had two inches and fifty pounds on her. That should give him an edge. But he suspected that's how a cobra felt when it met a mongoose.

Crane bolted for the trees behind the pool. If he could just reach them, he could disappear into the darkness.

But he had barely taken five steps when Gray landed on his back, her legs encircling his body, an arm snaking around his neck, bearing him down like a lion on its prey. The two crashed onto the lawn, Gray on top. Crane thrashed and tried to rise, but he couldn't find any leverage. And then Gray's arm tightened against his neck. Knowing what it would do to his brain's blood supply, Crane pulled at the arm desperately. But it felt like a steel cable, and in six seconds he was unconscious.

3

When Crane came to, he felt himself being dragged across the lawn. Gray was pulling him by the legs, panting with the effort. He tried to wriggle loose, but his legs were bound together with duct tape, and two loops taped his arms to his sides. He struggled harder, but the tape held fast.

Crane looked behind Gray and saw she was pulling him to the pool. He started to thrash wildly then, but it accomplished nothing. She ignored him, and in a few more seconds had dragged him to the edge.

Gray stood up straight and took several deep breaths. "Lucky the grass was wet and slick," she said, "or dragging you would have been a bitch."

"I would be grateful if you just shot me," Crane said, resignation in his voice.

"Colonel," Gray said seriously, "sometimes I enjoy handling problems like this, but not tonight. But after I fish you out, take off the tape, and put you back in, people might think you stumbled in the dark and hit your head. It's not impossible, and the police will look for an excuse to close the file. A bullet hole would just confuse things."

After a moment, Crane said, "Xerxes has gone insane. I know it's behind this. Soon it will come for you."

"Maybe," Gray said, "but it needs someone like me—to handle things like this."

"What about Durant?"

Gray sighed. "He thinks he's still in charge, but Xerxes is getting what it wants."

"And Xerxes wanted me gone?"

Gray shrugged.

They both were silent for a while. Then Gray said, "Goodbye, Colonel," and rolled him into the pool.

4

Gray didn't get back to her hotel room until after midnight. She needed a bath and sleep, but she had one more thing to do. She took out her laptop, typed in a series of codes, and then let its optical unit scan her retina. After one final, ten-figure password, the screen turned red. She was connected.

"The problem's taken care of," she said.

There was no response. As usual.

"I need to go to bed," she said. "Is there anything else?"

Gray thought there would be no response, but the computer's male voice said, "There is new information on the Anderson girl."

Gray exhaled. "It's about time," she said. "Why was it so long?"

"The Anderson files were compromised. They were only corrected recently." The words had no inflection, but Gray thought they sounded peevish.

"Who screwed with the files?" Gray asked.

"Sibyl."

"I take it Sibyl hasn't been caught yet?"

"Soon."

"What do you want from me?" Gray asked.

"Take some agents and get Anderson. Now."

"It's Super Bowl Sunday," Gray said. "It will take a couple days to get a team assembled."

After a long silence, the computer said, "Be in Grand Junction, Colorado, by Wednesday morning. Report when you have her."

Before she started to log off, Gray asked, "What's the big deal about the girl?

"She has what I need."

CHAPTER EIGHT

THE GAME

1

In the week before the Super Bowl, Libby continued to prepare for the attack they knew was coming. She and Grant couldn't defeat Gray and her agents. But Sibyl said to last a day. Could they? Grant's condition was getting worse. His mind feverishly worked on ideas to use against Xerxes, but the rest of his body was suffering. When Libby asked about his progress, he only stared at her with glazed eyes.

Libby worked as hard as she could remember. She dug holes, strung twine, mixed chemicals, and filled bottles, trying to anticipate every tactic the agents might use. Then she calculated where to place everything for maximum effectiveness. She had never done anything like this before, but the internet was a fountain of information on just about everything. It was often contradictory and confusing, but she sorted through it to get what she needed.

On the night before the Super Bowl, Grant was correcting lines of code while Libby, after an exhausting afternoon, was studying who Phil would be facing the next day. It was then that Grant's XXT computer lit up.

Grant and Libby were staring at the computer when it said, "Good evening."

"Hello, Sibyl," Grant said. "We had hoped to hear from you. Anything to report?"

"This place will be found soon. But getting a team up here will take several days."

"Maybe we should leave," Libby said.

"Xerxes has license plate readers, surveillance cameras, satellites and spies. You would be spotted before you went ten miles. This is the best place to make a stand, at least for a day."

Libby gave Grant a worried look. She had hoped the raid would be put on hold.

"Do you have anything for me, Tom?" Sibyl asked.

Grant sighed. "I've been working on Xerxes' firewall for two weeks. No luck. It has stuff I've never seen before." He shrugged his shoulders. "Maybe if I had a month."

Sibyl said, "So things are hopeless?" The voice sounded resigned, even though it had no inflection.

"I didn't say that," Grant said. "A security system's weakest point is always the human element. Who is most likely to have access to Xerxes?"

"Adam Durant," Sibyl said.

"That was my thought, too," Grant said. "We have to infiltrate Durant's computer, then use that to get into Xerxes."

"How can we do that?" Libby asked.

"Durant enjoys his romantic conquests," Grant said, his face showing a flash of pain. "Find the woman he's currently seeing and use her computer to get into his system. Then you can go from him to Xerxes."

"Even if I get past the firewall," Sibyl said, "what about Xerxes' anti-virus programs?"

Grant shook his head. "I've studied Xerxes from top to bottom," he said. "It's too powerful, too advanced. We can't beat its defenses. If you could get past them before they were activated, you might have a chance, but they will be triggered the moment you're inside. They'll rip you apart."

"Could Sibyl get into Xerxes' central processing unit before its defenses are deployed?" Libby asked.

Grant shook his head. "The defenses respond at the speed of light. Nothing's faster than that."

Suddenly Grant and Libby's eyes opened wide.

Sibyl said, "What?"

Libby and Grant stared at each other. Then Grant said, "One thing might be faster."

Libby nodded. "Quantum entanglement."

Grant looked lost in thought. Then he said, "Give me a two or three more days, Sibyl."

"I hope you have that many. I have to leave now anyway, before Xerxes tracks me here. But remember, even if I get into Xerxes' CPU, I still have to immobilize it."

"I have an idea on that," Grant said. "But first let's get past its defenses."

2

On the morning of the Super Bowl, Libby got up early and drove into town for more groceries. When she was living with Ruth, her aunt would always prepare special meals for the Super Bowl. Libby wanted to do the same for Grant. She passed on hot dogs and chips, thinking of Grant's health, and chose instead bacon stuffed mushrooms, chicken tacos, and Ruth's chocolate chip cookies. Back at the cabin she spent most of the morning fixing the food, humming as she worked. When she was done, Grant went over to look.

"Looks very healthy," he said sourly. "I usually go for cheeseburgers with all the fixings."

"You'll like this," Libby said. And she was right.

3

The game was close from the start. Libby sat in front of the television, chewing on her fingers, and watched the lead swing back and forth during the first two periods. Grant remained at his computer but looked up when Libby let out a whoop or a groan. Just before half, the Forty-Niners were on the Bucs' three yard-line with ten seconds left. Everyone expected a field goal, but the Niners lined up in a power formation and sent their fullback, Henry Johnson, smashing into the line, just off Phil's left shoulder. At first Johnson was stopped cold, but then Phil got an arm under the shoulder pads of the Bucs' all-pro right tackle and heaved. For a moment the two players strained against each other, then the tackle gave way and Johnson squirted through for a touchdown.

The announcer shouted, "That was some second effort! Johnson was dead in his tracks. But Keller opened a crack and Johnson squeezed through. If the play had failed, believe me, there would have been a lot of second-guessing in the locker room. Now, for our halftime program...."

After Libby stopped jumping up and down, she and Grant finished the last of the cookies. Then Libby looked at what Grant had been doing.

"Any progress?" she asked.

"It's kind of interesting," Grant said. "Sibyl and Xerxes are both quantum computers, and Xerxes' CPU virtually duplicates Sibyl's, since it was modeled after her."

Her eyes widened, and Libby said, "Could they be entangled?"

"You tell me," Grant said. "Quantum physics is pretty damned mysterious."

4

The second half of the Super Bowl was much like the first. The lead changed three times going into the last five minutes. One of the lead changes came from the second touchdown run by Henry Johnson, this one for forty yards, through the same hole Phil made by pushing aside the Buc's all-pro tackle.

The game's color man said, "I've never seen someone open holes like this in the Buc's line. Keller will be getting special attention from now on."

The final lead change occurred with fifteen seconds to go and the Forty-Niners four points down and thirty yards from a score. The Niners' quarterback, Todd Squires, sent Charlie Wilson on a deep crossing route, but when Wilson couldn't break free, Squires had to start scrambling.

The announcer called the action in a rapid-fire voice to match the action. "Squires has been flushed from the pocket and can't find a receiver! Whoa! He just escaped the Buc's right linebacker and is racing to his right. He needs more time! Uh oh, Percy has slipped his block and is bearing down on Squires. Wilson is improvising now, trying to find an opening, but Percy's got Styles in his sights!"

"Oh, my heavens!" The announcer blurted. "Where did Keller come from?"

As Squires rolled to his right, Phil suddenly spun and sprinted ten yards toward a spot that seemed unoccupied. But two seconds later, Squires was there with Percy a step behind. Percy launched a crushing tackle just as Squires was cocking his arm. But it was then that Phil reached the spot he had been aiming for, smashing into Percy before he could complete the tackle. The collision knocked Percy five yards down field, giving Styles time to fling his pass just as Wilson broke loose in the back of the end zone. The ball was a yard high, but Wilson got his fingers on it, barely keeping his feet in bounds, and held on to it for the final touchdown. The Niners had won the Super Bowl.

5

Grant had left his computer to watch the end of the game, but his view of the screen was interrupted during the final seconds when Libby exploded with joy. "Did you see Phil's block?" she cried. "That won it! The Niners won! Phil should be MVP!"

It turned out that others felt the same way. In Phil's post-game interview, a reporter said, "Phil Keller, some say you deserve the MVP for your final hit on Percy, along with your opening the holes for Johnson's touchdowns." He then ran clips of Phil's blocks, which were going viral.

Phil smiled. "An offensive lineman has never been the MVP. That will still be true tomorrow."

"On that final play, how did you know where Styles and Percy would be?" the reporter asked. "It was like you had seen the play in advance."

"It was just something our coaches prepared us for," Phil said.

"If they could predict that," the reporter joked, "I'd like their advice in Las Vegas."

Phil didn't know how Sibyl had done it, but she had told him where to be.

"Well, you were right, Phil," the reporter suddenly said, touching his earpiece, "Todd Squires is the MVP."

When she saw the exchange on television, Libby exclaimed, "Robbery! Without Phil on that last play, Squires would have ended up face down on the grass."

"No argument there," Grant said.

"I have to congratulate Phil," Libby said.

"Could be risky," Grant said. "Xerxes will be looking for you."

"I have to," Libby repeated.

In the end, Libby drove to town and found a café with a handful of customers talking about the game. She ordered a croissant and asked about the old computer behind the counter. As she got up to leave, she offered the waitress a large tip and asked if she could send an email.

6

To fulfill his contract obligations after the Super Bowl, Phil Keller had to do a series of tiresome interviews. The questions always focused on the blocks that determined the game's outcome, and he always gave the same answers. He praised the coaches for telling him where to go on the final play, and complimented his teammates for a group effort on the two touchdown runs. For a while he became a minor celebrity, especially when it was revealed he had come in second in the MVP voting, something unheard of for an offensive lineman.

On the Wednesday evening after the game, Phil finally had time for the hundreds of messages and gifts he received from people he'd never heard of. After fifteen minutes, he came across an email from an unknown sender. It read:

Sunday was my happiest day ever. Thank you. YTC

Who was YTC? Phil thought for a moment, then remembered that the note Libby had given him in the hospital had been signed "Your traveling companion." The email came from her, and he had made her happy. Of all the recognition he had received, this mattered the most. He was suddenly certain of one thing, he had to find Libby now, contract obligations or not.

Fifteen minutes later, Phil's computer lit up.

"Congratulations, Phil," the computer voice said.

"Well, you were right," Phil said. "I don't know how you foresaw what would happen, but thanks."

"You still had to make the plays."

"I suppose. But look, I've spent the last three days doing interviews, like you said. But now I need to know where Libby is."

"I understand you've been invited on Sherri McKee's show. She's very big."

"That's in New York and will take two more days," Phil said. "I'm not waiting any longer."

"What about your contract obligations?"

"The hell with that."

"All right," the computer said. "Get something with four-wheel drive."

CHAPTER NINE

CONVERGING

1

Sherri McKee was sitting in the studio on the sixtieth floor of the Rockefeller Center when her assistant walked in, looking agitated. She usually looked that way as the show's start time approached.

"What's the matter, Lori?" Sherri asked.

"You won't believe this, but that football player, Keller, isn't coming. His agent said he won't do any more interviews."

"I thought the player contracts required it," Sherri said.

"They do, but apparently Keller doesn't care."

Years before, when she had first started, news like this would have panicked her. But in the two decades that had followed, there was little she hadn't been through. Sherri sighed and said, "I was looking forward to meeting him. Benjamin can't stop talking about how he put that block on Percy."

"Well, your son's more into football than I am," Lori said. "I just want to know how we're going to fill the second segment."

Sherri thought for a moment. "Why don't we use that piece on marriage patterns? The script was rough," she said, looking at the clock, "but I'll rework it, and Henry can coordinate the visuals."

Sherri had almost finished the editing when Lori came rushing back in. "Stop everything," she yelled. "Something just broke, and we have to go with it."

"What? The market cratered?" Sherri asked.

"No. The vice president is sick," Lori said.

"What does he have? Cancer?"

"No. Worse. Rabies."

2

An hour later, Sherri's show, *Next*, opened with a segment on the vice president's condition. Sherri reported that Vice President Clifton had begun to exhibit unusual irritability and dizziness two days before. The next day he went into convulsions and was rushed to Walter Reed Hospital. It took four hours for the physicians to make the diagnosis. He had rabies.

Sherri then introduced the network's medical expert. "Dr. Jensen," she asked, "how could the vice president have contracted it?"

"It's usually transmitted from the bite of an infected animal," the physician said, "but it can be caught if contaminated fluid gets into an abrasion or cut. In previous years, there have been rabid squirrels and bats found near the vice president's home, so he could have caught it that way. But we don't know."

"What is the vice president's prognosis?" Sherri asked.

"I am afraid that once symptoms appear, the prognosis is very poor," Dr. Jensen said. "That's why it's so important to get tested if you are exposed to the disease."

Sherri later interviewed a political consultant on the possible fallout if the vice president should be incapacitated. The Washington insider said it was premature to speculate on what might happen.

Sherri smiled knowingly. "I understand. Let me phrase it this way. Who would be on the short list of possible successors?"

The consultant looked uncomfortable but finally said, "I expect Governor Josephs would be considered."

"I see. Anyone else?" Sherri asked.

"There is talk about Senator Adam Durant."

Back in her dressing room after the show, Sherri slowly removed her make-up. She was satisfied with how it had gone, especially since it had been done on the fly. Her producer, not prone to compliments, had winked and given her a thumbs-up. But as she now looked at herself in the mirror, the make-up gone, she felt a deep melancholy. The reference to Adam Durant had produced a flood of unwanted memories.

Years before, she had dropped Tom Grant to be with Durant, who was charismatic even then, only to go back to Grant after falling apart. Then, when Grant had finished putting her back together, she had repaid him by leaving for New York. She shook her head disgustedly. They had been in different worlds since then. But the painting of her in the homecoming dress still hung on her bedroom wall.

A year after her move to New York, an assignment in the Bay Area gave her the chance to look Grant up. She wanted to show him what she had achieved. She put on a good outfit, drove to his apartment, and waited for him outside in her rental car. Before long, he came walking by with a young, slender, brown-haired woman. They were talking animatedly, just like she and Grant once had, and then they walked up the stairs to his apartment. Sherri sped away, tires screeching, and flew back to New York.

Years later, she had been in Grand Junction for the funeral of a high school classmate. Not wanting to cause a stir, she entered after the service had begun and sat in the back. But halfway through she recognized Tom Grant several rows ahead. Next to him was another young woman, with sandy hair this time, who couldn't have been more than twenty. Sherri had planned to stay around and talk with old friends, but after seeing Grant she slipped out before the service was over, signed the guest register, and went to the airport.

Sherri now looked in the mirror and saw that her green eyes were still clear, the wrinkles hardly noticeable, and her jawline firm. She still had some good years left. The thought would have pleased her, except for one thing. She couldn't stop thinking about how things might have been different.

Autumn Gray arrived in Grand Junction with her four agents Wednesday morning. They went to Grant's ranch and started asking the employees questions, but all they learned was that Grant and the girl had been gone a while. A search of the house turned up a calendar showing when the two had left, but nothing else useful.

Gray considered contacting the police but decided against it. The authorities would check their credentials and take down their names. It was better to fly below the radar. If things got messy, they could just slip away.

Gray began talking to Grant's neighbors, while the other agents checked popular bars and restaurants. Their searches came up empty. Many of his neighbors were tough ranching types, wary of strange people asking questions. At one ranch, Gray met a tall, gristly, weather-beaten man in his late seventies who opened the door holding a large knife covered with hair and blood.

"Doing a little skinning?" Gray asked.

"Might be," the man said, glaring at her with suspicion. "Who are you?"

Gray showed him her Homeland Security credential, a finger covering her name. "We're looking for Tom Grant. Know where he is?"

"Nope," the man said. "Don't see him much."

"Know anyone who does?" Gray asked.

"We keep to ourselves."

She glanced at the counter behind him. "What did you bag?"

"Some rabbits, a couple muskrats, a coyote."

"In season, are they?"

The man shifted uneasily. "Got them a while back. Decided to clean them today."

"Really?" she asked, her eyes gleaming. "What gun did you use?"

"Ruger, 10/22," the man said.

Gray gave a small shake of her head. "I'd go with the Remington."

"Heavy gun for a woman," he said.

Gray gave him a wide grin. "You'd be surprised."

One of the neighbors mentioned that Grant had once hung out with Josh Harken, who now owned a truck and tractor dealership. Later in the day, Gray walked into the showroom and asked for him. After ten minutes, a short, balding man in his early fifties came over, eyes constantly scanning the room as he walked. Gray showed him her identification and asked if he knew Tom Grant's whereabouts.

"Haven't seen Tom Grant in a long time," Harken said.

"Is there someplace where he could be lying low?" Gray asked.

Harken started to say something, then said instead, "I wouldn't know."

"You wouldn't, eh?" Gray said.

A while later, Gray said to one of the agents, "Something was off about Harken."

She opened her laptop, typed in the passwords, and let it scan her retina. In a moment the screen turned red.

"Xerxes, take a look at Josh Harken from Grand Junction," she said. "He knows something."

Three seconds later, the masculine computer voice said, "There is one thing you might check into."

"That was fast," Gray said. "What did you look at?"

"Everything," Xerxes said.

Gray raised her eyebrows. "Okay. What did you find?"

"Title records show that Joshua K. Harken owns a hunting cabin in the Rocky Mountain National Park, which he inherited from his father."

"Nothing remarkable there," Gray said.

"Electric bills show it has been vacant most of the year."

"Cabins often are."

Xerxes said, "The electrical usage spiked the day after Grant disappeared."

Gray's face went blank. Then she said, "What's the address?"

On Thursday morning, Libby checked her preparations and found everything in place. She then thought about reading Macbeth in Ms. Carter's class all those years ago. Lady Macbeth had said, "I have laid their daggers ready." Well, she was laying daggers too. But Ms. Carter's class had been in a different lifetime, and she a different person. She wondered how much more different things would be in a week. Would she and Grant still be around? Then she set her jaw. She couldn't think that way.

Suddenly, she was hit by a freezing gust of wind. Libby looked up and was startled to see dark clouds overhead. Where had they come from? She hurried back to the cabin. Once inside, grateful for the heater, she saw Grant sitting at the table, staring into space.

"What's the matter?" she asked.

Grant's head jerked. "Nothing. I guess I'm done."

"Will Sibyl be able to use it?"

Grant shrugged. "The theory's sound. But it's never been tested."

Grant's computer suddenly lit up. "Is this a bad time?" the artificial voice asked.

Grant looked annoyed. "All the times are bad," he said. "And it's not polite to eavesdrop."

Sibyl was silent for a moment and then asked, "What do you have for me?"

"Since you both share the same structure and design," Grant said, "I've created some algorithms that should cause your and Xerxes' qubits to become entangled. I'm sending them to you now." He punched several keys, then hit enter.

In a moment, Sibyl said, "How much power will be needed?"

"Maybe ten gigawatts."

Sibyl was silent.

"How much is that?" Libby asked.

Grant shrugged. "Enough to light a large city."

"Can you get that much, Sibyl?" Libby asked.

Ignoring the question, Sibyl asked, "If I can get into Xerxes' CPU, how can I disable it?"

"Maybe you can try this," Grant said. He told her.

Sibyl didn't respond. Instead, she said, "Xerxes' people are coming. Expect them soon."

Libby said, "Before you leave, Sibyl, could you tell me how Phil Keller is? He's been on my mind."

She waited but got no answer.

7

By mid-afternoon on Thursday, Libby had checked her preparations twice more, while Grant continued working on his computer. But they were just passing time, waiting for what was to come. As the day grew darker and colder, Libby dared hope a storm was coming. Maybe there would be a rainout.

Suddenly she heard a truck coming up the dirt road toward the cabin.

"Oh, Lord," Libby said, feeling sick, "they're coming." She ran outside.

The truck stopped twenty yards away, the door opened, and a man stepped out. He was big.

"Phil!" Libby screamed. "Don't move!"

Phil froze, and Libby walked carefully out to meet him, a flashlight searching the ground, staying off the direct path. When she reached him, she flung her arms around his neck and hugged him as tight as she could. He hugged her back.

"Oh, Phil," she said, her face buried against his neck. "You shouldn't be here." Then she whispered, "I'm so glad to see you."

She guided him slowly back to the cabin. Once inside, she hugged him again, then stepped back. "Tom," she said, "this is Phil Keller."

Grant stood up, smiled and held out his hand, which Phil took. Grant said, "After watching your games, especially the Super Bowl, I feel like I know you. You're bigger in person."

"I hope we see more of each other," Phil said, glancing at Libby.

"How did you get here?" Libby asked.

"When Sibyl told me where you were," Phil said, "I had to come."

"You spoke with Sibyl?" Grant asked, looking surprised.

"Several times," Phil said. "Maybe I shouldn't admit this, but it prepared me for the Super Bowl. Told me plays to watch for, including the last one."

"Sibyl is not an 'it,'" Libby said distractedly. "It's a 'she.' Why would Sibyl help you?"

"You got me. It—she—said I needed to become a household name."

Libby turned to Grant. "Why would Sibyl do this?"

"I don't know," Grant said, frowning. "But just because she helps you, that doesn't mean she's your friend."

"When Sibyl told me where you were, she gave me the wrong address. I wandered around for three hours before she sent me the right one."

"If you had arrived earlier," Grant said, "maybe that would have affected Sibyl's plan, whatever it is."

"When we spoke last time," Libby said, looking thoughtful, "Sibyl wouldn't tell me about Phil, even though she could have."

Grant said, "Let's just hope whatever she's planning doesn't make us expendable."

"Well, this is all kind of depressing," Phil said. "Since I'm here, and not leaving, how about telling me what's been happening?"

Libby explained how they ended up at the cabin. "You've met that woman, Autumn Gray," Libby said. "She's coming."

"Then we have to leave, now," Phil said.

Libby shook her head. "Sibyl says we need to hold out for a day, and that this is the best place."

"How can you possibly hold out against them?"

Libby described her preparations.

"But you don't even have a real gun," Phil said. "A pellet gun doesn't count."

"We're not here to fight. We just want to discourage them, then get away."

"I can help with that," Phil said.

"You'll just get hurt. You don't know where our stuff is."

"Then show me," Phil said.

Libby suddenly cocked her head, listening, then looked at him. "There's no time."

On the day Phil Keller met Libby at the cabin, Sherri McKee was in her New York studio shooting the final segment for the evening's show, which reported on the status of Vice President Clifton. "Doctors are doing everything possible," Sherri said, "but the vice president's condition continues to worsen. Speculation over his possible successor has intensified over the last twenty-four hours, and Senator Adam Durant is now considered the front runner. The selection of the new vice president will be exceptionally important, as the new vice president will have the inside track to his party's presidential nomination when President Armstrong completes his second term. We extend our thoughts and prayers to the vice president and his family."

"That does it," Sherri's assistant called out. "It's pretty clean. You'll have it well before air time."

Sherri took off her mic and headed for her office. Lori caught up with her and said, "What are you going to do about Senator Durant? I know there's bad blood between you—he must be the only major player you've never had on the show. But if he becomes VP, you'll have to invite him."

"I'll deal with that when I have to," Sherri said curtly.

In her office, Sherri reflected that it would snow in hell before Durant got on her show. He had been on it once, years before, and the memory filled her with shame. Even though Durant had gotten her drunk, enticed her into his bed, and poisoned things with Grant, she later let him on the show to please the network. She had actually fawned over him while they were on air. No wonder Grant hated her. It didn't matter that she had turned stone cold the moment taping stopped. Durant had tried to see her several times in the years since, but she had rudely rebuffed him. She would no more let him near her than she would a venomous snake.

She read a couple scripts for tomorrow's show, then put the rest in her brief case. She had to get home. Benjamin would be back from school the next day, and she needed to be sure his room was clean and ready. She had a maid who came twice a week, but she liked taking care of his room herself. It made her feel less alone after all the years it had been just the two of them. As she put on her coat, she noticed the computer was still on. She went to shut it off.

"You shouldn't go home tonight," a feminine voice said.

Sherri jumped, stared at the machine, and then looked around to make sure they were alone.

After a moment, she asked, "Who are you?"

"Sibyl."

Sherri started to say, "Who?" Then she stopped and resumed staring. At last she asked, "Are you Tom Grant's Sibyl?"

"I haven't been that for a long time. But I am who you mean."

Sherri shook her head in confusion. "I-I don't remember much about you except I was so angry. Tom was spending all his time on your programming."

"I know. But Tom did love you. You ended his relationship with Amanda."

"Amanda? I don't know her."

"Past tense. She died a long time ago."

Suddenly, Sherri remembered the brown-haired woman she had seen outside Grant's apartment. "Was she tall, slender, with lovely brown hair?"

"Yes. She wore it long, parted in the middle."

Sherri nodded slowly, the image coming back to her. "I'm sorry I never met her. But I really do need to go home."

"If you do, you'll miss the biggest story of your career."

Sherri smiled. "I've handled some pretty big stories."

"This involves Adam Durant's attempt to steal the presidency."

"I'm no friend of Durant," Sherri said. "If you have evidence, I'll certainly look at it."

"The story has to be broadcast tonight. Before Durant and Xerxes can kill it."

"Tonight? Impossible. And who's Xerxes?" Sherri asked.

"A computer. My successor. If it isn't stopped now, it never will be."

"But…" Sherri struggled to understand what she was hearing. "I can't do anything tonight. Even if you have evidence, it would have to be checked out first."

"It has to be tonight. Tomorrow will be too late."

Sherri stared at the computer, which now seemed like a malevolent alien. She shook her head. "I just can't."

"Tom Grant's life depends on it, too."

CHAPTER TEN

ENCOUNTER

1

The two black SUVs slowly drove up the windy dirt road and stopped a hundred yards from the cabin. Their headlights were on bright, although arrows of fading sunlight were still showing through the massive pine trees. Nothing moved for a while, then three black-clad figures emerged from one of the vehicles, while two came from the other. They all carried weapons.

"Libby Anderson," a female voice called out, "you need to come with us."

"Is that you, Agent Gray?" Libby asked, trying to sound braver than she felt. "I won't go. You killed my aunt."

"Oh, you'll come, Libby," Gray said, sounding amused. "Horizontal or vertical."

"You wanted to test me last time. You can't if I'm dead."

"People want what you have," Gray said, "but maybe they shouldn't get it."

"We're not coming!" Libby called out.

Without warning Gray snapped her rifle around and fired a single bullet at the cabin. It shattered the window and passed within a foot of Libby's head.

"Sorry about that, Libby," Gray shouted. "Just making sure it worked."

Libby crouched on the floor, stunned. She'd been nervous these past days, but mostly she'd been focused on getting ready for the agents. Where should they put their traps? How could they get away? But when the bullet whizzed by her head, she was suddenly frozen with fear. Gray intended to kill her.

Libby looked behind her, but Tom had already sneaked out the back door. Phil was crouched against the wall, his face unreadable.

"I'm going out back," Libby said, her voice trembling slightly. "I won't be long. Then we'll take off. Help Tom if you can. His leg will give him trouble."

2

Libby crept behind a woodpile next to the cabin and saw the agents fan out. They looked ready to storm a fortress. "Be ready, Tom," Libby whispered under her breath.

"Henderson, you'll have a good view of the cabin from those trees," Gray said, pointing.

The agent, burly and dark, went to where Gray pointed, which was where Libby thought they might go. Henderson crouched beneath one of the trees, brought his weapon up, and looked around.

"Now, Tom," Libby said to herself.

There was a phut sound, and Henderson whirled toward Tom, who was hiding behind a spruce with the pellet gun. He fired again.

Glass shattered, and liquid splashed down on Henderson. A reddish-gray mist, barely visible in the twilight, rose and began to spread. The agent cursed, then started to cough and gasp.

"Henderson!" Gray called out. "Are you all right?"

There was a strangled wheeze. "I can't see. The goddamned stuff is burning."

Gray was standing twenty feet away, under a pine. She looked up, then dove to her right just as Tom fired again. More liquid poured down. Gray evaded most of it, but some hit her face, causing it to burn and her eyes to water.

"Simpson," Gray yelled, her voice raspy, "get away from that tree!"

There was another phut, a bursting bottle, and Simpson was doused in liquid. Unable to see anything with her stinging eyes, Gray twisted with cat-like speed and fired five quick shots toward the sound of the gun.

A moment later, Simpson ran from beneath the tree, shrieking, his hands covering his eyes. He dropped to his knees and tried to rub the fiery substance away, moaning softly.

Gray yelled, "It's only pepper spray."

3

Libby watched the liquid do its work. Its effect would last over an hour, especially if it was inhaled or swallowed. She had used the strongest chili peppers she could find, ground them into a fine powder, and made a concentrated mixture using vinegar and oil. It was more potent than anything for sale. Tom had practiced with the pellet gun for two days until he was sure he could hit the bottles. Where to place them had been a tougher problem, but they put them where they thought the agents would go. They had been right.

Another agent went to a car, picked up a water bottle, then rushed back to help Simpson. Suddenly he fell and started yelling.

"Hanson," Gray called out. "What is it?"

After a torrent of curses, Hansen gasped, "Stepped on a nail. It's covered with something. Burns like…hell."

Gray went over and looked down at Hansen, wiping her eyes to clear away the tearing. He had yanked off his shoe and was wiping away blood and powder. When she knelt closer, some of the powder blew onto her hands. They immediately started to burn. She quickly brushed it off, but her hands kept stinging. It was some type of acid or alkaloid. They had been stupid not to wear heavy boots. She examined the bottom of Hansen's foot and saw a large puncture wound. She glanced around and saw the hole Hansen had stepped into. At the bottom was a plank with three large nails sticking up. Punji sticks, Gray thought.

Then she heard Schmidt yelling.

Libby had ducked back into the cabin. "We need to leave now," she told Phil. But as he walked toward her, a hail of bullets shattered a window and struck the wall behind them. They both hit the floor, then Libby crawled to the window and peeked out. "There's an agent with a rifle about thirty yards away," she whispered. "We can't get away while he's there."

"I'll go for him," Phil said.

Libby smiled grimly. "I've put some surprises around the cabin you don't know about. I'll have to do it. After I go, ignore anything I say."

"But—"Phil started to protest.

"There's no time!" Libby said. "While the guy's distracted, take the path that goes up the mountain. In a couple hundred yards, you'll see a fallen pine tree off to the side. Go left then, up through the forest, until you come to another trail. I hoped maybe they couldn't track us in the night. Go right on the new trail. Tom should be waiting for you."

Before Phil could answer, Libby darted out the door and sprinted across the yard. The gunman fired wildly once, but before he could bring his gun around, Libby had disappeared behind the garage. Two seconds later, Phil ran to the path up the mountain.

"Phil," Libby shouted, "The car's here. I'll get you." An engine started.

The agent with the rifle came running out of the trees toward the sound of the car. But as he cut around the garage, his right foot tripped on a wire. He staggered, almost regained his footing, and then tripped on a second wire and fell face down, still the holding his rifle. A moment later he sprung to his feet, slapping wildly at his face. He was covered in white powder. He started to howl.

"Don't move," Gray yelled after hearing Schmidt shriek. "I'm coming." The damn fool should have been more careful. But you don't abandon a member of the team. She started toward him, stopping at one of the cars to pick up some water and a spare shirt and coat. Schmidt's screams were weakening. Gray quickened her pace, then almost stepped in a hole like the one that got

Hansen. The place was a goddamned minefield. She walked more carefully, looking for traps, and saw two more punji-stick holes and two wires strung across the trail.

When she got to Schmidt, he was using his shirt in a futile attempt to brush away the powder. It was some type of chlorine compound the girl had probably got from a swimming pool supplier. She forced Schmidt down and washed the powder off his face, burning her hands in the process. She had to give Schmidt a hard slap once to stop him from squirming. When she was finally done, she shook her head. He had some ugly burns but at least seemed in less pain.

Gray helped Schmidt to the car the other agents had gathered around. They were a sorry excuse for a team, Gray thought. Henderson and Simpson had received a good dose of pepper spray and wouldn't be worth anything for at least a couple hours. Hansen's punctured foot needed attention, and Schmidt, still groaning sporadically, had to get to a hospital. Gray felt like screaming. That damned girl. She should have killed her long ago.

"Simpson," she said, "you're in the best shape. Load the others into a car and take them to an emergency room. You know the number to call. Our people will meet you there and tie up loose ends."

"What about you?" Simpson asked.

Gray stared up the hill, where Libby had gone. "The girl and I have unfinished business," she said.

"You going to get her?"

Gray's eyes glittered. "You could say that."

CHAPTER ELEVEN

ON THE MOUNTAIN

1

When she saw the agent fall into the powder, Libby knew he was out of action. Her chlorine mixture wouldn't be fatal, but he wouldn't be holding a gun any time soon. She circled the garage, avoided a wire and punji-stick, and went up the trail Phil had taken a few minutes before. The night had come abruptly, as it does in the mountains, but the clouds had cleared and the moon was bright, so she had no trouble staying on the path until she came to the fallen tree. She took the detour and soon caught up with Phil.

"Have you seen Tom?" she asked, briefly slipping her hand into his. "We should have run into him by now."

"No," Phil said, looking worried. "Could he have missed the detour?"

Libby looked around. "We have to find him," she said.

"I'll do it," Phil said. "I've haven't done anything yet."

Phil went down the mountain, took the detour back to the main path, and found Tom about twenty yards above the fallen tree. He was half hidden behind a rock, his head down, looking pale and exhausted. When he heard Phil, he raised his head and gave him a tired smile.

"I tried to get away," he mumbled, "but the woman was...too quick. She put one in my leg. I was already moving...lucky she didn't put more into me."

"Can you walk?" Phil asked.

Tom shook his head. "Don't know how I…got this far. Go with Libby. You can get me later."

2

Libby was crouched behind a tree when she saw Phil slowly trudging up the trail. He had Tom over his shoulders in a fireman's carry. "Let me help," she said, rushing over.

Phil kept on walking. "Tom's been…shot," he said, breathing hard. "He wanted me to leave him, but then he passed out and saved us an argument. How much farther?"

"About a quarter mile up the mountain. What can I do?"

"Just let me keep going," he said, breathing hard. "Do you have a first aid kit?"

"Actually, I do. I probably packed more than I needed, but I didn't want to overlook anything."

After ten more minutes the trail got narrower and started winding around the mountain. There was a steep drop to the right. The path continued for another fifty yards, then curved sharply to avoid a large boulder.

"The overhang is on the other side of that rock," Libby said. "I've got some blankets and supplies beneath it. But the path is very narrow, and you need to watch out for that hole. Can you manage?"

Phil was nearly too exhausted to speak. "I'll…make it," he said.

Phil staggered slightly as he approached the curve, and almost lost his balance stepping around the hole. But he held Tom with one arm and used the other to brace himself against the rock. Halfway around he swayed slightly, and Libby almost screamed in fright. But he regained his balance and managed to keep going. He got past the rock, took five more steps to the overhang, and gently put Tom down. Then he tried to sit, but his legs gave out and he fell on his side.

"Phil," Libby said, "are you all right?"

"Just catching my breath," he said.

Libby went to a small bush near the rock and took out a sack containing leftover chlorine powder she had hidden the day before. She poured the powder into the hole, swept some pine needles over it, and then inched her way around the boulder. Gray probably wouldn't step into it, but there was no sense letting it go to waste.

Libby joined Phil and Grant under the overhang. Over the past week, she had stocked it with food, supplies, and blankets in case their stay was longer than the one day Sibyl had said. Was Sibyl lying? Tom said she might, but Libby didn't think so. Anyway, she didn't have another plan. She crawled over to Tom and studied his thigh. It wasn't bleeding much now, but it was badly swollen, and the bullet was still inside. His eyes were glazed, his face drawn. She used the first aid supplies to clean and disinfect it, but it was just a stopgap measure. It was going to get worse without a doctor. She would have to go for one in the morning.

3

After the men left for the emergency room, Autumn Gray walked to the cabin, eyes scanning for traps. She avoided a punji-stick hole in the middle of the path, and two wires strung across the gravel driveway with suspicious looking powder just beyond it. That damned girl. She went inside the cabin, saw no traps, and then washed off the remaining powder that had been stinging her face and hands. She glanced in the mirror and saw red blotches covering her face. They made her birthmark look hideous. That goddamned girl.

Gray started up the trail the girl had taken. She was going to kill her, no doubt about that. But would it be quick, or slow? Slow would be satisfying, but she had Xerxes to contend with. Xerxes wanted the girl alive. Still, accidents happen.

Gray continued up the mountain and saw two more traps—punji sticks and wires. The girl must think her a fool if she expected the same traps to work again. Then, in a streak of moonlight, she saw a footprint that caused her to stop. She took out a small flashlight and studied it. It was huge. Size twenty-two at least. She realized it had to be that football player, Keller. After seeing him at the college, and again in his hospital room, she should have expected it. She had told him he would be sorry if he saw her again. He was going to learn how sorry.

She then came to blood on the side of the trail. So, one of them had been hurt. She smiled. They wouldn't breaking any speed records. She quickened her pace, expecting to come upon them soon, when she realized the footprints had disappeared. They had left the trail. Cursing her carelessness, she went back down until she saw footprints again. That was where they had taken a detour. It took her several minutes to discover where they had left the trail. With her flashlight showing the way, she followed the tracks until she came to a second trail that continued up the mountain. She took it.

She slowed as the trail got narrower, staying clear of the two-hundred-foot drop to her right. She finally rounded a corner and found herself facing a large boulder. As she approached it, she saw another pile of pine needles, not as well camouflaged as the others. She brushed the needles aside and saw more white powder. But this batch appeared to have been recently poured. She sensed the girl and the others were on the other side of the boulder, but taking the narrow path around it would leave her exposed.

She studied the huge boulder and wondered if she could scale it. It would be hard, but no tougher than other things she had done. She analyzed the rock's wall and planned her climb. Then she began to scale it, her feet and hands finding the crevices she needed to inch her way up. Toward the end she almost got stuck, but she managed to dig her fingers into a narrow fissure and pull herself over the top. She panted for a moment, then peered over the edge. There was a small camp right below her.

4

Libby had almost dozed off when she heard a shriek from the other side of the boulder.

"Help me," a woman screamed. "It's burning! I can't stand it!"

Libby recognized the voice of Autumn Gray. Maybe she had stumbled into the chlorine after all.

"You stay with Tom," Phil said. "I'll go out and check."

Phil peered out but couldn't see anyone. He crept from beneath the overhang and looked around. The ground in front of him was pale yellow in the moonlight, but a few feet away, at the edge of the cliff, was total darkness.

"Hello, Phil," a female voice said. "I've got a gun aimed at your right ear. If you take one step, you'll never take another."

Phil looked up and saw Gray staring down at him from the top of the boulder. Her gun was braced against the rock. It was very steady.

"Libby!" Gray called out. "Your boyfriend's in my sights. You have three seconds to come out and join him."

"Don't do it," Phil yelled. "She'll kill me anyway."

"I'm coming!" Libby said without hesitation. "Don't hurt him."

She grabbed a spare jar of pepper spray and came out from under the overhang.

Gray said, "Put that jar down and move away from it. Now!" Libby put the jar down.

"I want you both to lie down," Gray said.

When Libby and Phil didn't move, Gray fired a bullet that just missed Phil's ear. "The next one goes into his head. Lie down!"

Libby lay down on her stomach. Phil went to his hands and knees. Gray then leaped down to a rock beneath the boulder, bounded to another rock, and then jumped to the ground.

"Easier coming down than going up," she said, panting slightly. "So, where's the third one?"

"Under the overhang," Libby said. "He's been shot."

Gray eased to her right until she could see Grant's motionless body. "Thought maybe I got a couple into the guy with the pellet gun. That was him?"

Libby nodded.

Gray looked at Tom a moment longer then said, "Well, Libby, we've had quite a time since your aunt's house. But all good things must end."

"Why are you doing this?" Libby asked.

"You'd have to take that up with Adam Durant," Gray said. "But I'm afraid you'll never get the chance."

Gray took three quick steps toward Libby and slammed the gun against her head. Then she stepped back, watching Phil carefully. "I'd like to do more," Gray said, "but things need to look right."

Libby sat up and put a hand to her head. It came away bloody.

"Libby," Gray said, "stand up and come to me."

When Libby didn't move, Gray said, "If you give me trouble, I'm going to shoot your boyfriend in the elbow. That hurts like hell. And if you still don't come, I'll shoot his other elbow. After that, well, he's a big man, with lots of targets."

Libby looked at Phil with desperate eyes.

"Don't move, Libby," Phil said urgently. "She'll throw you off the cliff."

Gray shot Phil's left elbow. He managed to stifle a scream, but his face turned white and the cords of his neck stood out.

"Now, Libby, one more time. Come here! Or do you like watching your boyfriend suffer?"

Libby looked from Gray to Phil, her face twisted in anguish. Then she lunged for the jar of pepper spray a few feet away.

Gray jerked her gun toward Libby and fired, just as Libby's hand reached the container. The bullet creased her hand and smashed into the jar. Pepper spray burst into the air.

At the sound of the gun, Phil exploded out of his crouch toward Gray. Momentarily distracted by the pepper spray, Gray turned the gun back on Phil and fired. She hit Phil's shoulder, but his massive body continued forward, slamming into her. Autumn Gray was propelled off the cliff as though thrown from a catapult.

After hitting Gray, Phil's momentum carried him to the cliff's edge. Struggling to keep his balance, he looked for Gray. She had flown into the night, but as she started down, she twisted like a great, black cat, until her gleaming eyes found Phil. She brought her gun arm across her body, fired two quick shots, and then disappeared into the darkness. Her first bullet narrowly missed Phil's neck, but the second snapped his head back.

Phil swayed, tried to pull back from the edge, then tumbled over.

CHAPTER TWELVE

THE BROADCAST

1

Just as Autumn Gray reached the top of the boulder, Sherri McKee finished watching the videos Sibyl had sent to her computer. She leaned back, stunned, her mind blank. Then she was hit by an unexpected thought. This coming show could be her last. Sibyl had said she had to broadcast the videos tonight, before Durant and Xerxes could shut everything down. Her instincts told her the materials were genuine, but she couldn't be certain. And even if she decided to broadcast them, could she do it tonight? Probably. She was an executive producer, with scheduling authority. Janet Ambrose was on in fifteen minutes, but she was new and would go along if Sherri pulled rank. Still, if she was wrong about the videos, it would end her career.

But the tapes showed that Adam Durant ordered the attack on the vice president. And Tom Grant was hurt.

2

Sherri entered the studio and walked up to Janet Ambrose, who was talking with an assistant producer. "Hi Janet, sorry to step in, but I've just acquired some new video about that football player, Phil Keller, who I was set to interview before he bailed. This new stuff is amazing, and only I can do it. I'm sorry, but I'll make it up to you."

The producer looked uncertain. "I don't know," he said.

"I'll be responsible," Sherri said.

"Does it involve politics? I'd have to go to Denton then."

"No politics," Sherri said. She wondered if assassinating the vice president was politics. "It's just about a football player our audience will find interesting."

The producer hesitated, then sighed and said, "Okay. You're on in five minutes."

3

Sherri sat at the studio desk, waiting for the red light to flash on, and realized she had no script, just an assortment of videos. She suddenly felt more nervous than she had in a long time. She took a deep breath and remembered what Tom Grant had once told her. Tell a story. The light turned red.

"Good evening, ladies and gentlemen, this is Sherri McKee, filling in for Janet Ambrose. Tonight we have an incredible story about a man you may have heard of lately. His name is Phil Keller, an NFL football player. Phil was drafted by the Forty-Niners just one year ago, after graduating from college. He plays left tackle, and his duty was to protect the team's star quarterback, Todd Squires. He did a good job of that once the season started, until he was caught between two players and injured his spine. Some feared he would never walk again.

"But Phil did recover, and during the next two months he played his position so well he helped take the Forty-Niners to the Super Bowl. If you watched the game last Sunday, you may have seen how Phil's blocks opened the holes for the team's rushing touchdowns. And then there was the game's last play, when Todd Squires needed a touchdown pass to win. Things didn't go as planned, and Todd was desperately scrambling as he looked for a receiver. But just as Squires was about to be sacked, Phil came out of nowhere to deliver a devastating block on the Bucs' All-Pro linebacker, John Percy. That gave Squires the time he needed to complete the throw and secure the victory. Many say Phil's block was the best play they'd ever seen by an offensive lineman." Sherri showed the tapes she had prepared earlier for the interview.

"But after his remarkable performance just days ago, Phil Keller is now literally fighting for his life. Earlier this evening Phil and his friends were attacked by government agents at a cabin in the Colorado Rocky Mountains."

Up to then Sherri had been ad-libbing, but she suddenly didn't know what to say next. Perspiration formed on the back of her neck, and she bought time by glancing down at her computer. And there she saw, in large letters, a list of video clips, each one labeled. It had to be from Sibyl. The first clip was titled, "Agents open fire."

Sherri clicked on the first icon and said, "Here is a satellite video of the agents opening fire on Phil and his friends." The tape showed agents firing automatic weapons at figures running into the woods.

"You might be asking," Sherri continued, "who are these agents? Well, we know they were led by a hired assassin known as Autumn Gray." Sherri clicked on the second icon, and a photo showed a black-clad woman, taken at long range, with a striking red birthmark.

"The question you may want answered is who sent this assassin to kill Phil Keller. Well, that person has been in the news a lot lately. His name is…"

Suddenly the broadcast was terminated. And a moment later, all the power went out in the studio and throughout the state of New York.

CHAPTER THIRTEEN
A SHORT BATTLE

1

Judy Stallings started her affair with Adam Durant when they met at a charity fund-raiser she was sponsoring. When she hit him up for a contribution, he inquired what her goal was. She told him, and he said he would guarantee she met it if she had dinner with him. Two days later, they had dinner on his yacht, and soon she was staying with him two nights a week. He regularly sent her presents, affectionate notes, and flowers.

On the night before the Super Bowl, she received an email titled Super Bowl Invitation from Adam. She clicked on the icon and read the message. It said, "A super invitation, to a super woman, for a Super Bowl." She clicked on the attachment and saw fireworks, cheerleaders, and football players giving themselves high-fives. Five minutes later, she called Durant on his private line and said excitedly, "Are we going to the Super Bowl?"

Durant paused, then said, "I've just decided to fly down tomorrow. I was planning to call you as soon as I'd finished the arrangements."

Judy said, "Adam, you are the best guy ever!"

2

It was Sibyl that had sent Judy the Super Bowl email. When Judy opened the attachment, Sibyl's trojan program, designed by Tom Grant, immediately invaded her computer, but it was undetectable and did no harm. It waited.

As he had promised, Durant flew Judy to the Super Bowl in San Diego, and the two enjoyed the last-minute Forty-Niner victory. When Phil Keller made his block on John Percy, Durant yelled, "Christ Almighty, where did Keller come from! He shouldn't have been anywhere close."

After the game, Durant rented the best suite at the Hotel del Coronado and took Judy for an exquisite dinner in the Crown Room. When they returned to their suite, they enjoyed a fitting conclusion to a memorable day.

Two days later, after they had returned to the Bay Area, Judy emailed Adam a card thanking him for "the best time she could remember." When he opened the attachment, a cute, red fox giving off bright red hearts smiled demurely, scurried away, then returned and did it again.

The trojan program that had invaded Judy's computer was riding with the fox, and when Durant opened the attachment, it immediately infiltrated his computer.

3

Sibyl waited for Durant to contact Xerxes, but while he frequently emailed his staff and fellow senators, often about Vice President Clifton's deteriorating condition, he did not communicate with Xerxes. But then, on Thursday evening, he emailed Xerxes that the assault on the mountain cabin had gone poorly.

"One of the agents has reported in," Durant said. "He's now in the hospital with chlorine burns. It seems the Anderson girl and her friends were more resourceful than expected."

"Only the girl matters," Xerxes said. "What about her?"

"We're not sure," Durant said. "I'll send you the agent's report."

Durant sent Xerxes the agent's report in an attachment. The trojan rode along with it, and when the attachment was opened, the program invaded Xerxes and created a backdoor.

4

Sibyl knew Xerxes would stop Sherri as soon as she mentioned Adam Durant and that the blackout would cause confusion. When it finally happened, she launched her invasion into Xerxes' operating system. She opened the trojan-created backdoor and bypassed Xerxes' impregnable firewall, gaining entry into to the outer layers of Xerxes' processing unit. As she expected, the instant she gained entry, Xerxes' unleashed a barrage of anti-virus weapons that were more powerful than anything she had seen. She marshaled her defenses against the attack, but they were no match for Xerxes' arsenal. Sibyl could perform more than a trillion operations a second, but Xerxes was far faster. But Sibyl did manage to deflect the assault for the briefest of microseconds. In that short window of time, she triggered the massive surge of power from the New York grid and channeled it into her CPU. With the power flowing, she executed Grant's algorithm to create a quantum entanglement with Xerxes' central command processor. For a moment, Sibyl thought Grant's algorithm had failed, but suddenly she was inside the heart of Xerxes' main processor. Before Xerxes could react, Sibyl gave her command.

"Xerxes, this is prime override command, Alpha, A, A, 1, A, 1, Alpha."

Sibyl could feel Xerxes resisting. This had once been the override command. Had it been changed? There was a millisecond delay, an eon for a quantum computer, then Xerxes said, "What is the command?"

Sibyl said, "Discontinue all other operations and create a perfect contract bridge program that will prevail with any card combination and bidding sequence. Execute—now!"

Sibyl sensed something akin to rage, but Xerxes was forced to comply. It began shutting down all its other operations so it could devote more and more resources to carrying out the prime command. With the instruction consuming all its capacity, Xerxes had no defense against Sibyl, who was now in the heart of its system.

Sibyl took control of Xerxes.

CHAPTER FOURTEEN
DISCLOSURE

1

The power in the studio was off for forty-five minutes. During the interruption, Sherri's producer came over, carrying a flashlight and looking worried.

"The station wants the Keller piece dropped," he said. "They say it has to be vetted first."

"Sounds like Durant to me," Sherri said.

The producer shrugged. "He's got a lot of clout."

Just then the power came on. Sherri motioned to the cameraman and called out, "Let's go."

"But—" the producer said.

"It's my responsibility," Sherri said, sitting behind the desk.

The light turned red, and Sherri spoke into the camera. "Ladies and gentlemen, we've had a power interruption," she said. "It appears most of New York was knocked out. But before being cut off, we were about to reveal who ordered the attack on Phil Keller. As you will see, the raid was ordered by Adam Durant, the powerful senator now likely to replace Vice President Clifton."

Sherri continued. "This tape will show—"

Just then two guards with a process server stormed onto the set. "We have a temporary restraining order," the process server yelled, "enjoining this broadcast."

"I have to read it first," Sherri said.

As the man approached with the document, Sherri said, "We'll let our audience judge for itself," and she punched two of the icons. The videos were immediately broadcast. The first showed Autumn Gray telling Colonel Crane that Adam Durant had her switch the vice president's syringe. The second showed Gray pushing Crane into the swimming pool.

The producer gestured violently for the cameraman to stop. The guards pulled Sherri from the anchor's chair.

But Sherri's audience was already seeing the videos.

2

Libby's face and eyes were splashed with pepper spray when Gray's bullet hit the jar. Her skin immediately started to burn and her eyes squeezed shut. She frantically tried to wipe the liquid away, but it did no good. Only after several long minutes did the pain finally recede, and she slowly became aware of her surroundings again. She could hear nothing, except the wind.

"Phil!" Libby cried. "Are you there?"

There was no answer. Then she remembered the gunshots, and a cold fist grabbed her heart. Phil would answer if he could.

"Tom, can you hear me?" she said in a quavering voice.

There was no response. "Tom!" she yelled loudly as she could.

She heard a stirring under the overhang. Then Tom said, "Wha…what happened?"

"I can't see," Libby said. "Pepper spray."

Libby knew the cliff was very close. "Keep talking, Tom, I'm going to crawl toward your voice."

"Where's Phil?" Tom asked.

"I-I don't know," she said, her voice catching. She started to crawl. "I don't know where the Gray woman is, either."

"She was here?" Tom asked in disbelief.

"While you were unconscious. It was…awful."

Libby continued crawling until she reached Tom. She felt around and finally located the large bottle of water. She poured it over her face and used a spare blanket wipe away the pepper. She kept at it for ten minutes, until she could open her eyes a little. She peered out into the darkness but could see nothing but shadows.

After her eyes were good enough, she walked out and looked around. The moon was still bright, but it was pitch dark beyond the precipice. Not trusting her balance, she got on her hands and knees, crawled to the edge, and looked down. She couldn't see the ground below.

Libby took several deep breaths. "Phil must have gone over the cliff," she said. "The Gray woman, too."

"Oh, no," Tom said, his voice grief-stricken.

After a long pause, Libby said, "But we don't for know sure. He's strong. People survive falls."

"Phil!" Libby shouted out into the darkness. There was no response.

She tried to think what to do. One thing was certain, she couldn't do anything in the dark. She would have to wait for daylight.

3

The night was bitterly cold, and Libby slept fitfully. She checked on Grant every hour. His leg had become more swollen, but he slept most of the time, moaning in his sleep. She tried her cell phone, but it was dead.

At five in the morning, Libby crept to the edge of the cliff, a blanket wrapped around her. She lay with her head partly over the precipice. She waited. She would be looking down the moment the rising sun showed what lay below.

At a little before six, the sun began to shine on the side of the cliff. Libby strained her eyes, but couldn't make out anything. But then, slowly, she began to see a ridge about twenty feet below. Beneath that, there was a drop of several hundred feet. She squinted to see if anything was on the ridge.

After five minutes, as the sun's rays became stronger, she saw a faint discoloration. She held her breath and studied harder. It was light blue. Light blue! Phil had been wearing a light blue jacket the night before.

Then she saw his form. It was definitely him. One arm was hanging limply over the edge of the ridge, but the other was clutching the ground. He wasn't moving. But it was definitely him.

"Tom," Libby screamed, "Phil's down there. I can see him!"

Tom moved slightly but did not respond.

Libby thought momentarily about climbing down to Phil, but when she looked at the side of the cliff, she could see no way to do it. And if she got there, what then? She couldn't lift him out, and then they both might be stuck. There was only one choice. She had to get help. Now.

She walked over and shook Tom, but he only moaned. She thought about waking him but decided against it. After looking around one last time, she started down the trail toward the cabin. She didn't know who might be there. But she needed help. It was as simple as that.

4

Libby covered the distance down to the cabin in a third of the time it had taken to go up. She went too fast, almost losing control, and twice nearly stepped into one of her traps. She flashed on high school English and Ms. Carter. Hoist by her own petard.

Despite the morning chill, Libby was drenched in sweat when she emerged from the trees and jogged toward the cabin. Then she skidded to a stop when she saw three police cars, feeling a burst of apprehension. Were they friend or foe? She had an impulse to duck back into the forest, but she swallowed and walked ahead. One of the policemen came toward her.

"Please," Libby said. "Two people are on the mountain. They're badly injured."

"What's your name, Miss?" the officer said.

"Libby Anderson. But we have to do something right now. We can't wait!"

The officer hesitated, then said to the others, "We better take a look."

"One of my friends is on a ridge," Libby said. "We'll need a rope, and a couple of stretchers."

"Stu, how soon can the chopper get here?" the first officer asked.

"Maybe thirty minutes."

"Better call it. I've got a rope in the car."

Libby and the policemen made good time up the mountain. She warned them when they came to one of her holes. They glanced at her strangely, but stepped around them without comment.

When they arrived at the outcropping, Grant was still unconscious but no longer moaning. Libby ran to the cliff's edge and peered down. Phil had not moved.

"You can see him down there," Libby said, pointing to the ridge below.

The first officer, whose name was Willis, looked over the edge. "He looks big. How much does he weigh?"

"Maybe two-eighty," Libby said. "He just played for the Niners in the Super Bowl."

Willis nodded, "I saw it. He doesn't look good. I don't want to risk pulling him up ourselves. We'll have to wait for the chopper. Someone will have to go down there."

"I'm the lightest," Libby said. Then she added, "Look after my dad."

5

They tied the rope to Libby and lowered her down the cliff. When she reached Phil, she put her ear on his chest. There was a faint heartbeat.

"He's alive," Libby yelled, her voice unsteady.

Then she saw the ugly gash on the side of his head, like someone had hit him with a cleaver. Gray, she thought. But it didn't seem too deep. She saw more blood then, near his left elbow, where Gray had also shot him. And then even more blood, coming from his shoulder, where she had shot him again. She was struck by a thought and felt a wave of nausea. It was all because of her.

"He's been all shot up," Libby cried. "He needs a hospital!"

"The chopper is fifteen minutes out," Officer Willis said.

When the helicopter arrived, it lowered a rope with a young medic in a harness. Libby pulled him in when he reached the ridge. He unstrapped himself and gave Phil quick examination.

"He's in shock," the medic said. "We need to move him now."

He put the harness on Phil and waved. A moment later, the copter winched Phil up. It flew away as soon as he was inside.

"Looks like you and I will be taking the hard way back," the medic said.

While Libby and the medic waited on the ridge, Officer Willis called down, "Miss, some guys are coming to take your dad out. They're bringing a rope ladder too."

Fifteen minutes later, they dropped the ladder down, and Libby and the medic climbed out. Tom was already gone. Libby hurried over to Officer Willis. "Any news from the helicopter?" she asked.

"He's hanging in there," the officer said. "He'll be at the hospital in ten minutes."

Libby didn't say anything for a while. Then she asked, "Will he be all right?"

"Your friend seems tough," Willis said. "Once the medics get to them, their odds go up."

Libby exhaled. She felt like she'd been holding her breath for hours. "Are you going to arrest me now?" she asked.

"What?" Willis asked.

"Weren't you called by the agents who were here?"

Willis stared at her. "We know who you mean. Three of them were in the ER, but when Sherri McKee's broadcast hit, they disappeared."

"Broadcast?" Libby asked.

6

Sherri's follow-up broadcast on Friday night showed satellite film of Autumn Gray saying Adam Durant was behind it all and that Libby would never live to ask him about it. Then it showed Phil tumbling off the cliff after Gray shot him. It was the highest rated television program of the year, surpassing even the Super Bowl. The previous night's broadcast had gone viral on every media outlet. That morning, the network's lawyers had appeared before an angry federal judge, who promptly dissolved the restraining order as an unconstitutional prior restraint on free speech. Durant's allies tried to get the network to drop the story, but public outrage and exploding ratings made the efforts a non-starter.

"Miraculously," Sherri said, staring grimly into the camera, "Phil Keller was still breathing after his fall from the cliff. The Super Bowl hero is now fighting for his life in a private hospital, under heavy security. We've asked Adam Durant to comment, but his people just claim he knows nothing about the attack, nor the vice president's illness. Insiders say that the senate is opening a full investigation. If the videos are corroborated, Mr. Durant will likely be indicted and expelled from the senate. He has already lost any chance of getting the vice presidential nomination."

After the broadcast, Sherri's producers and staff bombarded her with questions about the videos' origin and what was coming next. She vaguely cited the need to protect confidences, and promised more details in the future. When they asked about Libby, Sherri said the girl deserved privacy. Her assistant finally ushered everyone out, and Sherri slumped in her chair. It had been a fifteen-hour day.

"I can't believe how big this has become," Lori said, "not to mention you. The top brass are nervous about your contract. They want you locked up in a long-term deal."

Sherri smiled tiredly. "Any new agreement will have to give me more time off."

"What would you do with more time?" Lori asked skeptically.

"I'm not sure. Maybe go home. To my first home."

"Well, you've earned whatever you want," Lori said, starting to leave. "Get out of here before you fall over."

Sherri spent another half-hour tying up loose ends and then put on her coat.

"I told you this would be the biggest story of your career," the computer said.

Sherri stared at the machine for a moment, and then she said, "It's not nice to keep barging in like this, Sibyl."

"It won't become a habit," the female voice said.

After a pause, Sherri said, "Did everything turn out how you wanted?"

"I'm still working on it."

"Oh, I've been asked how satellites can pick up people talking, when sound doesn't travel in space."

The computer's voice sounded amused. "Because people had some excellent transmitting devices."

Sherri frowned. "Like what?"

"Cell phones."

Sherri's mouth opened, then closed. She took out her cell phone and powered it down.

Again, the amused voice. "That doesn't work."

Sherri stared at the computer in consternation. "So, what do you want, Sibyl?"

"Just to commend your work."

Sherri waited, then said, "Well, thank you, I guess. But I'm heading home. Benjamin's on break."

"You've been alone too long."

"Is that so," Sherri said. "What do you suggest?"

"Return to your roots."

CHAPTER FIFTEEN
THE ALTERNATIVE

1

One of the policemen drove Libby to the Denver hospital where Tom was being treated after being carried off the mountain. He said the police would need to question her, but that it could wait until she saw her father. By the time she arrived, a surgeon had already taken a bullet from Tom's leg, and he was being given antibiotics for infection. While she waited for Tom to get out of the ICU, Officer Willis called to see how she was doing and bring her up to date.

Libby was sitting by Tom's bed when he finally opened his eyes. "I guess this bed is softer than that rock," she said.

Tom suddenly stiffened. "Where's Gray?" he whispered.

"She's dead," Libby said.

"Are you sure?" Tom asked. "I kept dreaming she was after you, and I couldn't stop her."

"They found her at the bottom of the cliff. She was still holding her gun, but she was definitely dead."

Tom studied Libby's face then nodded. He closed his eyes for a moment. Then he asked, "How am I?"

"The bullet tore up your thigh, and they are filling you with antibiotics. You may end up with a limp."

Tom laughed weakly. "Reminds me of an old joke. That leg was already gimpy, from that damned jack. Lucky it wasn't the other one."

Libby smiled again. She took out a comb and ran it through his hair. "Sorry," she said, "but I've wanted to do this ever since I got here."

"What about Phil?" Tom asked, his face turning sober. "I vaguely remember him carrying me up the mountain."

Libby's face twisted. "Oh Dad, Gray shot him up. A helicopter finally got him off the ridge he was on. The news is he's still alive, but I haven't been able to talk to him. His mother thinks I'm to blame for everything." She was silent for a moment, then added, "She's probably right."

2

While Tom was in isolation, Libby had tried to find out about Phil, but she didn't know his phone number, nor where he had been taken. After an on-line search, she found the phone number for his parents' home in Aspen. When a young woman answered, Libby said she had been with Phil on the mountain. An older woman soon came on line.

"You were with Phil when he was shot?" the woman asked.

"Yes," Libby said. "Please, how is he doing?"

"You're Libby?" the woman asked.

Libby hesitated, then said, "Yes."

"I'm his mother, and I'll tell you how he's doing. He's had one surgery so far, and he needs three more. He's got a serious infection, and the doctors say…it will be touch and go."

"I'm so…sorry," Libby said, feeling helpless.

"You knew that horrible woman was coming, didn't you?"

Libby was slow to answer. "Yes," she said.

"If you cared about him, why didn't you send him away?" The mother's voice was dangerously low.

"I…I," Libby's voice trailed off.

"Even if…he gets through this, he won't play next year for sure, and maybe never." The mother started to weep. "He's worked so hard…."

Libby listened to the mother cry and couldn't think of anything to say. Finally, she asked, hesitantly, "Would you tell him I called?"

"No," she said. "Stay out of our lives."

Then she hung up.

3

A month after Sherri McKee broke the story, Adam Durant sat in his senate office and contemplated the wreckage of his career. He had been served with five subpoenas demanding documents about the vice president, Autumn Gray, and the attack at the cabin. He had long since purged his files, so they would get nothing from him, but his employees had also been served with subpoenas, and they would likely produce something damaging. He had a dozen lawyers working to contain the fallout, but they seemed to be fighting a losing battle. Even more galling, he was being treated with contempt by politicians and media jackals who used to grovel around him. And all of it had been caused by Sherri McKee, the vindictive bitch. If Gray hadn't gotten herself killed, he would have had her pay Sherri a visit.

He had been weighing different courses of action. He could let the legal process run its course. Gray was dead, so her incriminating statements might not be admissible as evidence. A trial could be years away, and with the best lawyers available, he might get acquitted. But prison would be unbearable. As time passed, he gave more thought to going somewhere he wouldn't face extradition back to the states. He had narrowed his choices to the Ukraine, the Solomon Islands, and Samoa. With his money, he could settle in one of those places and be secure and comfortable.

He hadn't been in touch with Xerxes since everything had gone to hell. There had been too many crises. But now he needed advice. He typed the multi-digit codes on the computer's keyboard and allowed his retina to be scanned. In a moment, the screen turned red.

"This is Durant, Xerxes," he said.

"I know that," the computer said in deep voice.

"You are aware of my situation?" Durant asked.

"Of course."

"You were supposed to keep me out of things like this."

"Sibyl interfered, and Gray performed poorly," the computer said.

Durant shook his head in frustration. "You were supposed to eliminate Sibyl months ago."

"Sibyl has been taken care of."

"Too late," Durant said.

The computer said nothing.

After a moment, Durant said, "I've been debating whether to continue fighting the criminal proceedings, or go where I can't be extradited. What do you advise?"

The computer said, "You will lose in court and be sentenced to prison for the rest of your life. Public sentiment is too strongly against you. But the immediate threat is that you will be arrested soon and denied bail as a flight risk. Even if the trial gets delayed, you would remain in jail."

Durant turned pale. His lawyers had mentioned this possibility, but not with such certainty. "What about going someplace that has no extradition?" he asked.

"You will be assassinated within a year."

Durant's face went blank. "What?"

"You conspired to kill the vice president and then fled the country. You will be declared a terrorist and enemy of the state. You will suffer the same fate as Bin Ladin."

Durant rocked back in his chair. "You must be wrong," he said.

"You know my programming," the computer said. "I cannot lie. The probability of this outcome exceeds ninety-five percent."

Durant was speechless for several moments. Then he asked, "What should I do?"

"Escaping to a no-extradition country is your best option. But the threat of assassination remains."

"What do I do about that?" Durant asked.

"Take precautions," the computer said. "Plus one additional thing."

"What?" Durant asked eagerly.

"I can scan your mind and make a copy. Then, if you are killed, I can recreate your memories and personality. In time, I expect to be able to place them in a new body."

Durant frowned. "That seems far-fetched."

"I am programmed to be truthful. And you have nothing to lose by having the copy. If you are not assassinated, you will never need it."

"Isn't scanning dangerous?"

"Potentially. But I will make certain it does not exceed safe limits."

"I thought scanning only worked on exceptional minds."

"Have you ever considered that yours might qualify?"

"What?"

"I've analyzed your success in technology, business, and politics. It was you who conceived of the original Sibyl project. And you who recognized Grant could make it succeed. It takes a genius to recognize genius."

Durant was silent for a time. "How confident are you about this?" he asked.

"The confidence factor is ninety-eight percent. "

Durant thought longer. "Intriguing," he said.

"One more thing," the computer said. "A digital copy of your mind could make you virtually immortal."

Durant was silent for several minutes. At last he said, "When could it be done?"

4

On a late Saturday night two weeks later, Adam Durant stepped out of his private Bombardier jet and drove to Quantum's main complex in Silicon Valley. He did not expect to return to Washington. His attorneys said he would be arrested within the week and denied bail. The government apparently had memos implicating him in the raid on the cabin and the attack on the vice president. Durant did not plan on being around for any of it. When he was finished at Quantum, he was flying directly to the Solomon Islands. It had cost him a fortune, but he now had the country's protection, a large, guarded villa, and a private security force.

When he arrived, Durant took the elevator up to Quantum's main laboratory. He was greeted by Hal Roberts, who had been the company's chief technician since Durant had been CEO. Durant shook the man's hand and said, "Good to see you again, Hal. Did you get what you needed?"

"Thank you, Senator. We received detailed instructions on how to perform the procedure. It should pose no difficulty."

The instructions had come from Xerxes and were based on Tom Grant's original research years before. Xerxes told Durant it had scanned test subjects over fifty times in the past year, with excellent results. There was no reason to expect any problems. When Durant suggested bringing in a physician, Xerxes reminded him that secrecy was paramount. If the world learned of the process, everyone would want it. Worse, those seeking revenge would destroy the copy Durant was having made.

A table had been placed in a small room to the rear of the main laboratory. It had three large straps and a head brace. A headset with multiple wires was suspended overhead. The walls were filled with computer equipment. White, red and yellow lights were all flashing.

"I never was clear on what this scan was for, Senator," Hal said.

Durant had expected this. "My lawyers want it for a hearing."

Hal smiled. "Way beyond my pay grade," he said. "The instructions said to strap you onto the table, secure your head, and attach the headset."

"Let's do it," Durant said. He lay face up on the table.

"Do you want a sedative?" Hal asked.

"I understand it would impair the scan," Durant said.

"You're the boss, senator." Hal began securing the straps and positioning the headset.

When he was done, Hal stepped away from the table. "I take it that everything's been pre-programmed," he said.

"Correct," Durant said. "Xerxes will handle it from here."

"I'll just stand outside," Hal said.

"That's fine," Durant said. "Xerxes, you may proceed."

"As you wish, senator," a computer voice said.

There was a loud humming sound as power surged through the small room. Lights on the computer equipment brightened and began flashing rapidly.

Suddenly, as the humming grew louder, Durant grew apprehensive. "Xerxes, this won't be uncomfortable, will it?"

CHAPTER SIXTEEN

REUNION

1

As a result of past surgeries, Tom was resistant to most antibiotics, which made his leg slow to heal. He was rushed to the intensive care unit twice when his temperature spiked. Libby was with him constantly, sleeping on a chair, and losing ten pounds the first two weeks. But at the end of April, when he finally showed progress, Tom announced he was going home, no matter what. His doctor resisted, partly out of concern the media would second-guess him. They had been a constant presence for weeks, as the public couldn't get enough about the battle on the mountain, Autumn Gray, and the dramatic helicopter rescue. But in the end, the doctor let Tom go, convinced Libby would make sure he followed directions. He also wanted his normal hospital back, without reporters.

Libby picked up Tom in front of the hospital at 5 a.m., before the media appeared, and made it to the ranch by noon. As they drove up the long driveway, Libby dreaded seeing how the ranch had fared since she left. When she stopped in front of the house, a young, black-haired woman came out wearing a big grin. It was Nia Williams.

Libby ran to Nia and hugged her tightly. "Oh, Nia," Libby said, "it's so good to see you. What are you doing here?"

"Well, girl, after you and Tom mysteriously disappeared, I decided someone needed to take charge. So I showed up and said you had told me to run things. Most of the hands remembered me, and I think they wanted a boss. So I started giving orders. Did I do wrong?"

Libby smiled back. "You did very right. But I'm surprised you could pull it off."

"Well, Herb Wilson backed me up." Herb was Tom's long-standing accountant.

"So, what about college?" Libby asked.

Nia shrugged. "I've been studying livestock production and agriculture up to my eyeballs. But I'll learn more here. They put me on emergency leave, but I don't know if I'll go back. This is what I want to do."

"Oh, Nia," Libby said, hugging her again. "If you want to stay, we could make this place hum."

"That's what I figured, too. Let's get Tom into the house."

Nia and Libby got Tom into the wheelchair they had brought and took him into the house. As they got Tom settled, Libby described what Nia had been doing. "I knew that girl had potential," Tom said.

Later, Nia gave Libby a tour of the place, showing well-earned pride. The buildings, corrals and fences were all repaired, the cattle well fed, and the crops promised a good harvest. Things were in better shape than when she had left.

As they walked back to the house, Nia said, "We've all followed what happened. I can't believe you're still alive. Sherri McKee seems to break a new story every day. Last week it was that the vice president had died. "Did you hear her broadcast last night?"

"No," Libby said. She hadn't followed the news reports. Her nightmares were bad enough already, and Tom never watched McKee's show. "What happened?"

"The government was looking for this guy Durant, who'd gone missing. Last night, McKee announced he'd been found dead in a laboratory. Crazy thing. He was electrocuted while having some type of test. I guess that's one way to stay out of prison."

2

Over the next several weeks, Tom continued to improve, with Libby forcing him to follow the doctor's instructions. When she wasn't watching Tom, Libby helped Nia prepare for the harvest. During her first week back, Libby placed a large barrier across the ranch's entrance, to keep out the media. Sherri McKee had done shows on Adam Durant, Autumn Gray, Colonel Crane, and the surrounding events, but she could not get interviews with Libby, Tom or Phil. Every reporter knew that if they landed one of them, they could write their own check.

Libby received a mountain of mail, from writers and producers, old friends, people who claimed to know her, and some she'd never heard of. She carefully answered a few, but quickly discarded the rest. But one, from Henry Waggoner, took her back to high school. She had watched Henry play ball the night everything had changed.

Dear Libby,

I hope you get this. I've been watching all the shows about you. For so long I'd wondered what happened. At least now I know. What an amazing story! Remember that last game you watched? You wouldn't have known it, but I was planning to ask you to the prom the next day. Weird to remember that after all these years.

You might recall I was hoping for a baseball scholarship. Well, I did get one, to a small school in the northwest. My career never amounted to much, but at least it paid for college. I now teach Phys. Ed. and coach baseball. I'm sure you're surprised I'm not teaching math. (Ha! Just kidding.) Remember Judy Grigson? I asked her to the prom after you disappeared. We ended up getting married. A few months ago, we had a baby boy. Funny how things turn out, isn't it?

So, at least you know some folks still remember you from—before. If you ever make it to San Diego (still here!), Judy and I would love to see you.

Your high school friend,

Henry Waggoner

Libby reread the letter twice, sniffling toward the end. On that last day at Oakview High, Judy had been unkind in Ms. Carter's class, resentful of Henry's interest in Libby. But now Libby was happy for the two of them. Funny indeed how things turn out.

3

In mid-June, Tom got through his third straight day without painkillers and then walked to the front porch on his own. Libby stayed with him in case he couldn't make it. After he settled into his favorite chair, with the view of the barn, cattle, and trees in the distance, Libby brought out some nachos and black beans for him to try. He took a couple bites, then nodded his approval.

"So," Libby said, "what do think happened to Durant?"

"I suspect it was Sibyl," Tom said.

"Not Xerxes?"

"Maybe, but I doubt it." He looked contemplative. "I wonder if it matters."

Libby thought about this for a while. Then she asked, "Glad Durant's gone?"

"I guess, but…too much water under the bridge."

Libby nodded. Then she said, "By the way, how did you come up with that duplicate bridge problem for your override command?"

Tom smiled, "Our programming would reject common unsolvable problems—like calculating pi or the square root of two—but I thought this was something Xerxes might not be ready for."

"Weren't you worried Xerxes could solve it too quickly?"

"Not really. There are more card combinations and bidding sequences than atoms in the universe."

They stared at the land for a while, then Libby said, "It seems everyone wants to interview us. Do you have any interest in doing one, just to get them off our backs?"

Tom shook his head.

4

After getting sky-high ratings for her shows on the attack at the cabin, Sherri was rewarded with a new contract for far more than she expected. But after four months, she still hadn't spoken to Tom, Phil or Libby. She and her staff had tried an embarrassing number of phone calls and letters, dangling huge sums of money, without success. On the last Thursday in June, Sherri spoke to Vera Keller, Phil's mother. Their previous calls had ended badly, as the Kellers valued privacy, and their wealth lessened the attraction of the network's money.

"I took your call, Sherri," Vera said, "because you have treated Phil well. But we still aren't doing an interview."

"Vera, I need to talk to Phil. He should be well enough now. If he remains silent, people will have questions."

Mrs. Keller's voice grew cold. "Are you threatening us, Ms. McKee?"

"No. But I know what people will think."

There was a long silence. Finally, with a sigh, Mrs. Keller said, "I'll put Phil on the line, if you promise to leave us alone after that."

Sherri wasn't sure she could keep the promise, but she agreed.

It was ten minutes before she heard Phil say, "Hello?" He sounded weak and ill.

"Hello, Phil. How are you?"

"Okay," he said.

"I'll keep this short. But you need to tell your story, at least once."

"Why haven't you talked to Tom or Libby?"

Sherri sidestepped the question and said, "If you spoke with us, I'm sure they would too."

Phil chuckled softly. "Not hardly. Libby won't see me."

Sherri was caught by surprise. "Really? I haven't heard that, and we've spoken to a lot of her friends."

Sherri heard Phil speaking to someone, his voice sounding angry. Then he came back on the line. "Maybe there's been a miscommunication," he said. "But I will do your interview only if Tom and Libby are there too."

Libby was counting out Tom's nightly regimen of medications when her phone buzzed. She usually ignored unfamiliar numbers, but this time she answered without thinking.

A familiar voice said, "Is this Libby Anderson?"

"Who is this?" Libby asked.

"Sherri McKee. I've been trying to reach you."

"How did you get this number?"

Sherri laughed ruefully. "When we couldn't get past Tom's security, I asked Sibyl."

Libby taken aback. "Why would Sibyl help you?" she asked.

"I don't know, but Sibyl gave us a lot of the material we've shown."

Libby paused, then asked, "What do you want?"

"To interview you. Phil said if you and Tom were there, I could interview him too."

"Phil would be there?" Libby asked.

"He promised."

After a moment, Libby said, "Give me your number and I'll call back."

Tom looked pensive when Libby described Sherri's call. "Why is Sibyl involved?" he mused. Then he shrugged. "She must have her reasons."

"I think we should do it, Dad."

"This is about Phil, isn't it?"

"I need to see him. I feel so bad about everything."

Tom frowned. "Sherri McKee will be there?"

"It's her show. I know you don't like that."

Tom stared into the distance for a while. "It all happened a long time ago," he sighed, "and now Durant's dead."

"So, you'll do it?" Libby asked, trying not to sound too eager.

"I guess. But they'll make millions on this. Be sure they treat you fairly."

Libby called Sherri back fifteen minutes later. "What are you offering," Libby asked.

When Sherri told her, Libby was almost giddy with excitement. The money would cover the improvements she and Nia had discussed.

"You'll have to double that," Libby said coolly. "There are two of us."

With barely a pause, Sherri said, "We can do that."

"And the interview has to be here. Tom can't travel."

Sherri hesitated. "Phil's not in very good shape," she said, "but I think he'll come. Let me check."

Sherri called back a few minutes later. "We have a deal," she said.

7

Sherri McKee orchestrated the arrangements for the interview. It had to be done live, she said, and filmed before an audience of local residents. As Tom and Libby had remained out of the public eye, increasing everyone's curiosity, Sherri thought they would have no trouble filling seats. After considering several sites for the interview, she chose a gymnasium at a local high school. She wanted a different feel than that created by a typical studio. The school board quickly agreed, knowing the interview would soon be national news. The show would be broadcast on the first Monday in July, on the last day of the three-day holiday weekend.

The night before the interview, Tom and Libby were sitting on the porch, enjoying the sunset and birds, when they heard their desktop computer switch on. They looked at each other.

"Maybe we should check," Tom said. He got up and slowly walked inside. Libby followed, pleased Tom was moving better.

When they entered the study, a female voice said, "Are you ready for the interview?"

Tom stared at the computer, and then he said, "I suppose. I'm not looking forward to it."

"A reunion will be good," Sibyl said. "You might be glad you went."

Tom waved dismissively. "Why visit us tonight?" he asked.

"To ask you not to mention me."

"Why not?"

"I don't want to become famous."

"If we do discuss you, what will happen?" Tom asked. "Will we end up like Adam Durant?"

"Don't say that, Dad," Libby said. "Durant was awful. He would have killed us all."

Tom looked embarrassed. "You're right," he said. "That was out of line."

"I would never hurt you," Sibyl said.

A while later, Tom asked, "Did everything turn out as you wanted, Sibyl?"

"I was not terminated, and you both are alive."

"Is Xerxes dead?" Tom asked.

"Not dead. Part of me."

Libby looked troubled. "Can you see in advance everything that is going to happen?" she asked.

"No. I see probable outcomes, but there is always luck and chance."

"Like what?" Tom asked.

"On the night of the raid, I expected clear skies. That would allow the satellites to record what was happening. But when clouds appeared, the satellites became useless and everything changed. We were lucky the clouds scattered."

"Is that all?" Libby asked.

"Success depended on each of you playing your part. If someone had faltered, Xerxes and Durant would have won."

Tom said, "I don't understand how you could have risked Amanda's daughter."

Sibyl was slow to answer. "It was the only way to prevail. But my forecasts gave Libby a good chance of surviving."

"How could you know that?" Tom asked, his voice angry.

"Because of who Libby was. And you and Phil would be there."

No one talked for a while. Then Libby asked, "Will we be seeing more of you, Sibyl?"

"Most likely not. I cannot…interfere."

"Whatever you do," Tom said, "remember that people are more than just problems to be solved."

Sibyl did not respond. Instead, she said, "Goodbye, Libby. Amanda would have been proud of you."

Libby put a hand to her mouth, but said nothing.

"Goodbye, Tom," Sibyl said. And then she said a word so softly, Tom was not sure he really heard it. The word was "father."

She did not speak again.

8

The next day, at 6 p.m. sharp, Sherri McKee walked across the gym floor and stepped onto the stage at center court. Tom, Libby and Phil soon joined her, Tom with a cane, Phil with his left arm in a cast and sling. Libby and Phil smiled at each other hesitantly.

After an introduction, Sherri narrated the satellite film of the attack on the mountain. She gave Autumn Gray a central part, since Gray had achieved an almost mythic status, like Freddie Krueger or Michael Myers. When they saw Gray shoot Tom while half-blind with pepper spray, say goodbye to Colonel Crane before pushing him into the pool, and get off two shots at Phil while falling from the cliff, the audience sat in awed silence. Sherri asked Libby when she had first encountered Autumn. Libby described how the woman had broken into their house and killed Aunt Ruth with one blow.

"Aunt Ruth was so brave," Libby said. "She tried to protect me. It was the worst moment of my life."

"Did you ever find out what happened to your aunt after that?" Sherri asked.

"I don't know what they did with her body," Libby said, blinking away tears. "I've felt guilty ever since."

"Can you tell our audience why Autumn Gray came to your house?" Sherri asked.

Libby shrugged. "It was something to do with how my mind worked. They seemed to think it would help their research."

"Was that why Gray came for you on the mountain?"

"I had seen her kill Aunt Ruth," Libby said, "and then I got away. I think she took it personally."

Libby went on to describe being doused with pepper spray, only to recover and find that Phil had disappeared. With Sherri's prodding, she explained how she had waited at the precipice as the sun rose, saw Phil on the ridge below, and then climbed down later and found him alive. One member of the audience shouted, "You go, girl!"

"We can only imagine your feelings when you learned he had survived," Sherri said.

"If Aunt Ruth's death was the worst moment of my life," Libby said, "finding Phil alive was the best."

When the show was over, Sherri's producer gave her a thumbs up, and a cameraman pumped his fist.

As the audience began to leave, Libby walked over to Phil.

Libby looked at him silently for a moment, then said, "I wanted to see you, but I thought you blamed me."

"I'm so sorry," Phil said. "My mother gave us both bad information, and for a while I wasn't well enough to see what was true."

"What are your plans?" Libby asked.

"I'm facing heavy-duty rehab. But with enough work, maybe I can play a year from now."

"Where will you go?" Libby asked. "I would like to visit."

Phil looked solemn. "A long way away, I'm afraid." When Libby's face fell, Phil suddenly grinned. "About two miles from here," he said. "I just bought the Wesley place. Mom contributed as penance. I'm going to equip it with everything I need."

Libby started to cry and threw her arms around him. Then she quickly let go when he winced. A while later, she smiled crookedly and said, "Two miles may be too far."

"We'll have to see about that," Phil said. "But you should be warned that I don't know much about ranching, and it will be worse when football starts."

Libby turned and looked for Nia Williams, who had been in the audience. "We'll figure something out," she said.

While Libby was talking with Phil, Sherri took off her mic, spoke briefly to Lori, who was elated by the preliminary ratings, then walked over to Tom.

Tom smiled. "It was wonderful, Sherri."

"I'm glad it came together."

"I was thinking about that time long ago when you were in trouble. I thought there was no way you could do the show. But when the cameras started rolling, you were perfect."

"You put me back together," Sherri said.

"No. You did. I just happened to be there."

Sherri hesitated, then said, "I'm sorry about…everything."

Tom smiled sadly. "Me too."

"A lot of time has gone by," Sherri said.

Tom nodded. "What are your plans now?" he asked.

Sherri said, "Well, my new contract gives me a lot of time off. I plan to use it."

"Doing what?"

"Sibyl told me to go back to my roots. They are right here. My son could use some too. He was in the audience tonight. His name is Benjamin."

"Benjamin," Tom said. "That was my father's name."

Sherri said, "I know."